TOR BOOKS BY DORANNA DURGIN

The Reckoners

Storm of Reckoning

Storm of
Reckoning

Doranna Durgin

TOR®
paranormal romance

A TOM DOHERTY ASSOCIATES BOOK

NEW YORK

This is a work of fiction. All of the characters, organizations, and events portrayed in this novel are either products of the author's imagination or are used fictitiously.

STORM OF RECKONING

A Tor Book
Published by Tom Doherty Associates, LLC
175 Fifth Avenue
New York, NY 10010

www.tor-forge.com

Tor® is a registered trademark of Tom Doherty Associates, LLC.

ISBN 978-0-7653-6165-3

First Edition: February 2011

Printed in the United States of America

0 9 8 7 6 5 4 3 2 1

Many of my books are dedicated to family, and it bothers me not one whit to do it again. So: to family, to changes, and to that journey.

Chuck, Mona, Nancy, and Tom

Acknowledgments

With many thanks to superagent Lucienne Diver, Torfolk Heather Osborn and Melissa Frain, and Secret AlphaReader. This was fun!

And with thanks to those who lent their names to the cause. These "tuckerizations" resulted from a contest I ran at my website, but the, um, *lucky* few (that's my story and I'm sticking to it) had no control whatsoever over their characters and are very good sports indeed!

Disclaimer Disguised as Author's Note

Yes, I've done it again. I've taken an extremely cool actual place—Sedona, Arizona—and I've let myself play around there. But all the dorky bits are mine, and all the cool bits are theirs, and all the bits I couldn't stomp through with my own two feet or research or Google to death, I *made up*. We do that sometimes.

The Reckoners Cast

Our heroine: Lisa McGarrity (Garrie), a natural reckoner, once mentored by a ghost named Rhonda Rose.

Our hero (we're pretty sure now): Trevarr, half-human bounty hunter from another dimension.

Our hero's bond partner: Sklayne, an energy-based creature of curiosity and appetite, often appearing as an Abyssinian cat.

The Bad beings: Oh, how to choose . . . Humans can get into such trouble. But don't forget the lerket, who really just wants to snort sparklies.

Reckoner crew: Lucia Reyes, spiritual empath.
Drew Ely, ethereal historian, recently resigned.
Quinn Rossiter, researcher and trivia master.

Guest location: Sedona, Arizona—home of red rocks, canyons, crystals, and vortexes.

Glossary

atreya (feminine) *or* *atreyo* (masculine): heart partner.

atreya vo: *atreya* mine.

atreyvo: a bond-mate.

atreyva: Hmm . . . See what you think it means.

blood token: a powerful clan object.

caray: a Spanish interjection, "!!!"

chakka: a parasitic darkside entity that invades smallish predators and hulks them out, then controls them in a hunt for atypically large prey for its own consumption.

chicalet: Lucia's nickname for Garrie based on the Spanish *chica* and the English diminutive, not to mention an allusion to a certain brand of wee gum.

darkside: a place vague in Garrie's understanding from which invading entities come. They all have the same flavor to her. She has thought of it in terms of spiritual planes rather than dimensions. This may change.

darksiders: entities that come from the darkside.

eatsll: a nasty living substance from Kehar.

Eye, the: a dimensional travel tool.

fark: every culture has a word for this . . .

Gatherer, the: a hunting tool; it detects energies and can "store" and transport beings in an ethereal state.

ghosties: what Garrie calls ghosts.

Kehar: Trevarr's world.

kirkhirra: a record of clan history kept in knots and formed into a ceremonial belt. The most complex macramé *ever*.

Klysar, Klysar's blood: an irreverent curse. Trevarr's people should have a name, don't you think?

Krevata: a clan of semiethereal demons, particularly ill-formed and excitable.

lerket: a mild-mannered and guileless creature bred for use on Kehar. Think guinea pig, elephant, and tentacles. Sort of.

memory stone: one of Trevarr's clan objects. He seems to have the responsibility of carrying his people's important things.

nibblers: a darkside entity; an aggregate creature that nibbles away at the energies of other beings.

pajarito: Spanish for "little bird." Lucia is not, perhaps, being entirely benevolent here.

petirrojo: Spanish for "robin." A definite promotion from *pavarito*, in terms of assigned nicknames.

reckoner: those who take care of a final reckoning for spirits who need it. Someone who can manipulate ethereal breezes to accomplish this, although Garrie considers her team to be reckoners beside her.

spive: an air-based darkside entity.

Storm of
Reckoning

1

Lisa McGarrity stuck to the shade.

Never mind the strong Arizona sun, never mind the summer heat beating down at the Sunset Point rest stop heading north out of Phoenix, or the fact that she wasn't wearing sunscreen.

It was the reflective shimmer of her skin that concerned her.

Nope, she still hadn't gotten used to it. And shoot, who'd even known the consequences she'd face from those moments in San Jose? Blown through a dimensional pocket, buffeted by the tsunami of energy channeled through her body, and hey, presto! Permanent starlet shimmer in strong light. Not to mention that the funky electric blue streaks once dyed into her gamine-short hair now grew a permanent silvery-blue from the roots out.

Yeah. Lisa McGarrity stuck to the shade.

Lucia Reyes, on the other hand . . . a creature of the sun. Basking in it, her exquisite features and model-perfect body—not to mention that damned J-Lo ass—drawing stares from travelers who until that moment had thought themselves weary.

Right. *What's the worry?* As long as Garrie was with Lucia, no one would notice a little shimmer.

And then she bit her lip on a sudden smile, because what had she even been thinking? Once Trevarr strode down the sidewalk to ponder the sundial memorial with them, no one would be looking at Garrie or Lucia at all.

There'd been a *reason* Garrie had gone into that portal.

That reason now stood in the full heat of the sun, deep blue shirt slightly iridescent where it wasn't inset with leather panels, crossover bib front making him look like both a trendsetter and an exile from someone else's past century.

That last wasn't so far from the truth, although Garrie wasn't sure if he was an exile as much as a rebel waiting to return. She knew only that things unspoken still rode him—needs and obligation and intent. That he carried himself tensely when he thought she wasn't looking; that he held himself wary when there was no evident need.

His out-of-place, out-of-time theme carried on through, just as the first time she'd met him—fall-front leather pants, high boots with enough buckles along the outside to satisfy any biker wannabe, wide leather belt riding lean hips, black leather half-finger gloves. There'd be a caped leather duster over it all if Garrie hadn't informed him it would draw serious attention in this heat.

Trevarr was used to a warmer clime. A *much* warmer clime.

Sunglasses added a little bit of Terminator to the mix. He'd pulled back deep brown-unto-black hair; myriad silvered braids were completely obscured within the mass of it, but Garrie knew of them. Likewise obscured, the tattoolike marks at his wrists and torso . . . the ones that sometimes changed. He still owed Garrie a good explanation about those.

She wasn't holding her breath.

And when he strode out toward that sundial after Lucia, the Bradshaw Mountains stretching stalwart and picturesque before them, the rest of the overlook platform mysteriously emptied of other visitors.

"Pikers," Garrie muttered, and went out to join him. No one left to see her shimmer after all.

"Good," Lucia said in response to Garrie's arrival, her face still tipped to the summer sun. "You have to get used to it sometime, yes? They all think it's makeup, anyway. I'd use it, if I could get it."

"*You* should know better than to want it," Garrie said, maybe just a tad bitter. Things lost, things changed . . . things still confusing.

For when they'd originally departed Albuquerque for San Jose, they'd been a team. A little ragged at the edges, with Quinn Rossiter staying behind to run the research, but nonetheless—not just Lucia by her side, but Drew Ely. Drew, whom they'd just left back in San Jose—his choice. No longer part of the team. No longer one of Garrie's reckoners.

Trevarr wasn't anybody's anything. Not then, not now.

He gave away nothing as he looked down at the sundial memorial. "This celebrates life lost."

"Commemorates," Garrie told him, aware all over again of how his indefinable accent edged his words—crisp here, inflection slightly misplaced there . . . a little bit Russian, a little bit German, a whole lot *Trevarr.* "What, they don't do that on Kehar?"

"Kehar," Lucia said, a dreamy tone in her voice. "A whole 'nother *world.* You still owe me details."

"Seriously . . . not," Garrie told her. "Not safe."

"That's what you said about *him*." Lucia lowered her face to give Garrie a brief if pointed glance. "Look how that ended up."

Right. Reckoner power mingling with the power from another world. Shimmering skin, streaky hair . . . and other changes, not yet truly known. Drew, opting out.

But that's not what Lucia was talking about. Not really.

"On Kehar," Trevarr said, without concern for their byplay, "they set *warnings*."

"Of course they do," Garrie muttered, tugging at the hair just behind her ear.

But she believed it.

Sklayne sulked.

Left in the farking car, as if he couldn't be trusted out at the rest stop.

As if he might be tempted by someone's little foo-foo dog.

::O fine snack!::

Maybe not such a bad idea, staying here.

It wasn't as if the car could keep him in. Not with locks, not with closed windows. Trevarr knew that; the Garrie knew it. The Lucia person had yet to learn it. The Lucia person understood not-cat . . . but she didn't yet know all that not-cat could encompass.

Not-cat was as big as the world. As small as the crack where the car window met the door. As solid as he wished, or pure energy and flow. Appearing as cat merely because it pleased him, as Abyssinian because it was what he had seen first.

Perhaps because it suited Trevarr. *Atreyvo*. Bonded.

Just as they were here because it suited Trevarr. Never mind that healing was best done in the sweet woods of Kehar, the safe warded cave lair where they'd never been found and never would be. *Stubborn Trev-*

arr. Never mind that the food here lacked the vital spirit that fed Trevarr's other. *O stubborn*. Never mind that Kehar was the only place he and Trevarr could overturn what had been done. *O foolish stubborn*.

Because of the Garrie. All her fault. Because she knew nothing of the tribunal or its ways or its wants.

Or its threats.

Sklayne experimented with disliking the Garrie. Small person of much power, the Garrie. Experimented with mean thoughts and making himself bristly.

No. Maybe not.

But he still wanted to go home. To *be* home.

Trevarr's self-voice rolled into his head, not far away at all. *We cannot leave her unprotected. Hunted.*

"Mrrp!" Sklayne made a surprised noise into the stuffy, muffled silence of the car interior. Thinking too loud. *Not my fault*. Bored. Homesick and bored and . . .

Hungry.

He eyed a small mahogany dog with a long body and pointy snout and wagging, whip-thin little tail. *Tasteeeee.*

No. Trevarr. Implacable. Paying attention.

Sklayne growled to himself. He knocked the cigarette lighter aside, sipping at the hot power that gathered in its wake and eavesdropping—ever eavesdropping, listening through the lightest thread to Trevarr.

Listening . . . and watching over.

Hunted.

With the next round of hapless tourists meandering along, Garrie moved away from the pipe-rail safety barriers of the overlook and circled through the shaded picnic shelter. Maybe a hat would help. She already wore a tissue-thin shirt in a watercolor wash of blues over her camisole top, tucked into low-slung trail shorts with all the pockets she could ever want and barely covering the braided leather bracelets she habitually donned on one wrist. Lightweight, sneakerish hiking boots and thick white socks, and wasn't she just the perfect blend of funk and tourist?

Then again, she'd long ago quit comparing her wiry, petite self to elegant Lucia. Because Lucia would somehow walk the Sedona trails alongside Garrie in her slim-cut clam-diggers and espadrilles and little cap-sleeved shirt with the eyelet panels, and she wouldn't trip, turn her ankle, or acquire so much as a smudge of dust.

"Whatever," Garrie muttered.

"Aie," Lucia said. "Grumpy!"

Garrie cast a look back at her, raised an eyebrow. The other one tried to join it. So much for practice with the Spock eyebrow.

"Oh, not *you,* chicalet." Lucia nodded at the rest rooms. "In *there.*"

"I haven't been paying attention." Garrie scowled at herself. Stupid, that—failing to sweeping the area for out-of-place breezes or darkside presence.

Lucia had no problem raising that single eyebrow. "Bathroom break means off-duty. Drive to Sedona means off-duty, too. It's just that you have to *look,* while I have to remember not to."

True enough. It was why she was on Garrie's team in the first place. Just as Quinn had an incredible head for supernatural trivia and ghostly details, and Drew could instantly read the history of a place.

In fact, Drew already had his first freelance gig back in San Jose, thanks to a connection through his new girlfriend: vetting a potential construction site for inconvenient ancient remains. Or even worse, those more recent.

But Lucia understood Garrie the best. Lucia read the emotional resonance of a place—of the energies there. Whether she wanted to or not. Like Garrie, Lucia couldn't *not* do this work.

Garrie glanced back at Trevarr—still imposing, even

if he still healed from what had gone down in San Jose—an arm still stiff, a side still tender, the scar over his eye angry but fading faster than it had any right to. He lingered at the pipe railing, gazing out on the long, lean desert mountain ridges. *Not exactly anything like it, back at home.* All deep gloom and black fog and heavy-branched trees over rugged ground, the air spicy and thick, the sounds muffled and threatening.

She'd been there once. She still wasn't sure if that visit had been just long enough, or if what she felt now was the yearning to see more.

Not much chance, with Trevarr exiled. Or if she didn't pay more attention to the here and now. She cast her awareness over toward the grumpy bathrooms— long, low, pale brick, recently remodeled . . . *surrounded by a deep glow-stick green morass of nastiness . . .*

Creeping tendrils trailed from the heels of the unsuspecting, a proverbial spiritual toilet paper trail. She wrinkled her nose. "It stinks."

Lucia reached into her Burberry tote, all details and buckles and D-rings and the faint plaid imprint on supple leather. "Time for the secret herbs and spices?" As if she ever went anywhere without their own special spirit-containment system—storage bag based for the modern disposable age. A little petroleum jelly, a few carefully chosen herbs . . . tried and true and field-tested.

Garrie shook her head. "Grumpy darkside visitors, that's what we've got." No containment worked for darksiders. Intimidation, dissipation—those things worked, both accomplished by ethereal breezes at Garrie's command. Breezes, gusts, and, if need be, gale storms.

Even if it was all somewhat erratic in nature since San Jose. As if she'd just learned to shout, but no longer knew how to sing a fine sustained note.

As if, every time she opened her mouth, she wasn't sure exactly whose voice would even come out.

She made her words firm. "Nibblers, I think." Business as usual, shortly after . . .

Well. After saving San Jose, and thus the world, channeling power that had changed her nature in ways she hadn't yet begun to explore. Or maybe to admit to herself.

Business as usual, because what else was there to hang on to?

Garrie's gaze flickered over Trevarr. Standing at that railing as though his mind were a million miles away, and knowing it was probably even further.

And yet he'd come back here to be with her.

I think.

Garrie headed for the bathrooms; protecting energies circled around her and questing energies reached out— letting them know she was coming. Letting them run for it, if they would. Better that than a pitched battle in a public place.

"Eep!" Lucia hastened to catch up with her. Trevarr jerked around, and those sunglasses did nothing to hide his subtle frown.

Didn't do anything to stop her, either.

Trevarr wasn't the boss of Garrie.

Especially when he had things he wasn't yet telling.

What happened to your people, Trevarr?

"Garrie!" Lucia said, catching up just in time to grab Garrie's arm and spin her away from the bathroom's dark, cool shaded doorway. "Men's!"

Oh. Right.

An elderly man exited the facilities, giving them a startled look. He'd be even more startled if he could see what clung to his shoes, trailing behind in ribbons of darkness and threat.

Nibblers . . . not such a big deal for a virile young man. For a Trevarr. Even for a Garrie or a Lucia. But for an elderly man? *He just went downhill,* they'd say. *No one knows why.*

Garrie knew, and she wasn't about to let it happen. A quick, precise puff of power severed the darkside ribbons at the man's heels; if he stumbled a little, he regained quick dignity and didn't look back. The darkness recoiled into the men's room like a snapped rubber band, radiating indignant offense.

"Not happy," Lucia whispered, effort in her voice. She, too, was a little off her game. "Maybe Trevarr's cat is hungry—"

As if she needed help. "You might want to step back." Tendrils of darkness emerged from the bathroom—appeared around the corner, coming from the ladies' room as well. "Because the sneaky little bastards are going to get a whole lot more *not happy* before I'm done."

Laced through with electric green and steaming in a particularly unhealthy fashion, the energies were for her eyes—and nose—only. Or maybe also for Trevarr's, as he came up from behind; she wasn't sure. She cast him a warning glance. "Might be some splashback."

Because of course her breezes . . . his energies . . .

Not exactly oil and water. Something more combustible than that.

He said, "Sklayne hungers—"

"I don't *need help*." Garrie felt an unexpected thread of fraying temper, individual strands snapping . . . *ping-ping-ping*! She pushed a breeze at the aggregate collection of nibblers and watched with satisfaction as they recoiled.

A man fled from the facility, towing a reluctant little boy behind him. "But, Daddy, did you see? Why did the toilet do that, Daddy? Can we go back and watch? Did Mommy's toilet do that, too? Daddy, my pants aren't done yet!"

Whatever Daddy muttered, he kept it under his breath—except to aim at Trevarr, "Go find a cactus, man. Trust me on this one." And then no time for more than a quick double-take at Trevarr's appearance, swinging the kid up for a quick rescue before the pants went entirely south.

Garrie took a deep breath, trying hard to pretend everything was as it had been not so very long ago—even if *as it had been* didn't include bold nibbler aggregates of this size. As Trevarr headed off to check the building perimeter, she stalked forward, straight-arming the door without actually entering the facility. "Blundering woman, incoming!"

"What? You can't!" A curse, scurry, and slam followed those panicked tones; her hapless social victim made good his escape through the opposite exit.

"Doing you a favor, buddy," Garrie murmured, sticking her foot against the open door. An eye-watering incredulousness of stench wafted out of the building.

Lucia intercepted someone behind her. "Sorry, the restrooms are closed." Her voice grew less certain with every word. "Because seriously, you don't want to—oh, Garrie, this large person really wants to—"

Garrie looked over her shoulder. Tall. Beefy. Biker-like and scowling, one hand already hovering near his fly. He'd crowded Lucia off the sidewalk and left her off-balance in the deep decorative gravel.

"Maybe Trevarr . . ." Lucia suggested, but faltered at the look on Garrie's face.

Since when did they *need* a strong-arm? A *warrior*? *Dark-blooded bounty hunter from another world.*

"Hey, no problem," Garrie said. "I think repairs can go on regardless." She pressed herself back against the door frame, one arm out to keep the door open, and gestured him through.

"Weird bitch," the man grunted. "Want to watch me take a piss, too?"

"Completely unnecessary," Garrie told him. "And we're busy. Repairs. You'll understand."

He disappeared within, but his fervent curse over whatever sumbitch had left the deviant-sexual-act odor turned Lucia uncertain. "Maybe you should wait, chi-calet."

"Still busy," Garrie told her, pulling in swift breezes from all around—completely aware of Trevarr's return as he stationed himself near her elbow. *Right.* Strong-arm. Warrior. Dark-blooded bounty hunter from another world. *Hard to miss.* "Can't hear you. La la la."

Whatever Lucia said then, Garrie truly didn't hear. Nibblers were simple, all right . . . but intense. They took a clean strike or they bristled back like darkside porcupines, flinging energy quills of nastiness. She stripped her awareness down to the aggregate huddled there inside the building . . . nibblers thinking themselves so sly. *You can't see us! How clever are we!*

Not so much. The breezes piled up around her, stirring her hair in the hot, dry air . . . stirring the thick miasma to make her eyes water. Didn't matter; she wasn't seeing with her eyes. She stockpiled those breezes, pulling them in tight, winding them up . . . winding tighter, deep within herself, a familiar tug of feeling . . . invigorating.

Suddenly, sharply tempting.

It startled her, that temptation. It threw her out of rhythm, threw the gathered breezes into turmoil. Rather than lose them, she flung them—hard and fast and *wham.* Not tidy; not neat. Not restrained.

Trevarr stiffened, taking the hit of it. Guilt washed through her; she struggled for better control—following through before she lost control altogether. Riding the storm she'd created.

The nibblers fled. The aggregate broke into a myriad pieces, hockey pucks of slick darkness racing frantically for escape, rebounding off each other in a black Three Stooges comedy of panic. But they went deep rather than going darkside—and that meant they'd return, stronger than ever, if she didn't stop them.

She went for them. She circled the entire foundation with breezes; she threw in a wicked spiraling twist. She gathered up the darkness, enclosing it; her hand, reaching out into the suddenly frigid air of the facility, clenched into a fisted gesture of finality.

Nibblers . . . imploding. Crushed, sucked into themselves, and then exploding free as undefined energy.

Garrie took a little stagger-step back, awash in turbulence—riding it out. She didn't need Trevarr's steadying hands on her shoulders. She sure didn't need them closing down, an extra, infinitesimal hint of . . .

What was that? Possessiveness, or—? She twisted around, caught the look on his face, the rising scent of smoke and ash. Didn't need to see behind those sunglasses to know the pewter eyes beyond shone bright . . . or to know the breezes had hit him solidly, rousing those things he tried to keep in check.

They had things to work out, he and she.

From the bathroom came a cry of horror. "Holy fucking shit! Oh God oh God oh—"

Lucia was, somehow, halfway to the parking lot. "We're done here, right? Right. ¡Caray! I feel that we are."

Garrie came back to the überbright sunshine with the heat set to broil, sand and pebbles crunching underfoot and giant armored stink beetles trundling with oblivious intent across open ground. And there in the midst of it all, Trevarr—tensely alert, keyed into Garrie and the dissipating energy, watchful of the area of incursion. Predatorial, and yet restrained by some invisible thread.

There was no warning when he moved—he reached out, snagged her arm, and jerked her away from the door. A mere heartbeat later, the interior erupted with a great banging of metal stall doors, a tremendous bloated gurgle . . . a sudden muted roar followed by breaking glass and ceramic shrapnel pinging off tile—

The biker dude bolted from within, his pants precarious and unfastened, his belt flapping . . . his clothing soaked. "Gah!" he said. *"Gahhh!"*

Uh-oh.

She'd set off her ethereal fireworks in the *plumbing*.

She pulled herself from Trevarr's grasp and straightened her shirt, giving him the most casual of glances. "Should have used a pointy-toed shoe."

He merely looked down at her, sharp sunlight coasting along the strong, lean angles of his face.

"Never mind." She straightened, aiming herself in Lucia's wake. *Dignity, be mine.* "My work here is done."

2

Communication skills should be foremost in your arsenal.
— Rhonda Rose

Spill it, ghosties.
— Lisa McGarrity

Ay Dios, do you think I don't already know?
— Lucia Reyes

Lucia Reyes. Desperate for something normal.

Then again, life hadn't exactly been normal before this, had it? Never mind the princess convertible at home, or the wardrobe and the massive walk-in closet that held it. Never mind flirting with the handsome gardener or the pool boy. They'd all known the unspoken, the whispered. Her whole family, their employees, her teachers . . . Lucia Reyes, Latin American princess, heading for implosion.

They whispered it behind closed doors. They murmured it on the phone, the rapid Spanish of family secrets. And they thought Lucia wouldn't notice, so lost in her own worlds—between the fashion and the cheerleading and—oh, right. Her increasing tendency to become completely overcome with emotions she insisted weren't her own.

Garrie had changed all that. Rhonda Rose, her long-dead mentor, had changed all that. If Lucia hadn't actually *seen* Rhonda Rose before her departure soon after Lucia's arrival, she'd still have known her through Garrie . . . learned from her.

And if the five years since hadn't exactly been normal,

they'd nonetheless been a life Lucia had, all unknowing, been desperate to live.

And desperate now not to lose. No matter what had
happened in San Jose.

She tucked in behind the wheel of the rental car, a low-
budget PT Cruiser that did at least have a moon roof.
And satellite radio, though she hadn't turned it on.

Garrie had driven out of Phoenix and headed north,
but after the I-17 rest stop—after what *happened* at the
rest stop—Lucia took the wheel, with Sklayne sprawled
beside her and looking exactly like the Abyssinian cat
he wasn't.

What he *was,* Lucia hadn't quite worked out. That he'd
saved her from a terrible fate in San Jose—gooey, predatory *eatsll* going after her new Taryn Rose shoes—she
knew. That he could communicate clearly with Trevarr—
that they were familiars of a sort—she also knew. The
rest was pretty murky.

Aie, *chicalet, what have we gotten into?*

Nothing more than a trip to Sedona to meet Quinn
and his ex-girlfriend, Robin, driving from low, flat
browned desert and up challenging steep curves—over
the Mogollon rim to red rock country. Garrie and Trevarr sat in the back with trail maps and hotel directions,
spewing conflict, crazy want, and worry. No poker face,
her chicalet—her eyes wide and a little worried in the
rearview mirror, her nut-brown hair gone spiky, especially behind her ear where she'd been tugging. Bad habit,
that.

Plus she was just pretending that she hadn't sliced
through the Cruiser's backseat with that absurdly sharp
knife—strong, sweeping edge, shimmering watermark
patterns on metal not quite earthly, black horn handle—
even a new sheath hadn't been able to keep it out of
trouble.

"Feeling anything?" Lucia asked, and at the flicker of vulnerability on Garrie's face, she *so* wished she'd said that differently. Garrie the reckoner, fierce in the face of ghosts and hauntings and invading entities . . . clueless in the face of personal matters. No matter Lucia's best guidance, her style remained stubbornly entrenched in *funky sprite* and her social life . . .

Well, it was more of a social *after*life.

She sighed. "You know . . . *Sedona?* Quinn's friend making the big SOS call?"

"Not that we know anything about this friend," Garrie said. Her expression went distant a moment, and she shook her head; the sun through the window shimmered off her cheek. "Can't feel a thing. Waste of time, maybe."

"Then why do you go?" Trevarr's voice had a rumble behind it sometimes; it did now. He wore those damned sunglasses; Lucia couldn't read his expression for anything. He hid himself better than most, but even more so, she'd come to realize, when he was unsettled.

Not a good sign.

And was that his stomach growling?

"You should have gotten something at the airport," she told him, distracted enough by a new series of curves, complete with a drop-off and canyon on the edge of the road.

Garrie didn't bat an eye. "We'll stop at Cordes Junction," she said, waving the map. "And we're going because Quinn asked us to, and how often does that happen? He even got time off from the bookstore, which is Not Heard Of." She fiddled with the knife, sighed, rolled her eyes, and said, "Oh, o*kay.* I always did want to know what it would be like to stand in a vortex." She gave Lucia a quick, defensive look in the rearview. "Hey, Winchester House was real enough. Maybe this is, too."

Lucia would have raised both hands in capitulation

had they not been so busy at the wheel. "Don't have to convince me, chicalet. If it's vortices you want—"

"Vortexes," Garrie said, looking, if anything, slightly more defensive. "Here, they say *vortexes*."

Lucia bit her lip on a smile. "Not that you've looked into it."

"How could I *not* know? That would be like you being unprepared for the shopping in any given location. You've got a list ready, right?"

"Chic, there *are* no trendy shopping sites in Sedona. There are gallery tourist traps, New Age tourist traps, Indian crafts tourist traps—"

"There's Tlaquepaque," Garrie said, a little too hearty with the cheer. A little too determined. Hiding something, as if she thought it would even work. Some worry she'd taken into herself. Lucia needed to corner her alone and rip it from her.

Beside her, Sklayne stretched one silly long front leg as far as it would go and tucked it back beneath, looking over his shoulder at Garrie.

"Tlaquepaque," Garrie repeated.

"I heard you," Lucia said. The cat's tail twitched. Too innocent by far. Just as innocent as when they'd returned to the car at Sunset Point and found the battery dead. "I know you had something to do with that," she muttered at the cat. And, to Garrie, "Tlaquepaque—art galleries, restaurants. Excuses to spend money. You know that's not what it's about for me."

Not in the least. It had be a bargain. It had to be something she was looking for. Something she needed. And then it had to be the best.

Garrie seemed unperturbed. "Lu, you know you're going to love it. Your *abuela* has her birthday soon, right? So, perfect. You shop, I'll soak up some vortexes, and Quinn can see his lady friend, knowing we're right here to back him up." She sat, a small figure snugged in by the seat belt. Beside her, Trevarr filled his own seat, knees bumping the front seat and one arm stretched along behind Garrie—and Lucia wondered if Garrie truly didn't recognize the possessive curl of his half-gloved hand just beyond her neck. Not touching, but . . . nonetheless possessing.

Ay Dios. They had to talk.

Sedona. Vortexes, crystals, auras, guided spiritual journeys and all.

Garrie hesitated in the shade of the Sedona Journey Inn office cabin, squinting out from the shadows to the surf-blue rental car gleaming in the sun. Trevarr stood at the hood, ensconced in his duster even if the marginally cooler air at this forty-five-hundred-foot altitude gave him no excuse to wear it. But she knew it wasn't so much about *wearing* the duster as it was about having his hands in the pockets.

She knew about the pockets in that thing. Those pockets held not only the Eye he used for his dimensional journeys and the Gatherer he'd used to suck up the semiethereal Krevata, but an heirloom sword named Lukkas and on occasion Sklayne himself, all without so much as breaking the sweeping line of the leather as it fell away from broad shoulders.

The Tardis of coats. The endless pockets to solve any traveler's needs.

The purse of Lucia's wildest dreams.

And now Trevarr stood with his hands in the pockets, and he no longer looked casual. Just the way he stood . . . the way he lifted his head and scanned the small parking lot of this family run inn . . .

Hunting something, he was. In the way of a man who knew there might be something to hunt.

Ah, crap. They had to talk.

*   *   *

::Spptt!:: Sklayne crouched inside the cat carrier and savored all the ways he could be *not there*. The ways he could spark the door open, blow the little carrying crate apart, or simply become something to which the crate wasn't relevant at all. ::Not happy.::

"Be of silence," Trevarr said. "There is something . . ."

::Nothing. There is nothing. Tell me yes and I will eat squirrels.::

"Nothing . . ." Trevarr repeated, and his expression had the hard look. He pulled the tracker from his pocket, holding it just so . . . reading it, from the sensations of it against his hand. He glanced at the Garrie, the barest tilt of his head. "We would not be here if this was a place of *nothing*."

::Not truth.:: Sklayne settled down over curled paws and fanned his whiskers wide. ::Wherever the Garrie, then us.::

Trevarr stilled. Not a good thing, that. "Was there somewhere else you wanted to be, little friend?"

Careful, careful. Distraction, the best thing.

::Mighty.:: Sklayne said it with deliberate disdain. ::And of *all* sizes.:: And then, more subdued, ::Could be home.::

Startling, the complexity of expression, flashing so fast over Trevarr's features—so fast through his being, there where Sklayne always had at least that faint connection. But his face settled hard. His hunter's face, his hunter's stance . . . hunter's awareness. "We do what we must."

But if they'd stayed . . .

Maybe his clan would have a chance. Maybe personal efforts—made by a fugitive in the night—would speed justice taken on a tribunal's broken vows. Maybe Sklayne and Trevarr would be safer, hiding on familiar turf and nurtured by a familiar land.

But then the Garrie would be alone. Unprotected.

He felt her awareness now—one of so few to whom he could connect directly. She'd seen Trevarr's wariness, his shift from traveler to bounty hunter—here in the parking lot, surrounded by mountain squirrels and red rock and pines. She was aware and concerned and questioning—wanting to know.

But no. Klysar's blood! There was no farking way they were going to talk.

3

Some of your choices, you will surmise, are already made.
—Rhonda Rose

This is what we do.
—Lisa McGarrity

You don't know the half of it.
—Lucia Reyes

"And this is our cleansing circle." Innkeeper Feather Middleton stood proudly at the area tucked up against an abrupt weathered red rock formation, the sedimentary layering readily apparent. Not tall or majestic, it faded back into a rugged slope of junipers scattered thickly with smaller formations and loose rock.

Garrie could all but hear Drew's irreverent and hopelessly untrendy words in her head. *Way phat. This is where we sit and wait for rocks to fall on our heads?*

As if to punctuate her wistful thought, several rocks trickled down the slope and into the circle. Feather carefully added them to the artistic arrangement of rock in the center of the circle—one of which was, alarm-

ingly, of significant size. The collection also held a clut-
tered variety of tokens, smooth painted river stones, and
kitschy faded dream catchers. "We consider the stone
falls to be a gift of the red rocks," she said. "Each piece
adds to the cleansing circle."

"Dammit, she never gets the point." That youthful
voice was new and cranky, imbued with the sound of
wind in the trees. It was directed not at Lucia, who lis-
tened politely to their hostess, or at Trevarr, who stood
back with such an unapproachable air that Feather had
apparently decided to pretend he didn't exist at all. But
at their hostess herself.

Oblivious, Feather gestured at the chaotic little cluster of items. "I hope you'll feel free to leave your own
token here."

A faint echoing crackling of broken brush. "That is
not groovy. This is *my* pad, not some establishment
happy place."

There she was, perching impossibly against the side
of the hill, flanked by a juniper on one side and a scruffy
little scrub oak on the other. Torn clothes shouted classic
hippie chick—tight, low hip huggers, huge pant bells
festooned with mod embroidery, a tie-dyed shirt knotted
at her midriff, a headband askew on her brow. Darned if
that wasn't a peace sign dangling around her neck on
a leather thong, and sloppy leather sandals on her feet.
"My blood. *My* broken bones." As if to make the point,
the rocks in the cleansing circle shifted slightly.

"Oh!" Feather cried with delight. "The circle wel-
comes you!"

Blood crept out along the edges of the stones. Not
blood anyone but Garrie could see—but Lucia gave
Garrie a glance that said she felt the *cranky.*

"It's nice to feel welcome," Garrie said, and glared at
the spirit.

"You *do* see me!" The young woman jumped to her

feet, sticking to the side of the hill as though she wore
Letterman's suit of Velcro. Her energies grew indistinctly
foggy at her lower spine and pelvic area; her eyes whirled
with black stars. "Groovy! *You* tell her. This is my spot!
My death pad!"

"We love enthusiastic guests," Feather said, beaming
at Garrie. Twenty years earlier—and in the right
generation—she might have been this same hippie
chick. Now she had short layered hair, dry and fine and
gone a natural gray, and lines weathering the soft skin
of her eyes. Her jeans were smart but practical, and her
cute front-button shirt owed more to her position as innkeeper than to a freewheeling spirit. A tattoo peeked out
from beneath a short sleeve—a hint of color and ink.

"Ohh," Garrie said, only moderately desperate at
this doubled conversation, "it's clear that this is a special spot." Shaded by ash trees, wind chimes scattered
throughout, and the bluff rising at the rear of the
property . . . it was beautiful. And although the space
also held a covered gazebo with the inn itself beyond,
the view off to the southwest was unimpeded, spreading
out below Sedona into vast, open red rock country.

Quinn's friend, she thought, was paying a pretty penny
to house them here.

The ghost woman scowled; her frown stuck there,
grew and distorted, and ended up dripping off her chin.
Charming. The loss of those lips didn't slow her words.
"Dig it, girl—I've been waiting a long time for some
respect here. Kicking stones down on these people just
isn't doing it for me anymore, you get that?" Her face
recoalesced with a jarring snap. "It's not like there's
anything rad going on around here. You've got time to
rap with me."

Don't jump to conclusions. Garrie would do a sweep
of the place tonight—once they were settled, and had
privacy. For now, she turned away from Feather, osten-

sibly to admire the hillside, and took the chance to make a face at the spirit—and to tap her with the faintest of breezes. *Be polite.*

Feather clasped her hands together beneath her chin. "You're going to love it here, I'm sure. So many people find the energies of Sedona to be refreshing . . . the perfect place for a vacation."

"That's exactly what I said, yes?" Lucia cast Garrie a sunny smile. *"Refreshing."*

"I'm pretty sure you said something about shopping."

"Same thing." Lucia waved her off. "Now, we need to find Quinnie, and we need to find his friend. Were you meeting someone here, too, Garrie?" She gave the rock pile a significant glance.

"Later," Garrie said, and passed the significant glance along to the ghost—sulking now, in the wake of that ethereal tap, but not truly deterred at all. "Once we've settled things with Quinn."

If at first she'd resented Quinn's call for help—diverting them to Sedona on the way home to Albuquerque from San Jose—she now felt quite abruptly grateful for the work he'd dumped on them. A nice easy job, easily resolved . . . getting her back in the Garrie Groove. She took a deep breath, tipped her head back . . . let the rising breeze of the afternoon wash its dry heat over her skin.

The ghost's voice came directly in her ear. "You don't frighten me. You're one of her bleeding-heart squares. You don't have the nerve for more than that little tap. And *I'm not waiting any longer.*"

"Are you all right, dear?" Feather asked, even as Trevarr reacted—not to the ghost, but to Garrie. If he didn't take a step closer, somehow his attention tightened the tension that always seemed to stretch faintly between them.

Sometimes not so faintly.

"I'm fine," she said, ostensibly in response to Feather. "A little distracted." She stirred the breezes, hunting resources—finding them; letting the ghost woman know she'd found them. *I don't want to hurt you. I'm here to help you. But you don't get to hurt anyone else, either.*

"Aunt Adrianne!" The cheery call came from the flagstone walkway winding along the side of the inn, a looping path through trees and wind chimes and beautifully xeriscaped grounds. The young woman behind the voice moved briskly toward them, clearly on a mission. She briefly missed a step, looked abashed even from a distance, and said, "Er . . . I mean, Feather!"

Feather didn't seem the least disconcerted. "Family," she said, with no notice of the new trickle of rock down the side of the bluff. The *bigger* trickle. "They call you what they want to call you, don't they? Well, you've seen most of what there is, and there's a schedule of activities, guided meditations, and à la carte enhancement services in your room." She turned to her niece, a woman in bangles and braids and plenty of each. "Caryn, you left the desk open?"

"I'm checking in Quinn Rossiter. He's unloading, but he said something about meeting someone here—"

"Us?" A smile lit Lucia's face.

It took the woman up short. "No," she started, but at Lucia's obvious surprise and disappointment, hesitated on her next words.

"Forgive me," Feather said. "This is my niece, Caryn. Caryn, these are our guests in cottages five and six—and, in fact, Mr. Rossiter is in number six with Mr. . . ." She lifted an inquiring eyebrow at Trevarr.

From up the bluff came a faint grinding noise, rock against rock. Dust trickled down, an avalanche in micro form. Garrie sent out a puff of a breeze . . . not only warning, this time, but the foundation for more, should she need it. If she could just get Feather out of here . . .

::Sptt sptt!:: Sklayne. Of course, Sklayne, coming out from the direction of the hotel, where he'd quite distinctly been left in the carrier, his independent nature reasserting itself at the worst possible time.

"Is that someone's *Abyssinian*?" Caryn said. "Oh, poor thing—it must be frightened. I'll just—"

::Yess! Better than squirrels!::

Garrie made a choking noise. Her grasp on the breeze slipped; it curled around—flicking past Caryn, flicking through Trevarr. She'd come to recognize that particular cant of his shoulders, that particular stillness as he tried to absorb and not react to it. *Sorry, sorry.*

Dust clouded the air at the base of the bluff, so fine that no one else even seemed to notice. Dark, clotty manifested blood welled up among the rocks, rising over tokens and offerings, for Garrie's eyes only.

"Garrie," Lucia warned.

"I know," Garrie muttered. Too many things, too close to teetering askew.

But Caryn wasn't looking at Sklayne any longer. She'd turned to Trevarr, her face awash with sympathy. Feeling . . . what?

Surely not a genuine sensitive. Not now.

But Caryn had already taken those steps closer to Trevarr, entranced.

Trevarr's jaw flashed into hard lines, and his hand flashed out, snagging her wrist—as fast as Garrie had ever seen him, and a damned sight faster than Caryn had ever expected. A mere instant, he held her, frozen like a startled deer, and then he released her with a snap of his opening hand and stepped back. "Trevarr," he said. "My name is Trevarr. But my silent ways are private."

Garrie flushed with protective heat, turning on her. "What did you *do*?"

"Caryn, dear," Feather said, a remonstration that ended there.

"I—" Caryn flushed. She looked down at her wrist, as if just now realizing it was free. "I didn't mean anything by it. He was so . . . *turbulent*."

Feather cast firm disapproval at her niece. "I've told you for years, dear. Hands off."

"But I barely . . ." She rubbed her arm, ever so lightly—but Garrie knew she hadn't been hurt. Knew of Trevarr's quickness and precision. She'd be broken if he meant it. "He couldn't have . . . it wasn't—" And damned if she didn't do it again. Sklayne spat a protest.

"Hands *off*," Garrie snapped, and for that moment she forgot about the angry ghost, the growing trickle of stone dust, the dull grind reaching her more through the vibration than through the sound. This woman had *trespassed* on Trevarr. Thought she could interfere with his energies when she had *no idea*—.

"Quinn!" Lucia cried, and ran past Caryn, Trevarr, and Feather to throw her arms around Quinn Rossiter— tall, blond, utterly composed of handsomeness.

"Lu," Quinn said, catching her up for a good hard hug—but over her shoulder, his expression wasn't nearly as welcoming where it settled on Trevarr.

Ah. Time to get out the measuring stick again.

"Note my surprise," he said, still looking at Trevarr, "to find you in the middle of a socially uncomfortable moment."

Garrie was too far away to kick his shin, so she held out her arms and said, "Me?"

"Yeah, babe," Quinn told her, and brought Lucia along for a hugfest.

::Sptt!:: Sklayne flashed between them, winding around legs, putting Quinn into a stumble—emerging unscathed with the three of them quite suddenly separated. The grinding grew louder behind him, evolving into a rumble. ::Reckoners. *Reckon*.::

"Oh, shit!" Garrie whirled around to glare up the hill.

"I told you!"

"Oh, *shit!*" Garrie, so very stuck for vocabulary. She grabbed Lucia's arm; she grabbed Quinn's arm. "Get away from the circle!"

And because Quinn knew her, and Lucia knew her, and Trevarr trusted her, they ran, and they swept Feather and Caryn up with them, and Sklayne was already long, long gone.

So when the massive red rock boulder came crashing down onto the cleansing circle, it didn't quite crush anyone.

::Sptt!:: Sklayne's disdain drifted through the settling dust. *::Reckoners.::*

Their half-cabin room closed in around Garrie—closed in around them all, here where they'd fled as the dust settled. Full of southwestern patterns and chakra colors and baubles, a cluster of handblown witch balls in the corner, and more bed than the room could hold with other furniture tucked in around the edges. Lucia felt it even more keenly than Garrie, visibly fighting for her Latina princess insouciance. It came out in Quinn's temper; in Garrie's restlessness.

Although in truth, Garrie would have been surprised to find herself anything *but* restless, after a solid day of travel and sitting and confinement. The breezes got to her; the energies stirred her up within. If she wasn't pounding it out on pavement or a treadmill or a workout bag, it built and swirled and ate at her.

Trevarr stayed by the door, very much on watch. His sunglasses hung from the second toggle hold of his duster; his startling silvered gaze seemed cool and distant.

Garrie wasn't fooled.

Sklayne, barely cat around the edges, had found dust bunnies beneath the bed. He worried and battled them, and when he stuck his head out to check the room, those rich green eyes were more perceptive than any cat's.

::Not dust bunnies.:: His prim voice broke into her awareness—hovering there, as it often had since he and Trevarr had returned from Kehar. Only yesterday. Or had it been the day before.

Out! She scowled the thought his way. A few weeks earlier, who had even known of an off-world creature—*demon,* Trevarr had said some might call him—who could be anything and everything and who habitually chose *cat* . . . and who had become privy to her thoughts once she'd entwined her energies so thoroughly with Trevarr's?

"Mow!" he said, out loud at that, startling in the glaring silence of the room. ::Not dust bunnies.::

She gave him a look. *Just eat it.* Whatever *it is. It's what you're going to do anyway.*

::Talking to me,:: he informed her in a smug *gotcha* tone, and disappeared under the bed with a squeak and a rustle and a disturbing rush of cool ethereal breeze.

What—? But no. She didn't want to know.

As if Sklayne's vocalization had broken the skim on their silence, Quinn shifted his hip off the dresser and crossed his arms. "What the hell was that, anyway? Do you really think we'll get anything done here if everyone hears about us before we even start?"

The hurt of it surprised her. "Wow, harsh," she said, trying to make it casual. Desperate failure, even with the deliberately distracted attention to her dust-covered arms and shoulders . . . grains of red rock sandstone, gritty on her skin and in her hair. Brushing at it proved futile, so she quit. It hadn't been convincing, anyway. "That ghost has been haunting this place for decades, and she hates that circle—"

Trevarr's voice hit the room with a granite quality and no apology. "He speaks of me."

Lucia's eyes widened slightly, alarm showing. "Quinnie—"

"No, he's right." Quinn's gaze bore into Trevarr, blue clashing with darkening pewter, and Garrie wanted to slap her forehead at the bald testosterone stupidity of it. "That stunt with the niece? Grabbing her? What were you thinking?"

"I thought," Trevarr said, and Garrie was probably the only one to recognize the edge of dark amusement in his voice, or to understand that it was one of the things that kept this moment from exploding on all of them right here and now, "that it would stop her."

"Quinnie," Lucia repeated, perhaps a little faintly. Garrie knew the look; she was blocking. Already exquisitely sensitive to lingering ethereal emotions and wisps of spiritual wants, since San Jose she'd struggled to block on-the-spot live emotional impact as well.

"Was she *hurting* you?" Quinn demanded of Trevarr. "Was making that point worth the trouble it's going to cause?"

Yes, it had hurt him. On a deep, intensely personal level. But Garrie knew he wouldn't say as much.

And he didn't. He flicked his gaze away, a dismissive gesture that matched the subtle shift of his weight. "Trespassing is not a thing done."

"Neither is grabbing!" Quinn snapped, taking a step forward and oh, really pushing his luck. "If we're going to help my friend, people have to talk to us. Do you know how small this town is? Do you know how many people already know that woman doesn't feel safe around you?"

"Quinn," Garrie said, her voice low, "as long as she's interfering with people, no one else is safe around *her*. It's about time she was stopped—"

"At Robin's expense?"

"Quinn!" More exasperated now. "He won't be the one asking the questions!"

Lucia shook herself into something that was probably supposed to emote asperity and didn't quite make it. *"Hola,"* she said sharply, and the sarcastic whip behind her voice was more successful. "We are friends, yes? Reuniting? Here to help Quinn?" A desperate glance at Garrie, easy enough to read. *Are we going to fall apart right here, right now?*

Garrie sent her a fierce look back. She wasn't giving up that easily. Just because suddenly nothing was the same—

What would Quinn think if he knew about that moment at the rest stop? That temptation?

Or how close she'd come to following the impulse . . .

Trevarr, watching her, had gone unreadable—no matter how adept she'd become at interpreting the subtleties of a face not given to revealing the man beneath. He reached for his duster, casting a meaningful glance at the bed—covered with Quinn's overnighter, a heavy crate of books, a laptop case, a tangle of battery chargers and AC adapters—and, off to the side, Trevarr's satchel.

Or not *at* the bed. Beneath it.

::Important busy here.:: The tip of Sklayne's tail briefly appeared, quivering in predatorial zeal. Either he meant for Garrie to hear his response to Trevarr's silent question, or he was getting sloppy. The result was the same—Garrie realized just in time that Trevarr was headed out. Smooth, decisive . . . the door quietly snicking closed behind him.

"What—?" Lucia said, baffled.

"Just giving us some space," Garrie said, more brusquely than she meant to. "Quinn, here's your chance. You know? As in, *hey, Garrie! Lucia! I've missed you!*"

For an instant, he looked baffled—still standing his ground, not quite realizing that there wasn't anyone left to stand it against.

Lucia understood. Lucia always understood. "Just because you were there," she said, "and he was *here* . . . it doesn't change anything, Quinn."

Vulnerability, that's what that was. Just a flash of it. Easygoing Quinn, never had to worry about his place in the world. Had the job he wanted, had the moonlight reckoning gig on which he thrived. Had his health, his looks, his smarts, his personal sense of invincibility. Nothing had ever threatened that.

Until now.

But the uncertainty, here and gone again. "Garrie!" he said. "Lucia! I've missed you guys!"

"Right answer," Garrie muttered, and discovered she'd been tugging on her hair again. Or had she never stopped? "Because I was just about to get out a ruler and start measuring—"

Quinn arched a look her way. "Can't you just go by experience?"

The words slapped at her; her eyes narrowed down. She rued the fact that ethereal breezes had no effect whatsoever on living humans and she rued it hard—a flash of temper so twisty, so sudden, she reeled in the aftermath of astonishment.

The bed rustled. Sklayne's thoughts, though preoccupied, came with warning. ::Bad for you, the Garrie.::

But Lucia came to her rescue. She poked Quinn hard, adding a little hiss of warning.

Quinn had the grace to look abashed. "Sorry," he muttered, and gave his sneakers some attention. "Seriously. I don't know what got into me."

"How about," Garrie said, her words tight in spite of effort, "we just say that you're worried for your friend?"

"I'm worried for you!" Quinn blurted.

Oh.

So then she hugged him, and Lucia hugged him, and

he ruffled her hair. His fingers stilled, and it warned her; they lingered over the crown of her head where she knew the hair had gone streaky blue silver, thoughtfully rolling a few hairs between his fingers. But when she stepped back, he said, "I haven't been able to find Robin. She's not answering her phone or her e-mail."

"I'll do a sweep as soon as we settle in." Right. Quinn and Trevarr, sharing a room. Great. She and Lucia had the room on the other side of this split cabin, not nearly close enough to stop trouble if it started. "Don't you have any idea . . . ?"

He threw his hands in the air, a subdued gesture. "Someone in the area getting out of hand—that's all I've got. Don't think I haven't been looking—but mostly I've been driving. Puts a damper on the keyboarding *and* the reading."

"But she convinced you to get us all here," Lucia noted.

He hesitated, giving that some thought. "It wasn't what she said." He looked at Lucia, hunting understanding. "It was how she said it." He sat back against the dresser, which creaked slightly. "I know I'm asking a lot, bringing you here, especially after . . . what you've been through."

"You don't know the half of it," Lucia muttered.

Garrie could have said more . . . didn't. Things Quinn didn't know; things even Lucia and Drew hadn't learned. Had she told them that those faint tracings of faded tattoos, feathered scale patterns across his arms and torso, came to life? Not damned likely. Did they know that the occasional rising scent of wood smoke meant those things within Trevarr that he worked so hard to control were momentarily rising closer to the surface? *And don't even ask about the eyes.*

Even Garrie didn't know what made the other half of Trevarr.

"Quinn," Garrie said. "It's okay. This is what we do. We're damned sure going to do it for a friend."

"Tell us more, yes?" Lucia flounced onto the bed, toeing her sandals off and shoving Quinn's things aside without remorse. "You met her when? What's she like? Will we like her? Were you lovers?"

Quinn made a strangled noise.

Lucia stretched and wiggled her toes, dangling her feet over the side of the bed. "Oh, Quinnie, you set yourself up for that one when you were so rude to Garrie. So, spill."

Quinn sent a desperate look at Garrie, who merely crossed her arms over her chest and smiled . . . and waited.

Quinn jammed his hands into his back pockets, retreated to charmingly modest—another of his skills—and said, "The year before I met Garrie. She's good people, she just . . . couldn't quite bring herself to believe what she really knows. She left instead. Bought into half of the Crystal Winds."

"You *did* like her," Lucia said.

Quinn scowled. "You didn't used to peek."

She gave him a sunny smile. "I didn't." Her foot twitched. "Hey! Cat! Knock it off!"

::Innocent, I am.:: Something like a growl curled through Garrie's mind. ::Hunting. Don't move.::

She coughed. "Pull your feet up, Lucia. He's got something under there and he's using you for bait."

"Dios, my every nightmare." Lucia instantly curled her legs up on the bed. "There *is* a monster under the bed."

Quinn had on his *what the fu—?* face, but he shook his head, an unconscious gesture. Later, he'd ask. For now . . . he reached out again to her hair; barely touching it. He ran fingers lightly over Garrie's arm—a freedom that lingered, speaking of what they'd once had, however brief. "Your skin . . ." he said. "Your *hair.*" A flip of the light switch in the waning evening, and there was no question about it. "So that's what Drew meant."

She didn't say to him *those aren't even the things I'm worried about.*

"Things have changed, Quinn," she said, touching an arm that had once been remarkable only for its wiry nature and scattering of freckles. She looked up, saw the dawning realization of it in his eyes. "Things have *changed.*"

"Mow! Spptt!" A startling bass rumble, a brief shudder of reality rippling through the room, a *pmmmf!* of struggle. ::Got it got it *gotit pouncing I am!*::

Right. Really, really, changed.

Garrie sat on the rock.

Not just any rock. The huge and newly deposited rock, still reeking of spiritual influence.

Their hosts hadn't appeared to have noticed. For all of Caryn's sensitivity to living auras and personal energies, she was obviously blind to the ethereal. The postliving.

Garrie was anything but. The breezes brushed against her, disturbed and sorrowing . . . undercurrents that told her as much about the not-departed-enough young hippie ghost as the anger she'd felt earlier in the day. So hard to sit still after a day of long sitting already and the energies stirring up the jitters in her blood. But first this, and then she'd find the little health spa area and pound the jitters into exhaustion.

The long, slow desert twilight faded into deep black; Quinn was off down 89A, gathering up basics for their kitchenette and with instructions to bring generous takeout on the way back. Something for everyone and twice as much for Trevarr, because it had been hours since Cordes Junction and that hadn't been enough. The *food* wasn't enough, whatever he ate of it. "We'll find Robin tomorrow," Garrie had told Quinn. "We'll hit the shops, after I sweep the area tonight. We'll have daylight. We'll split up and cover the whole town."

It wasn't, after all, a very big one. Tons of main street crammed into one short stretch, a few more typical Southwest shopping strips down 89A, and south down the infamous Y intersection to the few establishments past Tlaquepaque. Lots of vistas, lots of red rocks, lots of tourist action, Pink Jeeps everywhere.

So Quinn had gone shopping. Lucia had breathed a sigh of relief and set about putting both the rooms to rights—and if Sklayne hadn't yet emerged from under the bed, sparkly waves of energy lapped out to inform of his presence and his state of mind

And Garrie had come here, to soak up what information she could from the rock before taking a closer look at the energies of this town.

She had no idea where Trevarr had gone, but if she worried for him, she didn't worry *about* him. Riled he might be; tense he might be. *Hungry* he might be. But none of it such that Sklayne found concern.

Breezes brushed softly against her shins. She sat, a small person on a large, lumpy rock, absurdly comforted by the presence of the knife beside her, even if Lucia had made an exaggerated warding sign when she'd tucked the sheath onto her belt. The faintest of solar LED lights dotting the edges of the garden walk as it joined with the path around the inn; the crushed tokens beneath the rock gave off their own persistent energies—Garrie wouldn't have termed it a cleansing effect, but she wasn't sure either Feather or Caryn could discern the difference.

No doubt the ghost could.

For people seemed to have found their peace and cleansing by leaving behind those things they didn't want. Tangled knots of anger, thickly bubbling resentments . . . deep, sucking sorrows. A dark spectrum of color and pattern and movement, clinging to this spot. *Just groovy.*

She hadn't seen it earlier in the day; she rarely opened herself to such things in the presence of strangers—not to mention when off-balance herself. Looking this deeply meant finding quiet within and without.

But now that she had, she wasn't surprised at the ghost's distress, or her impatience. Her death spot had been persistently, profoundly defiled. *But that's not all of it.* "Bobbie," she murmured, assigning the spirit her official ghostie moniker, "Why did you stick around in the first place?" Because surely that's how it had happened—Bobbie had fallen, and some years later Feather Middleton had created a cleansing circle. As oblivious as Feather had been to the ethereal breezes, she seemed sincere, and kind enough. Garrie couldn't imagine her deliberately creating a cleansing circle on the very spot where a young flower child had fallen to her death.

And that meant the ghost—Bobbie, because they were *all* Bob the Ghost until she learned otherwise—had been hanging around long before then.

Drew would have been able to tell her when the woman had fallen. When the inn had been built. When the circle had been formed. At his fingertips—and until recently, therefore at hers.

Well, *fine*. She'd do it how she'd always done it. Come morning, she'd find Feather and ask some questions. Because if Bobbie had been here before the inn, then cleansing this cleansing circle wasn't going to resolve anything in the long term.

It didn't stop her from whispering in a few quiet breezes, clear and gentle, and washing them across the area—the stone beneath her no hindrance at all—

brushing away at the stains left behind by those who had polluted as surely as the toss of a cigarette butt onto pristine land. A whole series of breezes, each leaving the area cleaner than the last. When Garrie finally released a long, slow breath and let her focus go with it, there still remained a smudge of reminder . . . but she'd let it settle, and see what was left of it in the next day or two.

Surely they wouldn't be here any longer than that.

Unless, of course, she didn't get off her reckoner ass and do her area sweep.

She shifted on hard rock, stretching her arms out all the way to her fingers and settling them loosely across her knees, shoving the bracelets back out of the way. She centered herself back in, filling her lungs with the scent of hot earth and junipers, tipping her head back to take in the dramatic splash of stars against a deep sky. Still air left the night open to a plethora of subtle sounds—water trickling in the little garden fountain near the inn, a sporadic but confident mockingbird nearby, the rustle of something in the native flowers near the inn. Garrie took it all in, breathing deeply—and then she reminded herself, sternly, what had happened on her first sweep in San Jose.

She wouldn't be that careless again.

But then she forgot all that, because that last deep breath . . .

Wood smoke and leather. Only the faintest hint of it, but Garrie untangled her legs and popped up to her knees, twisting—searching the darkness.

Trevarr, she knew, could see her perfectly. Those eyes didn't need light. Those eyes weren't human at all.

"Hey," she said.

He said nothing, but she'd expected that. She found him, moving in the darkness, no sooner than he meant her to.

"Everything okay?" she asked him when he hesitated there.

"I wondered," he told her. "If she was here."

"The ghost, or Feather's pushy niece?" Garrie's tone left no question how she felt about the niece. The ghost . . . okay, she'd brought a giant rock down on their heads. But that was how ghosts were. They sometimes lost track of how such things played out in the corporeal world.

Caryn had no such excuse.

"I thought the spirit who owns this rock. But if you have warning of the other . . ." The wry humor told her he knew just how problematic that meeting had been.

"Sorry," she said. "Ghostie radar, yes. Idiot radar, not so much."

He took a breath, didn't quite say the words behind it—and then, when she held her silence, finally asked, "Are you able to hide from them?"

She repeated herself with a little smile. "The ghost, or Feather's pushy niece?"

"Either," he said, blunt and immediate this time. "Can you keep yourself from them?"

"Sure," she said easily. "Can't do much from that place, so I don't do it unless I really have to. But sometimes it's best for that first look around." She shrugged. "Doesn't really matter now. Caryn's stuck on you, and Bobbie ghost knows I'm here."

From the faint intake of his breath, she thought he might have something to add. But as he kept his silence—as the night kept its silence—she went back to where she'd started. "I was talking about you, by the way. You know. Everything okay with *you*?"

And if she'd spoken those words with the last hour in mind, they suddenly referred to so much more than that. The last hour, the last day, the last *week*. All those things they'd had no chance to discuss since his return.

An enthusiastic greeting in the San Jose hotel, yes; a babble of conversation and planning, a crush of logistics, yes. And then a rush to the airport, the flight that should have taken them home to Albuquerque had not Quinn needed their help here.

And then there they'd been, jammed into the PT Cruiser rental on the way to Sedona, everyone silent . . . recovering. Rehydrating. And Garrie, *not* checking his injuries to see how much scary-fast healing remained. *Not* touching him, or taking stock of how their differing natures and differing energies had settled out in one another. *Not* feeling the strength of him beneath her hand.

He was closer than she'd thought. His low voice startled her, as did the sudden gleam of his eye. "It is complicated."

She snorted. "I know what *that* means." She stuck her hands on her hips, her head just barely topping his from this perch. "It's either *don't fill her perky little head with details* or *I've got me some secrets and I'm not telling.*"

"Perky," he said thoughtfully, exploring the word in his accented tones. "This might not be the word I had in mind."

"Make it good," she warned him.

"Fierce," he said. "Full of . . ."

"Hey!" She scowled, knowing he'd see that, too. "That's not a phrase that generally ends well."

"And I am uncertain how to end it," he admitted. "Full of that which I crave enough to call to me across worlds."

Oh. *"Oh,"* she said out loud, barely enough breath there to do it. "I thought . . ."

She'd done her best not to think at all when he left, that's what. To be realistic. To understand he had a world, and he had people, and he had obligations.

Come to think of it, he still had all those things.

Later. Much later. She closed her eyes, giving way to the rising conflict of energies between them—born in the Winchester Mystery House, when he'd saved her life and fed her his own incompatible energies to do it. They still lurked, not so much tamed as intermittently quiescent. Sometimes they just burned along her skin; sometimes they merely scratched to be free. But when Trevarr was near? *This* near? A cold burn, rising to spark along her ribs and collarbone and twine sweetly in places so privately erotic that she'd never imagined she could be touched there at all.

She released her breath on a sigh; she opened her eyes to discover he'd reached for her face—his fingers hesitating a hairbreadth away.

Slowly, he dropped his hand, never taking his gaze from hers.

For whatever his energies did to her, she returned to him tenfold. The merest breeze was one thing . . . and a very fine thing indeed.

But true strong gusts, that was something else altogether. They pained him; they brought out that which he fought so hard to suppress. That which reminded anyone who saw it—all the people on his world who so reviled and feared their half bloods—what he truly was.

A turmoil beyond that which she could understand, even seeing it reflected on his face.

Even seeing what those energies had once pulled out of him.

"Twice already today, I've hurt you," she said, wishing she could see him better in the darkness—wishing her voice didn't sound quite so suddenly ragged. "And me . . . there are moments I'm not even sure who I am anymore . . ."

"I know," he said.

That sat in the silence a few moments, until he threaded his fingers through the hair that had been tugged into spikes just behind her ear. "How it is now," he said, with an obvious hunt for words in this language, "is perhaps not how it must always be. Now . . . we have been hurt." Right. Garrie, blasted clean from the inside out by the plasmic energies for which she'd been a conduit. And Trevarr—battered and shot and poured full of the very energies that so distressed him.

Acknowledgment of those things showed in his gaze . . . the way it went half lidded, watching her. Still gleaming. No longer camouflaged as human, but pupils more as a cat's. Or more . . . other things altogether. "We are raw," he told her; his voice held that little bit of rumble. "Still healing. Reactive."

Reactive. Yeah. You can say that again.

But she didn't. Instead, she said, "Are you going to kiss me, or what?"

Maybe it was more of a demand. Such as it was.

Features so habitually hard barely flickered toward a smile, the low light painting along strong cheek and jaw and nose.

She drew breath—*I'm not gonna say it again, buddy*—when he took that final abrupt step closer. His hands closed on her waist, tightening to pull layered shirts loose of her shorts. The cold burn burst to life beneath his touch, sparking outward from his hands; Garrie made a surprised and completely inarticulate sound. He drew her close with a startling little jerk, and his breath warmed her lips. "You are mine, now."

"I—*what*?"

"Whatever comes," he told her.

If she'd thought the thing that flared to life between them in San Jose—in the dimensional pocket in which they'd been trapped, in the Keharian shelter he called sanctuary—if she thought that had been a passing thing, *worried* about it, even . . .

Wrong.

He met her with *strong* and *warm,* and Garrie quite suddenly couldn't feel her feet. She couldn't feel her knees. She barely felt her hands clutching at him, pushing at his coat and his shirt, hunting toggles and laces and skin. A pure flush of emotion shuddered through her, pushing out a frantic little noise.

"Sah," he whispered against her lips, barely interrupting the kiss to do it. *"Atreya vo."*

All the cold sizzle rushed along nerves and bodily meridians, swelling into an uncontrollable rush far too big for her own modest body. She'd stopped kissing him, she realized dimly, which was absurd because at this moment there was hardly anything she wanted to do more—but there went her eyes, rolling back in her head. *"Atreya,"* he said, or maybe not, maybe something else, startled words in a language she didn't know, strong hands owning her body for the sake of supporting it—and here came that sudden cold explosion of power, bursting through a door barely cracked open, and she realized one damned farking instant before it happened that she was going to—

Dammit!

Faint.

4

Personalizing your subject can ease the path to solutions.
—Rhonda Rose

It's better than Jane Doe, right?
—Lisa McGarrity

Turmoil disrupted Sklayne's sleep. There from the place of fallen rock and angry spirit and petty spiritual slights, rising and twining and fluttering like the beat of a heart.

Turmoil similar to that in which Trevarr sometimes found physical release, and which he seldom kept from Sklayne, even if from a distance.

Bonded, they were . . . knew much of each other. Even quiet, crude rutting with strangers and convenience mates.

But this was nothing like that. Right from the start—sweeter than any stranger, more enticing. Bringing Trevarr back here when they needed to be *there*. For the first time ever, making decisions that didn't exclusively map out their personal survival.

Sklayne sent a pointed comment in Trevarr's direction. ::Tried to warn you.::

But if Trevarr heard him, he wasn't listening.

Typical.

Or maybe not so much, with that turmoil now rising and tasting of Trevarr but not of Trevarr, tasting of that which burned within him but now lacking his lifelong mastery over it.

"Mow!" Sklayne extruded claws into the thin carpet from every juncture . . . went polydactyl and added a few more for emphasis. "M-ma-mow!"

"As if," said the Lucia person, busy-busy in the room, moving the Quinn person's things from this spot to that as they persistently defeated her purpose, leaving a tangled trail of cords no matter where she put them. Neat little contained bricks of power, that's what they were.

Sklayne thought he could help things look much neater. Much.

"I heard you burp, too," she said, and she had *the voice*. The haughty princess voice. "How rude was *that*?"

::Bigger than you,:: he thought at her—not that she could hear. ::Bigger than the world.:: Big enough, inside and out, to emerge proudly from beneath this bed and stalk over to the door and demand that the Lucia person open it, never mind her haughty and *the voice*. Big enough to expect it as his due, full of all the different powers of his world and her world and others beyond. Big enough to—

The Lucia person. Between here and the door. Tall, slender . . . haughty and self-knowing and full of a *look* to go along with the *voice*.

Sklayne sucked extra claws back into the cat shape. Maybe not the door, no. He turned himself to glass and he . . .

Oh yes. He ran for it.

Straight to the power outlet he went, the Lucia person crying out in surprise—a quick Spanish curse and a gasp as at the last minute he *POOF!* let go of *cat* and became merely Sklayne diving into a power trail. The facility lights flickered, dimmed, and recovered and ::Yesss!:: Sklayne built speed and sparkle and popped out the nearest exterior outlet—short transit of much indulgence and sudden glee.

Poof! back into *cat* and slap and crash and that little bush had been ugly anyway. And then silence.

Darkness.

The sweet turmoil, fading so abruptly . . . leaving only the familiar, controlled taste of Trevarr.

Tidy cat face, emerging from battered brush. Ears perked, face of innocence.

Sklayne had been practicing.

From here, he could see—so clearly, in a night of many bright stars. From here, he could sense—so clearly, in a night so silent of energies other than these now directly before him.

So far, Sedona had been all of silence. Not impressive, this place of *vortexes* and energies.

But there, on the fallen rock, the small person of much power lay slumped against Trevarr. He purred. ::Tasteee?::

Trevarr shot tight censure Sklayne's way, tinged with snarl and worry.

Sklayne's tail lashed; whiskers twitched, fanned wide in thoughtful surprise. There, Trevarr's hand cradling the Garrie's head, the other supporting her back, wrapping around her shoulder . . . careful. There, he murmured regret into an unhearing ear.

Startling, to see it—half-blood Trevarr, man of neither this nor that and now literally living between two worlds. Hunter Trevarr, bringing in bounty for the tribunal lords. Fierce Trevarr, making those tribunal lords fear him with the very breadth of his successes.

This very same Trevarr, now bent over the small person who had more power than any nonethereal being Sklayne had ever met.

More power over *Trevarr* than any other being, anywhere.

So odd did it strike him, this tableau, so completely did it capture him, that he lost track of the night . . . and did not notice the Feather person coming, tiny dog in hand, until she was upon them. Fifteen feet away from the rock and quite obviously able to see, with her feeble human eyes, just a little too much.

"Is everything okay out here?" she asked, her tone sharp enough to indicate she very much thought not. The little dog yapped a few times, startled itself with its own temerity, and hushed. Sklayne's tail twitched, rustling dry leaves at the base of the battered bush. Tiny dog, much with the hair, russet and black, round black eyes and dark punctuation of a nose. ::Play with it, or eat it?::

Neither, Trevarr growled at him.

Sklayne winced, whiskers prissing, as the Feather person flicked on a flashlight and shone it straight at Trevarr. Ugly bright light.

If Sklayne felt the instant wash of energies that signified camouflage applied—shuttering the glow, hiding elongated pupils—the Feather person evidently discerned none of it. Though she saw enough of his expression as he turned on her, one hand blocking the light and the other still supporting the Garrie, to take a step back.

But only that one step. *Brave or stupid?* Sklayne settled in to find out. Especially as the light played over the Garrie—her hot energies still uncharacteristically uncertain as she stirred.

The Feather person said, "Exactly what's going on here?"

Sklayne felt the impulse as true as if it had been his own. All the threat, the growl . . . the tang of things hidden within, rising. Trevarr, not about to let anyone near the Garrie.

Always before, it had been easier. Always before, it had been impersonal—not circumstances to stir and prod the wild nature within. Trevarr's other half . . . seldom tame at all.

But this was the Garrie's world and they were here

for the Garrie's people, and Sklayne felt the restraint
as well as the impulse. Trevarr said, "She did not travel
well."

A truth, perhaps, if you had in mind the kind of travel
that Sklayne and Trevarr knew about, and that this
woman would never even imagine.

The Feather person hesitated, and said quite firmly,
"I'm sure you understand that if one of my guests is ill,
it's my responsibility."

"I do not," Trevarr said. "You know nothing of us."

"I do know something, don't I?" the Feather person
returned with some asperity. "I know that my niece was
distressed by your influence on this place of peace. And
I know how you reacted to her. What you did."

"You may tell your niece," Trevarr said, a matter-of-
fact voice with hard, cold metal behind it, "that I will always defend myself—and those who are mine—against
such invasion." He didn't add that on Kehar, it would
have meted a punishment more severe than the Feather
person was likely to imagine. Kehar was not something
to talk about here, where people were so secure in their
existence.

He shifted a hip onto the rock, pulling the Garrie to
him as she stirred. Sklayne felt the return of her, the
awareness sifting in—a befuddled confusion, rising
embarrassment and even shame. ::All is safe,:: he said
to her. ::Listen first.:: And then, to Trevarr, ::She comes
back.::

Not that the Feather person knew any of it. "Until
now . . . I wasn't even sure she was *doing* anything.
Maybe I indulged her, but—" She stopped herself,
straightening slightly. "It doesn't matter. I'm not about
to leave any guest passed out in the cleansing circle!"
The little dog yapped a fervent agreement.

::One swallow,:: Sklayne told it, and sent a hint of
threat its way.

"I'm not passed out," the Garrie said, although her voice was far from steady and her energies instantly flashed hot, a confusion of conflict and yearning.

::Trevarr has said you did not travel well,:: Sklayne told her, hasty at that.

The Garrie immediately took up his words. "I didn't travel well today. Maybe . . . the altitude . . ." She sat, still shaky, and leaned into Trevarr. The Feather person could not possibly fail to see her message.

The Garrie counted on his Trevarr. The Garrie trusted.

And unless the Feather person was blind even with her flashlight, she saw, too, Trevarr turning to the Garrie, running a thumb along her cheek . . . assessing.

"The altitude does strike some people that way," the Feather person finally allowed. "Even here at five thousand feet. You'd best give yourself a couple of days before you head up to Flagstaff, if you want to."

"We have to find Robin," the Garrie said, still sounding confused. Distracted. All the hot and bright, lingering effects of that bright flash of energy.

"That's right," the Feather person said, fresh realization in her voice. "That's what Caryn was coming out to tell us when . . . well, when—" She gestured at the rock, a loopy flash of light that made the Garrie close her eyes. "*You*—you warned us about the rock before anyone could have possibly known. And you—" The flashlight beam pinned Trevarr again. Sklayne's ears went flat.

"That," Trevarr said, ever so gently, "is enough of the light."

The little dog made a surprised sound as the Feather person clutched it suddenly tighter. Not at Trevarr's tone, oh-so-careful. Not at his calmness beside the Garrie.

But at that thing Trevarr couldn't hide. The taste of who he was, coming through.

The light drooped, gleaming off the wide leather belt

and satin sheen of worn metal that made the buckle, knots worked behind a sharp, fierce design of much meaning. The Feather person blurted, "Who *are* you people?"

Slayne purred into the darkness. Loudly.

The Garrie sat straighter. The subtle tension building between them raised the hair along Sklayne's spine, popping out an extra claw or two—on his paws, at the end of his tail. ::Tasteee,:: he told Trevarr, and gave a hedonistic stretch to let that sweet tight energy wash through him, rolling off every interior nook and cranny.

But the Garrie asked her own questions—still jittery inside, and that, too, reaching Sklayne. The strain of it sounded in her voice. "Who died here?" She looked up the steep bluff, into the entrenched scowl of energy that time had soaked into rock. "A woman. Before you bought this place . . . before you turned it into an inn. Maybe before anything was built here at all. Do you know? A flower child . . ."

"That girl!" the Feather person blurted. "Yes! I mean . . . no. I don't recall her name. My, it's been years since I thought of her, but when we first got here, of course it was all anyone could talk about. *Oh, you've bought the place where that poor girl died.* In fact, I started this garden with her in mind, although over time it's grown to be so much more." She looked at the rock with sadness. "I don't know what we'll do with it now."

"Leave it this way," the Garrie said. "She didn't like it much the way it was." Her voice had taken on a remote nature. Sklayne well knew why, feeling the faint riffle of a breeze she'd set up, pinging up the hillside to confirm that the ghost hadn't returned. So careful, was she, to send that ping away from Trevarr—and Trevarr knew it, bracing himself for the traces that found him anyway, eyes flashing, for an instant, like a cat's pinned by light in the darkness.

Quickly enough, the Garrie gave herself a little shake,

bringing all of herself back to this spot. "Give me a chance to deal with her."

"Who *are* you?" the Feather person repeated . . . baffled. Wary.

As well she might be, suddenly faced with she who had just channeled all the gathered power of a plasmic portal, burning herself from the inside out . . . branding herself with Trevarr.

Still learning the price, she was. Right this moment, learning the price.

Not that Sklayne allowed any responsibility for such things. He had done the necessary. He had paid his own price. This world was saved; so was his own. Now there were new things for Trevarr to face, and on which Sklayne would counsel him.

Trevarr, he thought, was going to need such counsel.

As for the Garrie, she said simply, "We're guests who'll be gone after we figure out what's going on with Quinn's friend. It's just that sometimes I talk to ghosts; sometimes Lucia feels them—and then Quinn digs up what we don't already know. And seriously, I wouldn't mess with this place until I've resolved Bobbie's problem."

"Bobbie?" the Feather person said oh so faintly.

The Garrie made an impatient gesture. "The woman. Ghost, I mean. It's better than Jane Doe, right?"

"I . . ." The Feather person's voice faded, and when she spoke up again, Sklayne found her hardly convincing. *Yawn.* "I don't know what to make of any of this. I think . . . you should take it easy tomorrow and drink plenty of fluids. I'll just—" and she bent to put the dog down, completing her sentence with action rather than words.

::Yes!::

"Oh," the Garrie said dryly, "I wouldn't." The Feather person hesitated, while Sklayne hissed in silent annoyance. "I heard something out there. Don't you have coyotes in this area?"

"Maybe the courtyard," the Feather person muttered, pulling the little dog in close.

::Yes, tiny dog. Tremble you should.:: Sklayne lashed his tail in annoyance.

The Feather person turned to go, the doglet tucked safely in her arms. But she hesitated, looking back at them. Looking at Trevarr. "You, and the other girl, and your blond young man. You talk, she feels, he finds out. What about *him*?"

"Oh." The Garrie didn't need to give that much thought at all. "Him." A shrug, a glance at understanding and protectiveness and awareness, there under the gaze of those faintly gleaming eyes. "He . . . *is*."

Oh, yes. Trevarr was going to need Sklayne's counsel.

5

Discretion is paramount.
—Rhonda Rose

Nothing to see here. Move along.
—Lisa McGarrity

Me. Sklayne.
—Sklayne

"I can't help it," Garrie said, refusing to acknowledge embarrassment as she yanked open the door to exit into the bright morning sunshine from the disconcerting Sedona version of a McDonald's. "Drink fluids, she said!"

"Maybe we should split up." Quinn glanced at his

phone, as if there'd be a message waiting since the last time he checked. Not. He pocketed it. "Seriously. We'll cover more ground. This town has over fifty galleries, eateries, New Age shops, specialty stores, antique shops—you get the picture. And we're running late."

Lucia balanced her coffee. "As if it's our fault that we missed this place the first time past."

"I was looking for *golden* arches," Garrie said, casting the building a baleful glance as she stepped into the parking lot. "I mean . . . turquoise on adobe. Who even knew?"

"Chamber of commerce," Lucia said wisely.

"Are you taking this one bit seriously?" Quinn snapped. "You do realize I still haven't even heard from Robin?"

"Quinn," Garrie said sharply—and just in time, for Trevarr had looked over from his shade path at the tone of that last, his morning quiet falling away to make way for awakening *I don't think so,* there behind his sunglass-hidden eyes.

Lucia fussed with the coffee lid as they approached the rental car. "We have come here specifically to help your friend Robin, yes? But her store doesn't open until nine. *Nothing* here opens until nine. So surely we can offer Garrie a pit stop, after all that energy tea this morning—because we all know that's what our Garrie needs, is *more* energy—"

"I didn't sleep well," Garrie muttered.

"Mm-hmm." Lucia took a delicate sip of the coffee, made a face, and swallowed it anyway. She gave Trevarr and his Dr Pepper in the morning a glance she probably thought discreet.

Quinn and Trevarr had been quiet neighbors, but Garrie had no illusions about the cool hostility in their room. And she well imagined that Trevarr ignored the bed, draping himself over the short couch for its vantage point, and still counted it plenty comfortable relative to the usual.

She knew damned well what had kept her awake. *How do I count thee . . .*

And it all led back to that rock. That cleansing circle. "She is gone," Trevarr had told her, when Feather finally and truly left them alone in the darkness.

"Gah!" Garrie had let the sound out in a rush, all the pent-up frustration and reaction and horrified realization, although it didn't do a thing to release the jittery energies urging her to run, to swim, to find an elliptical . . . to pound her way back to reality, one way or the other. "Oh. My. *Gawd.* I fainted. I farking *fainted.*"

There was far too much understanding in his silence. She struggled through it . . . couldn't find a way to break it. After a long moment, he held up his hand, palm out. A tentative hesitation later, Garrie held hers up to mirror it—not touching. Leaving that choice up to him.

Not touching it was. Just close enough to feel the cold burning tingle crackling between them, tracing up and down her fingers . . . raising sensation along each dip and whorl of each individual fingerprint. Sitting on a rock in the Sedona night, touching . . . without touching at all.

She forgot to breathe.

Trevarr only smiled—the faintest hint of a shadow at the corner of his mouth in darkness. "Come," he said, and then he did touch her—and suddenly his hands were nothing but hands. Strong, long fingers, nicked with scars and rough with calluses—not insistent, but asking. He turned her around and tucked her up close—burning warm in the cooling desert night, the duster falling around her shoulders and the belt buckle up against her spine.

Her bones soaked up strength and presence . . . muscle lean and tight behind her, reminding her once more that he did not thrive here. She absorbed the faint movement of his breath; the natural scent of him closed in around her, a smoky tang now faint enough to tell her he was under no particular stress, free of any inner battle between dual natures.

"Do your sweep," he told her. "You will be safe here. I will see to it; Sklayne will see it to it."

::Me. Sklayne.::

As if Garrie could have forgotten him, hiding in the bushes in his favorite guise of *cat,* amusing himself with gustatorial threats against Feather's poor little Yorkie.

::Hungry!:: Sklayne protested. But his mental voice held far too much satisfaction.

She settled back against Trevarr and put herself into a looking-around frame of mind, but she found herself completely and entirely grounded by—

"I feel that," she told Trevarr.

"Atreya," he said, patience in his voice—and just enough of a pause in his phrasing to clue her in to the deliberate word choice. "So it is, when you are this near. But I will not faint of it."

"Oh." She would have elbowed him, had she not been so bemused to find he could even *be* mischievous. *"Oh!"* But there was no way to stomp her foot—not with her legs still folded beneath her—so she gave it up and enjoyed the rare lick of his humor, quickly taking her awareness high above Sedona for an expert survey of energies—colors, sounds, feelings, and ever-present breezes. Vortexes, viewed from on high. Except . . .

She saw nothing.

Oh, a faint wash of cheerful color here; a bubble of activity there. A few dark blobs with watercolor edges bleeding into the pale foundation energy state of the area—darkside entities, but not strong ones. Here, where the Journey Inn sat, a mild roil of clashing colors, a taste of sorrow and the short, strong gusts left behind by anger. The white-heat of brightness that was Garrie herself; the more subtle layering beside her—smoldering warmth, scintillations rising to the surface . . . glimmers of an inner being, emerging and submerging in buried depths. And not far, a Fourth of July sparkler that could only be Sklayne.

But relatively speaking? In an area that should have had four major vortexes and three more nearly as significant, not to mention oh so many unmapped smaller sites . . . in an area brimming with energies and activity . . .

Nothing.

And it had kept her awake, so she had beaten the dawn—all full of rise if not shine—to grab an hour's hard run, hitting the dirt road beside the inn and heading back into the small canyon there.

She was not, after all, truly suffering from altitude sickness.

But she'd sucked down plenty of precautionary water nonetheless here in this high, dry air, devoid as it remained of curious breezes or interesting energies. And on the way back she discovered Trevarr in the cleansing circle—well, what was left of it—working forms.

Sword forms.

Of course.

Sword forms with Lukkas, the blade he stashed away in an impossible coat of many pockets. And while it didn't look particularly strenuous, Trevarr—he who eschewed air-conditioning, wore the duster without regard for the high summer Arizona heat, and made his home on a world Garrie had found oppressively steamy—had not only stripped off his shirt, but worked up a gleam of sweat.

Not that she stared or anything. Not at the feather scales patterning his torso, not at recent scars still wicked red—a puckered bullet hole, the slash across his biceps, the deep stab angling in under his ribs.

None of which should have been nearly so healed at all.

The cut across his back looked older, ragged . . . not part of their San Jose adventure. His hair fell over it, braided back from the sides and loose at his neck— a quick, sloppy braid tied off with leather, revealing the glimmer of silvering in the myriad thin braids normally hidden within the mass of it all. His belt sat low, following the contours of sleek muscle—and if his pants gave him plenty of room to move in the leg, they also hugged his ass on the way past.

Okay, yeah. *Now* she was staring.

And she'd been caught at it, too. No hesitation in his movement, so practiced and smooth and flowing, the sword an extension of his arm—now in one hand, now in two; now extended, now dropping point in an extreme guard position, now cocked over an outstretched arm with the hand reaching, just so. Ritual. But his gaze found her, and held her. Unhidden, those bright eyes and their slitted pupils.

She returned the regard . . . meeting, quietly, the challenge in it. Until he finished, and returned to a basic guard, and then straightened, offering her the slightest of bows.

A flush crept over her neck—a prickle of cold heat. She'd stood her ground; she'd given him a dry, wry little smile. And *then* she'd made good her escape.

She thought of it all now—the silence of the area, the smooth power of him . . . how she could see it in him even now, walking the scant shadows across this already hot parking lot in his hunting clothes—the rugged boots, leather pants, indigo blue shirt with an asymmetrical cross-bib front and lacing.

He only glanced at her—as if he'd been completely

aware of her scrutiny all along, and no more bothered by it than he'd been that morning.

"Hey." Quinn came up short, staring hard at the rental car where it hugged a tiny blot of shade. "I thought we locked this car. I'm damned sure we didn't leave the windows open."

"We did lock it." Lucia regarded the PT Cruiser with coffee in one hand, the other resting on a cocked hip—a model's saucy pose. "Who would break into the car in order to roll down windows? And is everything still there?"

"Everything and more, I would guess," Garrie said dryly.

"Sklayne," Lucia realized, a dramatic gesture away from spilling her coffee.

Quinn cast Garrie a quick frown. "What? The cat? We left it back at the inn."

"Mow!" said Sklayne from within the car. His tail alone appeared above the bottom edge of the window, unfurling in pleasure. Sklayne, it seemed, had been practicing—although perhaps not quite enough.

It seemed there was an eye at the very end of the tail, wide and unblinking . . . watching them.

"Is that—" Quinn said, and if he'd been reaching for the door handle, now he hesitated.

Trevarr didn't. Trevarr took one swift stride, reached inside the car, and came up with Sklayne—hanging by the scruff, tail gone limp and extra eye vanished. Trevarr lifted him to eye level and said nothing . . . just raised that one eyebrow.

::Had to come.:: If there was anything more sullen than Sklayne, caught, Garrie didn't care to hear it. ::Get into trouble if you leave me.::

"You get into trouble no matter where you are, as far as I can tell," Garrie told him.

The tail lashed. ::*You*. Get into trouble. Trevarr, gets into trouble. Always.::

Quinn snorted. "It's almost as if you're talking to . . ." His words faded as Garrie looked at him; as Trevarr looked at him, that eyebrow still raised. As *Sklayne* looked at him. ". . . That . . . *cat*." Quinn took a breath, gave them a look of equal parts glare and obstinance. "*Abyssinian* cat. Ruddy coat with ticking, particularly distinguished by its lack of patterns. Medium-sized cats, wedge-shaped heads, often considered to be the breed that ancient Egyptians worshipped—"

"Quinnie's been researching," Lucia said, singsong and under her breath.

Trevarr tucked Sklayne up in his arm, an absent move, one hand scratching along the ruddy cheek. Sklayne leaned into his fingers. "You brought the book?"

Garrie heard the subtle meaning there. *The* book. She thought Quinn did, too. Somewhat baffled, he said, "You mean the one you sent and then wouldn't let me study?"

"Wouldn't let *others* study." Trevarr was at his most remote, his features hard; Garrie rued the moment she'd so casually mentioned that she and Quinn had once been an item. "Study it now. But do not think of Sklayne as mere *cat*." He looked down, realized he was chin-scratching the mere cat at the same time the mere cat realized he was enjoying it, and both instantly arranged a parting of ways.

Distracted again, thinking of silence over Sedona, Garrie added, "Look under *made of awesome*. He talks back to us, too."

"Us?" Quinn said, looking not the least mollified or reassured. "*Us,* who?"

"Me," she told him. "Trevarr."

"Not me," Lucia reassured him.

::But I borrow your sight.:: From within the car again, unchastened.

"You what?" Garrie asked him, startled.

::Not you. You would know.:: Smug now, with only his ears showing over the bottom edge of the car door.

Quinn closed his eyes. "He's talking to you."

"He—well, yeah," Garrie admitted, deciding a quick change of pace might be timely. "Say, how about we hit your friend's shop now?"

Quinn opened his eyes; he took a deep breath, slow and deliberate. "How about we do that," he said. "I'll drive. I scoped it out last night while I was grabbing food. Much of which seems to be gone already."

::Still healing,:: Sklayne said absently, jumping lightly to the front seat to meet Lucia and take a proprietary interest in her coffee as she slid it into a cup holder.

"Purchases will not be a problem," Trevarr told Quinn, closing the door firmly behind him. "The things you hold dear here are more common on Kehar." Then, as Quinn craned around to question him with a look, he added, "Metals."

"That explains those airline tickets to San Jose," Lucia said with satisfaction.

"Metals," Garrie said. "But not silver."

"Why not silver?" Quinn started the car, backed it out in a tight turn, and gauged the traffic on the main street—Highway 89—shooting out into the street with abrupt speed.

Lucia snatched at her coffee, simultaneously grabbing the handle over the door. "*¡Caray!* Quinnie!"

"Silver belt buckle?" Garrie asked him, briefly bouncing against it as she fumbled for the seat belt.

He steadied her. "Not silver."

Lucia turned back with a quick, expert glance before settling herself more firmly behind her own seat belt, ignoring the tucked-away malls and shopping centers on either side of the street—a strip mall was a strip mall to Lucia Reyes, no matter how prettily the chamber of commerce dressed it up. "Platinum," she said wisely, even as Garrie took in the hard sheen of the bright metal, the crisp edges of the design overlay and the hard knotted lines of metal around it. Not softened and worn and tarnished, even though it had the look of something long used.

"It is older than you think," Trevarr told her.

::Older than you want to know,:: Sklayne intoned from his decently secure perch between the seats, claws suspiciously long and stout as they anchored him there.

"Oh, stop that," Garrie said—only to earn a look from both Quinn and Lucia.

::Answer in silence,:: Sklayne advised her. ::That is best.::

Trevarr slanted a look her way—hidden behind the glasses, but there in the faint tilt of his head. "It is his nature," he said, as if that was any explanation at all.

"Gotta read that book," Quinn muttered, slowing the car to navigate the big *Y* of an intersection between 89 and 179, the town's two and only major streets. Here, the road narrowed slightly, bottlenecking traffic with slant parking, slowing down the tourists so the lure of food and shopping might draw them in even if they'd thought they were headed to Oak Creek Canyon or Flagstaff beyond.

Quinn said, "Gotcha!" and slung the Cruiser around into one of those slanted spots, barely slowing to do it.

"Nice," Lucia said, approval in her voice. "Prime parking turf. And no meter, either!" She looked up and down the street, rescuing her coffee from the holder— not a drop spilled, although Garrie knew that had it been *her* coffee, the slosh factor would have gone off the scale—and giving an approving nod. "I may have under-estimated them."

"It happens," Garrie said, straight-faced. "We were tired when we came through yesterday."

"I was looking for the hotel," Lucia said, archly enough to let Garrie know she'd never be too tired to notice good shopping.

But Lucia had it right. The shops . . . they begged for a day of exploration. Double tiered with outdoor entries and raised walkways and charming adobe architecture, the shop names scribed in classy desert tones and elegant scripts, the shop contents beckoning. Unique artisans, funky clothing, New Age allure, trendy little restaurants . . .

Lucia gave a happy sigh.

Quinn cast her a quick frown. "Luce, we've got work to do."

"And work we will," Lucia said, still in arch shopping princess mode. "Don't ever insult me by suggesting I can't multitask when it comes to *shopping*."

Quinn held up both hands in quick capitulation. "It's just that Robin—"

Lucia instantly softened. "We'll find your Robin," she said. "What was the name of her store, did you say?"

"Partly her store. Crystal Winds."

Garrie gave him a squinty look.

Quinn gestured around—not at the storefronts in the foreground, but out further—red rocks rising all around them, grand vistas in every direction. "Hey, considering what this place is . . ."

"Considering they probably have no idea what real wind *is*," Garrie muttered.

"Chicalet's got her back up," Lucia observed, striding out with long and elegant legs until she found the very best vantage point to peruse the shop names. "Do we look here, or—?"

"One of these little side streets." Quinn consulted a much-folded printout and pointed vaguely; he and Lucia headed down the street.

Trevarr still regarded the scene with such silence that Garrie felt compelled to catch his eye across the top of the Cruiser, sunglasses and all. "Okay?"

From within, unmistakable tones, unmistakable glee. ::*Tasteee!*::

Garrie closed the car door. Hastily. Firmly.

Trevarr said, "There are moments . . . when I know for certain how far from home I am."

Garrie's chest felt a little tighter. "I'm sorry," she said. "The exile . . ."

He gave her a mildly surprised look. "I have goals beyond," he said. And he, too, closed the door.

Garrie bit her lip and swallowed with a throat suddenly gone dry. She couldn't have said just why . . . only that Trevarr had somehow told her more than she understood. And she'd find out, too—but not this moment. "I suppose there's no point in worrying about him in the hot car."

"No point," Trevarr agreed.

::No point,:: Sklayne echoed, although if Garrie hadn't been familiar with the little *poof* of a bright ethereal breeze, she might have missed it. She might even have been surprised to find Sklayne waiting for her when she rounded the front of the Cruiser to gain the sidewalk.

"I hope you locked it behind you," she told him, walking right on past.

Lucia stood on the corner, impatience in her modelesque hip-shot stance. "Down here," she said as soon as they were close enough. "Crystal Wind. Quinn went ahead."

But they found Quinn ducked off to the side of the store's forced adobe charm, thumbing impatiently at his cell phone. "I missed a call," he said. "The *can you hear me now* people need to do something with the reception holes around here."

Garrie thought of the other holes she'd seen—those where the breezes should have been playing and dancing. She raked perceptive fingers through the local energies. "Yeah," she said. "Holes everywhere."

Quinn frowned at her in a distracted sort of way, stabbing through the phone menu. "Ought to be a missed call number here—no. *No.* Don't even try to tell me the battery is going! I charged this thing all night—" He lifted his head, sudden and sharp, eyes narrowing. "Where's that cat?"

"Good luck with that," Garrie muttered, not quite loud enough for anyone but Trevarr to hear. She extended her awareness into the storefront—into the collection of geodes and crystals, meditation lamps and candles and incense, beautifully illustrated tarot cards and meditation CDs and rune stones and—

She closed her eyes. She turned away. She was startled at the realization that she would have to shield herself in this place, where a maelstrom of differing influences pelted her with conflicting needs. *Ugh, nausea.* A deep breath and she was as ready as she'd ever be. "I'm going in while I still have my nerve."

Quinn scowled between phone and store. "I'm going to try a few places, see if I can get some reception and reach my voice mail."

"*I'm* going in." Lucia headed through the door with a jingle of bells.

A strangely disquieted look crossed Trevarr's face. "There is a smell—"

"Patchouli," Garrie told him, and sighed. "It's not a bad thing . . . in moderation." And then she laughed at his disbelief, and pushed through the bell-laden door—shields up, for sure. Not shields that would protect her from physical harm—or an overuse of patchouli—but anyone pushing at her privacy would be in for a rude surprise.

Not that she often kept shields up. Took too much effort, too much concentration . . . it wasn't second nature, not like her manipulation of the breezes.

But here, she didn't expect to be using breezes at all . . . just words.

"Chicalet, look!" Lucia held up a jumble of disjointed, irregular ceramic disks on monofilament, a flat length of tapering wood in the midst of them. Garrie's blank expression made it to her face before she could stop it, and Lucia held it all a bit higher. "Wind chimes! The tree of life, yes?"

The components settled more properly into place and suddenly there it was, a branchless tree with ceramic leaves and a bamboo trunk. Garrie's confusion cleared; Lucia looked at it with satisfaction. "*Mi abuela* will love this. And she has a birthday coming up." A glance over at Garrie. "Oh, stop. Multitask, remember? It'll be easier to talk to her if we're buying something." She nodded toward the back of the store, where the single clerk was ringing up someone else's purchase.

"Well," Garrie said, trying not to sound grudging, "if they have some good lavender-scented soap . . ."

Lucia collapsed the wind chime down into a puddle of ceramic and string in her palm. "Funny thing, about that missing soap of yours," she said dryly.

"Isn't it, though." Garrie matched her tone and rather than face questions about Sklayne, she headed toward a display of candles, figuring if this place had specialty soaps, this would be the—

"Oh," she said. "Handmade goat's milk soap. Lavender and oatmeal. *Oh*."

Lucia laughed softly. "Now," she said, "we can go talk to that woman. She looks hassled, yes? So we'll make her day better with a couple of sales."

She looked hassled, all right. She finished up the transaction at the register, mustering a marginal smile.

Medium height, profoundly sturdy . . . pushing the limits of zaftig, in flowing lightweight harem pants, an equally flowing blouse, and a remarkably snug, tailored bodice that thrust her ample charms first and foremost. Bright blond hair that didn't quite look natural, makeup that could have been a little less intense . . . and faint lines of worry bringing out the age she was trying to hide.

"*Buenos días,*" Lucia greeted her. "We're not too early, I hope?"

"Not at all." Smooth sales talk, another smile without any feeling behind it. "What can I get for you?"

"Respect!" said a male voice, heavy on the gutterals. The entire display of wind chimes sounded off, ringing wildly in the breeze. *Ah, ghostie.* Busy little town on that account, given how quiet it was otherwise. Garrie lifted herself to the breezes, cold and stuttery and carrying a stench like rotting incense; a hazy roil of waxy presence hung in the corner, melting away but never diminishing.

The saleswoman's smile took on a brittle nature. "Odd drafts we get in this place."

Garrie read that expression; she took the chance. "It's not a draft. But I expect you know that."

Oh, more brittle yet, as she stepped back behind the glass-topped counter. "Was that a threat?"

What? A *what*? "I don't—"

Candles. Melting. Everywhere. The rising scent of ghostie excretions mixed with the rising scent of released perfumes.

"Did Huntington send you?" the woman demanded, her eyes going narrow and her brittle going hard. "Because you can just turn right around. I may not be what he's becoming, but I know how to defend myself!" The hand reaching under the counter . . . might have been going for a phone. Might have been going straight for a weapon.

"Aie!" Lucia said, and her horror spoke more to the lack of propriety than to the potential danger. "We're your *customers*."

"Not anymore you're not." The woman's grim tone left no room for discussion. "Or maybe you brought a great big wad of cash to pay for this damage? Your credit sure isn't good here anymore."

"Respect!" the ghost gurgled out.

In a way, the woman was probably right. Often times a disgruntled ghost, upon realizing that Garrie perceived and reacted to its presence, immediately changed states— went from biding its time and pissing and moaning around to acting out. Causing damage.

Melting candles.

Dropping rocks.

"Bob!" she snapped, not even thinking before she hung her all-purpose name on the man. "Behave yourself, or I'll—"

"You!" the woman pointed. "How stupid do you think I am?"

::Watch!:: Sklayne's voice broke into Garrie's thoughts right through her shields, adding to the whirlwind of ghost and confusion. ::Weapon!::

The woman's pointing finger now jabbed at the door. "Put down the damned soap and get out of here! Tell Huntington that we don't scare that easy, and he'd better stop his stupid damned scheme to rule the world from freaking *Sedona,* and—" She broke off with a gasp.

It wasn't easy to slam open a heavy glass shop door, but Trevarr had done it—setting the bells to a frenzied jangle, filling the doorway—and then filling the shop— all dark and tall and leather and the hard lines gone predatory.

"Oh my *God*," the woman said, gaping at him. "What has Huntington *done*?"

Trevarr didn't bother with words. He strode through the wind chimes and past the racks of cute batik shirts and past the melted candles and right through the burbling wax manifestation of the ghost—past Lucia and her helpful exclamation of, "Aie! *¡Caray!* No, no, no!" Directly up to the counter, where the saleswoman—caught between feisty and horrified—fumbled with whatever she had behind the register in the first place.

Trevarr planted a hand on the glass and leaned over the counter with such swift, fierce purpose that he'd clamped down on her wrist before she did anything more than utter a few breathless words that Garrie only belatedly realized were meant to be a warding.

Garrie opened her mouth to say something sensible. Something like, "This is all a huge misunderstanding," or "No, seriously, a ghost did it," or "Trevarr, don't break her!" but the woman dropped what she'd been holding—a startlingly pink, boxy object—only to scoop it up with her other hand and jam it onto Trevarr's arm, her face contorted with fear and her eyes wild as she squeezed her hand until the knuckles popped white.

It was the sound that gave it away—revealed what it was. Electric cackle-static, sharp and loud.

Stun gun. Garrie cried a wordless and angry protest as Trevarr stiffened, an involuntary grunt kicked out of his lungs. But there he still stood, to the woman's obvious astonishment. "Go down!" she cried, plump features distorted with fear, oblivious to the ghost's moans of annoyance. She jammed the stun gun forward again even as Garrie leaped to join the fray.

She wasn't the only one.

Sklayne appeared from nowhere, phasing from glass cat mode to visible cat to leaping cat, all flattened ears and snarling countenance. He leaped not at the woman's hand, but at the stun prongs. She shrieked and might well have jerked back had her reflexes been quicker—

but they weren't, and her thumb spasmed down on the trigger.

POOF! Puffer fish cat, every hair standing on end, legs splayed in all directions—and if he absorbed most of the second jolt, he didn't get it all. Trevarr jerked back, stumbled, and fell against a display of wind bells; both went down in a jumble of sound and motion. Sklayne dropped straight to the floor, balled up, and rolled away like a tumbleweed.

"Respect!" said the ghost, gargly and offended. *"Now."*

Garrie finally clamped onto the woman's wrist, more wiry strength in her body than people ever gave her credit for, and she twisted fiercely; the pink stun gun fell and clattered away. Through gritted teeth, she told the ghost, "It's not about *you,* thank you very much! You get out of line again and I'll show you what it means to demand respect!"

She shoved the woman away from her, barely able to catch a glance at Trevarr—had she ever seen him look *ungainly* before? "Dammit," she said, torn between them all, finally giving Bob a quick shove of a breeze just for the buffer it gave them, and blowing out an equally quick exasperated breath, glancing at the woman just long enough to say, "The problem is, from a ghostly perspective, Bob has no concept of where the line *is.*"

"Who *are* you?" The woman backed away, rubbing her wrist. "What do you want?"

Lucia reappeared from between two racks of clothing, not a hair out of place, stun gun in hand. "Aie, Dios, maybe you should have asked that *before* zapping at us?"

Garrie scowled at the woman and went down beside Trevarr, in disheveled disarray down there with the wind bells, his sunglasses knocked off along the way.

Not getting up just immediately, either, eyes dazed and exposed and so thoroughly not *human*.

"Look at me," she said, as much to keep his gaze averted as to assess him as she groped around for his sunglasses. He seemed to try . . . but no, no focus there. He'd found her left ear, perhaps.

There was, for an instant, silence.

And then Quinn came bouncing through the door. "Nope, I just can't get a—"

He stopped short, just as astonished as Trevarr with the stun gun jolting through him, or as the woman now faced with Sklayne hovering to absorb a second jolt in puffer fish mode. "What the *hell*? Are you *kidding* me?"

"Hey," Garrie said, surly on Trevarr's account. *"She started it."*

Well. And Bob. Because truly, Bob's timing . . . totally sucked.

"Are you *kidding* me?" Quinn said again, incredulousness swelling. And then he saw Trevarr's unshuttered eyes, and his jaw did that weird little thing where it jutted just a little bit sideways, and Garrie knew *uh-oh,* Quinn had really reached his limit and she did the only absurd thing she could, which was to swiftly cover Trevarr's eyes with her hands *la la la you don't see that . . .*

Yeah. Real grown up, Garrie. So was the defensive tone in her voice. "Can I help it if they come out of the woodwork when I'm around?" For Quinn wouldn't need to be told who *they* were, or what had truly been the catalyst here . . . if he chose to listen. If he chose to stop glaring at Trevarr, who wouldn't take it kindly if he ever stopped staring stupidly at nothing.

"Garrie's right, Quinnie—she *did* start it." Lucia cast an annoyed look at the saleswoman. "And I was trying to *buy* something, too."

That, if nothing else, got Quinn's attention. And the

saleswoman's, too, as she tended her wrist, backed up against the wall behind the counter like a frightened animal. Something of the big-eyed sort, like those in a children's movie. "Quinn?" she asked, as Trevarr did, finally, lift a hand to uncover his eyes.

He missed and lurched over to set the bells to jingling in protest beneath him, but still. Progress.

"Quinn?" the woman said again, taking a step forward. "Robin mentioned a friend named Quinn . . ."

"Exactly," Lucia said. "And here we are, to buy things and let you know we're here, because Robin asked for help and then she didn't meet us last night at the hotel."

The woman frowned. "I said she mentioned *Quinn.* She didn't say anything about a shopping princess or the Terminator or . . ." She looked at Garrie. "I give up. Or you."

Garrie glared back. "The one who can make sure the rest of your stock is melted like those candles if you don't find a nicer tone of voice, that's who."

"And what *was* that?" the woman asked, pretty much as if she hadn't heard. "That . . . that . . . *puffer cat.*"

Lucia said sweetly, "Sklayne."

Quinn bent to pick up one of the fallen display trees, leaving half the stock behind. "It doesn't matter."

::Be sorry if you think not.::

"Behave," Garrie muttered. "You and Bob both."

Trevarr tried again, a clumsy hand coming up to bat at hers, and this time it landed—but she held firm, leaning in to murmur, "Your *eyes.*" That she could resist him at all spoke volumes.

Farking hell, he was going to be mad when he pulled himself back together.

::Klysar's farking bloody hell mad,:: Sklayne said, with the air of someone pleased at stringing so many profanities in a row.

"Listen," Quinn said, stepping carefully away from the display tree he'd righted; it gave a listless, creaky half-turn. "I don't have time to untangle this. I need to find Robin—I need to know what's going on."

The woman took a deep breath, still rubbing her wrist, and gave Garrie a pointed look. "I want to know what that was all about, first." The pointed look switched to Quinn. "You want trust? Fine, Robin trusts you. I don't."

Garrie thought that under other circumstances, she might admire this woman. As it was, she found her damned annoying. Explaining ghosts . . . explaining reckoning . . . *right*. Just like that. "What's your name?"

She hadn't expected that. She pursed glossy red lips. "Nancy Barber."

"All right, Nancy. Here you go. You have a long-term ghost. He's unhappy. He recognized that I would be able to communicate with him, and he pretty much wet his pants over it. He wants respect. I'm not sure what that means, but given the really wicked cross-drafts you've created in this store, my guess is you need to pay a little more attention to your ethereal feng shui."

"My . . ." Nancy Barber looked just as dazed as Trevarr.

"Ethereal feng shui," Garrie repeated impatiently, daring a peek at Trevarr's eyes. *Not yet.* Even if his grip did tighten around her wrist. "All of the things—okay, some of the things—in this store are meant to *do* something. But you've got them arranged by the shiny factor and not by how they might affect the space. So maybe you ought to think about that, huh?"

"I . . ." Nancy said, looking around the store. Things melted, things overturned, things shoved aside, the sales counter all but cleared of their tidbit displays.

"Maybe this is for the best," Lucia told her. "Now you can put it back together right."

"You *think*?" Nancy's look might possibly have been more disbelievingly aghast, but Garrie wasn't sure how.

"Hey," Garrie said. "It's up to you. You're the one with a ghost. You can ignore him if you want—"

The waxy melting blob of Bob emitted a discordant sound.

"—but I wouldn't, because he's not likely to back down after this."

"Do you think we need to get help?" Lucia took a step closer, making it clear—the question wasn't about Bob or the store at all. *Trevarr.*

Garrie shook her head, an absent gesture. "Maybe Sklayne . . ."

A small pile of shirts shifted and belched, then groaned, a sound reminiscent of too much Thanksgiving dinner.

". . . Or maybe not. I think just give him another moment." She peeked again at Trevarr's eyes, found the dark rims and pewter shading easing back over silver, the slitted, catlike pupils fading to roundness. Relieved, she let her hand slide away, pushing back the carelessly short strands of hair that framed his face. His other hand came up, finding her free wrist with unerring accuracy.

Ah, yes. He was on his way back.

But not quite. Because there, for that instant, he didn't hold her wrist—he clung to it. His eyes shone not with hard self-assurance, but with need and vulnerability and even yearning. More intensity than she'd thought any one being could carry; more emotion. More *need*. It swelled up around her like a rising breeze, filling her with eddies of sensation—more than the chilly brisk heat gathering where it would, tightening across her skin in contrasting layers of shivers. Much more.

Garrie broke away with a gasp, moving nothing but her eyes, but it was enough. A faint wash of energy trickled past her, and then he was just as she would have expected to find him—here in the broad daylight, in the exposed open ground of a strange land. Eyes fully camouflaged, expression unreadable.

At least, unreadable to anyone else. Garrie could see well enough the anger behind it, the awareness that he'd been taken by surprise, an unfamiliar weapon wielded by inexpert hands.

The door bells might have jangled warning, had not the door remained jammed open. As it was, Garrie had only the peripheral glimpse of someone's approach.

The woman's voice was husky alto, pleasantly commanding, and just a tad incredulous. "What, if I may say, the *fuck*?"

Maybe it was because Garrie had just seen what she'd seen in Trevarr . . . *felt* it. But she was startled to now see even a faint watermark of the same in Quinn—only a flash, quickly covered by the rest of what Quinn was—self-confident handsome guy who knew it. "Robin," he said, even as Garrie exchanged a quick glance with Lucia.

The faint wrinkle on her forehead said *yes, I saw it, too.*

Only then did she turn her complete attention to Robin.

In the back of her mind, she must have been expecting Quinn's usual type—everyone but for his brief fling with Garrie herself.

In a flash, she suddenly understood that all of those *usuals*—tall and slender, vaguely vacuous, as blond as he—were a cover-up for this one woman. Very much like Nancy—not so tall, lush curves encased in snug jeans and an equally snug bodice. *Store theme?* Smooth brown hair shone with chunky honey highlights, a casual bob with heavy bangs, casually mussed. She wore her makeup more lightly than her friend . . . and nothing would have been enough to hide the fatigue and strain on her face.

"Quinn," she said, taking obvious stock of the chaos of her shop. "Do I have to say it again?"

Quinn's mouth quirked. "Ghost," he said, just like that. "If they're at the tipping point and Garrie comes through, they blow. The rest of it, I think you can call collateral damage."

Nancy said, ever so faintly, "I'm sorry . . . I saw him and I thought of—you know—"

"But *we* don't." Garrie climbed to her feet, wishing she didn't bear the imprint of several chimes in her bare shins. Trevarr rose to his feet with stiff awkwardness; she put out a hand to steady him and it was enough to draw Robin's sharp gaze to the pink stun gun in Lucia's hands.

"I thought—" Nancy blurted, and then silenced herself, opting to stand pat on words already said.

"Robin," Quinn said, "This is Lucia . . . and this is Garrie."

Damned if Robin's eyes didn't widen slightly, as if their names meant something to her. As if she'd known about them all this time, while they hadn't heard a thing about her. Her gaze slanted to Trevarr.

Lucia stepped in to fill that empty space. "This is Trevarr. We worked together in San Jose." It sounded moderately lame, so she added—no better—"That's where we were when Quinn called. So we came."

"Just stop talking," Garrie muttered at her. "It's the only way out."

"I was going to buy a wind chime," Lucia added, a final uncharacteristic blurt of words. "It's around here somewhere."

"Find it, and it's on the house," Robin said dryly. She looked at Quinn. "Coffee shop and talk?"

"Right here," Garrie said firmly. "Right now. We've gone to a lot of time and trouble to show up here, because we're trying to help the friend of a friend, and I've already dealt with one ghost for you. But so far we've been stood up—that would be by you—and we've been accosted, and we've been outright attacked. And meanwhile, there's nothing going on here. *Nothing.*" Even if it wasn't entirely true. Not with two ghosts boiling up into temper mode at the catalyst of Garrie's presence, and not with things being so very quiet in a place known for its activity.

But she had a point to make. So she said, "Unless I hear something interesting damned farking fast, I believe I'll make plans to see the Grand Canyon. And oh, Meteor Crater, and right! Sedona isn't the only place around here with really cool rocks, either. There's that old volcano thing up past Flagstaff."

::Crunchy!::

Robin's generous lips thinned. "She always like this?"

Quinn said gently, "Expecting to be treated like the skilled professional she is, you mean?"

Garrie loved him all over again for that. Even Trevarr cast a grateful glance his way. Okay, it read more like a momentary cessation of ever imminent threat, but it was enough.

Robin sighed, pushed her ruffled hair back with one hand, and gestured something that might have been apology. "Things have been a little stressed around here."

Garrie just looked at her. Lucia just looked at her. Even Quinn just looked at her. The customer who came to the doorway behind her and lingered just long enough to see the interior of the shop looked at them *all,* and fled.

Robin threw her hands up. "I'm sorry, okay? I'm *sorry.* You're right. It sucks that I wasn't at the hotel last night. I got caught up in this thing. I—I'm so used to *not* talking about this . . ." She took a breath, stepping closer to them . . . checking behind her in a reflexive glance that spoke volumes. "You know how it is here . . .

this place is so full of New Age practitioners, all peace and love and vortex energy."

"Not you?" Lucia asked.

Robin shrugged. "I do what I do. But I've never seen the need to be *cliquish* about it. Walk the walk out where it's hard to do, in real life."

Garrie frowned. "Okay, so there's a lot of incestuous peace and love here. Not seeing the problem so far."

"The problem," Robin informed her, "is when they're too literal about it. And when they decide they all want more than their fair share. Like, what happens if they each suck in a little personal store of energy . . . what can they do with it? Can they hold onto it? Use it? Abuse it?"

Garrie thought of Krevata plasmic portals. She thought of the hot white energies of a star's heart, pouring through the conduit of her body. She thought of the remaining storage stones, left behind by the captured Krevata. The ones she hadn't mentioned to Trevarr.

And while she was doing all that thinking, Robin watched her, and her wary expression slowly eased. "I thought you would laugh."

"Robin," Quinn said, "if you knew even half the stuff we deal with . . ."

"Ghost poop," Lucia said glumly.

"Ghost snakes," Garrie added. "Aunties who wished they were haunted. Grannies who wished they weren't. Families who want to dial up the dead to berate them for how they died." She gave Robin a look. "We didn't, of course."

"The sororities!" Lucia said. "Remember that? *It's hell week and we want to make it real.*"

No one said anything about plasmic portals, Krevata, or the Winchester Mystery House now mysteriously cleared of its habitual ghostly population.

Even so, Robin held up her hands in defeat, exchanging a glance with her friend—it could have been relief, or it could have been *but they don't get it yet.* "Okay," she said. "The thing is, whether you think we have a problem. Whether you think what they're doing can be *done.*"

Garrie shrugged. "Maybe two weeks ago, I would have said no. But now I'd say . . . it depends. You know . . . on who's trying, and how they're trying it. It's not my thing—"

Trevarr made a sound. "It is not your thing, *atreya,* because you don't need it to be. These people have no true sense of your breezes—they feel only the strongest gales."

Quinn crossed his arms. "You certainly seem to have picked up a lot."

Trevarr said flatly, "If the woman at the hotel represents the skilled here, then I have *picked up* enough."

"There are always exceptions," Garrie murmured. She brushed again at the bell imprint on her leg. "The thing is, I went looking last night." She glanced at Robin. "It's this thing I do . . . a sweep of the area. And last night . . . I don't know where you were, but there was nothing going on."

Robin rolled her eyes. "I never said they were doing the nefarious deed last night. Last night, as it happens, they were *plotting* their nefarious deeds. And I was . . . well, I was spying on them. And then I got caught there, because they decided to celebrate their extreme cleverness with lots of self-congratulatory sex." She squinched up her nose. "But they've had some success. They've been sucking life out of these red rocks . . . can you feel it?"

Garrie cocked her head, thumbs hooked in her shorts pockets. "Can you?"

Robin looked away. "Not so much. But you know . . . I can *see* it. So can everyone else—they just think it's the drought. But last year was pretty good—the snow didn't leave the San Francisco Peaks until well into June!"

A child of the high desert herself, where the high mountain snows of the northern state helped to feed the Rio Grande through the year, Garrie well understood the significance of this. She thought of Sklayne the evening before, tumbling into the dead, brittle bush . . . there in the well-watered landscaping.

Waxy Bob shuddered, shedding globs of himself. "Truth," he said, his reverberating voice gone all the more creepy in its thoughtfulness. "Meant to melt it *all*."

"Well, thanks for sharing," Garrie told him. And in response to Robin's narrowed eyes, she told them, "Your ghost. Bob. He's agreeing with you. In his unique way."

"Are you quite sure," Robin said, each word distinct, "that he's *our* ghost? He didn't show up until you did, after all."

Quinn lifted his gaze to the heavens.

"You mean I'm either lying about it or I *didn't notice* I had a ghost trailing me?" Garrie shook her head. "For the record? That's strike two."

And while Robin, startled, tried to form a response, Garrie turned from her. "We need food," she said, meaning *Trevarr needs food.* "And I need somewhere to run this off." She didn't care that Robin and Nancy wouldn't understand her shorthand.

Robin, it seemed, didn't truly need to understand. "Hiking?" she said, eyebrows raising, opportunity seized. "Rugged hiking?"

"Better than not."

"Then," Robin said, "I have just the thing. If you don't mind stumbling into the fug left over by the self-congratulatory sex." She made a face. "Did I say, *lots* of self-congratulatory sex?"

6

Appropriate equipage is paramount.
— Rhonda Rose

Best invention ever: stain-resistant clothing.
— Lisa McGarrity

Shoes! It's all about the shoes!
— Lucia Reyes

If Lucia had expected some meandering tourist trail along dry desert bluffs, artistically scattered with juniper, cedar, and stunted little scrub brush . . .

Wrong, wrong, wrong.

But Robin had said hiking shoes, and she herself had been wearing sturdy lightweight trail runners. When Lucia had hesitated, measuring the effect of canvas tennies on her cute little spring outfit, Robin had repeated herself in no uncertain terms. So while Garrie pulled out a bag of hot, spicy jerky and tossed it to Trevarr, rummaging for water bottles and a dorky hiker hip pack that didn't seem to have much chance of hanging onto Garrie's wiry frame, Lucia reluctantly changed out of her sandals.

And still Robin had given the tidy little canvas tennies a hairy eyeball. Lucia had no idea what she thought about Trevarr's boots—the scarred leather of well-worn working boots, perfectly fitted and long maintained, complete with their surfeit of buckles. And if Trevarr was possibly the only person in the world who could carry them off, that was okay. Because he was definitely the only person in the world who had them.

Next to him—and next to Lucia—Garrie was probably a relief. She had regular high-top hiking sneakers.

She didn't hesitate to buckle on her water bottles. She wore those ubiquitous trail shorts, full of pockets and slung low on her hips, somehow defying gravity. And while the paper-thin long-sleeved shirt layered over a snug spaghetti-strap tank covered the new shimmer of her arms in the sun, sunscreen dulled the same effect on her face.

Lucia wore sunscreen, too. But she never let it dull her face. For Lucia knew how to distract people from her occasional . . . *lapses*. Even if they were much more occasional than they used to be.

Quinn was probably just plain normality. Jeans, an outdoorsy short-sleeved pullover with macho detailing at the neck, and plain old big feet in plain old cross-trainers, laced up tight for the hike. Normal. Totally guy. Was what he was.

She gave Robin's back a quick glare. *He'd better be much more than that to you, if you're using him like this,* pajarito. *If you're using* us *like this.*

And then she sighed, gave her unaccustomed ponytail—high off her head, swingy and fresh—a tug, and reached for the most convenient tree to haul herself up the trail.

Meandering little tourist trail. *Wrong, wrong, wrong.*

"I can't believe," she found herself saying out loud, "that you made it down this trail after dark."

Robin, just ahead of her—behind Quinn, who was behind Trevarr, who was behind Garrie, who was naturally leading the way as if she'd been in these woods all her life and beyond that as if she could barely keep herself slow enough to suit them—hesitated before her own picky footing, giving Lucia a startled glance.

Lucia was somewhat gratified to see the woman was as out of breath as Lucia herself, her face flushed with effort. She, too, wore a water-bottle pack, and she reached for the bottle now. She shook her head even as she squirted a stream of water into her mouth, swallowing. "You must be kidding. Sterling Pass is the hard way in. I took the Arch trail. Short and easy."

"What?" Lucia felt her eyebrows climb. "Aie, Dios! There's an Easy button?" She dabbed at the sweat on her brow. "Why, oh *pajarito,* are we not *using* this Easy button?"

Robin narrowed her eyes. They were far too quick, those eyes.

Lucia waved a hand. "Little bird, yes?" But she, too, had eyes that could speak, and she used them, pinning Robin hard. "And *why*?"

Robin glanced up ahead, where Garrie scrambled over a tough, steep section as though gravity were an imaginary thing. Sklayne bounded up an impossible vertical beside her, his claws glinting suspiciously long against an emerging slab of deep red rock. So it was all around them—a forest most gorgeous, deep green Ponderosa pines with stunty little maples peeking out where the sun hit the sides of a pass full of high cliffs and fancy rock formations, all red and sand and rich color.

Lucia followed her gaze, abruptly understanding. "Surely not because she liked the words *rugged hiking.* Oh, please no."

Robin returned her water bottle to the small of her back. "Not in those words themselves. But Quinn said . . ." She hesitated, glancing ahead as if to gauge whether they might be overheard. "He said she gets this way. That it's the price for what she does."

Lucia took a sudden deep breath, lips pressed together, guilt coming on hard. Of course Garrie needed this. Of *course* she did. She'd spent the entire previous day sitting in vehicles. The plane, the car. And then dealing with that cranky ghost to top it off . . . and finding out that the inn's little gym room closed at eleven.

Maybe Lucia would speak to Feather Middleton about that later today.

If she survived this hike.

"Right," she said to Robin. "Energizer bunny, that's Garrie. Abs of steel. Legs of steel. Buns of steel."

"That," Robin said, "might be more than I want to know." She looked up, where Garrie, Trevarr, and Quinn now looked back at them. "What I *do* want to know—"

"Oops," Lucia said, because she knew what was coming next. Trevarr. Of course, Trevarr. "Looks like they're waiting on us." And she passed Robin on the narrow trail and scrambled her way up the next treacherous bit of rock-strewn excuse for a path as though her feet actually knew what they were doing.

Another mile of that and she was more than ready to flop down where the trail topped out. "I can't feel my feet," she said, primly rotating an ankle as she perched on the convenient rock instead. Let some other woman *flop*. Not Lucia Reyes.

"Maybe that's a good thing," Garrie suggested. "Anyway, it should be easier going from here." She pulled a trail map from one of those many pockets and handed it over—breathing lightly, moving easily.

"I could hate you, chicalet." Lucia snatched the map.

"Probably not," Garrie said. "Catch your breath, take a drink. I'm going to scan ahead."

Code, not that they needed it here. Check out the landscape, maybe. Check out the etherealscape, for sure.

Garrie didn't go far, maybe not as far as she thought, before the landscape caught at her—Sterling Canyon, spread out beneath in a gaping space defined by rugged cliffs and bold conifers. Red and buff and green, with gashes of paler rock windblown into swirling rock hollows and forms. Sipping water, Lucia rotated her toes within her shoes, taking note of them all—Quinn and

Robin, off to the side together in awkwardness; Trevarr barely even close enough to be called *with* them at all, expression forbidding . . . and Sklayne, conspicuous in absence. Garrie tipped her head back, standing square, arms lifting gently from her sides, hands turned out . . . a receiving stance, with those funky braided bracelets creating the perfect punctuation. The canyon fell away before her; bright blue sky raised up around her. The breeze ruffled her hair—as spiky as it ever got, after this morning and after this rugged climb.

Lucia found she was holding her breath. Found she felt suddenly privy to and even part of something much bigger than it had ever seemed before. The exertion of the climb, the intensity of the sky, the harsh beauty of the canyon . . . it put Garrie in a framework that matched the power she held.

¡Aie, caray! Maybe there was something to this Sedona vortex thing after all.

And yes, maybe Garrie thought she'd moved farther out than she truly had. For she relaxed her stance and lowered her chin, looking out over the canyon with the head tilt that meant she was thoughtful and not entirely happy about it. And then she spoke to Sklayne, who had shown up at her feet, chewing on a pinecone. "I'm worried," she said, which got Lucia's attention right away, and after that the incidental eavesdropping became purposeful.

Sklayne stopped chewing to regard her. After a moment, he gave the pinecone a single precise pat of his paw that sent it skittering over the edge of the trail and bouncing down who knew how many hundred feet of dirt and rock.

"Don't tell me you're not," Garrie said to him. "I've seen the difference in him. Before it seemed like the food wasn't quite right, but at least he could eat enough of it. Now? I swear it does nothing for him."

Sklayne flicked an ear, then a tail. Lucia knew he spoke, in some manner . . . she knew Garrie could communicate, if not as well or freely as Trevarr, at least with effort.

She knew, too, that Sklayne had also insinuated himself into her own awareness, back in San Jose. She didn't like that, thinking back on it, she still had no sense of when he'd done it. Nothing other than a few odd impulses while shopping.

Come to think of it, maybe she was glad to know those hadn't been her impulses, after all.

"You mean, because he's healing?" Garrie's voice dropped even lower; she tipped a quick look over her shoulder, angled directly at Trevarr.

It didn't escape Lucia's notice that she hadn't had to look for him. She'd simply *known*. Okay, that was a little spooky, too.

And then she paid attention to what she was hearing. She remembered that back in San Jose, Garrie hadn't even been certain of Trevarr's survival. He'd taken the Krevata back to Kehar in a battered state about which Garrie wouldn't talk—but when he'd returned days later, he hadn't moved like a man who'd been sorely wounded in fighting for his life—for *Garrie's* life. And now, mere days later, he was apparently as he had ever been—a lethal hunter in the middle of an unsuspecting civilization. Tall, silent, hard. Not safe, just as Garrie had warned Lucia from the start.

"I *know* he needs something," Garrie said, in that tight way that meant her temper was rising—even as she fought to lower her voice.

Lucia got it: really she did. Garrie was protecting Trevarr. What they'd been through together, Lucia didn't know. She knew it had forged something between them, and hey, *bueno* for them. But long before Trevarr had shown up, Garrie and Lucia had been through plenty, too.

She deserved a little trust, she thought.

"Then *get* it," Garrie said, lowering her voice even further even as the intensity of her words carried. "How is it not safe? How can you not go back? You know, it couldn't be any more obvious that there are things he's not telling me. And you, too. How stupid do you think I am, anyway?" An indignant huff, there. "Dammit, Sklayne, I don't like being in the dark."

Funny. That makes two of us.

Garrie found herself grateful that Sklayne made himself scarce as they descended into Sterling Canyon. Some stinky herb from Kehar would likely help with the whole food thing, would it?

But *no,* it would be too easy to simply go to Kehar and bring some back. And it would be too easy to tell her why that wasn't an option just now, either.

Did that apply to Trevarr's personal lair, too? A place from which he had seemed to draw strength, and where—although she drew attention outside it—she'd been safe and unseen? A place she'd hoped to visit again . . .

Stupid mysterious hero type.

She kicked at a stone or two, but generally she kept her feet on the rugged trail. She wasn't ready to try reckoning from the other side of life.

Behind her, the others straggled out. Robin had been tired before the day started, and Lucia was now as disheveled as Garrie had ever seen her—in truth, the glow of exertion on her cheeks was looking more and more like plain old sweat. Quinn hung near Robin, and Trevarr brought up the rear.

She'd worried at first, until she realized it had nothing

to do with the stun gun. No, he was covering twice as much ground as the rest of them . . . watching the back trail, checking different vantages, on occasion just plain disappearing into the woods.

Hunting mode, Garrie realized. Watching mode. And while she didn't think there was anything to watch *for,* it spoke to her of his life. Trevarr in default mode.

Ha. A hike—great idea. It had been rugged. It had taken the edge off. But it had left her far too much time to think.

"Wait up!" That was Robin, making no attempt to increase her pace as the trail pitch eased. Garrie hesitated, discovered the nagging impulse also somewhat abated, and pulled a few quick stretches. By the time Robin—and Quinn and Lucia—had caught up, Trevarr, too, had pulled in from his outrider position.

"Oh, good," Garrie said. "The pregame huddle."

"It's not a game," Robin said sharply. "Tell me, what did you see? Up at the top, when you looked around? That's what you did, isn't it? *Looked* at things?"

Garrie turned to Quinn. "Tell me again why she came to us for help? If she doesn't believe?"

"I came to *Quinn* for help," Robin said distinctly. "He has a knack for putting things together . . . for figuring them out. For knowing what to do."

All true. All part of what made him so valuable to the team. But still. "Oh," Garrie said, tight and offended inside. "Okay, then. Never mind." And if she hid her reaction from Robin with a matter-of-fact tone, she didn't hide it from Trevarr. He drifted subtly closer, one hand briefly touching her back. *Cold tingling heat.*

She couldn't hide it from Lucia, either, whose casual question hid all manner of subtle rebuke. "What was it you wanted to tell us?"

Robin opened her mouth; closed it. She tried visibly

to sort whether she'd been *telling* or *asking,* and finally took Lucia's lead. "The trail we just took isn't highly traveled."

"*Ay* Dios, I wonder why?" Lucia looked over her shoulder at the steep angles they'd just traversed.

"But we're about to hook up with Vultee Arch trail." Robin gestured vaguely downhill, where two slashing canyon walls cut toward one another and left a wide V in the center. "The walk in from the other side is easier, and it's a really popular spot."

Quinn put on his trivia face. " 'This plaque is dedicated to the memory of Gerard "Jerry" Vultee, pioneer aviation developer, and his wife, Sylvia, who lost their lives in the crash of their airplane near this site on 29 January, 1938.' "

Lucia shuddered. "Here? They didn't have a chance. I hope we don't meet them."

Garrie said nothing. But she didn't think this was about them. If it had been, she'd have seen exacerbated activity in the area, sinkfests of ethereal energy. And she'd seen nothing.

"The plaque went up in sixty-nine," Quinn said. "If there was going to be a problem, I think it would have shown up by now. And the actual crash site is on East Picket Mesa—that's a mile north of here, and up higher. Besides, Robin already knows what's going on. What we have to do is figure out how big a problem it is, and what to do about it."

Robin cast a look at Garrie, one that quite clearly said *and* that *is why I called him.*

Okay, then. Garrie rocked back on her heels slightly; pushing back into the warmth of Trevarr's hand on her back. She allowed her mind to wander, taking herself off-duty to consider what, then, she might do for Trevarr and his inability to get what he needed from their food.

A moment later she realized that Lucia still watched her expectantly, and Quinn as well. Habit. It was a shame that Drew wasn't there, too—his ability to read this site might provide them with significant information about recent events.

Of course, with the bunny-sex in the bushes vibes from the night before, it was probably just as well that Drew was nowhere around. She might keep an eye on Lucia at that.

For the moment, she turned her own gaze to Robin. Waiting.

And if Robin grew a little uneasy at the shifted gestalt, she nonetheless squared her shoulders and stepped out ahead of them. "It's this way," she said. "We'll hit Vultee Arch trail, and then we'll head out a little farther to the arch itself. You'll see what I mean." And she led the way.

Garrie let the others go ahead, lingering simply to feel that hand on her back before she started that decent stretch of steep downhill still before them, the trail now cutting through scrubby growth, manzanita and cactus on this lower slope. She didn't expect Trevarr to lean in from behind, his other hand landing on her shoulder— just as warm. She *really* didn't expect him to move in close to her ear and say in that low rumble, "She has angered you. Shall I kill her?"

She froze, at first aghast. And then she snorted, and then she laughed, and when she dared to look back at him, she found the faint quirk of his mouth. Without much thinking about it, she rubbed her cheek against his knuckles and walked out from beneath the hand, heading on down the path.

There, Lucia offered exclamations of relief as the terrain bottomed out and met up with the Vultee Arch trail, spreading wide to bisect a broad, beflowered meadow. Now a faint steady uphill, it nonetheless felt easy; it lured Lucia into conversation. She told Quinn of her shopping scores in San Jose—Burberry and Taryn Rose for starters—and they wondered aloud how long it might take that city to put itself back together after experiencing the epicenter of Krevata misdoings.

Robin pointed them at a side path, where a central gash in the rugged formation—red stone, deep green growth spread above the deciduous trees directly before them—turned into a minor slash of a water-worn canyon. A sandstone bridge spanned the sides of the mini-canyon, as level as any road. And if Robin took the view for granted and would have moved on, the tourists from New Mexico had to stop and gawk.

"Drew would have liked this," Lucia said, a little sadly.

Garrie took a breath. "Drew is happy," she said, firmly enough to convince herself. *I hope.* Because really, who knew? And how long had he known Beth before making the decision to change his life? To stay in San Jose?

It hadn't only been about Beth. It was about Drew, still looking for his place in the world, and maybe never quite finding it with the Albuquerque reckoners.

Besides, who was Garrie to doubt? How long had she known Trevarr before making decisions that changed *everything*?

Starting with travel to another world.

Beth, at least, was innocuous. Tour guide and mild sensitive. Someone who could understand Drew's odd moments. Although honestly, with Drew, there were a lot of those.

"Forty feet high," Quinn was saying. "Fifty feet long. Not an arch, per se, but a geological bridge—creek water washed out the rock beneath it. Twenty minutes, and we'll be there."

"Can we climb out on it?" Lucia asked.

Quinn gave her a surprised look. "Do you want to?"

"No," Lucia admitted.

"Yes!" Garrie said, and laughed as Sklayne exploded out from beneath a bush on the trail of a lizard, batting frantically at it every step and catching nothing but dust. The hike was settling her, all right, and if she'd come here as a misunderstanding . . . well, she could play tourist while Quinn worked. And she was good with a hike that meant more clambering and climbing than walking; she was good with the giant blue sky and the intense colors and the hot, juniper- and cypress-scented breeze.

She hitched her water bottles up at her hip and headed down the side trail at a trot.

So many little footpaths spawned from that main path that she gave up trying to decide which was the right or the best and followed her nose. Soon enough she found herself scrambling the last steep steps up to the arch itself, well-worn sandstone just barely wide enough to avoid the balance beam effect. High above the ground, it offered her the perfect vantage to watch the others approach.

Well, those whom she could see. Sklayne was nowhere to be found, of course. And she didn't find Trevarr until she realized he wasn't far behind, quieter than a man of strength and height should be and standing at the end of the arch to endure the full sun. She gestured out at the view of opposing canyon side—troll-like rock formations jutting up from a rounded red hillside of pines, brilliant blue sky above. "Not much like home for you, is it?"

"No," he said. Not one for wasting words.

"Here they are," she murmured, as the others closed in, coming past the humped red rock with the memorial plaque. Lucia waved up to her as they spread out beneath the arch. Quinn walked slow circles around an area that Robin indicated, while Robin and Lucia eventually sat. Lucia was fading; Robin looked beat.

No little wonder, really—she'd been up half the night spying on this place, no matter if she'd come in and out the short length of Vultee Arch trail. Plump and lush and made of stern stuff. After a moment, she rose and pointed a few specific places to Quinn's attention.

"Ironic," Garrie murmured. "This isn't even one of the main vortex sites. Though supposedly there are little ones everywhere. Normally, anyway."

"But not now."

"No. Not now. Either Robin is right and something's going on, or the whole vortex thing has been an astonishingly successful hoax all this time." Below them, Quinn crouched, pulling up a piece of trash; disdain washed over his face about the same time Garrie recognized the limp, worn object.

Well, at least the group had protected themselves in their wild frenzy.

Lucia, too, reacted—not with the pretty flush that Garrie had expected, but with distress that gave her big dark almond eyes that worried-puppy look.

Huh.

Garrie sat down cross-legged, glancing over to Trevarr—looking for the ever-subtle signs of his reaction. To the place, to the situation.

He hadn't come any closer. He looked, if anything, wary. Something of the same expression he took on when they flew, and yet not quite. More certain. About flying, he hadn't yet come to a conclusion. This . . .

As if he knew better.

"Don't tell me you're afraid of heights," she said, realizing it even as she spoke.

But he shook his head, barely discernible. Sunlight glinted hard off his hair, black and darkest seal brown and the occasional glint of braid, the wayward shorter sections in front falling away from the rest of it, the sides scraped back and fastened. Sunlight glinted off his new sunglasses. "It is a different thing," he said, as bluntly honest as he was often obscure. "It calls to me."

Garrie snorted an incredulous laugh. "You mean the way some people have that impulse to see if maybe they can fly after all?"

He hunkered down where he was, all loose-limbed and easy; she'd seen him this way in the San Jose night, too, with cross-dimensional fires blooming overhead in the darkness. A habitual posture. A waiting posture. Perfectly balanced and ready to move, startlingly grace- ful. "Some part of me," he said, "*knows* it."

::Wise Trevarr.:: Sklayne's voice floated out like an echo in the canyon, from everywhere and anywhere.

A hint of wood smoke rose on the air, faded. Not wood smoke at all, of course. Just . . . Trevarr. What- ever part of his heritage slumbered within.

A part that knew it could fly.

"Can you go back?" she asked suddenly. "Back to your lair, whatever you call it? Back home at all? You're so damned good at *not saying* things . . . it's easy to forget to ask. At least until it becomes obvious that one of you is *not saying*."

"Sklayne." He said it flatly, a decided nonanswer.

::Not my fault!:: A mere whisper on the faint breeze, trickling in with the sunshine.

And Garrie, because she'd learned something of Tre- varr, let the moment stretch out. She found her awareness of him—the cold joyful burning, the tension between them—and she let it hum. Ostensibly, she watched Quinn and Robin and Lucia's growing frown, and she said noth- ing.

Trevarr said, finally, "My *lair*. So your Rhonda Rose called it, the time she was with me." Rhonda Rose, trav- eling spirit . . . mentor extraordinaire, and the being who had planted the seeds within Trevarr to find Garrie at all. "The lair, I think, could be safe. A place or two like it."

Garrie's chin gave a startling and unexpected little quiver as the impact of his words hit her. "I'm right. You can't go home."

His expression didn't change a whit. "That isn't what I said."

No, it wasn't.

It wasn't *safe* for him to go home. That's what he'd said.

"Do you think they'll get over it?" she asked, and the words couldn't make it any louder than a whisper.

Maybe he would have answered. Maybe not. With the moment stretching out tight between them—

Maybe, if she hadn't stiffened, struck offsides by a cold ethereal breeze. An angry, haunting breeze . . . one that made Lucia gasp in surprise audible from below. Garrie instantly went into ethereal mode—checking for threats, checking for presence.

"We have company," Trevarr observed.

"You feel it?" She looked at him with only half her attention. Not just the one ghost—a primary, trailing his own ghostie gang.

It seemed as though a veil had dimmed the sunlight around them. "I see it in you."

Garrie shook it off. She put up light shields, letting the effect of their new visitors slide away without touching her. "Probably just another old ghost, stirred up by my presence."

"You believe that." His tone made it clear enough; he didn't.

"Well, no. But I don't particularly want to think about the alternative." She glanced down in the old dry stream-bed below them, a tumble of rock and scrub growth and areas beaten down by hiker feet. Robin spoke urgently to Lucia, who shook her head, her mouth tight and her eyes on Quinn. Waiting for him to figure it out. *No longer alone.* But he didn't; he didn't pay any attention to her.

She glanced up at Garrie, thrust herself to her feet from her rock perch, and headed back down toward the trail.

Robin looked up at Garrie, too.

Trevarr stood—a fluid motion, without hesitation or fear indeed. "What will they find without you?" He held out a hand, as if in acknowledgment of the inevitable—that they could not linger here forever.

Garrie took a breath, trying to loosen her chest. Solidifying the light shields so she wouldn't have to think about them while she climbed her way down. "Lu knows there's unhappy ghosts bumping around," she said. "Quinn's picked up as much from the area as anyone not on *CSI* can. But that's as far as they'll get." Neither of them had the wherewithal to untangle the subtle ethereal threads woven around this place. "Unless they find some keen sex toys."

"Sex toys," Trevarr repeated, the faintest hint of humor around his mouth.

"Oh, sure." Garrie kept her reply as bland as possible, which wasn't very. "Let's talk about that sometime, shall we?" She stood, brushed the dust off her shorts, and took a conspicuous drink, pulling her second bottle from the hip pack to toss at Trevarr, who plucked it out of the air.

He tipped his head back and squirted it down his throat, letting water trickle from the corner of his mouth and absently wiping it away with the back of his wrist. He returned the bottle to her as she walked by—only he didn't release it right away, stopping her if not in her tracks, abruptly nonetheless. "Yes," he said, looking down at her in a way that created all manner of unexpected sensations, only some of which could be blamed on the wayward energies within her. "Let's talk. Some-time."

Holy farking smokes.

She thought she heard the faint echo of Sklayne's amusement on the ethereal breeze.

She took the water bottle. Snatched, more likely. And scrambled up the barely stepped rock at the end of the bridge, heading for the spur trail to descend and double back to where Quinn and Robin now stood—hoping to meet Lucia on the way.

She didn't. Lucia had been swift in retreat and no doubt already waited in the broad area of the dry wash that held the trail, sipping water in the shade and look-ing regal, a mystery to those who might pass by.

Or better yet, discouraging anyone who might plan to come this way.

Soon enough, Garrie found herself looking up at the arch, surrounded by canyon walls. She trailed her fin-gers along the plaque for the Vultees, checking past her shields enough to know the ghost she'd stirred up with her presence not only lingered, but had gathered strength and more cronies. A fresh ghost, struggling to focus, so full of resentment and fury that it created microbursts of ethereal wind, enough to manifest and stir the dry grasses of this area.

For dry they were. In spite of this decently wet year. In spite of the stream trickling down through the center of the wash, easily navigated. Crispy dry, even singed, in this area where there was no other sign of life, either.

::No lizards,:: Sklayne informed her. ::No crunchy beetles.::

Robin's mysterious band of ne'er-do-wells were mak-ing their mark, all right.

Whether it was Garrie's problem remained to be seen.

"Hey, Garrie," Quinn greeted her. "See anything from up there?"

The pattern of intensified withering, for sure. But here, in the middle of it, it had even more impact, so it wasn't anything he hadn't already discovered. "Not so much."

He hesitated—a double-take kind of look. Sensing that things weren't right, bright eyes narrowing, mouth working up to a question as Trevarr came up behind her, already in the shade and already settling into silent.

Robin said, "Luce thought she felt something."

Garrie stiffened, struck anew by that startling hot wild flare of energy—impulsive, wanting action. She said, as carefully as she could, "*Lucia*. Her name is Lucia. Sometimes her friends call her Lu, but—" And she got stuck there an instant, teetering on temper, before she could add, "She didn't *think* she felt anything. She *felt* it."

"Go be with her," Trevarr told her, his voice low and just a little rumbly.

Garrie flicked a glance at him—gratified, seeing his awareness of it—and found no forgiveness for Robin in his expression.

No. Of course not. In a world where shunning meant death, where simple survival came hard . . . in a world that gave even less to its mixed bloods . . . such stupid social games probably cost lives.

Even here, the distraction wasn't wise. Wasn't welcome. Garrie went sideways a moment, sending her attention to the ethereal front, where—before she even had time to think whether it was a good idea or not—that surging impulse came live again, fast and strong; her physical body broke into a brief cold sweat.

No, she wouldn't deal with the primary ghost here. Now. Not with distractions and upset and the subtle interference of someone who didn't truly want her. Safer to deal with it all later. On her own.

Quinn took a step toward her. "Garrie—"

She cast a look at Robin . . . gave him the merest shake of her head.

"Don't be a hard ass," he told her, proving again that he could read her as well as anyone.

"Twice, Quinn. Twice. At the store and on the trail. And I like me way too much to go for a third." Garrie turned away, buffeted by breezes—diverting them even as she took in their angry, mournful nature.

Betrayal. Sudden death. Disbelief. Revenge. Blackish purple ethereal sludge washed over the rocks and the bridge itself. *All right then. This is a live one.*

So to speak.

Best if she left, actually, if her presence was stirring up the primary—just like at the inn, like Robin's store.

Quinn sent a desperate look at Robin. "Robin, you need them. You need a lot more than *me*. Given time, I can maybe put together what's going on here, but what do you think I can *do* about it?"

"Listen," Garrie said, already picking out her path to the wash, "I don't *think* you should hang around. But have it your way." Quinn's wry wince told her he got the message—but a glance at Trevarr took her completely by surprise.

A man distracted, a man wary . . . looking from arch to bluff and across the wash to the top of the cliffs there, as if he thought he'd find . . . *what*?

Not the ghost. He wasn't a man to waste time on futility. *Sklayne?* she asked. *What's up?*

::Sitting with Lucia,:: Sklayne told her, sounding smug as only he could. ::She pets my whiskers.::

Behave, Garrie warned him.

Robin stood beneath the arch, hands on hips—choices made. "Quinn and I will be down when we've seen everything we can. We have to figure out how to counter these idiots."

Garrie nodded. "That makes perfect sense. But really,

I wouldn't hang around. Maybe come back later. When it's less crowded."

"You know," Robin said, flashing her own scowl, "I'm *tired*. I was up half the night, hiding, hoping not to be seen . . . and then desperately wishing *I* couldn't see. So no, I don't want to *come back*. I want to *finish* this." She hesitated, and went for it, still hanging on to that scowl. "I *get* that Lucia thinks there's a ghost lurking. I *get* that you think she's right—"

So many subtle pricklies. Garrie's temper fluttered around inside her like a wild thing, beating to get out. She grit her teeth and tamped it down again.

Robin didn't notice, even if Quinn had winced. Robin was sharp, intelligent, and educated, but she was clearly not a woman who interacted with the ethereal.

At least, not on purpose. At the moment, she stood in the middle of a microburst, her expression vaguely uneasy . . . the words still coming. "But I don't think this is about ghosts, anyway, so it doesn't really matter."

"Sometimes it does," Garrie observed. Robin had made her choice, several times over. And while Garrie wouldn't abandon a spirit in need, she also knew to choose her moment.

Not this one.

As if the spirit sensed the departure of the one person who could truly interpret for it, it whipped up to a frenzy, stirring not just the ethereal but the corporal world. Dried, brittle grasses rustling, dead twigs rubbing together, wilted leaves flipping around . . . Robin looking warily around herself and Quinn closing his eyes in reluctant acquiescence to the inevitable.

And Garrie walked away.

7

Learn to recognize the correct monsters.
—Rhonda Rose

I know what I am.
—Lisa McGarrity

¿Qué huele?
—Lucia Reyes

Sklayne stomped away from the bridge on noisy paws enlarged slightly just for that purpose.

Too much sharing.

Not prone to *sharing,* Trevarr. Not prone to anything but resolute *self-is-enough*—even when it so obviously wasn't. Not prone to such a crystal clear awareness of another's presence and physical nature so that the effects bled strongly through to Sklayne—Trevarr, a being of appetite and a strong body with strong needs, suddenly tuned to the small gestures, the brush of a hand.

Too much sharing.

So Sklayne kept his thoughts private, and he left.

But still, it set up a longing. *Home.* That which they would likely see again only in stolen moments, fraught with danger. Home with its strong scents and thick dark fog and lurking dangers.

With others of Sklayne's kind.

His own fault. He'd forfeited his time with them long ago, when he'd first come to young Trevarr in that clearing—lured in by curiosity and Trevarr's extraordinary patience.

And by his own nature. Even Sklayne—untested and untried and barely fully grown into himself, thinking himself wise nonetheless—had sensed the conflicts lurking within the being who had taken possession of his clearing. And he'd wanted to know more.

Now he knew more than any of them. Any of his kind, and very nearly any of Trevarr's kind.

A lonely thing, knowing. Sometimes. Lonely enough so for even a short while, it seemed entirely worthwhile to follow the Lucia person as *not-cat,* remembering to check that he had left off the extra claws—so convenient!—and the extra eye.

For the Lucia person would not deal well with the extra eye. He made his paws tidy again, too, and found her dabbing her eyes, searching for some small remaining dry spot on her paper cloth.

Sklayne twitched with the impulse to *poof!* and take his natural state long enough to clean and dry the paper cloth for her. Easily done, for a creature that consumed any and all. Trevarr's clothes started each day fresh; his nightly camp spots stayed free of infestations. No fleas for Trevarr.

A sudden purr startled Sklayne's throat. *Fleas.* He liked fleas. They tickled going down.

The Lucia person looked down at him. "There you are!" she said. "I was afraid the hike was too much for you. Trevarr seems to think you can do anything."

::Can,:: Sklayne told her, even if she couldn't hear it. No cleaning of things for the Lucia person, then. Too late if she'd already seen him.

She folded her long legs, so graceful, and sat on hard gritty ground that really wasn't meant for people-sitting. Her long hair swung freely from the gathering point high at the back of her head.

Sklayne lifted a paw toward it, another impulse. *Shiny.*

"Yeah," she said. "It hasn't really been the day I expected it to be." She lay her fingers beneath his paw and gently stroked the top of it with her thumb.

Sklayne maybe fell a little bit in love.

No! Fiercefiercefierce Sklayne!

But he was already pushing his head against her hand.

"I wanted to like her," the Lucia person said, scratching behind first one ear, then the other. O gentle fingers. "I wanted her to like *me*." Sadness drifted across her features, all eloquent eyes and smooth skin. "I wanted Quinn to stand up for Garrie. For *me*. For what we all are together."

::Stupid Robin person,:: Sklayne said. ::I will eat the thread from the seat of her pants.::

Not that he'd ever done this thing to anyone before.

No, nono.

But the Lucia person didn't hear, so she didn't leap at this fine suggestion, and Sklayne was left without anyone to enable him in those things for which he'd get into trouble anyway. And besides, she had such gentle fingers, such a fine touch. The ruffle of the fur beneath his chin, the little dance of her fingers between his ears. And all the while he could feel the dark, heavy energies around her—those that had come from the clearing and then clung to her as she fled it—growing lighter and fading away.

She sniffled again; she sat straighter. "I'm fine," she said. "I'm better. I just couldn't stand to have her see me like that. Not when she doesn't *believe*." Her voice gained assurance. "She's so sure of what she *thinks* she's seen, there isn't any sight in her for what is. Can you believe she didn't even get a ping of the nastiness up there?"

Sklayne had sampled, all right. He'd found cast-off scraps of ethereal refuse, corrupted beyond all use. Found formations that should have been bulging with rich life, now all but empty husks. And of course there was the ghost. Rising to the Garrie's presence, pulling together its young, fresh, power . . . as of yet untouched by whatever process sucked the life from this place.

Hmm.

Maybe he should have stayed there. Maybe there would be entertainment.

The Lucia person ruffled her fingers down his back; his spine rose to meet them and his tail flipped into the air. No, no. This had been the right decision. And the Lucia person no longer blotted tears from the corners of her eyes, so careful with what little makeup she wore.

Sklayne especially liked the mascara. Chewy. He plotted how he might obtain some—without getting blamed for it—and leaned into her stroking hand. Yes, this was a good moment. Plotting. Being touched. Being *Sklayne*.

A deep, subsonic shiver whispered through the trees.

"Oh," the Lucia person said, and Sklayne found himself suddenly five feet from her reaching hand, alert to the sky. To the rocks, to the looming canyon walls. To *anywhere*.

Not good energies.

Not of this world.

::Treyyyy,:: he said, a warning.

I feel it. Where?

::Can't find. Maybe only a poke.:: A tentative first probe from Kehar, by those not used to using the Eye.

Because they'd have had to have found someone else. Someone new. Not one of the other hunters.

The other hunters all knew Trevarr.

And that meant they all knew better.

Garrie didn't walk away alone. She didn't walk away swiftly, either. She dropped her light shields to keep close tabs on the ghosts—and she found herself a little wobbly in the turbulent ethereal effects. That, and something else?

"What's going on?" she asked Trevarr.

He might have gotten an award for that face. Just enough faint, dry skepticism there to imply what he thought of the chance she would get an answer to such an all-inclusive question.

"Yeah, yeah, yeah," she said. "Ghosts, check. Interfering civilian upsetting the team, check. Surrounded by ethereal theme park, check. But it's something—" *else, too,* she'd been about to say, if a whirling dervish of hot, lashing power—nothing from her ghost, nothing from Sedona, nothing from this *world*—hadn't snapped through her like a whip, wrenching out a gasp and, hard on its heels, a tremendous scowl.

"That was not mine." Trevarr's mouth flattened, the well-defined nature of it briefly turning hard.

But it had the faint taste of him all the same, and he knew it. Plain enough, he knew it.

Too much going on here. Garrie glanced back over her shoulder, frowning, and found Quinn watching her—exchanging words with Robin, and gesturing with some emphasis. "If they don't get out of there, they're going to find out things are more complicated than she thinks. Not that he didn't warn her."

He scraped loose hair from his face and twisted back to follow her gaze—as startled as she when another lash of hot energy smacked up against them, followed by a deep rumble. She gasped with it, floundering in unfamiliarity—not quite in tune with the depth of the lurking spirit's reaction. His awareness of the energies, his resentment . . .

Turbulent and furious breezes kicked up another notch, spiraling tightly into ghostie overload, and if Garrie now had no trouble buffering herself, she realized too late—

"Uh-oh," she said, suddenly understanding it—seeing that the ghosts had crossed the threshold into tantrum while she was one step behind and not even technically on the scene. She cupped her hands at her mouth and shouted, "Duck, Quinn, *duck!*"

Yeah. Too late, all right.

Robin shrieked, an undignified sound of surprise and disgust, and Quinn cursed soundly, and by then Garrie had swept in the breezes and thrown them out again in a shockwave effect to blow the area as clear as she could in case the ghost came back for seconds.

Damn, it felt good.

Damn, it felt good!

She tipped her head back to let it build, that feeling, feeding the power-hunger and suddenly realizing how easy it would be to put an end to the entire inconvenient ghost issue—suddenly impatient and imperious, finding it intolerable that the irritated ghosts of Sedona were acting out on her wherever she went. Breathing in power as easily as she breathed air, the cold burn intensifying along her spine and coiling into exhilarating knots, invading low in her belly, tightening along her chest—

"Atreya." A low voice in her ear, hoarse and affected; arm wrapping around her waist, drawing her in tight; a hand flattened over the low rise of her shorts, drawing her in even tighter.

All part of the moment. All part of the temptation. She drew him in, too, arching into him, hands reaching back—

He put his teeth on her neck.

Sharp teeth. Some of them pointy teeth.

Garrie froze.

She snapped back to herself. To her shallow panting and his breath gusting in her ear.

Farking damn shit!

Convenient word of his, that *farking.* Amazing how many times she'd had reason to turn to it since he'd gotten here. Even if he'd never defined it for her.

She had a pretty good idea.

Farking damned reckoner, doesn't even know who she is anymore.

Because yeah, maybe thinking of herself in the third person would make it better.

"Okay," she said, teeth gritted. "Okay, I've got it."

So had Quinn and Robin, to judge from the stench wafting their way. Gotten it, and gotten it good.

Ghost poop.

"You can let go now," she added. Not that she truly wanted it, but . . .

Ghost poop and all.

He released her as if surprised to find he'd still been holding her at all, strength peeling away from her, hands stroking lightly down her sides—touching her neck. He said, *"Atreya—"*

She said, "I know. You're sorry. You had to stop me."

"My hands were already full," he said simply, but when she twisted to turn to him—*holy Keharian crap, was that a joke he just made?*—she could read nothing from his face. So she scowled at him, fists clenched at her side, and she didn't, no she *didn't* poke him.

In fact, she thought she spoke with quite some aplomb when she said, "Well, then, let's go see how bad it is."

She didn't mention what she'd almost done. How it went against everything she was and everything Rhonda Rose had ever taught her. A childhood of knowing how different she was . . . of holding that identity tightly to herself, until she met the one being who could mentor her. Teenage years of sacrifice and broken social life and learning that along with her gift came a responsibility that was bigger than anything she'd ever expected. She wouldn't grow up to be a princess, a firefighter, or an athletic trainer. She was a reckoner, and who knew where that fell in the Myers-Briggs personality continuum.

And she knew that one day she'd woken up and realized that the drive to do this work didn't come from Rhonda Rose and never had. That it had been there all along—and if it hadn't, she would have turned into a monster so young, so strong, that instead of mentoring her, Rhonda Rose would have taken steps to remove the threat of her.

And soon after, Rhonda Rose had gone.

All that, she'd almost just thrown away.

Because *hurting* spirits wasn't what she did.

Stopping them, yes. And protecting them, and resolving their issues, and keeping the hard-copy world safe while she was at it.

She didn't say any of it. She didn't need to. She saw that much on his face, tension lingering behind the joke he had or hadn't made.

He knew.

He knew it wasn't over yet, either.

And so did she.

Lucia smelled it on the wind, shortly after Sklayne made a strangled, uncatlike noise and darted into the underbrush.

Ghost poop.

An unmistakable odor, not to mention unforgettable. Something like ground zero skunk mixed with whatever lived at the back of her boy cousins' closet and a little bit of the Rio Grande after an inadvertent sewage spill upstream. Times ten.

Poor Quinn!

Or maybe not so much. If *poor Quinn* had set boundaries with his friend Robin from the start, then Robin wouldn't have given Lucia such a dismissive and *aie, yes!* pitying look. There wouldn't have been that unfortunate allusion to counselor Deanna "I sense pain" Troi because of course Robin *would* be a Trek fan. And Lucia wouldn't have left them there to their own devices.

Not to mention Garrie wouldn't have already been so offended that she retreated to a forty-foot-high sandstone bridge, watching them fumble around as if she

weren't the one of them who could tell exactly what had
gone on in this place.

If anyone had bothered to ask.

But they loved Quinn. So they'd let him work through
this.

Lucia sighed, pushed herself off the ground, and
spent a few moments brushing herself off. She smiled
pleasantly at the hiker pair approaching from the easy
end of the trail, but when they would have turned toward the arch she said, "Oh, I wouldn't. Not today. Such
a mess."

"A mess?" said the woman half of the pair, not looking much deterred.

"Oh, terrible," Lucia said. "Not that they let me get
close. They're trying to clean it up. Something about
environmental conditions being just right . . . a giant
desert slime mold. Who knew!"

The man half of the pair said, with rightful suspicion,
"Giant desert slime mold?"

"And the smell!" Lucia fanned herself. "Can't you
just smell it from here?"

Bless the breeze that picked up, sending a good whiff
of that unforgettable odor.

"My God," said the woman. "That's terrible." She
looked at her partner. "Well, it was a pretty walk, but
it's awfully hot. We'll come back again another day."

"If the car can take it," the man muttered, looking
over his shoulder at the barely visible Vultee Arch as he
turned around.

Awfully, indeed. Lucia sighed, waited until they
were out of sight, and headed back up the bridge trail.
She might not be Deanna Troi and she might not be all
that Robin was looking for, but she knew enough to
know that with that stench came a whole new ball game.

They didn't notice her approach, but that wasn't sur-
prising. Not with the . . .

Wow.

It was everywhere. Effluvia, dripping off the entire bottom length of the sandstone bridge. Draped over rocks in contiguous sheets. Glopping off Quinn's shoulders. Totally in Robin's hair.

Lucia felt suddenly better.

"Ghost poop?" Robin was saying. She wiped the sticky, gloppy substance—a lovely murky lime green—from her cheek, and flung it to a rock beside her.

Garrie and Trevarr, Lucia was glad to see, were untouched. Well . . . except, possibly, by each other. She gave them a tired smile as Garrie heard her, and turned to spot Lucia with obvious relief. *"¿Qué huele?"* she asked. "What's up?"

Garrie narrowed her eyes. "That is *terrible*."

"Only if you know the literal Spanish," Lucia averred, pleased with herself again.

Trevarr looked to Garrie, and she muttered, "It's to ask what's going on, but literally it means *what smells*."

"Ghost poop?" Robin repeated, still lost in the moment and her voice tangled up in disbelief and horror and overwhelming disgust.

Quinn, in contrast, sounded resigned. "That which they excrete when they're really, really mad." He sighed, offering Garrie a look that would have been dry had it not already been so very . . . goopy. "In case you thought we were kidding when we said they act up around Garrie when they're already on the brink."

"It's convenient, really," Garrie said, and rocked up on her toes and back again, looking somewhat more mischievous than she probably meant to. The silvery blue streaks in her hair . . . no, those didn't help. "It brings them out into the open for us."

"Convenient," Robin said through her teeth. "I hope it'll be just as convenient if I *throw up now*."

"Be my guest," Garrie said, and her voice got a little

harder. A little more *you don't tug on Superman's cape*. "I guess I'll see you back at the hotel, Quinn. We'll hitch from the parking lot, or call a taxi. It's so close to the Slide Rock parking . . . we won't have any problem."

Ooh. Ooh, *yes*. She would do it, Garrie would. An exchanged glance told Lucia that Garrie was as offended for what Lucia had experienced as for herself. And . . .

Something else.

Something haunting her eyes. The same thing, maybe, that made Lucia think *protective* when she glanced at Trevarr, even though when she looked closer, she saw only what he was, a man out of place in this ruggedly breathtaking Arizona landscape, out of place in this world.

"Garrie," Quinn said, and let it trail off, his gaze sliding to Robin . . . understanding. Or at least accepting. They weren't going to make this right for her. Not that they could. Past the time for that, really.

And Robin sat down on the rock beside her—it made a squishing noise—and burst into tears. Sharp, smart, all-together Robin. Big fat noisy tears.

"Yeah," Garrie said. "Nice try."

Trevarr tipped his head . . . listening. To what, Lucia didn't know. "Close your eyes," he said, and looked at Quinn, who had checked his initial impulse to reach out to Robin simply because his own ghost poop factor couldn't possibly make the situation any better. "And you." Matter-of-fact nature of his words, all full of accent and mystery as they were.

Garrie looked over at Lucia. "And possibly you," she said. "Depending on your comfort zone right now."

Lucia got it, then. Another thing about which Garrie had somehow become cavalier but that was totally outside anyone else's experience. Her eyes narrowed. So had Quinn's, for that matter.

"I don't even have a tissue!" Robin said, wiping at her face in futility.

Oh, Lucia just couldn't stop herself. "It's not like anyone can tell," she said. But she clapped a hand over her mouth. "Aie, *caray!* It just came out!" She dug into her designer waist bag for the tissue she'd so recently used, offering it tentatively from her safe distance. "This is damp, but tears only, I swear—" But she stopped herself, because it wasn't damp at all. Not anymore. She stared at it, dumbstruck, and poked a hand back in the Roots waist bag, but she *knew* that had been her only tissue, she just knew it—

"Exactly," Garrie said, as if that made sense. "Sklayne was with you, I take it."

"For a few moments. But—"

Garrie plucked the tissue from her hand and passed it over to Robin, risking the edges of the ghost poop. Robin took it most gingerly, and then didn't even know where to start. "Quinn, just trust me on this one. Close your eyes." She glanced at Lucia; after a moment, Lucia, too, closed her eyes.

Sort of.

Because then she opened them again, letting in a mere glimmer of light through thick lashes. *Sklayne* indeed, bounding down among the rocks as if his feet didn't quite have to touch the ground, one final leap from the unaffected area directly at the gloppy, quivering goo. Lucia gave herself away, gasping in anticipation of that landing, cat into ghost poop deeper than he was in places.

Except in midair, Sklayne twisted, flashed brighter than bright, poofed out into nothingness, and recoalesced into a . . .

Lucia gasped again. She clapped not one but both hands over her mouth.

Bright. Bluish. Floating. Blanket?

It thinned. It spread. It settled over Quinn; it settled over Robin, who startled and squeaked a juicy half-sob. It encompassed the rocks and the dry creek bed and the hillside. It pulsed and shivered and a faint steam rose above it, and when it rose again, the motion looked more like a satisfied stretch.

In the wake of that stretch, it abruptly snapped closed, tumbling away in a ball of condensed motion that suddenly had clawed feet sticking out from all sides as it rolled off into the brush, picking up speed.

"Now," Garrie said to her. "You know how we cleaned up after that blood and gore business with Bob at the hotel."

Right. San Jose Ghost Bob. The drifter who'd been possessed by a Keharian chakka and tried to kill Garrie, very nearly killed Trevarr. Funny how Lucia had never before thought to ask what had happened to that body, or to all the blood. Now she thought maybe she wouldn't.

Because now maybe she didn't have to. Not with the hillside shining bright and clean before her, Robin's face fresh if pale, Quinn standing clear and clean beside her, no signs of exertion from the morning hike, never mind ghost poop.

Right. Not-cat.

Definitely *not-cat*.

Garrie didn't give them much time to think about it. "Okay," she said. "See you back at the hotel."

"No!" Robin said, jumping to her feet. "I mean—don't go!"

Garrie gave her a steady look. Arms crossed. Knowing what she was—a small wiry person, less than impressive appearance. No doubt her hair was sticking out in all ways, the blue-silver streaks an oddment in the sun. No doubt Robin with her well-turned outfit and her lush, padded body and her sleek hair hadn't ever seen anything worth noting at all.

But Garrie knew what she was.

No, said the sardonic voice in her head, nimbly evading her attempts to squash it, *you know what you* were.

Close enough.

"I tried to tell you," Quinn said, apology in his voice.

Robin's gaze didn't leave Garrie. "You aren't exactly objective, Quinn." She sighed. "Besides, you have to understand Sedona-speak. Hyperbole is the name of the game. I didn't realize you weren't doing it."

"She still doesn't get it, you know," Garrie told Quinn. "She thinks the ghosts left because they were done. She thinks, okay, they act up around me, but what's that really mean? And the clean-up . . . that wasn't me at all, which is true, and honestly, you gotta give her props for dealing with that so well. But mainly, she doesn't want you to come after me. You know. Gotta keep control."

And Quinn just looked at Robin, and something that had been alive in his expression all morning quietly faded away.

"Quinn—" But Robin didn't deny it. Props for that, too.

"Never mind," he said, struggling a little with it. Sad. "We've had a misunderstanding. It's my fault." He took a breath. "I'm here to help, Robin—Garrie and Lucia are here to help. But we work as a team, and we do it our way. Now, you're putting us up, so obviously, if that doesn't suit you, let us know right now." His expression grew briefly distant, and Garrie recognized it—the fact-sifting look. "Better to drive from here, I think. The rental's already in play, and gas is cheaper than trying to pick up a flight home."

Robin shot Garrie a resentful look. "I can't do this alone," she said, and the resentment made her words faintly bitter. "But Quinn, I *know* this area—"

"Good," Quinn said. "We'll need that." He straight-

ened his shoulders, opened an arm in a gesture to indicate the rocks all around them. "I don't know if there's
anything left after that little clean-up," he said. "But let's
find out."

"Sklayne took only the ghost . . ." Trevarr hesitated,
said it anyway. "Poop." No doubt they weren't words
he'd ever anticipated saying. "I will scout the area."

"I did already search," Quinn told him, but shrugged.
"I do better on sidewalks."

Trevarr headed for the base of the arch, and if the rest
of them looked hot and worn in the sun, she would have
sworn he soaked in the heat, even as he hid from the
light—even as he stood on tense alert.

Her gaze lingered; she pulled it away to look at Quinn,
tucking aside the questions she meant to aim Trevarr's
way as soon as utterly possible. *What's going on? Who's
messing around with Kehar-based energy that's not
us?* She didn't want to ask those in front of Robin, anyway. Not when Trevarr had that look on his face.

She turned her attention to the ghostie situation. "While
he's busy with that, I've got someone I want to talk to."

"The boss ghost," Lucia said. "He's angry, chicalet.
Betrayed. He doesn't want revenge so much as justice . . . and, I think, comfort."

"I think so, too." Garrie tapped her fingers against
her hip pack, pondering whether to lure the ghost or to
simply bring him. And how far away had she shoved
him, anyway? "What do you think? Our approach?"

"Give him something," Lucia said promptly.

"You—what?" Robin asked. "What do you give a
ghost?"

Garrie's fingers stilled. "This," she informed the
woman, "is the part where we don't stop to explain what
you don't believe we're doing anyway."

Quinn shifted, as though he wanted to intervene—but
he took a deep breath, tore his regretful gaze away from

Robin, and said, "Ready when you are," which just meant he'd put his observer's eyes on. He might not be Mark Trail in the desert, but when it came to ghostie doings . . .

"He's not close," Garrie said, finishing a quick local sweep. "C'mon, then, Bob . . . let's talk, huh? We think you have a story to tell."

"What I don't get," Robin said, "is how you think you're going to keep the whole ghost poop thing from happening all over again. He was here once and you didn't do a thing with him then."

Lucia gave her an odd look, a frown creasing her brow, mouth opening . . . words not finding their way out.

"Never mind, Lu," Garrie said gently. "It doesn't matter, does it?"

Lucia's mouth closed. Her eyes sparked with protective resentment, but she let it slide away. "No," she said. "Not anymore."

Garrie closed her eyes, went looking. "Here, little ghostie . . ." She took her perspective up, took it wide. Found them in the center of a sparkling spiritual clearing. *Farking yowza.* When Sklayne cleaned, he *cleaned.* And there was Sklayne himself, an überbright ball of presence sitting in the middle of the arch. *Digesting.* Down the trail, there were several hikers on the way; another pair headed down through the pass. And there, to the west, huddled in the ethereal camouflage of a tiny bubbling wellspring of butterfly color and light . . .

Yeah. Something that didn't quite belong.

She sent him a gift. A soft breeze, pleasant and comforting. Soothing. A ghostie version of herbal tea and chocolate muffins.

Because, really. Chocolate muffins. Who could resist?

"C'mon," she murmured. "There's more where this came from. We got off to a bad start, but I do want to help you."

Yeah. *Chocolate muffins.* He slipped out of the wellspring, over the cliffs . . . circled the blotty troll-like can-yon formations sitting on top of the opposite hill. Garrie followed him with eyes closed and senses extended, and if she looked like something out of a bad séance, suddenly aware that one hand was extended as often happened in a physical reflection of her energy manip-ulations, then she could live with that.

Right on cue, Robin muttered, "This looks like something out of a Saturday night SyFy movie."

Okay, *that* hurt.

But it didn't matter, because here came Bob, easing closer . . . wary. All the turbulence he'd created in the breezes now combined to make of him a solid little package—a reflective manifestation, rather than a rep-resentative one. If she looked with her eyes instead of her inner radar, she'd likely see nothing but a vague roil of air.

The others would see nothing. But there was nothing new about that. It was only new in that it suddenly seemed to matter.

"Gonnne," the ghost said, most mournfully, drawing out the word on the nasal consonant. His manifestation burbled slightly. "Taken!"

"I'll try to help," Garrie reassured him. "But I need to understand." She fed him another little sip of a breeze.

::Good,:: Sklayne said, the only one of them who could see the breezes as clearly as she, if without any control over the energies of this world. ::Make it strong again. Then mad. Then o happy mess and I will snack on—::

Ghost poop, Garrie finished for him, if in terms other than those he would have used, thinking the words with tight intensity to be sure he heard them.

Sklayne fell silent.

She added, *Making him mad again isn't the plan.*

It seriously wasn't. A nose could only deal with so much stink in one day.

All the same, it was a fine line. But the gift wasn't to make the ghost strong. It was for the sake of the offering. The reassurance. It wasn't this spirit's fault that he'd been handled so badly from the beginning.

"Will you talk to me?" she asked him, ignoring the faint exhalation behind her that might have been a suppressed snort. She didn't have to vocalize—as with Sklayne, she could focus in on her thoughts, project them. But for Lucia's sake, for Quinn's sake—and until recently, for Drew's sake—she'd gotten in the habit of working out loud. Robin wouldn't change that.

If the ghost didn't say anything in response, he nonetheless moved closer, his energies a little more buoyant. Assent enough. "Have you been here long?"

clap of thunderous sound universe wheeling around her chanting in the dark red and black Rorschach gore blown away by the wind oof—!

Garrie landed on her ass, rocky ground coming up to meet her, good-bye skin and hello *ow*!

"What the hell?" Robin said, a scowl in her voice, and a question overridden by Lucia's cry of dismay.

"Garrie! Chicalet, are you all right?" In she swooped.

"Fine," Garrie said, still gasping. "Aside from my bony butt." She sought out and found Trevarr, crouched off to the side and still, all his attention on her; she lifted her chin in acknowledgment. *No, seriously. Fine.* He tipped his head at her and went back to his examination of whatever rock had caught his attention.

Quinn extended a hand and Garrie took it, letting him pull her back up. "Cranky?"

"No," she said, mulling it over. "No, I don't think so. Just trying to answer my question. He's fresh, Quinn."

"Good, then maybe he saw—"

"No," she interrupted, letting the horror of it tinge her voice. "He's *really fresh*."

Lucia got it. "Oh my God," she said. "Last night—"

Garrie nodded. "I think so. Let me see if I can get anything else from him. He's struggling." Helping him, if she was right . . . it wouldn't be so straightforward.

As she dusted herself off and stepped forward again, targeting the ghost by the barely discernible wavering of the red rock cliffs behind it, Robin said, "What does she mean, fresh? Surely you don't think—"

"Not now," Quinn told her, not unkindly, brushing Garrie's shoulder clean in a wholly unnecessary gesture that she took, with a glance of surprise, for what it was. Support.

They were rattled, her little team. But they were doing their best.

She took a deep breath, pushed away all the myriad sensations that so persistently bombarded her—breezes and energies and proddings that no one else ever knew existed—and returned to their ghost. "Sorry about that," she said. "Nothing personal. Just one of those things . . ." She waited for him to shift closer again, pushing him the faintest of breezes in response. "Can you tell me your name?"

He hesitated, and she found herself breathing shallowly, leaning toward him . . . concerned she might miss it. Or that he wouldn't answer at all. Not all ghosts had enough sense of themselves to say who they'd been. Not all knew what they needed to find their peace, whether that meant resting here or making a transition.

She'd just about lost hope—and run out of air—when he managed, "Daaaaandy."

Ohh-kay then. No name. Well, Quinn could check around, see if he could come up with anyone missing. "Was it here?" she asked him, bracing herself for the response.

No uncertainty there—only rapid-fire imagery. All the *same* image, a grouping of rocks and brush and a glimpse of sky, strobing positive negative positive negative positive *gah*! Garrie held up one hand. "Got it," she said. "Seriously. Never going to forget it." Yiee!

"Takennn," he told her, tying himself into sudden dark knots of wind. *"Gonnne."*

"Is that what you need?" she asked, sudden inspiration—even if she didn't quite know what he meant. "Is that what would help you?"

He flashed bright, bright, brighter, a whirling minia-ture maelstrom, tightening down on the knots of wind so tight and tortured that he collapsed in on himself and disappeared.

Garrie blinked at the spot where he'd been, her inner vision gone flashbulb blind and interfering with her plain old eyes. She stumbled as she turned to Lucia and Quinn; Lucia reached out to steady her. "I hate when they do that."

"What is it he needs?" Lucia asked. "Did he say?"

"Not really. Something to do with being taken. Or gone. It's a starting place, once we figure out who he is and what happened."

Robin frowned at them from behind Quinn. "What's this got to do with the Sin Nombres?"

"Well," Garrie said, "either not everything's about you, or we'll find out." She blinked her eyes clear, scruffed her hands through her hair, and shook out some of the residual influence of the ghost, energies tingling along just under her skin. She bounced on the balls of her feet a couple of times for good measure and then, ignoring Robin's skeptical reaction—*farking crap, she thinks I'm staging*—she turned to her awareness of Trevarr, finding him unerringly. He'd moved; he stood not ex-amining, not searching, but waiting.

Framed by rocks that strobed stark significance in her mind's eye.

Ignoring Lucia, who'd reached out to her . . . ignoring Quinn, who'd said something . . . she eased to the side, head cocked . . . trancelike in movement. Moving, step by step, to match what she saw outside with what she saw inside.

And then it did. She blinked, came back to herself . . . found Lucia and Quinn on her heels, Robin hanging back . . . and Trevarr, close enough to feel the warmth of him. She thought he'd reached out, but blinked again and found him standing quietly, watching intently—understanding, as none of the others yet understood.

Because he already knew. He'd already found it.

"Death happened here," he told them, looking past her.

"Dandy," Garrie said, nonsensically enough. Not that Quinn and Lucia weren't used to it—but it was Robin who reacted.

"Jim?" she said. "Jim Dandy? That's not his real name, of course, but—" She stopped short. "Oh my God. Here?" Robin abruptly pushed her way to the front, looking down on the tufty dried grass and rocks and red gritty ground.

Garrie hadn't looked down, not yet—she hadn't needed to. She'd been full of the moment, the flush of sorrowing truth, absorbing what she'd felt from the ghost and integrating it into the reality around her.

Now, she looked.

She saw little. A vague jumble of smaller rocks in an area cleared of those larger; disturbed ground and crushed grass.

Robin saw no more, apparently. "I don't understand the significa—"

"The blood is of yours," Trevarr said.

"The blood is of—what blood? Of mine?" Robin frowned, both at the ground and at Trevarr, which was perhaps the boldest thing she'd done thus far.

"Human, he means," Garrie said, knowing she hadn't cleared things up one whit and not at this point caring.

But Quinn had circled around, and his mouth tightened down. "I missed this," he said. "I was here, and I knew it had been disturbed, but . . . I missed it."

"The rocks were a circle." Trevarr crouched, tracing a broad circle in the air a foot above the ground. "But for this." He picked up a chunky rock, hefting it slightly—careful to present the side with the rusty brown stain. "This rock killed."

"How—" Robin started, but cut herself off, her eyes a little wild and her expression grown wary. Finally, she had it figured out. Finally, she saw it.

If she asked questions of these reckoners, she was going to get answers.

8

Ethereal etiquette is paramount.
—Rhonda Rose

Sorry about the ethereal head-butt.
—Lisa McGarrity

Feed me.
—Bob the dog

"I changed my mind," Robin said stiffly, already taking a step toward the arch trail. "Let's go."

But this wasn't Robin's game any longer. This was Garrie on the trail of deeper rights and wrongs, with Quinn avidly, grimly watching Trevarr turn up traces from the previous night.

What Garrie found more than anything was silence. Not the quiet susurrus of the world breathing, but spots of absence. Dead, dull spots where her presence fell leaden and silent.

What the hell were these people playing at? Did they even know the impact they had on an ecosystem they likely couldn't even fully perceive? And if they were deliberately pulling out the land's specific regional energies, what were they doing with them?

Garrie had plenty of time to think about it during the silent hike back through Sterling Pass. True to form, Lucia made it through the whole hike with nothing more than a deep smear of red dirt on one hip—a mark that spoke of her time sitting out by Vultee Arch trail without them, and a mark about which Garrie had no intention of telling her.

If she could convince Sklayne to do a kindness, perhaps he would take care of it.

Garrie had, in the past day or so, put enough pieces together to realize that this was just exactly how Trevarr traveled so lightly, and yet never seemed short of clean clothes. And how her own nightshirt had shown up remarkably fresh in San Jose, smelling faintly of scents Garrie now recognized as coming from Kehar.

Sklayne. Questions waiting to be asked, that one.

As Lucia moved with deliberate care on the hard trail, Quinn fell behind to walk with Robin, whose sturdy reserves seemed to have failed her, and whose moderate extra padding had now clearly become a burden. Her face flushed, her steps overly careful as they descended back toward Oak Creek, she kept her silence—and she seemed to understand that Quinn's grim support came not because he'd withdrawn his declaration of solidarity with the reckoners, but because he simply wouldn't leave her hanging.

As they hesitated before the final steep descent, Garrie located Trevarr—obscured in the shadows he found so readily, relaxed and easy. Nothing in this place challenged or concerned him; for this brief moment, she might have even called him content.

But she wondered if he, like she, was thinking about those power surges near the arch, knowing they had come from the world he'd left behind. Or if he, like she, was thinking about the Krevata who had almost destroyed San Jose and the world with it, greedy for power and unheeding of the consequences, and how their mind-set might not be so very different from that of these Sedona practitioners.

Or if he even realized that she still had several of the Krevata storage ovals—brightly colored stone that wasn't stone, segmented by metal lacing that for all she knew wasn't metal. All crammed with the energy the Krevata had been hoarding away before she and Trevarr had stopped them.

Surely these people had nothing like that.

"Don't tell me it's all about the sex," she said, a lot more out loud than she'd meant to.

If humor lurked briefly in Trevarr's features, it didn't linger. "At first, perhaps."

"And now a man is dead."

Truth be told, they'd left the arch with too many questions unanswered. But they'd run out of privacy—hikers on the way—and they'd run out of time, and they'd run low on water, and only Trevarr hadn't been feeling the heat. For Trevarr was a creature of darkness and warmth and danger, and it clung to him as much as the unique smoky scent by which Garrie was learning to gauge his moods.

He eased past her on the trail—or would have, if she hadn't slipped a hand around his arm. "About back there—"

He knew damned farking well she didn't mean the ghost poop or the preternatural display of tracking. That he, like she, still inwardly frowned over the energy surges.

That he, unlike she, had a damned farking good idea of what had been going on.

He tipped his head down to consider her; that his arm remained within her grip was simple courtesy on his part; tension hardened the muscle beneath her hand. "Sklayne is watching."

And then the others were upon them, and the trail parking—a tiny turnout nudged into the nonexistent shoulder of Highway 89A—popped up at the bottom of the trail, and somehow Robin was pulling out her phone and ordering a variety of pizzas—and if she gave Garrie a skeptical look when informed that an additional large would be a good idea, she nonetheless ordered it.

They drove past the inn to pick up the pizzas, then doubled back to descend upon their rooms. Lucia all but dove into the bathroom in the girly side of the cabin, emerging moments later with hair loose and shiny, face freshly washed and apparently free of makeup. Garrie took a turn to scrub a washcloth over her face, arms and legs, and found just what she'd expected—an explosion of product, makeup everywhere, and her own toiletry kit buried.

Not that it mattered. She'd never gotten that soap. And she really didn't want Lucia poking around in the Crystal Winds gift bag she'd walked away with—there where several ethereal energy storage eggs of other-worldly origin hummed softly beside touristy geodes and crystals. The extraordinary, hidden in the mundane. Shoot, hidden in pure kitsch. Even if the geodes *were* pretty.

She wiped down the dust of the day and immediately felt better for it. She pushed the sheathed knife into her cargo pants and emerged to gather up the travel mugs they'd acquired on the road, then stuck her head into Quinn's room, where the pizza—and everyone else—had landed.

Quintessential Quinn's room. Research tools—electronic and hard copy, notebooks and papers and accordion folders, chargers and AC bricks.

As with the hotel in San Jose, very little sign of Trevarr.

All the easier to fade away, untraceable.

Garrie blinked at that. It hadn't come from any particular place . . . just an insidious little worm of a thought.

Stupid little worm of a thought.

She held up the mugs—size huge, readily available in a desert clime. "I'm going to find the ice machine. I think it's near the office." Another of the small buildings, paired with the modest workout center and a massage and treatment room. No, wait. *Enhancement activity room,* Feather had called it.

Quinn raised a hand in acknowledgment, his mouth already full, as Lucia nibbled the pointy end of a thin slice. For the moment, Robin simply sat, looking weary and wary.

Trevarr eyed the pizza, unconvinced. "Eat it," Garrie told him, and pulled out the knife to cut a corner off one slice—right through the pizza, the box, and into the wood of the dresser. *Oops.* Time to pretend *that* hadn't happened. She put the crusty bit into her mouth and pointed at the rest. "Cheese, bread, various meats. Sauce. Good stuff."

A sly paw hooked around the top of the end table, catching at the corner of the open box; she pointed a finger at it. "Haven't you had enough to eat today?"

::Never,:: Sklayne said, and she supposed that was the truth.

Robin only narrowed her eyes, making Garrie realize her mistake. Trevarr's accent, as exotically ticklish to the ears as it was, was far from enough explanation for a man who had not seen pizza.

Well, screw it. She didn't owe Robin any explanations. Not anymore. "Back in a mo," she said, and left the door ajar behind her, the knife sitting out for anyone who was brave enough to use it.

She trod the manicured path to the office cabin, circling it to hunt up the ice maker. The squat little machine sat on the north side, protected from the elements by a little painted plywood shelter. If she'd been just a little bit taller, she'd have been able to set the mugs on top of it, instead of jamming one under her arm and the other between her knees while she filled the third— until she heard an exclamation behind her, and Feather's niece Caryn came rushing up to help.

"Let me hold those for you," she said, not waiting for a response before she pried loose the one clamped in at Garrie's side. "Have you enjoyed Sedona today?"

So that's the way they were going to play it. As if the young woman hadn't trespassed all over Trevarr. And if Garrie had to guess . . . Feather hadn't said a thing to her niece about the night before. Nothing about *she sees dead people,* nothing about fainting or altitude sickness. At least, not yet.

"It's been intense," she told Caryn, quite truthfully. "We saw Vultee Arch. Maybe tomorrow I'll look for vortexes."

Caryn brightened. "They're everywhere, you know— not just the four main vortexes. There are some small ones right on this property. I can grab a special inn map for you, but basically, anywhere you see the junipers twisted up tight, or—"

Something on Garrie's face must have stopped her. Garrie, thinking of dead spots and yet another angry ghost, of Vultee Arch and ghost poop and misbehavior prompted by her very presence, of energy surges that had sent an answering call through the cold heat now residing within her, that which tasted of *dark green hot spice wild* and yes, Trevarr . . .

She bit her lip on a smile and said. "No, thank you. I won't have any trouble finding the vortexes."

"Oh," said Caryn in a small voice.

But Garrie thought again of Caryn's self-appointed aura healing duties and her very real ability to move energy around—even if she did it with all the finesse of a jeweler wearing oven mitts. She didn't know that. And just as important, probably no one else did, either. So, clutching the overflowing ice mugs, she said, "You must have quite the reputation around here."

Okay. Not smooth. Blatant flattery. Social duncery. But it got Caryn's surprised attention, if some confusion. "Because of what I did yesterday? That was nothing, really . . ."

Nothing? *Not for Trevarr.* Garrie swallowed her instant reaction, tried for better words. "Still, obviously . . . it's not as if everyone can do that sort of thing." *Or should want to.*

"I think most people are capable of things they don't even realize," Caryn said, an earnest expression widening her eyes; she moved closer to Garrie.

Garrie instantly put up buffers, a decent shielded zone. Probably just in time, to judge by the startled look on Caryn's face, and the way she stopped short—as if she'd stubbed not her toe, but her whole body. Garrie said, "I heard something in town today—kind of a warning. To watch out for Sin Nombre." Not quite accurate, but she wasn't about to tell Caryn what they were really up to. "I figured you must know what's going on in this place. Maybe you know what that's about?"

The question distracted Caryn from her stubbed psyche. She frowned. "Well, it's what they first called hantavirus, but you shouldn't have to worry about exposure while you're here. We keep our rooms free of mice. Did someone suggest that we didn't?"

Okay, maybe not so useful after all. Definitely not the

direction Garrie had expected to go in. "Oh, it was just a general thing. You know."

To judge by her expression, Caryn didn't . . . or else wasn't about to admit it.

Well, what the heck. *Go for it.* "Is there really a guy around here named Jim Dandy?"

Caryn shifted, crossing her arms . . . biting her lip and quickly realizing it, letting it go. "You did have an odd day, didn't you? Jim Josephs, but he goes by Jim Dandy. He's with the Canyonside tours mainly, but he does some vortex hikes on the side. With . . . *exclusive* clientele. I don't think it'd be your thing. If you want to know more than that, you'll have to ask someone else."

Ah-ha. Paydirt.

Not that Robin didn't know. Her reaction to the name out on the trail said as much, loud and clear. But as long as Robin was the only filter through which information came, she had far too much control over how Garrie proceeded.

And she had far too much invested to have far too much control.

"So . . . Trevarr. That must be the . . . I mean, your . . ."

Garrie didn't help her. Garrie felt distinctly and suddenly less amiable.

"Friend," Caryn said, finally landing on a word, and when Garrie's head lifted, she gave a little nod herself. "He really needs some attention, you know."

Hot. Surging. Wild. Temper.

Completely out of proportion.

It rose up within her, swelling against her throat and chest, curling her toes and fisting her hands. Garrie fought it back as she might fight a spirit gone mad; she fought it back as she might conquer a darkside entity running rampant. And though she won—she kept herself from lashing out at Caryn, from doing far worse than anything Caryn herself had ever considered in her do-good righteousness—she didn't manage to keep it all within the boundaries she'd created to protect herself from Caryn's interference in the first place. Sharp breezes licked past and dissolved those shields before they faded. Caryn gasped, her eyes going wide and her hand lifting to her throat, a surprised and vulnerable gesture.

"Best," Garrie said tightly, reining in the remnants of it all, "that you don't concern yourself too much with Trevarr."

Because that which now dwelled within her had no use for logic or sense or even restraint. A sleeping dragon, far too easily poked awake.

If only Rhonda Rose . . .

Right. Rhonda Rose had pretty much gotten Garrie into this. Never mind the mentoring, the preparation, the whole *mold the reckoner* project. Rhonda Rose was the one who had taken herself off to travel beyond boundaries Garrie had never understood—*still* didn't understand—but to which, these past weeks, she'd found herself abruptly introduced. Rhonda Rose was the one who had first met Trevarr—ill used by a tribunal that evidently had never had qualms about how often or how dearly they risked his life—and stayed with him. Kept him company.

Taught him.

And, in the teaching, introduced him to Garrie by proxy.

Big surprise, then—when Trevarr had need of help in this world, he'd come to someone he already knew. By proxy.

Garrie thought that Rhonda Rose would be quite smug if she knew.

So maybe, no. Not *if only Rhonda Rose.*

But still.

Caryn just stared at her. She'd taken a step back. She looked at her hands, as if she expected to be burned.

"What—?" she said, looking back at Garrie. "How could you—?"

"There's a whole world outside Sedona," Garrie said, mouth still tight around the words. *A whole world and more . . . and I've seen it.* "And in that world, people who interfere with the energies of others, whatever their intentions . . . those people are stopped."

By me.

But after that . . . well, then she was just embarrassed by herself. *Protective of Trevarr. Overreacting.* Wouldn't that go over well?

"So, listen," she said, clearing her throat and inching away from the ice machine. "Thanks for the help." *Sorry I almost gave you an ethereal head-butt.*

"Sure," Caryn said faintly.

Garrie had no warning—just a blur of motion; a sudden slam of fretful spiritual wind, the faintly familiar feel of Bobbie Ghost from the cleansing circle before she pounced. *"Felt you!"*

"Gah!" Garrie jerked back, jarring up against the weathered shade shack around the ice machine.

"Gah!" Caryn yelped, skittering away as she looked wildly around—not, obviously, as good with the postliving vibes. "What? *What now?*"

Bobbie Ghost: still cranky.

"Perfect," Garrie muttered. Out loud, still so casually awkward that it hurt, she said, "So, hey. Did your aunt find out anything about Bo—I mean, the woman who died on this property before it was this property?"

"She didn't mention it." Caryn's wariness . . . possibly justified.

A ripple of air, a tight, hard ball of roiling energies—new energies, also newly familiar. *"Takennnn."*

"Oh, come *on*. Both of you?" And both of them shouting, too. Shouting and intense.

They'd felt her, that's what. They'd felt the dragon, and they'd come to it. Supplicants . . . demanding, emotional, irrational supplicants. One who'd already dropped a giant rock on their heads and another who'd recently flung vast amounts of ghost poop across the picturesque red rocks.

"Are you . . ." Caryn stopped, quite obviously not certain it was a good idea to ask.

"Fine," Garrie said. "I'm just farking *fine*."

A dog suddenly sat at her feet, wagging a stout tail. Labrador mix, chunky and strong, broad head and lolling tongue. *Feed me.*

"Ah," Garrie said. "Bob the dog. Of course."

"Dog," Caryn repeated. She might have been reaching for her cell phone . . . maybe she was just backing for the office.

"Lab mix. Black. Kind of fat. Wants to be fed. Seems to be missing half an ear." Garrie could only wish for Lucia to be there, a hand on her arm—silencing her. Or for Quinn, speaking up to cover her babble.

Caryn blanched. "Feather's old Doogie Dog."

Feed me?

"Okay then. Gotta go." Before anyone or anything else showed up. She gave their visitors a gentle nudge of breezes, a silent message—*I can't help you right now*—and backed a few more steps toward their cabin, the dog in perfect attention at her side—big woeful brown eyes exaggerated as if someone had gone mad in a graphics program.

"Right," Caryn said, barely audible.

Garrie tugged somewhat violently at the hair behind her ear. "Well," she said, as matter-of-factly as she possibly could, "if you think I'm just this crazy, maybe you *won't* mess with Trevarr again. You hurt him, you know. And because you don't believe it, that's why I have to tell you I won't let it happen again. The rest of it?" She gestured vaguely at the dog, the ripple of air, the young woman now perched on the roof of the office. "Frankly, I'm playing it by ear. So maybe you don't want to be too close anyway."

"No," Caryn might have said. "Maybe not."

"We saved you some meaty pizza," Quinn said when Garrie entered the guy half of the cabin bearing her mugs of melting ice. He nudged an open box her way; it had seen much depredation, but several pieces remained separated and askew on the greasy cardboard.

Whoa. The meaty pizza. Garrie shoved aside Quinn's gear to jam the mugs into place on the rustic little desk beside the pizzas, reaching past Trevarr's Dr Pepper for her soda. With quick, no-nonsense movements, she popped the top and poured the contents over ice.

"That's not caffeinated, is it?" Lucia asked, alarmed.

Ah. It showed, then. The ghosts, roiling her up. The waking dragon, roughing her up.

What a luxury it would be, to be simply tired.

"It's something clear." Garrie took a big gulp of the soda and sighed in pleasure at the cool bite of it. "Pretending to be citrusy."

Lucia relaxed slightly. She dabbed a paper napkin to an invisible spot at the side of her mouth and sat against the headboard of what must have been Trevarr's bed. Neatly made, no electronic gadgets sticking out from beneath the pillows, and his leather duster hanging over the corner post. Over the duster hung the stained leather satchel he'd carried in San Jose—carried and left behind. That the leather held a patterned grain that Garrie had never seen before might have puzzled her once; now she merely wondered if Robin—who sat perched stiffly on the edge of Quinn's bed, a small pizza box balanced on her knees to hold what was left of her latest piece—would notice.

Trevarr sat backward on the desk's wooden chair, arms folded over the back of it, giving his usual impression—that he wasn't just *sitting* there. That he was, in fact, prepared to use the chair as a weapon at any time. Supposing the numerous knives secured about his person didn't do the trick, or the sword of which there was no sign, but that Garrie knew had been tucked away in the mystery pockets of the duster. The pockets into which she was careful to never, ever put her hands.

He'd made serious inroads on his pizza, for what good it would do; his shoulders had a hard, sharp look, and her body remembered the tight feel of him. He regarded her with just enough focus—a quiet, lurking smolder—that she realized, suddenly—*he felt it*. He, too, knew of the dragon.

She returned the regard, as steadily as anyone could with another gulp of ice-cold soda between them; his nod might have been her imagination. Maybe not a nod at all, maybe just a hint of change in his posture.

Okay, then. Garrie helped herself to a socially unacceptable bite of pizza, chock-full of sausage and pepperoni and tender chicken, closing her eyes to savor her carnivorosity. When she opened them again—a swallow, fingers pressed against her lips to suppress the attack burp driven by all that soda—she found the quiet acknowledgment turned to amusement, and she wrinkled her nose at him.

Two pieces of pizza later, and Garrie thought she could take a breath. From the way Robin was looking at her, she thought maybe she *should*.

Not your game anymore, Quinn's friend.

"So," she said, draining her soda and thumping it down. "Jim Dandy, aka Jim Josephs. Erstwhile tour guide." She ignored Robin's surprise. "Liked to dabble in things not mentioned in polite Sedona company. I get the feeling it started out being about power and sex, which is never a good combination, but it's gone beyond that now. Power and sex and death. An even worse combination." She cast a longing glance at the third and final piece of pizza. "The question is, what do we do about it?"

"I need to know more about what they're up to," Quinn said. "It doesn't really feel like necromancy, but . . . it could be some perversion of it."

"I can ask around tomorrow," Lucia said. "In shopping mode. We know a little more about what we're looking for now."

"Jim-Bob might be able to tell us a little more, given another night to sort himself out," Garrie allowed. Yes, that third piece was looking mighty fine. She reached for it.

Trevarr's voice rumbled a counterpoint to them all. "Give them what they want."

"Excuse me?" Robin asked. She'd neatened up while Garrie was off tugging her hair into unruly excess over ghost gang-ups and Caryn's cluelessness; like Lucia, she looked refreshed, her tailored bodice framing curves Garrie couldn't even imagine having, her back straight. "Do you even know what they want? And how would you go about giving it to them if you did?"

"Strength," Trevarr said. "They want strength. They want power. They want that which they think no one else has."

Garrie nodded. "Gotta go with that," she said around a bite of pizza, catching some of the meat from falling from the *meaty* and popping it into her mouth. "It's a theme this month. Twoferone. You know, mainly we deal with spirits who don't know how to handle who they are. Or who they *were*. But lately . . ."

Quinn scratched the back of his neck, his face screwed up in thought. Only Quinn could do that and still look like the all-American poster boy. "Rhonda Rose had you working in Albuquerque long before you were old enough to see the bigger picture. It's been *cleaned*."

Cleaned enough that she'd leaped at the chance for something challenging when Trevarr and his hard look and his exotic accent had walked into one of her paint-by-the-numbers spirit-clearance jobs.

"Yeah," she said. "Maybe we should have gone walk-about sooner."

"It's not your job to keep the whole world cleaned up," Lucia pointed out.

"Isn't it?" Garrie asked. Wasn't it? Or was it only Not in My Backyard, and everyone else could watch out for his own?

If she'd felt that way two weeks ago, San Jose would be a smoking crater, and most of the world would have been sucked in after it.

Robin put her hands to her temples, pressing gently. Visibly thinking, *na na na na na I don't hear this.*

"Given all that," Garrie said, leaving crumpled napkins behind as she got up to nab another soda, "I'm not exactly sure how we give them what they want. Or what good it'll do. Or if it's even smart."

"They dabble with powers they don't understand," Trevarr said. "Let them suffer the consequences."

Ah.

She saw it on Quinn's face; on Lucia's face, too. Understanding. Partial understanding, at least. "How?"

Trevarr gave Robin a long look. Assessing. Robin looked back, for which Garrie gave her props. Not an easy gaze to meet, all smoky pewter in this indoor light, pupils in their round disguise but the overall effect still decidedly startling. Or, once one learned to see past the startlement, riveting.

He came to some decision, for he abruptly shifted his gaze from her and back to Garrie. "There is a . . . creature, you might call it. Similar to the Krevata. Smaller . . . short lived."

Garrie froze with the soda on the way to her mouth. "Similar to the *Krevata*? Are you nuts?"

Lucia made a noise. "Chicalet, is this the one to ask such a question? Even if he is, pretend not!"

"He heard that, you know."

"Well, yes, of course," and here Lucia inserted an expansive gesture, very Latina for the moment, "but did it not sound like so much babble?"

Trevarr tipped his head at her. "Very much like *so much babble*. Perhaps a day or two from now, it will occur to me to take offense."

"There, you see?"

Desperation edged Garrie's voice. "But *Krevata*?"

Trevarr shook his head. "Like them in its attraction to energies, even to the point of its own demise. But only dimly sentient. Small." He held his hands apart to indicate something the size of a moderate dog, fingers spread and managing to imply a round pudginess. "Awkward. With a face full of . . ." A brief frustration narrowed his eyes; he brought his hands up to the side of his mouth and wriggled them with expansive vigor.

Garrie blinked. This was not a sight she'd expected to see. "Tentacles?" she guessed. Not quite, she could see from his face, but close enough. Dryly, she added, "I take it you don't consider this thing to be a threat."

A disconcerting snicker skittered across her mind—Sklayne, lingering on the edges of the conversation. Also not much impressed by Trevarr's creature.

"So it's not very smart and it's not powerful and it's not big and it's kind of ugly," Garrie said. "This does what for us?"

Now, he looked satisfied. "It is bred for use . . . a detection creature. We send it ahead into questionable areas. When it encounters stray energies, it—"

::Sparklies!::

"Ahh," Garrie said, understanding. "Visually spectacular. Impressive but unimportant."

Quinn had been watching—frowning, trying to follow . . . not nearly as accustomed to thinking across two worlds.

Not that she would consider herself *accustomed*. Because really, would *that* ever happen?

But now his expression cleared, and he nodded. "Let *them* think they've come up with something unpredictably dangerous," he said. "Make them think twice about what they're doing."

Lucia took up his frown. "You think that'll *stop* them?"

"I have no idea what you're talking about," Robin said. "I don't think *you* have any idea what you're talking about. But what makes you think success will stop them?"

"It won't," Garrie said. "But they won't be expecting it. It should at least buy us some time to figure out exactly what they're doing. You know . . . *before* they kill someone else."

"You don't know that they killed anyone at all."

"Well." Garrie tossed her thoroughly used napkin into the pizza box and put it aside, giving her tight stomach—no longer perfectly flat—an apologetic pat. "In fact, I do. *You* don't know it, but that's not my problem."

"But—"

"Robin," Quinn said, gently. "The situation has gone beyond what any of us thought it was."

Right. As if Garrie had ever had any idea at all. She'd come for Quinn.

"The problem," Robin said tightly, "is that in order for any of it to make sense—any single piece of it— then I have to accept every word you're saying on faith."

If Lucia could ever be said to gape . . . "The ghost poop wasn't enough?"

"The ghost poop left an indelible impression." Robin's nostrils flared. "But that doesn't mean it's related to the other things. Maybe she just made them mad."

"The ghosts," Garrie said, closing her eyes to speak through a clenched jaw, "are upset because the energy balance has been disturbed. That one ghost in particular is reeling from a murder you very nearly witnessed. Thus the ghost poop. Which we cleaned up for you, by the way."

Robin held her ground without flinching. "Why shouldn't it just go as suddenly as it came, on its own?"

Garrie saw it then, in a sudden flash of insight. What had drawn Quinn to Robin . . . what had pushed them apart. Her ability to believe in herself, to act on her needs. She was the one who had called out for help— the one to take action. But then she couldn't let go of what she was and what she knew in order to see beyond what she had established as her own reality. A strong, strong woman.

It cut both ways.

Lucia didn't yet see it. "I don't get you, *parajito*," she said, bluntly frustrated. "This is *Sedona*. If you don't allow yourself to think of these things, what are you even doing here? Working in that shop? *Calling* us?"

"That's exactly it," Robin said. "It's *Sedona*. Do you know how many crackpots I deal with on a daily basis? That doesn't mean there aren't people out there who are the real deal. But they're few and far between, and if I didn't keep a damned strong sense of my own reality, I'd be just another crackpot."

"Then get out of the way," Garrie said, a snarl harsh in her voice. "Because it's going to take this particular group of crackpots to deal with your little problem."

Silence fell over the room, which didn't then seem quite large enough to hold it. Silence, until Lucia looked at Trevarr and asked, "This thing of yours. It is called what?"

"Lerket." Trevarr glanced over at the coat. "It is not hard to obtain; they are kept in . . . holding. But we should be there. Where they will return."

Lucia moaned. "Back out to that stone bridge?"

"We'll take the Arch trail," Quinn said. "That's how they do it. The road to get there is pretty much an adventure in shock therapy, but the Cruiser should do it."

"Fine," Garrie said, ready to be done with this conversation. Ready to be hitting the treadmill—or conversely, trying to turn herself off and sleep. Ready to not be justifying herself to Robin. "Tonight, as it gets dark. Quinn, we really need you on research this evening, and Lucia, I bet some of those shops will be open tonight." Lucia brightened considerably.

Robin, she pinned with her gaze. "Trevarr and I can get this lerket thing done. And Robin."

They had the same expression, all three of them—Quinn, Lucia, and Robin. Dumbstruck—Quinn said, "Are you sure?" and Lucia said, "Chicalet" and Robin said, "Hell, no!"

"Hell, yes," Garrie said, absurdly proud that the cold burning energies did nothing more than lick around her bones, not affecting her voice at all. "Consider it a dose of reality."

9

It was an evening of reckoners regrouping. Lucia lay on the double bed, allowing herself to feel relaxed and flat in soft comfort. She'd cranked up the air-conditioning, again washed her face clean of the day's grit, passed the washcloth over her arms and throat and legs, and spritzed herself lightly with a nice coconut and melon hydrating body splash.

She pretended not to hear a small cat sneeze from some mysterious location within the room.

She'd left Quinn setting up his laptop and little portable printer, already working on research. It would rejuvenate him as much as anything . . . off in his own little world, the still, cool room silent but for his fingers tapping away at the keys. Robin lay on his bed, exhausted and—in this, at least—acceding to the group-mind decision that she should rest before checking on her ghost-torn shop or returning home to prepare for the evening.

And then there was Garrie.

Lucia knew that look. The one where the energies were getting to her but she'd already pushed her body as far as it would go to work it off. Out in the middle of the night, a run this morning, a brutal pace on that trail today, covering twice as much ground as anyone else under the hot sun. She needed rest, yet whatever assailed her here wouldn't let go long enough for her to get it.

Although Lucia was beginning to wonder if there wasn't something else to it. Those flashes of temper she'd seen . . . so very unlike her friend, leaving her struggling visibly for restraint.

Rhonda Rose had brought her up better than that. Different than that. And Garrie just plain wasn't that sort.

It had never been said, but Lucia had the feeling that had Rhonda Rose felt her to be of *that sort,* Garrie would somehow have failed to make it through her teens.

Lucia cracked her eyes open. No, Garrie wasn't on the other double bed where she should be. She'd stripped its quilt and draped it not over her shoulders, but— there, on the pull-out sofa—over the distinctly broad shoulders of the man who had so suddenly become part of their lives, if not truly part of their team.

Although Lucia was beginning to wonder if there wasn't more to that, too. Too many things about Trevarr that even *he comes from a different world* didn't quite explain. Including the way he seemed to set himself out as Garrie's . . . what, her *guard?*

As if Garrie ever needed one.

They sat on the sofa where Trevarr had invited himself, leaving Robin and Quinn their oddball privacy of one working and one sleeping. He stretched out long legs, but every bit of him still radiated an inexplicable awareness and *readiness.* Lucia wouldn't be the one to come up on him too fast. Ever.

But Garrie no longer hesitated when it came to Trevarr. Lucia's savvy girlfriend gaze told her the two hadn't yet been intimate, but . . . *Get it over with,* she thought, seeing Garrie settled in against him, head on his shoulder, his arm tucking her in close and his hand touching her hair, her cheek . . . a reverent touch. And Garrie, if not sleeping . . . relaxed, fingers splayed across the half-open laces of his shirt—the intensely dark indigo one, the one with a little sheen to it—twitching now and then.

Yeah. He had the look. Lucia had seen it often enough. The look of a man in restraint . . . the look of a man in want.

But she'd never seen it alongside such patience and contentment, either.

The snap of his gaze to hers came suddenly—unpredictably. Catching her there, pinning her with the eerie silver awareness and she could have sworn his pupils didn't look quite right, either, but from here who could tell? For an instant, she held her breath—waiting for annoyance, or censure, or a frown.

Instead she saw acknowledgment. Understanding. A common bond.

Lucia smiled slightly, closed her eyes, and fell into sleep.

Rest. Unexpected and cherished, moments when Trevarr's warmth and solid presence and quiet watchfulness had been just exactly the thing to ease her to . . .

Well, sleep would have been too much to hope for. But deep rest had been good, too, for as long as it had lasted.

But Garrie was damn sure awake now. And her teeth would rattle for a month after the pure rock and roll, rattle and slam of the dirt road back to Vultee Arch trail.

Of course, it wasn't meant to be taken in the dark, either.

Nor was the trail, for that matter. But they had more than halogen flashlights.

They had Trevarr.

And Trevarr had Sklayne. And if it had never been more obvious that Trevarr's eyes purely loved the darkness so endemic on his world, it had also rarely been more obvious that Sklayne, too, came from another place.

Garrie grinned wide when they disembarked, one of several cars at the trail access and none of them particularly supposed to be there at all. For Sklayne, climbing out behind her, stretching hugely and yawning with a great display of whisker and teeth, didn't stay *cat* long. And maybe Garrie should have warned Robin.

Probably.

But Robin had only hyperventilated a little, and not for long. Now—a couple of miles down the trail—she seemed fairly well adjusted to Sklayne's alternate form. Not his true self, Trevarr had told her, but one of his other favorites. The one he had taken the night the parasitic chakka had attacked Garrie, when Trevarr had been so sorely wounded in her stead; the one by which he had illuminated a dark night so Garrie could . . . well, rip Trevarr's shirt off.

Now he drifted before them, a soft blanket of localized moonlight, casting the trail into a distinct pattern of rock and shadow that made Garrie feel foolish for carrying a flashlight at all.

But you never knew. And she wasn't a reckoner prone to exploration of dark basements, attics, or cisterns unless she could farking well see what she faced. *Just don't go there.* She'd seen the movies.

Behind her, Robin fell into shadow, stumbled. "Hey," she told Sklayne, a scolding sound. "Pay attention."

Sklayne instantly dimmed.

"Be nice to the light source," Garrie muttered.

::Important. Me.::

For if dusk still lingered to the west, it was fading fast. Robin had said—had *hoped*—that if the Sin Nombre met this night, they would stick to observed pattern and be well settled by the time their little task force arrived.

Sklayne slowed, the edges of his blanket rippling in a fluttery backstroke. Robin still startled when Trevarr moved in out of the darkness, silent but for the faint sweep of the duster. With evening had come the desert night chill; Garrie had thrown on pants and an old army surplus jacket, and Robin had gone home long enough to phase from her daytime uniform to a nubby flowered thermal, jeans, and hoodie.

"They are there," Trevarr said. "Arguing about last night. One claiming accident, some believing and some not. Those some think things have gone far enough. The others think last night proves the worth of their efforts." He moved closer, ignoring Robin—closer yet, until Garrie had to look up—serious up—into the faint gleam of his eyes. *Wood smoke and leather.* "We do not engage," he told her. "You do not go close."

It took her a moment, but she got it. "Damn," she said. "This is you being protective, isn't it?"

He made a noise in his throat. It might have been a growl. "Do not push me on this, *atreya*. There are too many of them." She took that with some surprise, until he added, "Unless you want more to die. I cannot hold them without that."

Okay then.

Robin broke the silence. "Oh. My. God. Do you two even listen to yourselves?"

Sklayne extinguished himself into abrupt darkness with a *pfft* of a hiss.

"Right," Robin said after a moment. "Point taken."

"It is not far," Trevarr told them. "Use your flashlights. Keep them pointed down. And walk in my steps. There sleeps a snake I believe to be dangerous."

"Oh God," Robin muttered, an entirely different tone of voice.

Garrie thumbed her light on. "Just don't step on it."

Robin didn't. And after only a few moments of careful progress, they could hear the Sin Nombres—tension and raised voices and strife. Flashlights off. Moving more slowly yet . . . the trees, rocks, and twisty trail unfolded to reveal a cluster of LED camping lanterns. Backpacks lay scattered around, slumped and careless; a dozen figures of all sizes, details hidden in darkness, grouped together in disagreeable discourse. Voices mingled, male and female. "Not worth it—*dead*—didn't you *feel*—it's really there—accident—don't let it go to waste!"

Too many cooks in that kitchen, for sure.

She leaned close to Trevarr. "If they don't go for it . . ."

She barely saw his nod in the darkness. This lerket of Trevarr's could hardly show up as an ostensible result of Sin Nombre activity if the Sin Nombres didn't saddle up.

As if. The tallest figure stepped aside, his light clothing taking an odd cast in the LED lanterns and his voice taking a no-nonsense tone. "Brethren," he started.

Oh, *that* couldn't be a good sign. Far too cultish.

"We've come too far for second thoughts now. You all felt the startling accomplishment in the wake of that tragic accident—"

"Liar," snarled Jim-Bob Dandy, right in Garrie's ear. She stiffened, muffling her surprise; Trevarr's hand drifted across her shoulders. "Used me!"

"Dave Huntington," Robin murmured, completely unaware. "You great big fat fibber."

"Because you know something? Or because of who he is?"

"A little of both," Robin admitted.

"We've learned so much," Huntington said, with that extra lick of earnesty that made Garrie uneasy. "Did you feel it last night? Do you feel it now?"

"Shields up," Garrie muttered. But not very far. Just enough so she could slap them into place if necessary. Trevarr crouched beside her among the rocks, as graceful as ever; his hand on her arm brought her down, and she followed suit with Robin as she felt his intent. *Now.*

She heard just enough rustling to know he reached into one of those mystery pockets, and then every bit of her attention jerked back to the arch gathering, where the faint remaining breezes gave a sudden twist, a sudden pained spiral—crying out in a way Garrie had never heard before. Huntington took up a dramatic stance, his head tipped back, the muscles of his neck corded and tense, arms rising from his side with fists clenched, forearms taut.

Garrie was in midskeptical squint when it hit her. It hit all of them at once, sending a gasp of delight through the assembly and a hard grunt of impact through Trevarr and even wrenching a faint noise of surprise from Robin. And then it hit Garrie, a combination of pain and pleasure. Sedona's pain, Jim-Bob Dandy's pain, the pain of breezes contorted in ways they had never been meant to bear—inner essences drawn without. And then the pleasure of those breezes washed back in a gush of freedom, ready for gulping by those who could otherwise barely perceive them.

Nothing profound enough to knock her off her feet, or even to knock her off balance. Not normally. Not when she didn't have her own internal storm battling for freedom.

But she did.

And it leaped to greet such bounty, lashing out from within—making the hair on her arms stand up as she lurched forward unthinking. Trevarr caught her arm, hand clamping down tight, breath hissing through his teeth.

"Shields," Garrie told herself, the word riding a gasp. "*Shields,* idiot!" She slammed them up into place, not the least surprised by the strong gleam of Trevarr's eyes or the strong scent of him or the extra strength of his touch.

"Control it," he said, growling the words. "Be ready."

Ready, because it would be her job to provide the fireworks—the energies that would spark Trevarr's lerket into something spectacular, convincing this group that something new and completely unexpected had occurred as a result of their actions.

For like the Krevata, the lerket was semiethereal. Like Sklayne, its size and shape were mutable . . . but unlike either, it had little choice. Cultivated into extremism for the use of those on Trevarr's world, it responded to energies without conscious thought.

And after the Sin Nombres had had the shit scared out of them, they'd either think twice about what they'd been doing, or they'd eagerly try to do it again. Either way, they'd be completely distracted from their current plan.

Maybe not forever. But long enough.

"I'm ready," she told Trevarr. "More than. Poised. Teetering. Pre-pouncing. How about you?"

"Hey," Robin said, doubt in the darkness. "I'm not sure I'm comfortable with this—"

"Too bad," Garrie told her. "If you'd had enough trust in Quinn, you would have been prepared for this . . . for *us*." She shook her head. "Two minds like yours, sharper than sharp. I can see why you were together . . . I can see why Quinn broke it off. And I can see why you just lost him again."

"Hey," Robin repeated, totally different meaning.

"Too little, too late," Garrie muttered, and returned her awareness to the breezes outside her shields. As turbulent as Jim-Bob Dandy's, as twisted and tortured and ugly. With a gentle touch, she smoothed them, brushing the tangled strands into order, easing the theme-park twists into smooth curves.

Dave Huntington staggered slightly at the unexpected loss of connection, and instantly stabbed for a new hold—a child grasping a fork and trying to impale marbles. Garrie's soothed and cultured breezes slipped out from beneath his grasp, and his followers lost their frozen, enthralled postures—no longer emitting sighs of pleasure and exultation, no longer surreptitiously fondling themselves in the darkness. The couple that had drifted close now broke apart, somewhat befuddled.

So, no wonder the orgy that Robin had witnessed. Garrie cast her a look, and found her unaffected. Either this group had cultivated their reactions, or they'd been chosen for them.

Trevarr didn't wait to be told she'd set the stage; the evidence stood before him, the grumbles on the air. Huntington rallied quickly enough—damned clever, too. "You see?" he said. "You all think it's worth it. You all want more. You want every bit you can get. So who here still thinks we should withdraw from our efforts?"

"The real question is," said another man, zealously enough to make Garrie shudder, "do we see if a sheep suffices, or do we pull one of the summer transients off the national forest outside Flagstaff?"

Oh, *enough*. Garrie gave the breezes a shove. A proper shove. She shielded herself from Trevarr, working hard to keep the ripples from brushing him, and she sent a strong gust through the circle. A *clean* gust, tasting nothing like the ones Huntington spewed. And then she watched the reaction—who stiffened, who remained clueless. One woman took a step from the others to glance around, although she didn't seem certain what had prompted her uneasiness.

Huntington reacted the most strongly, eyes narrowing as he looked from face to face of his followers—looking for the source.

"Not even close," Garrie said under her breath, and

aimed another gust straight at him. She gave it a little spiral twist—smooth and steady and clean, but closer to the feel of what he'd been doing—and ooh yeah, he felt that one. He startled, stepping back—as if putting his back to the big smooth sandstone outcrop behind him might actually do some good.

"What's going on?" one of the others asked. "That's not—*you're* not doing that."

"It's different," agreed another, and when Garrie pulled in one gust after another in opposing directions, the fearful babble broke out large—and finally, *perfectly,* someone said it. "Huntington, what have you done? Did you take this too far?"

"We," Huntington said harshly. "And this is a learning process. We can figure this out—"

I doubt it. For Trevarr didn't need to be pointed at his cue. He held up the Gatherer—platinum and unearthly stone, the thing that imprisoned his ethereal bounty—and he worked the mechanism. It snicked like a cartridge jacking into the firing chamber of a semiautomatic; it gave a faint vibration of air and energy. There was something different about the way he held it; something about the focus of him. *Working it.*

Whispers of energy, gathering energy, a deep, distant hiss of wind . . . a faint and undefinable whining—

And in the distance, a subtle bass groan, felt more than heard. A subsonic cry cast out not by whale or elephant and traveling the miles, but by something that introduced the sudden sense of black fog creeping across the land, invading fingers of cloying demand, reaching and searching and—

Sklayne's cry came from a great distance. ::Treeeyy!::

Garrie startled, barely holding on to her modest breezes—protecting Trevarr and yet reaching out to him. "Did you feel—"

"Finish this." He snapped it, whipping up the tension between them. *"Now."*

She threw more energy at the babble of fear; Huntington went so far as to crouch slightly, as if protecting himself from a blow. "Center yourselves!" he commanded. "Calm yourselves! You're only making it worse!"

Garrie grinned a faint, fierce little grin—and knew instantly of her mistake, for the sleeping dragon sensed that weak point and came roaring up, a surge of *do it* that left her scrabbling for her own balance and fighting the impulse to fry them all from the inside out. *Dammit, no!*

She clawed back her control, Trevarr's warning grinding in her ears; Huntington's lips were drawn back in a rictus of a snarl as people fainted around him, and ready or not, Trevarr waited no longer—a barely heard metallic *snick,* a blast of cold, stale energy, and a straggly ball of an ethereal being ejected into the night air, arcing into the midst of them and instantly phasing into solidity.

The Sin Nombre reaction swallowed Robin's disbelieving cry of surprise, nearly swallowed Sklayne's still distant warning cries. The lerket rolled to a stop, hesitating a motionless instant just long enough for Garrie to take it in . . . small, pug-sized, stumpy legs and a misshapen elephant-like head with a limp and blobby nosetrunk. On each side of the trunk sprang a veritable forest of tentacley fingers, wiggling like a nest of disturbed worms; a matching set sprang from its rump where there might otherwise have been a tail. Disturbingly chartreuse eyes sat at the corners of its lumpy head, buried within translucent flesh and rotating independently of one another. Its skin crackled, revealing veins of glowing putrescence.

Or something.

"Throwing up now," Robin whispered desperately, and seemed to have taken a step or two away from them all.

::'Ware! Trey!:: Sharper, a bit closer. ::Coming!::

"Feed it," Trevarr snapped, even as he pulled out the sword they'd all agreed they wouldn't need tonight. "Quickly."

That, she could do. She might flounder in this muddle of Huntington's twisted aberrations and her own darkness and the invasive subsonics and creeping hot, dark fog—but pulling out the breezes to toss at their little distraction? Oh yeah.

But not the only one. A surge of subsonics, a tendril of dark fog—

The lerket squealed, a death sound that wasn't; it convulsed. Sparks rained upon the ground without igniting. All its tentacles snapped stiff and straight and those cracks . . . they *widened.* The creature foamed, blew vile spit from who knows how many places, and quite suddenly stood two feet tall instead of one, and then three feet tall instead of two, and damned if the Sin Nombre nerve didn't break—and it went down hard. Lanterns snatched, feet scrabbling over rock, wildly bobbing light—no way to tell exactly what was going on any longer, except that the lerket pitched and flung itself around, a tracery of glowing veins in the darkness. The stench of it wafted over them and Robin instantly retched noisily in the scrub to the side, sputtering, "Oh shit oh shit oh shit!" between heaves.

"Enough," Trevarr murmured. He held up the Gatherer, whose colorful stones glowed, quite impossibly, in the darkness; the lerket sparked and popped, made a horrendous sound of wrenching flesh, and phased to ethereal form.

::Coming!:: Sklayne's essence rang closer now, closer and closing fast. ::Coming coming fastfastfast*now*!::

"What?" Unanswered, Garrie went to frantic speed, withdrawing her efforts from the lerket here in this clearing full of already conflicting energies. Just that fast, she built shielding—hard and strong, and—

Maybe if she hadn't tried to extend it around Trevarr. Around Robin. Maybe then she wouldn't have been vulnerable when the black fog rolled in, obscuring bright stars above them and dark rocky silhouettes towering around them. Thundering in with a bass roll of threat and reverberating danger and crashing into the area's already tumultuous clash of breeze and ephemera and roiling hard around Garrie.

Garrie lost sight of it. She lost sight of all of it. Of Robin, quailing alongside the trail; of Trevarr, tall and straight and all the strength one man could pack into his determination. Of the lerket, of any hint of their surroundings. She floundered in the clash and slam of energies; she lost her hold on her own balance and control. She realized anew how easy it would be to end *all* of this—to scatter Jim-Bob Dandy, scatter the lerket, to swoop in on Huntington's people in their flight and scour their souls clean. So much easier, so much faster . . . so much more complete.

Do it. Just DO it! Be done with it!

And then glory in the power of it, the absolute and immutable power she called hers. Burning cold, swelling toward freedom, scraping along the insides of her nerves and chilling her bones and coiling up a strong and fiery liquid heat low in her belly.

"Garrie!" Trevarr's voice came sharply—more sharply than she'd ever heard. Fear behind those words. Fury driven by that fear. *"Atreya.* No! Protect yourself!"

If I use this power, I won't need to protect myself from it. It would become part of her—fully part of her. Dark, tempting . . . a storm of intensity and sensation and want.

::Trey—! Nonono, stop her! Stop the lerket! Be far from here! *All of those things!*::

Outright fear in that normally cocky little voice, and Garrie couldn't bring herself to care. Not when she could—

When she could—

Darkness swelled before her, filled her; brought her a maelstrom of sparking reds and bruising purples and smears of bitter, angry blackened orange. Glowed in her inner vision, gaining power, taking her—

She threw back her head and howled like a wild thing.

A curse tangled her thoughts. Metal snapped closed; a strong arm wrapped around her waist, lifting her off the ground even as she clutched the stone and grasses there.

::Yesss! Run!::

The world turned to utter silence. Her bones jerked from within, a vaguely familiar sensation, and she wailed at the sudden loss of the swelling power and potential, her mind gone primal and her body fighting him as she had never tried to fight that immutable strength before. His arm tightened; he struggled to maintain the hold on her writhing form.

Sound returned, an echoing cacophony of grief and fury that sounded not nearly human enough; it fed the chaos of her mind and fueled her efforts—heedless of his grunt of pain, heedless that his other arm finally closed around her, or that his every move restrained without hurting her—until, finally, he simply pushed her up against hard rock and held her there, panting as hard as she was. Finally stilling.

Sensations assailed her—told her more than she wanted to know. The deep, heady scent of sharp spice and hot dark woods mingled with faintly damp stone—no longer the Arch, no longer Sedona, no longer her world.

His body pressed up against hers, heat pouring off it, his breath even hotter against the side of her neck as he ducked his head alongside hers, buffering her. Restraining her even in that way. Bone and muscle, intimately familiar in its flat planes and lean strength and ready response to her.

Her breath hitched. Not at the nearness of him or the fury at his presumption or even in exhaustion, but on a sudden sob of realization.

What she'd almost done.

What she'd almost become.

No turning back from that. And after that . . .

Lisa McGarrity, reckoner no more.

Instead, the one to be stopped.

Another sob followed, and another, and Trevarr's hold on her changed—no longer restraining, but simply *there*.

Of course she drew back and hit him, as if it was all somehow his fault.

Wasn't it?

She hit him again, and she whirled away from him— and if he didn't stop her, he didn't let her go, either. He held her from behind, laying his cheek on the top of her head to let her tremble through emotions, all horror and self-recrimination and *gah*! She was *crying*!

She scrubbed her hands across her face and sniffled. She meant for the words to come out firm and distinct. They didn't. Muffled and throaty. Great. "I don't understand what's happening. To *me*."

He took a deep breath; she felt the movement against her back. He turned her around—not truly giving her a choice. For her, this cave—*his* cave, his lair and retreat, his *world*—was utter darkness, save for the faintest gleam of his eyes. But she had no doubt he could see her. His touch on her face—thumb unerring on her cheek, wiping away a final tear—only confirmed it.

She knew it anyway, when he ducked his head to hers. She wasn't surprised to feel the firm warmth of his mouth, or the confidence of his touch. She wasn't surprised to respond to it, whirling mind gladly giving itself over to this new turmoil. To this, which she'd wanted so badly to do since he'd returned to her. Not just a stolen kiss here and interrupted moment there, but a lingering, flirting, nibble and tongue and teeth and heady, heady touch. Breath coming harsh all over again, a new whimper in her throat, new neediness burgeoning within.

Not surprised at all.

The taste of blood, now *that* surprised her. She made a querying noise, pulled back . . . found his face with her fingers. Found the damp trickle from lip past the deep offset scar beneath it and down his chin.

"You," he said. "You *wiggle* most effectively."

Instant guilt. "That about sums me up, I think."

The noise he made sounded more like annoyed disagreement than anything else. He brought her in tight and hard, kissed her harder—one hand behind her head, the other sliding all the way down to firmly cup her bottom, quite abruptly pulling her in even closer. Instantly she wrapped her legs around his hips, let him tuck her up tight . . . squirming against him until his breath rumbled in his chest and his mouth grew demanding and she thought if she could just somehow get even closer, the heat building inside her might just ignite into pure white flame.

Just . . . might . . .

"Hey!" she said, startled away from his mouth—if just barely. "No fainting!"

"Not yet," he said, and it sounded something like a threat. Or intent. Or *holy farking crap what are his fingers*— She clutched his shirt, arching into him in a way that only made it all so much better, and doing it with a desperate, undignified sound of the squeaking variety. Just . . . might . . .

But he stiffened, holding himself with absolute care—absolute restraint. Ashy smoke scent suffused the air; his breath came panting and uneven. It was enough—just enough, for Garrie to snatch a single thread of sanity, sliding carefully back down to the ground.

Because they were in the middle of something here. They'd fled it, but not ended it.

Even if they'd managed to completely and utterly forget it for a moment.

Just . . . almost . . .

"Seriously," she said, clearing her throat when her voice caught. She forced her clenched fingers to open, flattening her hands against his chest. He didn't move—didn't dare, she thought. Control, hanging by a thread. "Yesterday all it took was a kiss. *That* was a whole lot more than a kiss." She ran her hand down his side, absorbing the feel of muscle, bone, and strength—owning, fiercely, the flutter of reaction to her touch.

His hand clamped over hers. "There is," he said, and took a deep breath—and then another—"a flow and ebb. I took the ebb time. The after."

She realized quite suddenly that her pants were unfastened and resting on the curve of her rump—one wrong step and they'd slide down altogether. "You certainly did," she said, and pulled her hand free to fasten and zip.

Before she knew it, he had her face between his hands—tilted up, looking into the darkness—searching it for him, knowing he saw her perfectly well. *"Atreya,"* he said softly.

Possibly the boldest thing she'd done in her whole life, her next move, and she didn't even think about it. He'd made a mistake, leaving her hands for her face. Because she did just what he'd so recently done—she wrapped a hand around behind to land right smack on gluteus maximus gloriosus; he jerked in response. She planted the other hand to evoke a startled almost plaintive noise. "Just so you know," she said. "It goes both ways."

He twitched beneath her hand, but otherwise seemed disinclined to move at all, his hands still cradling her face. He started to say something through clenched teeth, gave up.

Yeah. Like that. *Just so you know.* She sighed again, letting her hands slide away . . . one last caress. Also bold. The new Garrie. "Ebb time," she said. "I'll remember that. Now . . . *tell me* what's going on."

Slowly, he released her—not actually stepping back, but somehow not quite as close as he'd been. Not answering right away.

As if she wouldn't notice. She held up her hands. "Don't make me use these."

His short laugh cut the air. "And so you find your power," he said. "But ask me a better question. There is too much *going on* for that one to be of use."

Damn. Points to him. "Start with what's happening with me. Tell me you at least have some idea. This . . . this *thing* . . . I barely have control over it. I barely have control over *me*. And it comes from that . . . from at the Winchester House." When he saved her life, giving of himself to do it. "Tell me I'm wrong about that."

"It seems I have little left to tell you at all."

She couldn't read his voice and she couldn't see his face and damn, that made her crabby. She poked him. Right in the ribs. "Don't play games with me. Don't you dare. You of all people. *You know what this is like.*"

He went suddenly, totally still. Garrie winced; wanted to clap her hand over her mouth. But when he spoke, his voice was even. "Yes," he said. "I know." Mixed-blood Trevarr, shunned by Kehar's polite society—if there even was such a thing—and left to survive on his own. Honed by the process and then turned into a tool for his tribunal for precisely who he was. And fighting it every step of the way—keeping some significant part of himself buried, because his two halves didn't play nicely together.

But he reached out, then, and smoothed the hair behind her ear. "I'm sorry. I have no answer for you. This is not something of which anyone knows. I did not realize. I did not—" Maybe he looked away from her there in the darkness; she couldn't be sure. "I did not know," he said, "that it would bind us in this way. Or that it would change in nature, or nest within you."

She narrowed her eyes. "Did you just say this is a *mistake*? That it's *artificial*? That you'd just be some coldhearted bastard to me if you hadn't accidently passed along a little mixed-up mojo?"

"Atreya," he said gently. "I have known I would find you long before I ever set foot on this world."

I hope you're happy, Rhonda Rose.

Garrie swallowed hard, which was the only way to swallow at all. She made her voice as casual as she could. "But . . . is it going to get better? Or just worse, or—"

"I don't know what happens," Trevarr told her, touching her jaw. "But I am here."

It sounded more profound than she'd expected it to be. Words and layers and extra meaning.

And still. Questions.

She closed her eyes, darkness all around them, and imagined this place as she'd last seen it—barely furnished, a place to sleep and a place to heal; a place of rough comfort. A secure place, with a single, difficult physical entrance, dim light and scent of faintly damp stone and unfamiliar forest saps. "Are we safe here?" she blurted. The last time they'd come here, the cave—the stone around the cave, and something in its composition—

had kept this world from homing in on Garrie, and on her energies.

Energies that some of the entities here apparently considered a delicacy.

But this time, it was about more than Garrie. This time, Trevarr was the wanted one.

"They know the Eye was used," he told her. "They know I have a retreat. They don't know where. And this place, I hide from their detection."

"What about the Keharian energies at the Arch? They exiled you; you left. What's the problem?"

Dry came that voice. "They are a law unto themselves, at times. Or so they think. They may learn differently."

Garrie frowned, crossing her arms between them. "That's not really an answer."

"Time is short," he said. "Your Robin and the lerket may not be alone for long."

"*Quinn's* Robin," Garrie muttered. And maybe not even that. "But yeah. Okay. Be evasive. Let's go get that lerket; let's get Robin. Things didn't go exactly as planned, but . . . I think we made an impression. Ought to buy us a little time before those idiots start in on goats and sheep."

He pulled the Eye from his pocket, a sudden subtle gleam of color in the darkness. Clear, pure colors of the spectrum. She drew in breath, anticipating the fountain of color and energy, the black star pixilation and fade to dark . . . the encompassing silence.

She got an unexpectedly firm grip on her chin and jaw, lifting her face; an unexpectedly tender kiss, lingering just long enough to make the point. And *then* his arm wrapped around her, tucking her in tight and putting the Eye into her hand as he had once before. This time she knew to hold it up; this time she knew to expect that he would trigger it through her.

This time she knew he had filled his free hand with something else. And she didn't have to see Lukkas to know what—and she didn't have time to wonder why he had pulled the sword out at all.

O joy. O glory. O chaos.

Sklayne crouched in the Sedona brush beside the shrieking Robin person and decided not to have ears. He withdrew them, those fine cat ears of his, flattening the furry profile of his head, his whiskers tucked in tight, all prim disapproval.

Scheming humans, thinking themselves grand, not knowing how they stole and how they poisoned.

O, Klysar, he could stop them.

He could stop them *now,* if allowed. But *no.* No fixing things. No, no, no. Just because he'd misunderstood that one moment. How was he to know, that first time, that Trevarr made such a sound in mindless pleasure and not the throes of pain? How was he to know that the woman had not *trapped* that appendage of which Trevarr took such care?

::Not my fault.::

And so had the geas shackles been formed.

It mattered little that since then, their bonding had completed to the point that Sklayne so casually eavesdropped on similar dalliances, and that he now deeply understood that the appendage was good for much, much more than watering bushes.

Oh yes.

For a time he experimented with his own such appendage. *Appendages.* Here, there . . . of this shape and that. But in the end he found claws so much more useful. And if they did not experience the same sensation, then it mattered little when he could still mind-drop on Trevarr.

And still Trevarr kept the geas shackles upon him.

Too impulsive, he said. *Too much* you *for how little you think about it. There is a reason your kind do not otherwise live long.*

Whatever that meant.

So no harming sentients. No stopping this before it went any further, these humans with their blind and blundering theft who sickened this rich land and roused the spirits who had been slumbering among the living and left their trail of vile ethereal pestilence behind.

But these energies, he would not clean; he would not take into himself. Some things, even a being of his nature could not withstand.

Odd how the lerket seemed to thrive on it.

Trapped in an ethereal holding pen, it had been one of the tribunal's lerkets. But not a thing, missing, that should have gone noticed. The tribunal had a dozen in service; they had agents out using them. Trevarr's plan to withdraw and return one . . .

Easy plan. *Good* plan.

Who knew it would react to the Sin Nombre energies—to *transform* with them? Who knew the tribunal would send a probe roaring through these canyon lands, mixing with the sickened energies to make the Garrie go insane? Who knew the lerket would gulp those energies, too, and the Garrie's breezes along with them?

He'd never seen a lerket hold onto the power it ate. He'd never seen a lerket amass enough personal energy so it became a lodestone for more.

::Also not my fault.::

Too bad there was no one here to hear him. For once he was right.

The Lucia person.

Sklayne would check on her. See if she was well. Figure out what to do next.

He reached out to her, following the subtle tug of

awareness he now and always held of her. He did not go deep, careful with this body-free connection of his.

He didn't need to.

The Lucia person was in town, all right—had been to shop, spoken to people, persisted with people . . . holding herself straight and tall, yet reeling from the general onslaught of the evening. Not just people, but spirits, pulled from their rest by the Sin Nombre activity—resentful, grieving, confused—crowding up against her. He felt the exhaustion of it weighing on her—for if she lacked the skills and power of the Garrie, she could still pet those in unrest in her subtle way. Send them quiet offerings of better emotions than the ones they had.

And she knew they were riled. That they had a sense of age and sleep about them, the confusion of spirits long slumbering and recently disturbed.

She wasn't the only one, sitting now in the back room of this unpretentious little crystal and bead shop with too much incense swirling around, clammy in marginally cooled air. She perched at the edge of the folding chair, a circle of chairs around her and a man and a woman beside her. Wary.

The man wore his thinning hair in a tight ponytail. Nothing like Trevarr's, thick and horse-mane strong, encounter braids woven throughout but hidden—personal, as they should be. Private. The woman had hair enough, and had forgotten to do something about it. Occasionally she would flip it back over her shoulder, but it never stayed. They both wore loose short-sleeved tunics and baggy pants and an astonishing amount of patchouli.

Once they learned the Lucia person was working with Robin, they had hoped she would speak to them in this private space, with the doors of the store now locked. They probably didn't know that her hand in her beloved Burberry tote had closed around a small canister of fiery defense spray.

Now *that* would be a scent to savor.

But Sklayne sensed only the faintest power in them. The ability to perceive certain things. The ability to do something about it? *Noooo.*

"It's just," the woman was saying, "it's a small community. We know one another, mainly. Even those people who . . ." She trailed off, glancing at the man.

"Who feel differently when it comes to the responsibilities of beings of spiritual influence," the man said firmly.

Beings of spiritual influence. The man didn't even know what he didn't know.

The Lucia person cocked her head slightly, a faint awareness of Sklayne's reaction.

Oops. Be more careful.

The Lucia person put aside what she'd felt. Not forgetting, just moving forward. "Are there particular things you're concerned about?"

"Well," the woman said, "we were hoping you might tell us a little bit more about why *you're* here. Who you are. That sort of thing. This is a small community, of course. We know you were in Crystal Wind this morning, and the mess that came of that. But mostly . . . this is our home. *Our* place to nurture. So if you know anything, really, we should act on it as is best."

"Oh," the Lucia person said. She nodded. "Yes, I can see why you'd feel that way." And they smiled, thinking how smoothly this was going, eager for what she could tell them.

But Sklayne felt the Lucia person's rising anger, her resentment on behalf of all the spirits now so upset and disturbed, the land damaged. Her voice grew a crisp edge, one against which Sklayne wanted to rub his cat cheek. "Unfortunately, you wasted your opportunity to act. Your *people of differing philosophies* haven't been stopped, and now it will take a reckoner."

The man snorted. "You're out of line, young lady. And no one can—"

The Lucia person stood. "We're staying at the Journey Inn. When you want to help, come see us. When it sinks through to you that the distress of the earth and of the spirits is more important than your claim of jurisdiction, come see us. When you decide that your own son's suffering needs to be eased—"

Maybe she hadn't meant to say that; she stopped herself, very suddenly. Sklayne felt her chagrin.

Too late. They gasped, reaching for one another. The man's face reddened. "That's what this is," he said, virulently enough so the Lucia person withdrew the defense spray from her purse, keeping it hidden in her palm. "Trying to take advantage of our grief—!"

"No! Theo!" The woman clutched at him. "What if she can talk to him—"

"She can't!"

"I can't," the Lucia person agreed, easing toward the exit. Dignified. "But I can feel—"

"Nothing!" the man spat at her. "Don't you come into our town, our store, and think you can work us, just because this is a place of believers!"

The Lucia person stood her ground. "Your *believers* are killing this place! And this is your only chance to influence how the *outsiders* handle the problem your insiders have made!"

"Get out!" the man shouted, his worn face purpled into a strange color, the woman sobbing beside him.

The Lucia person paled, but not in response to his rage—flinching as emotions rose high, spirits on the brink . . . their son on the brink. Their *son* . . . knowing they turned their rage on the wrong person. Pleading, while the Lucia person put up a hand as though to shield herself.

All the lights in the room blew out.

All the lights in the shop blew out.

All the lights on the block blew out.

The Lucia person fled. Out of the room, out of the shop, fumbling with the doors and with the burdens and with the fear, all seeping through to Sklayne. He rode her shoulder with his presence, purring in her ear, not knowing if she heard. *Approval.*

Brave person of modest power, doing what she could.

But not doing it alone. And so Sklayne left her behind and followed the faintest of tugs to the Quinn person—splitting his awareness between the Arch where his not-cat-shaped energies crouched without ears, waiting for Trevarr's return and keeping track of all things here at the same time.

Ahhh, the Quinn person. Alone in the room, gear spread everywhere. Books across the bed, papers stuffed into an accordion folder perched precariously on top of the room phone beside the bed, a wirebound notebook flapped open beside the hefty laptop computer, printer, and scanner. Cords and wires and rechargers . . . a giant travel mug filled with stinging ice water. A constant murmur of voices and static bursts in the background.

Sklayne knew most of these things by the thoughts he stole, dipping into the Quinn person's mind. A shallow connection, borne of shallow acquaintance.

But here, this room, was the place to which the Lucia person now fled. Trevarr might say that Sklayne pushed his allowable boundaries, intruding and eavesdropping on this one who knew no better, but Sklayne had *purpose.*

This place must be safe for the Lucia person. Safe not just for her body, but for her vulnerable self.

The Quinn person tabbed away from a computer site on which he *chattered*—

No.

Not quite right.

Chatted.

Like Lucia, feeling around for local information. Pretending he had just moved here. Pretending to be one of them. On another page of his *browser,* he scanned information about the Garrie's newest ghost. Her Jim-Bob Dandy. His business on the far side of town, some personal tidbits . . . lots of photos. Lots and lots of photos.

The computer screen flickered, objecting to Sklayne's presence . . . he remembered the unexpected demise of the thing called *television* in their San Jose hotel room and moved away from the tickling energies.

Maybe later.

The Quinn person scowled, fiddling with the power cord . . . unplug, replug . . . settle back to work.

The staticky voices changed. No longer a trickle, they became a steady stream, a little fuzzy burst at the end of each clipped comment. Sklayne moved his attention closer. Teasing him, those fuzzy bursts were. If he could only catch one . . .

The computer pinged at him—pinged again, and again. "What the hell?" The Quinn person stuck his pen between his teeth and put both fingers to the keyboard, tabbing back to the chatter room, scrolling along through the quickly appearing messages. "Ahh, Garrie . . . what have you done?"

Fingers flying, he switched to a new screen, moving a little white arrow around and ooh. Fast. *Shiny.* Sklayne focused in on it, his metaphorical haunches twitching, raising in the air and ready to thrust—

But oh. He wasn't truly *here.* And now would not be the best time to eat the Quinn person's shiny.

Maybe later.

The voices grew louder—annoyingly loud. The Quinn person fiddled with something on the screen and the static cleared away and suddenly Sklayne understood.

The Quinn person was eavesdropping, too.

Stuck in his puny human body, he had found a way to listen to the people who took charge of things happening here. And now they talked fast, and they had urgency in their voices. They said things like *blackout* and *mass hysteria* and *gas leak* and *evacuate* and *unknown unknown unknown.* And by the time the Quinn person returned to the chatter page, enough words had poured in to scroll off the screen and most of them went *!!!!!!* and the Quinn person muttered, "What the *fuck*—"

The Lucia person burst through the door. She slammed it behind her and stood up against it as though she was keeping it closed with her body, although Sklayne knew there was nothing on the other side. "Oh!" she said. *"Oh!"*

"No kidding," the Quinn person said. "Do you have any idea—?"

She shook her head most vigorously. "No, no, no. I'm done here tonight. No more. I am closed!"

"Lu, I don't think—"

"Your Robin doesn't think, that's what!" She closed on him, stalking him—her finger out and aiming for a big poke on his arm. He braced himself. "Trying to use you! Trying to control us! Dismissing us and insulting us! If she had been open with us, we might have some idea what's happening here!" She threw her hands in the air. "Instead we have this! Sedona ghosts set to boil! Imagine if they hadn't been weakened by what these Sin Nombres do!"

"Lu—" said the Quinn person, holding his hands out—placating, for what it was worth.

Worth just about nothing. Sklayne admired the energy of her—that which had come from the ghosts, sparking around her hair in a constant glimmer and flicker of light and emphasis. Not like the Garrie, not a small person of much power. But perfectly suited to the Lucia person. "Lu, nothing!" she said. "You know I'm right! You could have set her straight from the start. You could have given us half a chance to do this right!"

"I know!" he shouted back, standing so suddenly that the chair scraped back. Not that the Lucia person took as much as a startled step back. "I know! You're right! I'm sorry! I just hoped . . ." He took a deep breath. "I kept hoping she'd *get* it. That she'd see. That she'd truly understand about what we are. That's what I thought, when she contacted me—that she'd finally lost that certainty she's always had. *This is what things are and this is how I handle them.* She's never been able to see that there might be more beyond, even when she's been in the middle of it. Why do you think we're not together?"

"Because she's a controlling bitch and you're better than that!" the Lucia person snapped, and then slapped a hand over her mouth as the Quinn person recoiled. "Oh. Oh, Quinnie, I'm sorry. I didn't mean—"

"You did," he said, resigned now. "Hell of it is, you're right. She doesn't get it and she hasn't changed and it doesn't matter how brilliant she is or what I feel when she walks into the damned room. I can't be with someone who thinks my life is a lie. I couldn't then, and I can't now. I just *hoped* . . ."

"Oh," the Lucia person said again, and Sklayne felt a startling little twitch at the sadness and understanding in her voice; his body lashed its tail. These were not *his* people. Not his bonded. Not his problem. What was he even— "Oh," she said. "I *am* sorry, Quinnie."

For an instant, the Quinn person looked desperate, even a little trapped somehow. Then he jerked the chair to the side and gestured at it. "Sit," he said. "Let me get you something to drink. Take some breaths. I don't know what's going on out there, but I have the feeling we're going to find out, And then I don't think we'll have much time for anything like pulling ourselves back together."

Sklayne thought he was exactly right.

And if he sat with them, purring at the Lucia person—only because it amused him and no other reason *at all*—he also watched at the Arch, where Robin had subsided to whimpers in the wake of the lerket's transformation. He went wide, a quick scope of the area . . . far enough to find the lerket. To find the person called Huntington. To see the two beings converge . . . interact . . . move away together.

Hmm.

But a surge of Keharian energy pulled him back, completely back. Out of the hotel room, away from the Lucia person, back to his not-cat form in the canyon, completely solidified unto self.

There, where a splurge of color filled the night and told him of the Eye—there, where he prepared to run or to greet. For Trevarr was not the only one with an Eye. And the probe that had swept through in the wake of the lerket's arrival . . .

Not a friendly thing, that probe. Not a good thing. Not for Trevarr.

Not for the Garrie.

But ah. This time, the familiar sense of Trevarr. The bond, slipping into a more comfortable place with proximity. ::Tre-eyyy,:: he purred, not meaning to, and wished that like the Lucia person he could clap his hands over his mouth.

Tried it anyway.

Paws.

Not the same.

By then the darkness sparked away; the colors faded. Trevarr stood with the Garrie, the two of them pulsing with lingering and incompleted sensations. Sklayne wrinkled his cat nose, flipped his cat whiskers. ::Just *do* it,:: he told them, startling the Garrie and earning one of those looks from Trevarr.

But not for long. Because Trevarr left the Garrie and ran to the spot where the lanterns and people and lerket had been. Nothing left of it now, only a spot drained scratchy dry and surrounded by ugly spots. Leftover ethereal litter.

The Robin person said dully, "They're all gone. Everyone. Every*thing*. Even you. I'd ask what the hell happened and where the hell you went and what did we even do here, but right now . . . you know, I just want to *go*."

"I think we'd better," the Garrie said, regaining some balance. "Back to the hotel. See what Quinn and Lu have found. See if we can figure out just what happened."

They'd need to know about the lerket and the Huntington person, they would.

But Sklayne sat with his tail tucked around his legs and his ears tucked into his head and his whiskers prim, looking at the Robin person all pasty-faced and the Garrie desperately trying to pull herself into nonchalance and Trevarr, standing tall and ready and wary by the Arch, knowing better than any of them the ramifications of what had happened this night even if he didn't even know all the facts yet.

Maybe later.

10

Assess your circumstances with an objective
and steady eye.
—Rhonda Rose

Hell, no, it's not safe.
—Lisa McGarrity

Garrie stopped for fast food on the way back to the hotel, swinging briefly the wrong way down 89A and then back again. Robin opened her mouth for a protest, but ultimately seemed too numb to complain.

She parked in the main lot instead of in front of their shared unit, jamming the shift into park. She glanced over at Trevarr just as he fed a final french fry to Sklayne, Sphinx-like on his lap. "I want to go through the uncleansed circle," she told him. "Get a sense for how things stand there." And then, looking at Sklayne's smug pleasure with the french fry, she mouthed an exaggerated, silent, *"Ears!"* at him.

Cat ears popped back into place, perky and perfect. He didn't even hesitate in his chewing. Garrie bit back on a smile. A mystery, Sklayne was. But in so many ways, a simple being.

She got out of the car with more energy than she'd gotten into it. This was her time of night, with the clock crawling on toward midnight and the world settling around her. Most people thought ghosts came out at night to pick up their haunting; the truth was, they were there all the time—unnoticed, with radios and televisions blaring, traffic noise in the background, phones ringing . . . even the heightened flow of electricity changed they interaction with the world.

At midnight? Not so much.

Trevarr emerged to join her, and Robin came a distant third. Sklayne . . . well, who knew. But at least he had ears again.

Robin spoke for the first time since they'd left the Arch. "Seemed like an awful lot of red and blue flashers out there tonight. And was half the town dark?"

"Quinn'll know." Garrie headed for what was left of the cleansing circle, past the hotel office and around behind, finding the path familiar in the darkness. She reached the huge rock in a few matter-of-fact moments, surprised to see there were already a few tokens placed along the outside edge. Feather didn't learn from experience, apparently. Or she still didn't understand.

Well, Garrie understood. She gathered the tokens—with respect, but without hesitation—and set them off to the side, under a pretty ornamental plum. The tree welcomed them; the ground welcomed them—a subtle drift of pleasing breeze that had not been present at the rock at all.

"Groovy," said Bobbie Ghost.

Ah, there she perched. On the rock, of course—high, of course. Barely discernable in the darkness, but with the same obvious dichotomy in clarity that she'd had from the first, the central muddle of energies that made Garrie think she'd taken a horrible lower back injury in her fall.

"You're welcome," Garrie told her, peripherally aware that Robin would have stepped in closer to investigate had Trevarr not simply put himself in her way. "Is there any other way I can help you?"

Bobbie Ghost scowled, fading out for a moment. "I don't—it's a *secret*." And then she disappeared, but only for an instant. "I slept," she said when she returned, and she sounded baffled. "For so long. And then something woke me. Changes here, tugging at me. Rad stuff. And I found this . . . this *stuff* here, man, it's all *wrong*!"

"There have been changes," Garrie agreed. "We're working on that. But it would really, really help if you didn't drop any more rocks on our heads while we're doing it. Because that's pretty distracting."

"I . . ." the young woman said, looking down at her feet, at the rock she stood on; her wild bellbottoms swung out of the way with her movement. "Oh."

"And if you happen to get a sense of what's going on . . . the more I know, the better I can counteract it."

"I'm—" Bobbie Ghost said. "It's—" And she scowled and blurted, *"Secret!"* in a voice that went all drippy around the edges as she abruptly disappeared.

Garrie sighed. "Well, maybe she won't drop any more rocks on our heads, anyway. Or maybe she will. She's pretty tangled up. Still, maybe I'm getting through to her. And she's troubled. I really, truly don't want this one to end in dissipation just because I couldn't get through to her."

"You care about them," Trevarr said, as if realizing it. "You could do away with them at any time—any of them. But you don't. Not even those remnants where I first found you."

Right. The fractured pieces of multiple spirits, killed by flash flood a century earlier and accidentally incorporated into the house construction. Garrie had seen them returned to the arroyo in which they had died, allowing them to rest.

"Right," she said out loud. "That's not what this is about. It's never been what this is about. But then, you know that, if you spent all that time with Rhonda Rose."

"I know that," he agreed. "But I learn it all over again. It is much different than things on—where I come from."

Garrie muttered, "That, I believe."

She followed him down the meandering path to their unit, where the darkened windows on the side she shared with Lucia pointed her exactly where she'd expected to go—Quinn and Trevarr's room.

Wouldn't Drew just be impressed—Quinn not only had the nerve to share a room with Trevarr, but had managed to take up most of the space.

Garrie knocked once for propriety and opened the door, not surprised to find Quinn squinting at his laptop and Lucia rising from what had been a curled-up nap on his bed, her face flushed in a way that told Garrie she'd been pushed to her limits this evening.

Yeah. Flashing lights, half the town in darkness. Their simple little task, grown out of control and rippling outward.

Trevarr's bed was, somehow—in a way that barely got a glance from Garrie but stopped Robin short—already occupied by Sklayne. The heavy leather satchel hung from the headboard; other than that, there was no sign of Trevarr in this room, and Garrie suddenly wondered if he slept here at all.

"Lots of activity," Quinn reported without preamble. "Heart attacks, fainting, accidents with electricity. Half the town is down . . . you probably saw that. Something hard rolled through here. Things go okay with you?"

"Well," Garrie said, and pondered a moment. "We got their attention."

"Okay?" Robin said, as if the words burst out of her. *"Okay?"* She looked as disheveled as Garrie had seen her, her thermal shirt rumpled and smeared with a reddish stain, her jeans sporting a small tear from the dark hike, her hair mussed. Through Quinn's eyes, she was probably damned adorable—rumpled, vulnerable, no longer tightly bound by that bodice, and her extra weight perfectly proportioned to maintain a figure that Garrie would never have. Lush versus tight and wiry.

Oh well.

But right. Robin was ranting. Pay attention.

"I get it, okay?" Robin said, gesturing at Garrie, and then at them all. "I get what you do. I get that I *didn't* get it."

"Ah," Lucia said, catching Garrie's eyes. "You were impressive, yes?"

"Inadvertently," Garrie admitted.

Lucia sat up all the way, tucking her feet beneath her. Naturally, her girlish summer outfit had not wrinkled. She pinned Robin with her gaze. "So, now you want, what? A medal? You want in the club? For that, you believe in us when it means something. Anyone can believe after seeing what Garrie does."

"It was Trevarr's lerket," Garrie said. "I just stirred things up a little."

Sklayne's laughter skimmed down the back of her neck. His cat form squeezed its eyes half closed at her.

"What I want," Robin said, rather desperately, "is to know what's going on. I want to know how you think you'll stop these people. I want to know what that thing was, and where it came from. I want to know who *he* is and where *he* came from, because don't think I haven't been trying to place that accent or that outfit or—" She threw her hands up.

"Gypsy," Garrie said abruptly. "Very old gypsy tribe of Russian lines. Hasn't been here long. They have a real way with animals, don't you think?"

Maybe that last was a bit much. Robin just looked at her. And then she looked at Quinn.

"Robin," Quinn said, ever so gently—and just in time to forestall Garrie's flat-out *too bad for you, it's not gonna happen,* "that takes trust."

Robin jerked as though she'd been slapped. She took in a deep, slow, breath, looking at them all. "I see," she said. "I messed up that big, huh?"

"Don't get us wrong, *pajarito,*" Lucia said. "We're

doing this thing. But now we don't stop to explain ourselves along the way."

When Robin looked at Quinn again, he lifted his shoulder in a quiet shrug, leaning back in the desk chair to watch her.

Robin's eyes filled. She got it.

Yeah, she definitely got it.

But she also wiped away the tears, brusque and no-nonsense. "Okay, then. What next? From me, I mean?"

"Have a seat," Garrie said, not unkindly. "We're about to figure that out. But . . . you think maybe you should stay here, instead of trying to drive home tonight?"

"I think she should," Lucia agreed. "After this past day? You and I can share one of those beds."

"I don't have . . ." Robin waved a helpless gesture. "Toothbrush. Soap. *Things*."

"We have an extra fancy welcome kit from the San Jose hotel, yes?" Lucia looked at Garrie to confirm it, then nodded. "Tomorrow morning, run home for *things*. Tonight, rest."

Robin went to the previously proffered chair and sat, heavily. She wiped her eyes again and said unsteadily, "Thank you. And . . . I'm sorry. I wish I could—" She glanced at Quinn. "But I can't. Undo any of it. I know that. So let's just get this solved."

"Did we buy some time, or not?" Quinn asked, and it was Trevarr he looked to.

Trevarr did as he'd done earlier—took one of the straight-backed chairs, flipped it around, and settled onto it backward, his forearms resting over the back of it. "Your Sin Nombres will be busy," he said. "But if they realize how to take advantage of the situation . . ." He shrugged.

Garrie felt the length of the day descend on her—the hike, the heat, the energies. "And how would that be?"

"The same way any group uses a weapon to its advantage. First, to reach out to those who might stop them." He looked directly at Robin, his head tipped ever so slightly to maintain a shadow from the lamplight.

She flinched. Either she had not truly noticed the impact of his gaze before, or she had not remembered it. She fiddled with the zipper pull of her hoodie—up, down, up. But her voice remained steady. "Honestly, there's no one. I mean, no one *I* can think of. I wouldn't even consider . . ." She took a deep breath, blew it out, and started again. "There are some who might *think* . . ."

Quinn said, "This town is saturated with pretenders. How are you to know who can do exactly what?"

"I live," Robin said starchly, "in a town saturated with *good people,* a great many of whom are wishful thinkers." But the starch left her, and she added, "But you're right. For the most part, people know who's who . . . and like hangs with like. But not everyone fits into a neat little clique."

"You don't," Lucia observed.

"Will your Huntington person take chances?" Trevarr asked, discarding the nuance of it all and cutting to the core.

"Not mine." Robin scowled, pretty features screwed into disdain. "This is all my fault. I never guessed . . . Huntington and Jim Dandy. Macho assholes, if you really want to know. As far as I knew, their biggest ambition was to convince cougars they were full of mystical energies that could be tapped only by fulfilling their wildest sex dreams."

"Then that is how it started," Trevarr said matter-of-factly, and seemingly unaware that the attention of everyone in the room had abruptly riveted upon him. Or maybe he was, for he glanced at Garrie. "It is not known, here? That pleasures of the flesh open conduits otherwise left closed?"

Garrie pretended she didn't feel herself grow hot. "It's not something that comes up," she said, and winced—*no, no, no, didn't just say that*—adding, "So to speak." And then, at his skepticism, "Seriously. People here just aren't used to dealing with discernible breezes. Certainly not enough to notice them if they're, um . . . preoccupied."

"People here," Robin said flatly. "You mean the States? Because I've been in Europe, you know. It's not *that* different. People don't exactly fart rainbows."

::Yes!:: Sklayne sat up with ears perked and whiskers fluffing out. ::Will try this thing!::

"You will not," Garrie told him, fiercely.

Robin crossed her arms, tilted her head . . . raised her eyebrows.

Oops.

Obfuscation. That was the ticket. "Right," Garrie said, completely out of clever. "People not *there*," she said.

Quinn snorted, letting it go. "So Huntington and his now-dead pal Jim Dandy had a schtick for pulling in older ladies—but he was enough of the real deal to notice when the schtick actually produced results." He nodded at the laptop. "That jibes with what I found this evening. Allusions, snide remarks . . . plenty of people know about their gimmicks, that's all they think is going on."

"So tomorrow we . . . what? March into Huntington's tour office and tell him to play nice?" Lucia's doubt spread over eloquent features.

"I'm still looking for a way to protect the area," Quinn said. "Big honking shields seem out of the question. They have to be fueled somehow, and Garrie can hardly do that by herself, never mind stick around to keep them going."

"The vortexes?" Lucia suggested.

Garrie shook her head. "Everything's running on dry already. I think we need to deal with this guy. The problem is . . . we deal with *ghosts*. Ghosts and darksiders. Not *people*." She shook her head again. "I can hardly dissipate him. And I have no idea what happens if I try to . . . well . . . *manage* him. And you know what? I don't want to know."

"Are you kidding?" Robin's voice came thinner than usual, and a little incredulous. "I know exactly what we do next. We put that *thing* of yours back where it belongs." Robin glanced somewhat accusingly at Trevarr. "I can't believe anyone thought that was a good idea."

"Hey," Garrie said, letting her miffed show. "It *was* a good idea. That interference came out of nowhere."

Quinn cleared his throat. He planted both feet on the ground and leaned forward, elbows on his knees. "What exactly happened?"

"Yes," Lucia said, looking straight at Garrie. "What exactly happened?"

"Er," Garrie said.

Trevarr broke his recent silence with a matter-of-fact tone. "The creature did not react well to the damaged energies of Huntington's people."

"Think of it as toxic waste," Garrie suggested, and Lucia made a face. "Hey, be glad you can't taste it yourself."

"Actually, I think it reacted *really well* to the toxic waste," Robin said, her acerbic tone ramping back up. "Like it went in there a nerd and came out a supervillain."

Garrie had to stop a moment and regard her with admiration. Resentful admiration—she wanted no part of admiring Robin at all, and she'd already had enough of feeling like Stick Girl next to Robin's plump voluptuousness. *Stick Girl* was *not* a good superhero name.

But Robin's analogy was . . .

"Yeah," she said. "That's it exactly. Then add in the other interference, which, seriously, came along at just exactly the wrong time—"

Trevarr caught her eye—something of reticence there, and she didn't trust it. An instant of panic swamped her—reality, striking hard. What was she doing trusting any part of him? This *not-safe* man with his *not-cat* and his leather duster and his *sword,* who had so recently invaded her world and her life, and who had told her so little of himself . . . hints and insinuations and spare, rare facts. Who had already changed not just her circumstances but her body—and who was quite obviously ready to claim the rest of her body as his own, too.

Please.

There, see? That wasn't her, that thought. It had never *been* her.

But when she looked at him, she saw beyond the obvious—beyond the startling first impression of fierce features and broad shoulders and strength on the prowl. Beyond the scattering of old scars, well-used hands often hidden beneath half-finger gloves that made a whole lot more sense now that she'd seen the sword and knives.

One wanted a good grip, after all.

She saw an equally startling vulnerability.

She must be insane.

That wasn't her, either. Seeing things in people. Accepting silences and games. Accepting that somehow, in some way, his need for her had created a need for him. Accepting that his very touch had changed her nature . . . and instead of snarling and slamming every possible door in his face, metaphorical and physical, letting him in again. And again. And—

"Chicalet?" Lucia asked, worry drawing fine brows together.

Oh.

But Trevarr was the one who seemed to blink, to suck in a quick breath; his shoulders twitched. Yet his voice was perfectly normal. "I believe the lerket's changes to be permanent."

::Permanent. Yes. No longer a thing of Kehar.::

How handy to communicate without a mouth, if one was to be cleaning one's nether regions during the conversation.

Trevarr aimed a look Sklayne's way, enough focus in his attention to make Garrie think he said something—and indeed, Sklayne lifted his head, a started expression widening rich green eyes, ticked-red fur rippling down his back.

He put his hind leg down and pulled his tail into a prim curl around his feet. ::Not a thing of Kehar,:: he repeated, looking at Trevarr as though it meant something.

It did.

"It cannot return from whence it came," Trevarr said.

"From whence it came," Robin echoed. "Does anyone really *say* that?" And when they looked at her, she waved them off with a hand. "No, no, never mind. Just having a reality-challenged moment."

"What, then?" Lucia said, her hands resting so quietly on her knee that Garrie recognized it for what it was—Lucia in self-control. Lucia worried. "And what exactly happened to it?"

"Oh," Garrie said vaguely, "it got bigger. It got kind of sparky. And it got ugly, but honestly . . . it was pretty ugly to start with. It's just that when it was small, it had that so-ugly-it's-cute thing going for it. You know. Like some of those monkey-faced dogs. Now . . . really not so much." She repeated the vague gesture Trevarr had made earlier that day, fingers waving around at either side of her mouth . . . decided against doing the same at her butt.

"A *lot* bigger," Robin said. "A *lot* sparky. And everywhere it went, it left . . ." She hesitated, looking at Garrie as if for help with the words, and finally said, "Unfootprints."

Quinn snorted. "What's that supposed to be? *Unfootprints?*"

Trevarr cocked his head slightly. "I believe it was removing energy from all it touched. Removing . . . order."

"What? Like an entropy machine?" Quinn gave a short bark of laughter, then his amusement died away. "You mean it. You mean just that."

"It resisted capture with—" Trevarr glanced at Robin, decided against finishing that sentence. "But it may be that we can worry it until I can control it again, as it was before."

Garrie got it. Got that he didn't want to say straight out that he had a device made of rare metal and inexplicable stones—the Gatherer—that would affect the lerket's ethereal nature.

And Quinn got it, too, though not without a doubtful frown. "You want to beat it up until it can't resist."

"What a fun plan!" Garrie exclaimed, and just barely restrained herself from clapping her hands together in sardonic glee.

"And then all we've solved is the problem we created in trying to solve the problem," Robin said, pointed words in a pointed tone.

"Why yes," Garrie said, so sweetly that Lucia winced and Quinn put his face in his hands and Trevarr's eyebrow shot up, the one that was so completely independent of the other, so very Spock. "Sometimes when we don't really know what's going on, we define what might work by trying different things and seeing how they don't work. For instance, if the person we've come to help insists on keeping all the juicy little tidbits to herself so she can have control of just exactly how we perceive the situation because maybe her whole goal wasn't *really* to get help because she never *expected* us to be capable of helping in the first place. Say, maybe if the whole thing was just an excuse to get a certain one of us here, and the rest of us simply proved annoyingly independent and resistant to manipulation. You know. Like that."

Robin closed her eyes. She sighed hugely. She flopped back on the bed, arms akimbo, her chest a substantial presence rising from the bedcovers. "Oh," she said, driven by an unvoiced *aurgh, "just shoot me now."*

"I think," Lucia said, quite sensibly, "it would just be better if you quit poking us."

Quinn raised his hand. "All in favor!"

"Aye!" Garrie said, raising both hers.

Lucia added a silent third. She gave Trevarr a meaningful look. A prod. With a baffled frown, he took one hand off the chair and slowly raised it, holding it there.

Garrie covered a smile. She composed herself to stern and cleared her throat. "Huntington may try a preemptive strike with his new entropy toy, supposing he survives the night with it. Robin wants to go home tomorrow morning, but then she can meet Lucia in town, and together they can warn the most likely targets. Quinn, I'd like you to monitor things as best you can. I'll check in with the ghost activity, and then do a little recon, see if I can pin things down that way. The entropy toy's location. Then Trevarr and I will go deal with the thing. And *then*—" She looked at Robin. "Who knows. Huntington might not even have any starch left by then, between handling the lerket and losing it."

But Lucia was frowning, and her quiet hands had folded together, knuckle-white. "The recon thing?" she said. "In these circumstances? Is that . . . safe?"

Garrie laughed. Huntington's toxic waste oozing

around, a lerket gone rogue and wild, and Kehar sweep-ing through to send her boiling. "Hell, no, it's not safe."

Farking bloody hell, no.

Lucia stared at the ceiling, and sleep mocked her. The pale outdoor lighting filtered through the curtains and painted the room in soft moon grays and black shad-ows, illuminating her state of sleeplessness.

Not that she had any trouble sharing a bed with Gar-rie. They did it often enough, for this reason or that, and in tighter circumstances to boot. One-nighters in Clovis or Alamogordo or Santa Fe, where those artsy Santa Fe ghosts like to make a production of everything. Garrie might have lost her financially sensible parents in a car accident at barely eighteen, but she'd still been under the guidance of the utterly frugal Rhonda Rose . . .

They'd for certain done their time sharing hotel beds. And Garrie, wiry and vibrating with energy when awake, was nothing more than a slender bit of a thing asleep—or pretending to be asleep—quiet and still. Lucia's long legs took up more room than she did. So it was now, Garrie beside her with a pillow over her head—she al-ways seemed to end up that way—and Lucia stretched out on her back. Staring at the ceiling. Unable to blame it on a restless friend, or even snoring. And Robin had cried herself to sleep in the second bed over an hour earlier.

It's a good plan.

Too sensible, that was the problem. La, la, la, head out to town and play Paul Revere with anyone Robin thought might need warning. It didn't matter whether or not they were sensitives or maybe even had skills—plenty of people did, if very few managed to cultivate them.

It only mattered that Huntington and his Sin Nombres thought they might be a problem.

Robin was sensitive to some things, blind to others. She'd noticed nothing of Sklayne; nothing of her ghosts. But the energies stirred up by Huntington—she'd most certainly felt those. The disruption of the mutated lerket . . . Lucia had no doubt.

At this point, the woman no doubt hardly knew which end was up. She'd expected Quinn; she'd gotten the team. She'd expected to take point on a mundane investigation; she'd gotten intractable, independent reckoners, headed by Garrie in her funky sprite persona—still glittering from her run-in with the Krevata portal, bursting at the seams with skill and power. Younger than Robin by at least five years—for if Lucia didn't miss her bet, Robin had a couple of years on Quinn, and Quinn had a couple of years on Garrie.

Lucia could almost feel sorry for her.

But not quite.

She sighed.

Tomorrow will be fine. She stopped her spinning thoughts, pinned them in place. *We have a plan. We have a good team. We have a decent idea of what's going on and we know who has to be stopped.* And if she was utterly surrounded by fresh, strong spiritual angst as she had been all this evening—disturbed ghosts everywhere, leaving her at peace only when Garrie returned, subtly creating her boundaries—well, that's what she was here for, wasn't it? To judge what was happening through what she felt?

This work is how I make peace with what I am.

The air-conditioning kicked on and off and on, a shift of motor noise beneath the circulating fan. Garrie sighed softly—not asleep after all, and no big surprise in the wake of a day of conflicting energies and no chance to pound them out on a treadmill or pool laps or any of the myriad ways she managed such things. But Lucia couldn't fix that; Lucia could only manage her own needs.

This work is how I make peace with what I am. She felt sinking in . . . finally felt herself relaxing. Dozing. Heading for sleep.

And then suddenly she wasn't.

She didn't move; she only slowly cracked her eyes open, found that she'd dozed enough to roll over, looking at the bundle of Garrie beside her. And she thought to warn Garrie—*something* had woken her, and that was never good—until she realized quite suddenly that the something was Garrie herself. That she, too, had come alert, and if she didn't move yet, it was because she still assessed. But she was *too* still, too drawn into herself. Gathering herself.

And then quite suddenly, she relaxed.

That's when Lucia knew. She hadn't seen him yet, but she knew.

Trevarr was here.

Garrie pushed the pillow from her head and slipped from beneath the covers, clad in a girl-next-door cotton cami and boy shorts set that Lucia had foisted on her in their final days in San Jose, claiming she'd gotten the wrong size.

They'd both known better, of course—it wasn't the first time Lucia had surrendered to impulse when it came to Garrie's wardrobe, even if she always tempered what she wanted to get with the knowledge of what Garrie would actually wear.

Now Garrie reached for the sleeveless hoodie at their rustic headboard and shrugged it over that revealing nightware as she stood. Ah, yes. There he was, then. Visible in clear silhouetted against the window. How the hell tall was he, anyway? Enough to be thoroughly imposing. Garrie's head came right about to his heart.

Well. Where Lucia thought his heart might be. But she was done making assumptions.

Garrie went to him without hesitation; he greeted her

silently. And that, suddenly, was when Lucia knew. That was when she saw it.

That everything was changed. Everything was *different*. This was not her friend flirting with the dark side of the Force for the rush of it. This was not Lisa McGarrity tired of her scattered, sporadic dating pattern and lured by the *not-safe* into a fling, wise or not.

No. This was Garrie giving everything and leaving herself wide open for heartbreak.

Because here, watching, silent in the darkness, she saw it reflected in Trevarr.

Everything. Changed.

She realized it with a flutter of fear at first. She *needed* this team. She *needed* the reckoning. And if it seldom paid well, Garrie had nonetheless turned it into a business—one driven by referrals and a portfolio of successes spanning more than half her life.

Not that the money mattered to Lucia. Not with trust funds, her own suite of rooms in a house large enough to hold them, a private entrance that kept her independent from Mami and Papi.

No, it wasn't about the money at all.

So, yes. Fear.

As Garrie went to him, he raised his hand to touch the side of her face. She tipped her head up to receive it—nothing studied about that interaction. Nothing uncertain. Then when Trevarr bent to her, Lucia thought, *Close your eyes,* impertinente, but her eyes didn't close at all. And so she saw that Trevarr kissed Garrie's brow, and she saw the hesitation before he gently kissed her mouth—a statement more of tenderness than of passion.

Dammit. Fear made room for a little kick in her gut. If she normally protected herself from the world, and if she generally found herself more vulnerable to lingering emotional imprints than to live emotions, she nonetheless had enough connection with her friend to feel something sweet and deep.

Oh, damn.

Don't you dare hurt her, Mr. Not-Safe.

Not because you have your own agenda. Not because you can't control whatever you're into. And not because you forget that this one isn't just another conquest. For if they hadn't been together yet—of which Lucia was certain—then she also guessed it wouldn't be long. That, too, was revealed in the deep and sweet.

She lost track of them for a moment—until the door opened, just enough to let Garrie pass, and then wider to let Trevarr through—closing again, without a sound. The old-fashioned porch swing wasn't nearly as quiet as they settled into it. But then, silence.

She couldn't help it. She slid from the bed, found her soft bunny flip-flop slippers with her toes, and eased over to the window.

Right. Who needed a hotel room, when you had the canyonlands moon overhead? Who needed a blanket, when you had Trevarr and that coat? And Garrie, unlikely to sleep after a day full of so much energy no matter how tired, once again appeared well on the way to doing just that. He stroked her shoulder; he rested his chin against her hair.

Just maybe, she thought, he would sleep, too.

11

Spirits in need have a unique perspective.
—Rhonda Rose

Me, me, me!
—every ghost, ever

Garrie opened her eyes to the bare hint of dawn—coral and pale turquoise spread along the eastern horizon.

Whoa. *Outdoors* dawn. Birds singing, check. Air kissed with dampness, check. The scents of the day—pine and juniper and cedar—warming around her, check. Her legs chilly, the rest of her humming with warmth . . .

Check, check, check.

Right. Sleepless night, Trevarr . . . and if it wasn't right for him to stay in the room where Robin and Lucia slept unaware, then the porch swing bench had been waiting. And so, apparently, had sleep.

A loud purr vibrated through the air, tickling the bottoms of her feet.

Not cold, the bottoms of her feet, tucked up on the bench as they were. Now she knew why.

"How is it," she said, "that I can sleep when I'm with you?" In San Jose. Here. No dreams, no jarring surges of unsettled energies.

He shifted slightly behind her. "Some things simply are."

::He doesn't know,:: Sklayne informed her, and smug at that. And then he purred ever more loudly, rendering impossible anything Trevarr might have said to him in response.

"Don't you?" Garrie asked.

"Should I?"

"You're the one who travels worlds. I'm the one who only recently learned there are worlds for traveling." She stretched her toes, and realized then that she hummed with more than warmth. That the toll for sleep had been a slow and subtle build of the wild pressure from within her, seeping into her every personal nook and cranny. Persistent, unrelenting . . . hunting release.

He shifted beneath her again, his arm over her shoulders, his chest beneath her face, lean stomach beneath her hand where her fingers slid along and under his belt—

"Oh," she said, pulling her hand back a few inches. "Sorry." *Persistent, unrelenting . . .*

He made a noise that sounded a little like *can't talk just now,* and for those moments they simply breathed in the dawn together—if somewhat unevenly. Until he took one final deep breath and said wryly, "Traveling worlds means nothing when it comes to the nuances of being with you, *atreya.*"

"Hmph." She tucked her light sleeveless hoodie around the snug little camisole Lucia had thrust at her in San Jose, and looked into his face. "I'm not sure if that's the best compliment *eveh,* or just plain rude."

::You choose,:: Sklayne suggested, and, "Mow!" when her foot happened to twitch just so, nudging him off the bench.

She, too, sat up, ignoring the protest of the persistence, the brief escalation of humming, and the faintly desperate nature of movements that tried so hard to be matter-of-fact. "I hate to wake Lucia. I might as well check on our ghosties before I go back inside."

Morning bladder might have something to say about that. But she'd see.

Trevarr stood, shedding his coat—draping it over her even as he drew Lukkas from one of those pockets, propping the sword briefly against the bench rocker to tug his shirt free, loosening the laces with a practiced hand and pulling it over his head.

Garrie resisted the urge to trace her fingers over the faint brush marks that weren't old tattoos at all—the feathery scales barely visible along the backs of his arms and fanning out over his ribs, growing darker along his forearms, darker where the pattern converged toward his spine at his belt line . . . ever, ever so faint along the sides of his neck. He put a hand against the porch over-hang and stretched against it, a ritualistic motion; mus-cle and bone rippled beneath skin.

"Oh," Garrie said, swallowing hard. "Right. Don't mind me. I'll just concentrate on ghosts with no trouble at all. Really. No problem."

He straightened; he looked over at her with slightly narrowed eyes. "This is something we will deal with," he told her. "Soon."

Oh, *really*? "Do you think so?" Okay, yeah. Maybe so. But— "And do you really think that's going to *help*?"

Something like amusement eased his expression— something fervent in there, too. "I *hope*."

"Huh," Garrie said.

And he leaned against the post again, but in that star-tling instant, all the taut strength seemed drained from him. He was not stretching; he was farking *being held up*.

Garrie dropped one foot to the ground, ready to push off—ready to rise and help. But a red-buff paw landed on her leg—good God, there was a *thumb*—and claws extruded, ever so gently. Not piercing skin . . . but stop-ping her.

"What?" she would have demanded, had not those claws pushed just a smidgen harder, rich green eyes catch-ing her attention. Something whirled behind the pupils, something not merely a cat's eye at all.

Sklayne's words came to her mind tight and precise

and strained—only between the two of them, she realized, and not an easy thing, to shut Trevarr out. ::The food,:: he said. His ears swiveled—perfectly normal cat ears this morning. ::We must make this better. Soon.::

She didn't have to respond. Not when her eyes widened in spite of herself and her chin trembled ever so faintly.

For she'd seen Trevarr hurt and agonized and wounded unto death; she'd seen him poisoned and stabbed and shot, surviving through determination and through Sklayne's gifts and through his own obviously preternatural ability to heal.

But she'd never seem him simply falter.

He straightened abruptly, glanced her way—his expression hard, the sharp edge with which he'd first introduced himself now fully in place. *Covering.* Or trying to. And checking to see just how much she'd seen.

Nothing. As far as he was concerned, nothing at all.

"Seriously," she said, wearing her oblivious face— Valley Girl Reckoner, on demand—and if she almost choked on the word and its blithe nature, she didn't let it show; she somehow found her sardonic tone of before. "Don't mind me. I'll just do my ghostie thing. No problem."

No problem at all.

The ghostie thing. Didn't go so well. Or maybe . . .

Went too well altogether.

"Find me," Jim-Bob Dandy implored her, garbled words with echoing vowels and bouncing consonants. "They *took* me."

Okay, nothing new there.

If you didn't notice how the tumbling gusts of energy that formed him now stuttered, guttering like a drowning candle.

"This is my place," murmured the flower child, visible

only in her upper body and the outrageous bells to her jeans—and only when Garrie walked out from beneath the short cabin porch overhang to find her perched above. She clasped her arms around invisible knees and rocked back and forth, but her voice remained only a whisper, nothing of the clarity and strength it had carried the first time Garrie saw her. "Someone needs to know."

"Me," said another ghost, clustering in close—and if she'd seen it here before, she couldn't identify it. A small entity, probably a child.

"Me!" insisted yet another, giving the impression that it shouted—that it shoved the others aside and jostled for the head of the line. But in truth, it was a voice so low that Garrie barely heard it. And it was one of many, all clamoring—or trying to clamor—for attention, all without managing to say what they needed at all.

Trevarr worked his forms off to the side, the sword slicing air—singing more loudly than the faded, frantic ghosts. Fast, accurate, deadly . . . precision and strength once more on the prowl.

Yet if Garrie saw anything, with the ghosts all around her and Trevarr's particular form of masculine beauty in motion before her, it was that moment when all the intensities of him had drained away and left him leaning against a porch post.

"Thieves!" Bobbie Ghost spat, the loudest of them. This was her death spot, her anchor. The others had, astonishingly, left their anchors to come here. To find Garrie. To demand that she *fix it*.

Damn. She wasn't used to them in herds. Even Winchester House had been different. There, they had been trapped. Preyed upon. Desperate to get away.

"You know," she said, "it would help if you *helped*. How about a nice sparkling trail of obvious to the guy who's causing all the trouble? How about a hint or two? You can all be pretty effective if—oh."

For there was Feather and her little Yorkie dog. On its own feet this time, bouncing along as though gravity barely managed to keep hold of its tiny form. "Good morn—" She stopped short, caught flat-footed by them both—Garrie in her scrap of boy shorts and the open hoodie over the camisole, Trevarr shirtless and—

Oh, yeah. Swinging a sword.

"Yap!" said the dog, stiff-legged and fierce. It bounced a half-circle around Trevarr, *yapyapyap,* no apparent bend in its legs at all. Just bounce. "Yap!"

::For-rr meee?:: Sklayne purred from the bench seat, no thumbs in evidence and eyes all slitted satisfaction. Garrie's glance at him was enough to direct the dog's attention—even as Feather pulled her startlement away from Garrie and Trevarr to tend the dog, reaching for it, it bounced off to challenge Sklayne.

::Ohhh yess.::

"No," Trevarr said, voice of law. "You will not."

"I—" Feather recoiled, startled. "I beg your pardon?"

"The cat," Garrie said, quickly stepping between them, closing her ears to the ghosts crowding around her—drawing her hoodie closed and still not feeling nearly dressed enough. "Sorry. We really didn't think anyone would be up this early. But—" Desperate distraction—"Since you're here . . . Caryn said she thought you'd found something about the young woman who died here?"

Feather finally scooped up the little dog. She blinked at Garrie as if the words made no sense to her at all, and that's when Garrie realized that Feather was still in her bathrobe, her feet in old flip-flops and her faded hair pulled back into a sloppy scrunchy. No doubt still half asleep—no doubt not certain she was seeing exactly what she was seeing—even as Trevarr settled his duster around Garrie's shoulders and tugged his shirt over his head, still breathing fast from his forms, sweat gleaming on his chest. The shirt fell casual and sloppy, rucked up on his belt buckle and so obviously an incomplete state of dress that the bare chest somehow might have been better.

"Me, me, me!" A never-ending chorus of need and demand, overlaid with the hiss and sputter of Jim-Bob Dandy's sporadically failing energies, the cry of flower-child anguish . . .

Just groovy.

Feather blinked again and said, "Yes, I do have some information. Not much. If you want to stop by the office once it's open, I'll be there today." She hesitated. "About Caryn—"

"I get it," Garrie said. "You've tried to stop her. We've had this conversation."

"No, that's not—" Feather made a reluctant face, wiped a hand across dry lips. Garrie didn't look back at Trevarr; she didn't have to, to feel his increased attention. Feather finally shook her head. "She's my niece, and I love her, but . . . she hurt you once, and I don't think she learned from that. I think it made her curious." Feather looked at Garrie, whose face inconveniently took the first hint of sunlight over the horizon and turned it into a shimmer. "Whatever it is you have, I think she probably wants it."

"That's never good," Garrie said, gripping the edges of the duster.

As if encouraged by this distraction, the ghosts surged up against her. *"Me, me, me!"* Plucking at her, imploring . . . growing petulant, Jim-Bob Dandy at the forefront of them. A new spirit, and one who, before death, had learned how to manipulate the ethereal world.

Even if in the manner of a man knitting while wearing mittens.

And when Garrie pushed a gust at them all, just enough to earn herself some space and some respect, he sucked it up with the same parasitic zeal she imagined him to have shown in life. "Damn," she muttered. "I should have seen that coming."

Feather didn't even give her a startled look. "I don't know how you could have. I've known her all her life, and *I* didn't see it coming."

Jim-Bob, swelling in size and intensity, grabbed onto Garrie's breeze—held it. Reached for more, drawing it in as if it were a rope . . . with Garrie on the other end.

"Oh crap," she said, voice rising slightly. *Cut the breeze, Idiot Reckoner. Throw it away!*

But Garrie was one with the breezes. For all she pushed the energy away, for all she waved her hands as though flipping away water droplets, there still remained the trickle of that connection. Jim-Bob sizzled a back trail, following energy to the source with the speed and fervency of a lit fuse. "Oh farking *crap*!" she said, a frantic tone creeping into her voice. "I am *so* not awake enough for this!"

"What—?" Feather asked, finally realizing this particular little dance had nothing to do with Caryn. She tightened her hold on the squirming little dog. "Trickle, no!"

Shields. "If I only had a brain," Garrie muttered, and threw up a set of rock-hard shields. Jim-Bob ran into them at full blast, hard enough to reverberate—hard enough to set her back a step or two. He flattened up against the dome of energy, spreading thin—seeking a way through. *Not these shields, mister.*

He slid back to the ground, a shrunken, pale version of himself. Puddling there.

::Rude,:: Sklayne observed, not a hair ruffled.

No kidding. She straightened, hunting nonchalance and dignity. Pretending none of it had happened at all. "So listen," she said, as if Feather hadn't already noticed. But so very few people would break the conceit if she held it out there. Just an extension of the social games everyone played, pretending not to see when someone had spinach in her teeth, or that a stranger's ragged bra strap was so totally showing, or worst of all the dreaded nostril malfunction. "Later in the office, you said?"

"Anytime past eight." Feather drew the little dog closer as it lifted a lip at Sklayne, its tiny soprano growl vibrating in the air.

"Great," Garrie said, a beat too late to be natural. "That'll be just—oh, *farking*—"

For there on the ground in his puddle, Jim-Bob had not yet given up. He pushed up against the shield, up against the ground . . . he made a sucking, slurping noise that Garrie could not—seriously could *not*—believe that Feather hadn't heard. A frantic glance in Trevarr's direction revealed that while he certainly knew there was ghost trouble, he hadn't heard a thing, either.

Until the very visible earth gave way to Jim-Bob. Gave of itself, because there was nothing else left to give, here where Huntington's Sin Nombres had already sucked the earth dry, a desert land now parched for more than water. The ground gave a deep groan, and bedrock, so near the surface, shuddered and shrank. The earth tightened into itself, leaving a network of cracks.

Garrie gaped at them, a long instant in which she failed to react at all. And then she simply bolted forward, using the shield to shove Jim-Bob away. "You stop that!"

Feather slowly backed away, holding her hand over

the little dog's eyes as if to shield it from an emotionally scarring sight, while Garrie snapped, "Get over yourselves! Yes, there's trouble! Yes, I'm working on it! But news flash—you're not making it any easier! And I'm not going to let *you* become the problem." She gathered up energy—legitimate breezes, those Jim-Bob didn't have the skill to shape and mold on his own, drawn by what she'd always had within her and now driven by that which struggled so hard to make its way out of her. Hands held before her, cradling breezes, massaging them with the lightest touch . . . she let them see what she had. "If I have to use this now, I'll use it for keeps. You got it?"

Dissipation. The ugliest threat she could use . . . the ugliest outcome. Dissipation meant failure, no matter how it seemed like victory to those on the solid end of the spectrum. No resolution, no completion, no passing beyond.

But she meant it.

And they knew it.

Within seconds, the area had cleared of ghosts. All but Jim-Bob, who lingered—chastened, but still reluctant. Still wanting. She gave him a poke, and that left only Bobbie sitting on top of the porch roof. Still faint, and now faintly amused. She'd asked, but she hadn't pushed . . . and this was *her* territory. Garrie gave her a warning look, but nothing more.

"Coffee," Feather said faintly, easing away from them—easing away from a reality she'd always claimed to believe, away from a truth Garrie had already explained but that hadn't yet been seen or truly believed. *"I need coffee."* And quite suddenly she was in flight toward the office.

::Fark,:: said Sklayne. ::Took my snack.::

* * *

Amazing how quickly a day could turn ordinary. Garrie jostled for the shower and lost to Lucia, but not before Robin grabbed a moment in the bathroom, scooped up her car keys, and promised to return in little more than an hour.

Garrie did calisthenics, waiting for her turn, flirting with the notion of hitting the office to see what Feather had learned but putting it off when she finally had the chance to head in for a quick clean-up. She found, to her surprise, a bar of the luxurious soap she hadn't had the chance to buy at Robin's shop—all handmade and olive oil and ginger scented with little flecks of cinnamon.

Sklayne's voice drifted into her head. ::Gift.::

She'd figure it out later. For now, luxury. And what with one thing and another and then adding breakfast to the mix, the day had turned its heat up to sizzle before they quit bumping around the two rooms and each other, preoccupied with their various morning things.

Quinn, already collecting information from the night before. Lucia, caught in a peaceful series of yoga stretches. Garrie, completely preoccupied by what had happened in the yard, what had happened the night before, what was happening in her body . . . what was happening to Trevarr.

Trevarr, hiding exactly that.

If not as successfully as the day before.

But then they were settling down, water bottles re-charged and chilling, sunscreen applied . . . Lucia's tote by the door and her person perfectly appointed, just the right delicate jewelry to set off her sun-kissed olive skin tones, a faint hint of lavender dusting her lids and tint-ing her lip gloss. Today's outfit was all flirty silk tiers in the top, slim crop jeans and itty-bitty sandals below, hair drawn back into a high ponytail with just enough deliberate rumple to make it interesting. Cool and classy.

Definitely ready.

Garrie's trail shorts—washed in the shower the night before and dried over the air conditioner—didn't look quite as crisp as they had. The filmy blue-tone top, also a rerun. The ribbed spaghetti-strap tank she wore beneath was the last of those she'd brought with her.

One way or another, she'd lost much of her clothing in San Jose.

Lucia gave her a critical look. "I should have picked up more clothes for you," she said, and when Garrie would have protested, said, "What was I doing but shopping? Shopping therapy." And if she had a satisfied gleam in her eye, it had also been nothing but the truth. "Where is our *pajarito,* anyway? She'll know the best places to stop today. She won't want to, I'm sure. But we can't have you running around without clothes."

"I have clothes!"

Lucia gave her nothing more than a silent *oh, please* and flung the door open. "Where *is* she?"

Not answering her phone, that's what. They'd already tried.

And there was Trevarr, in the doorway, looking nearly as startled to have it flung open as Lucia was to find him there. They collided; Lucia clutched at him to keep from going down, and almost did it anyway as Trevarr recoiled.

"What?" Lucia said, offended.

Sklayne yawned loud. Not in the doorway, not outside the room—but there, on the foot of the halfheartedly made bed, as if he'd actually entered the room in some fashion along the way. Garrie would have accused him of showing off if he hadn't said, his tone bored, ::Silver.::

"Silver!" Garrie repeated out loud, panic hitting a button she hadn't known was lurking. She pushed up against Lucia in the doorway. "Are you—did it—"

::Not stabbed,:: Sklayne said, still bored. ::Not

blooded at all. No blood and silver. You see? Not hurt.:: He seemed to consider this, sniffing the air with a contemplative expression. ::Much.::

"Silver," Lucia said, floundering. And then, "Like in San Jose." She shook her head, looked down at her rings and bracelets.

"It was nothing," Trevarr said, and his expression was as cold and distant as it ever got. As if he had to be more Trevarr than thou to prove his words.

Sklayne jumped from the bed, winding himself along the edge of the open door, tail held high. Along Garrie's leg, tail held high. So casual. A ruse, that. ::Stupid Trevarr. Burned. Should not be so. The food. We must fix.::

I know, she told him, and bent to scratch along his cheek—only belatedly realizing that perhaps it wasn't quite done.

But Sklayne was a creature of indolent hedonism, and accepted the attention as his due. It didn't change the resentment in his voice. ::I *could*,:: he said. ::I should be *allowed*. *Free*.::

But he hadn't stayed quiet enough for that one.

"Little one," Trevarr said, suddenly looming close; Lucia snatched her hands away and put them behind her back. "That was your bargain to make."

"Mrrt," Sklayne said out loud, a distasteful sound of no meaning at all.

"Rather than be left out of the conversation," Lucia said pointedly, "I believe I will follow through with my grand and dramatic gesture of stomping out into this little dusty yard with its charming new earth cracks to exclaim about Robin's absence."

"Oh, I think you should," Garrie agreed. "It's time to get this morning moving." She stepped the rest of the way outside, closing the door behind her.

In tandem, Quinn burst through the other door only a few feet away, veering off from Lucia by mere inches.

"Aiee!" Lucia said. "Oh! *Will* you men watch where you're going!" She gave it up altogether, grabbing the only moment she was likely to get. "And where *is* that Robin!"

"They have her," Quinn said, bright blue eyes gone grim even in the glimmer of the sun.

"I—what?" Lucia's grand and dramatic gesture petered out into *surely I didn't hear that.* "*Who* has her?"

"The Sin Nombres, who else? It has to be. I just heard it on the scanner—the police are at her shop. They're calling it a break-in. I called and got some lackey. She just got there, and the place is a mess. Not a ghost mess, a man-mess. And Robin isn't anywhere around."

"But Robin was coming *here,*" Garrie said, baffled. "Why would she be—"

"Because she lives over the shop!" Quinn interrupted, a desperate kind of anger in his voice. "She should be *there*—or here. And she's not either, and she hasn't been. Not for far longer than it would have taken her to get here from there." He hovered on the edge of something— Garrie didn't know what, and she thought Quinn didn't know, either. Of *doing.* Of *needing* to do.

"You need to go," Garrie said, making the decision for them.

He snorted. "What good will that do?"

She ignored that, pointing toward the parking area. "You and Lucia. Go. You might well see something in the shop that no one else would notice. Signs of the lerket . . . anything that ties to Huntington. See what her friend knows—Nancy, the one who zapped Trevarr."

Lucia tilted her head at Quinn—at his remaining hesitation. "Come, Quinnie. She wants to do some of her own looking, and we'll just be in the way. Besides, when you get back, you can check your little chat forums. Right now, no one even knows about it. But we can spread the word . . . stir things up."

"Stir things up," he repeated grimly. "Yeah. Let's go do that."

"Hey." Garrie caught his arm as he turned to go back into the room. "You find anything, you call. Right? Because this isn't a hero setup. There's nothing you can do with that lerket."

"Yeah?" he said. "And what about you? Is there anything *you* can do with that lerket? Or these *people*? You said it last night, Garrie. We do *ghosts*, not people. We're not prepared for this. I should have known better. I should have remembered—"

He cut himself off with a sharp shake of his head, wayward sun-brightened strands of Hollywood blond hair falling over his forehead. "Okay. I'll get the keys. And I'll call. But you find anything when you go poking around with that reckoner radar—"

"I'll call."

He gave her a look.

"I'll *call*," she said.

If she found something he could do anything about.

12

The human element remains unpredictable.
—Rhonda Rose

I do ghosts, not assholes.
—Lisa McGarrity

Talk, talk, talk.

It was a people thing, the talk. Sklayne wanted to *act*. He wanted to hunt the dry prickly desert, leaving not even bones behind; he wanted to taste the sharp shards of existence here. To shed the cat form and sizzle along the terrain, moving faster than the Garrie's people could even imagine, and then leaping the power lines to surf the miles.

Oh, wait.

Yesterday.

He had done that yesterday.

He wanted to do it *again*.

Not the talk, talk, talk. Accomplishing nothing. Why not let him go Kehar-ward, then, and search for the pungent, spicy leaves of which he had told the Garrie? That would be *doing*. It would be *fixing*.

And no more sitting here on this strange world—fun to explore, fun to eat, not fun to *live* in. No more feeling the gray crawl in along the edges of Trevarr.

::Tre-eyy,:: he said, his best wheedling voice.

But the Quinn person had returned to his room for only a moment, coming out with a water bottle and keys in hand. He jerked his chin in Trevarr's direction. "What about him?"

::Stays,:: Sklayne said, as decisively as if he was the one with the last word.

"I stay," Trevarr said, at almost the same time.

The Quinn person looked both resistant and relieved at the same time. Sklayne narrowed eyes at him. Thought about biting him. ::Cannot both stay and go.::

His comment made Trevarr give the Quinn person a second look—hidden behind those dark lenses now, with the sun up to burn eyes used to a soothing Kehar forest.

Well, not so soothing in the parts where it might eat you. But not bright. Dark fog, thick branches, dim sun.

Trevarr said, "She is too vulnerable when she searches in this way."

"He's right," the Lucia person said. "She doesn't have the faintest idea what's going on in the real world when she's out there in Garrieland."

And if Sklayne knew that wasn't what Trevarr meant—or at least, wasn't *completely* what Trevarr meant—he kept it to himself. But the Garrie looked at her feet, and then at her hands, fingers twined around one another at the level of her flat little stomach and twisting. The Garrie knew.

Unpredictable, she'd been. Since Trevarr had pushed energy into her at the Winchester House. Since she'd channeled enough plasmic portal energy to save a world.

This world.

And his own, if it came to that. Which it would have, eventually.

The Quinn person tossed the keys up, snatched them out of the air. "Let's go then." he said. "If those bastards have Robin, I want them to know we're on their trail. They're in *way* over their heads."

Sklayne wondered what *bastard* tasted like.

Garrie pulled the pillows off Lucia's bed and added them to her own, piling them up to create her own little soft throne. No-nonsense efficiency. "I can do this," she said, and heard the worry in her own voice. She stopped, took a breath, and found better grit. "I. Can. Do. This."

Trevarr stood in the open doorway—soaking up heat before the door closed on artificial coolness, keeping an eye on the other cabins as the guests stirred and emerged and started their own days. No particular concern, she thought . . . simply a lifetime of habit.

She had the feeling that the word *lifetime* was aptly applied. She could see him, suddenly, in this same posture, in some other doorway on another world—a child, skinny and bruised and hardly assured of survival, ever watchful of those around him. *Mixed blood,* he'd told her, *seldom survives on Kehar.*

And she was worried about a little area-wide sweep?

Just because it wasn't the same old comfortable routine, the same old comfortable *her*?

Yeah. She could do this.

She spread a towel on the bed so she wouldn't have to unlace her hiking sneakers, sitting cross-legged against the pillows and taking the moment to shake down her arms and let herself relax. Eyes closed. *La la la*. Reaching for that other plane of awareness, the one so familiar to her . . . the one where it seemed she spent half her time.

Hearing instead the ticking of the room's AC, the sound of a car motor starting in the distant parking lot, the arrogantly persistent song of a mockingbird in the tall ash beside the cabin. Light on her eyelids from the window, dimming somewhat as Trevarr finally closed the door. The faint scent of him; the leather of his duster at the headboard. What was left of the cinnamon bun she and Lucia had split at breakfast tickled her nose and sent her stomach into a growl.

Hmm. Still here.

Maybe she sighed. Maybe she shifted. Maybe she didn't make any sign of it at all, but still, Trevarr knew. He said, "You cannot shut it out."

She didn't open her eyes. She thought about *it*. "The dragon, you mean? Is that what I'm doing?" So determined to keep it from getting out of hand, she'd shut down everything.

"Dragon," he said, and his voice was distinct, dry irony. Not one he explained before moving on. "It is part of you now. You cannot simply separate it from yourself and still be yourself."

No. Apparently not. "It damned well better behave."

The AC kicked in, ticking away. The half-size refrigerator hummed. A bug bite on her knee itched. Carefully, fearfully . . . she let go of the tight control, allowing the feel of the whole—from her usual light clarity to the lurking chill that warmed her bones.

With it came the missing view—the sensations of what lay around her. Flooding in, a familiar rush of skill and power. Sedona, at first all vast silver-gray plains of unrelieved emptiness. She pulled her vantage point up and away . . . went satellite-view. The topographic energy map. It should have been teeming with differences, darks and brights and colors and textures. This place, of all places.

Garrie frowned at that fog—found it not so much representative as obscuring, and, on impulse, did what she had never done before from this place. *Interfered.* She pushed at the fog—steady, even thrust, a stirring of power that shifted her inner balance, allowing the dark heat to thrum along her nerves. The fog thinned before her, revealing a pale version of this land's original ethereal topography—the vortexes, clearly evident as whorls of bright color throwing sparks across the surrounding land and the canyons with their extreme variation of cold hidden darkness and bright streaks and soupy Crayola colors bubbling over the plains and trickling into the city. All washed out, and yet all with enough brilliance to let her know exactly what this place would be, had she seen it undamaged.

Vultee Arch shone starkly in the midst of it all, bright black impossibility clutching onto the land, full of spikes and claws and barbs all drilling their way into the heart of the red rock. A fainter trail led toward town—black so bright she could barely look at it, oozing into every available crevice along the way—blooming bright here and there, and then thinning out to wash across half the town.

There. That spot of activity in the middle of town—

"Breathe, *atreya.*" A quiet voice, low and meaningless to her ear. "Stay the balance."

That spot of activity in the middle of town . . .

Had to be Robin's shop. A pinprick of tortured energies all poured into one tiny spot; a gallon of hatred crammed into a thimble.

Why hatred, she didn't know. The root of it . . . resentment, anger, thrilling power trip . . . washed over her in a buffet of tasted emotion.

"*Sah, atreya.* Breathe. Here. Now." And, as she blindly responded, "Yes. Steady. Good."

Maybe he'd seen it coming before she did. He must have. Because there, with the throb of malignancy pounding at her, the knowledge of what had been behind it and who had suffered for it, that heat sparked up into cold through her belly, sent a shiver down her back. *Robin. Is she even alive?* Or had they—

"*Breathe* it." More commanding now, his voice, and so much closer to her. "It is of *you* now. It must ebb and flow, as with breath."

—Destroyed her, taken her . . . left of her nothing more than what they'd left of Jim-Bob Dandy? Sound stuck in her throat—effort, caught in a shudder. A wave of hot-scented electricity rippled through her, lighting nerves into fuses until she quite abruptly knew it would eat her alive from the inside out if she didn't—

"With me." His voice, so low, skimming her ear. His breath, warm and stirring her hair, tightening her skin, sending her hands into clenched fists. "Breathe with *me*. It is *us*, now, *atreya*." And there, below the surface . . . familiar dark energies, fierce and unquenchably wild, a tumult of emotion and intensity and its own endless conflict. And he, too, had gone breathless, the pattern of it fluttering against her skin.

She gasped with the effort of it—with the fear. She cried out with it, a woman running headlong at a cliff and plunging over.

But not falling.

Breathe. Breathe us. *Ebb and flow.* And he showed her—catching her up, enfolding her in sensation so profound she felt herself flutter and give way before it, forgetting ebb and flow and *us* altogether—eyes rolling back, head falling back, spine arching . . . clenched hands spasming out into stiff fingers.

He shook her. Not physically, but an effect that rippled through her from the center out. *Do it!* A demand, now, as fierce and wild as the energies surrounding her.

Take it in. Push it out.

Yes.

Take it in. Push it out. *I can't—*

Give it to me.

But you *can't—*

He shook her again. Sharply.

They were going to have to talk about that.

She snapped it out at him—too much, too sudden, so he reeled beneath it and she struggled desperately to hold back the surge of *more, more, more* that pushed to break free, felt herself losing control altogether—felt him tremble, not even touching her, and felt the groan of his pain and effort like a blow. *Reality strike.* He didn't do this *to* her, he did it *for* her. Damned farking right she was going to—

Breathe.

Ebb and flow.

Not her. Not him. *Them.* She fought the overflow down to a trickle . . . felt him absorb it and let it go. She took in what was left . . . let it go.

The rage of what was in her slowly settled . . . calming. No more storm surge . . . just lapping waves.

"Like so," he said, his calm not entirely convincing; his voice raw.

"Like so," she said, and the sound barely made it out at all. She opened her eyes, just a little surprised to find she was still on the bed. Not much surprised to find him on his knees before her, arms on either side of her and hands on the headboard—only now easing up on their white-knuckled grip. His mouth had been beside her ear; now, briefly, he rested his forehead on her shoulder. Without thinking, she tipped her head into his neck—acknowledgment and gratitude and connection.

It hurt when he sat back on his heels, hands resting on his thighs. Like something stretching, something breaking. She found his eyes all smoky pewter, the pupils gone wide in spite of the room's decent daylight.

Wide, not big . . . he wasn't hiding the reality of them from her, and she suddenly knew that for the gift it was. She found she'd lifted both hands to his face, touching it as if she'd never seen it before. Tracing her thumb along the hard beauty of his features, dark expressive brows with a new scar cutting through one outside edge, the faint lines of hardship at the corners of his eyes, the corners of his mouth. It had gone quiescent, that mouth, but for the faintest tug at the corner. She ran her thumb along the off-center scar in the distinct depression beneath his lower lip, and then she ran it along the lower lip itself. Once, twice. When that singular tug turned into a smile, she smiled ruefully in return and let her hands fall away, releasing a deep sigh.

"Breathe," she said.

"Like that." He turned her hands over in her lap and rubbed his thumbs over the palms, where her nails had cut deep, angry creases. "It is something I have always done." He glanced at her, in case she misunderstood. "To survive."

She got it then, startling a little with the thought. "When you said mixed bloods don't survive, I thought it was because of the cruelty you were shown."

His smile turned dark. "Yes. That, too. But a good number of us simply cannot exist with ourselves. Now, I think . . . now you can understand why."

She closed her eyes on a shudder. "I guess I do."

"It will be better now," he said. He relinquished her hands. "Easier."

Fear lurched at her chest. "But what if—" And then she couldn't say it. *What if you're not here?* And she reached for him again, to thread her fingers through the sloppy stout braid into which he'd again pulled the side sections of his hair.

::No, no, no!:: Sklayne howled disapproval from outside the room and for a confused instant Garrie thought he objected to *her* and by the time she realized *wrong*, Sklayne had caromed not off the window but through it, changing states so fast he was a mere blur of reddish-buff cat skidding off the top of the air conditioner and sending Lucia's things flying. In the shocked moment of silence following his arrival, the window gave a belated *creak* of protest; in the next instant, a spider web of cracks shot through the surface.

Trevarr jerked back, and if he shot a demand at Sklayne, it was so tight she couldn't hear it at all.

::Not my fault! Not not not! Who said to watch for trouble here?:: Almost a wail, that was, and if Trevarr's gaze shot to his duster, there at the headboard and out of reach, there was no time at all to act on it. Even as he flung himself at it—right over Garrie, crushing her into the pillows with weight and drive so she felt every leather tie, every buckle, reaching sinew and strength— the door slammed open, frame splintering. Trevarr scooped up Garrie instead of the duster, rolling them right off the bed and into a heap on the floor behind it.

::Not my fault—::

"Quiet!" Trevarr ground out, and quiet it was. Garrie sought to untangle herself, legs entwined, arms entwined, way too vulnerable—and yet somehow Trevarr's hand was beneath her head, saving her from a jarring blow against the floor. She scooted out from beneath him, caught briefly when their belt buckles clashed and stuck.

By the time she'd rolled to her hands and knees and peered over the bed, the several people on the other side looked uncomfortable and uncertain, as if they didn't quite know who should go first. Five men, all older than Garrie, all weathered. Men who knew this country and who kept themselves fit climbing around it for a living.

Garrie scowled at them. "Knocking," she said. "You should try it sometime."

"I knew Huntington should have come," muttered the oldest of them, a man probably in his early fifties but no less fit than the others.

"Oh, for Christ's sake," said the buffest of them all. "You. Lisa McGarrity. Come with us."

Garrie snorted. *You must be kidding.* "Give us Robin back first," she said, and didn't need Trevarr's hand touching the small of her back—a warning—to hold her position.

The older man started to nod, as if this all seemed perfectly reasonable to him, but he got a jab in the ribs for it. Buffest said, "You can talk about that with Huntington. Let's go."

Garrie thought . . . *not*. Trevarr crouched beside her, one knee to the floor, his hand filled with a knife that had come from who knows where. Too bad her own Keharian knife still sat in its ill-fitting sheath in the bathroom.

Or not. If she waved it around, she'd probably cut off her own hand. "Look," she said, "it's not gonna happen. Why don't you leave your card? We'll call later today."

Buffest's jaw muscles flexed perceptibly—expecting to make more of an impression, maybe. Not knowing just how very hard her heat pounded beneath two layers of wispy shirts and behind the mattress.

Trevarr knew. His hand touched her thigh, briefly. Tightened, briefly. She sensed in him no worry, just readiness. Poised and leashed and ready to spring, and if these men had any sense, they'd get back the way they came.

From beneath the bed, Sklayne hissed.

"You had your chance," Buffest said. He made an imperious gesture, and it took Garrie an instant to realize—he had played too many online games, grown up with too many dungeon adventures. He was, she realized, about to perform some *magic*.

Or something.

Shields up! Wide shields, encompassing both of them—and if she let them press against her, a comforting solidity, she kept the opposite edge far away from Trevarr. Conflicting energies, never quite tamed, leaped at the chance to rise within her; she didn't try to squash them down. She let them come . . . let them wash through. A hot flush, a cold sweat, but . . . flow, ebb.

Trevarr made a sound deep in his chest; she took it for approval.

And Buffest hurled his feeble attack. Dripping, corrupted energies, roiling around themselves with a faint acidic hiss and splashing harmlessly off her shields. *I counter your fireball with shields of doom,* Garrie thought at him. *Fool.*

But if she should have felt satisfaction, she didn't. Never had she defended herself against ethereal human malice before. Never had it occurred to her that she would have to do so. She swallowed the sudden sting of it and forced a light tone to her voice. "Seriously. You'll have to do better than that. I'm sure that impresses everyone around here, but I just stopped two worlds from imploding, and it's not doing so much for me."

His eyes widened—only for an instant, before he covered his surprise. The oldest man opened his mouth,

might even have been about to say something sensible—
if Buffest hadn't reached behind to his back waistband
and pulled out a small semiautomatic pistol.

"Damn," Garrie snapped, the sight of that gun kicking her pulse into fast overdrive and her mouth into
automatic—and now she was the one who reached out
to Trevarr—so aware of the snarl he hadn't quite voiced.
"You couldn't just bash us over the head like you did
to Jim-Bob Dandy? By the way, he misses his body."

Beneath the bed, Sklayne hissed—and as Trevarr
stiffened beside her, Garrie realized her mistake.

Now they knew how much she'd figured out. Now
they knew how much she could do. Now they had no
intention of walking away from here without her.

"Farking damn," she said under her breath, glancing
at Trevarr. "Sorry. I do ghosts, not assholes."

Trevarr spared a quick tilt of the head in Sklayne's
direction—a tight, private directive.

::No, no, not the pockets hate the pockets,:: Sklayne
said, unusually incomprehensible at that.

Do it.

She heard that, all right, even as Buffest said, "Gather
'em up!"

Oh, deceptively passive, that Trevarr, still on one knee,
hand splayed flat against the ground and knife beneath
it—the other leg crouched up beneath him and ready,
warm where it brushed Garrie. Deceptively, calmly passive as the four men approached, looking as stout and
macho as all posturing could make them and just really
having no idea at all. Garrie's pulse hit overdrive; her
throat tightened down. The surge of dark fierce wild
inside leaped to the surface, beyond any simple ebb and
flow, beyond controlling—but *not now, not now* and
she kept it in, kept it away from Trevarr.

"Gather 'em up," Buffest repeated, "and we'll go have
a little talk. C'mon, c'mon. They won't give you any

trouble now. And if they do . . . well, maybe that's just what we want."

And Trevarr pulled the glamour from hot pewter eyes and he told the men, "Maybe it's not."

Power fluttered against Garrie's spine, coruscating in her throat—and Trevarr surged forth. He caught up the bed and flipped it over, flinging it with such abrupt ferocity that they didn't quite believe it even as two of them went down. *Now!* Trevarr commanded, reverberating between Sklayne and Garrie and back again with the force of it.

::No, no, no!:: Sklayne wailed, even as he darted for Trevarr's coat—the coat that had gone flying along with the bed. And Trevarr flung himself over the bed and directly for Buffest and his gun.

The other two instantly turned on him, and Garrie cried a wordless warning, for they'd snatched out weighted leather blackjacks that would split skin and break bone. She scrambled over the upturned bed— askew across two men and tilting wildly against the other bed—to launch herself at a raised blackjack. The gun went off in the chaos of it all and her cry turned to rage; her wiry strength took the man by surprise and suddenly the crude weapon was hers. Even as she tumbled to the floor, she plied it, slapping it hard against the side of his knee not once but twice.

But the other man fell on Trevarr with a vengeance, as the gun discharged again and Sklayne cried, ::No, no, no!:: The gun flew to the side, clattering off a small dresser now jammed crookedly against the wall.

Garrie's howling target lurched for her as he fell, and all the while his pal whaled on Trevarr's back and ribs and shoulders, but it was Buffest who shrieked a high pitch as something cracked loud and clear.

In that instant, all the men froze—and Trevarr gave them the chance, panting, still poised, Sklayne muttering ::No, no, no, wrong pocket *scary pocket*—:: and ::*kkkktt!*:: and ::*spptt! spppt! sppttt!* no no no Treyy!:: Garrie knew it for what it was—the moment when these men could leave, battered as they were, and call it victory simply because they were still alive.

The instant ended. Garrie's target twisted away from her, smart enough to see that it was indeed Trevarr who really mattered. The other man renewed his attack from behind and Trevarr whirled—a thing of deadly beauty and grace, the knife trailing his hand in a gleaming slice of metal and suddenly spurting blood.

It took the man an instant to realize he'd been cut— arm gaping to the bone and pumping blood, the slash skipping across collarbone and chin and flaying the far side of his face.

Garrie stuttered in conflicting impulses—to stop that horrifying spray of blood, and yet simultaneously, driven by the roiled-up furies battering around inside, to glory in the swift, clean efficiency of what Trevarr had accomplished.

But what she did was stand aghast at the blood spreading across Trevarr's side. "No!" she cried. *Not again!*

And she lost control of the burning cold charging along her spine and igniting her soul. The dragon rose up and overtook her, laying dark red blood over her vision and drawing a crackle of lightning along her skin, tracing the lines of sensation that tightened her skin beyond bearing, tugged at all things intimate. Power demanded power, drawing upon the parched earth until it groaned beneath them.

Trevarr, suddenly earthbound, suddenly with the look of someone needing a porch post for surreptitious support, cursed resoundingly in a language she still didn't know, but that suited his sharp cut of consonant and vowel so perfectly.

Buffest stretched for the gun from the floor. Bleeding Guy fell slowly to his knees. Limping Guy shoved Garrie aside, wrested Bleeding Guy's blackjack for his own use and faced off against Trevarr—not making any attempt to close . . . just distraction while Buffest went for the gun. A third, battered man made it out from under the upturned bed.

They're going to nibble him to death while he thinks of nothing but protecting me.

She knew, then, that she could end this. These were sensitives, no matter how they'd chosen to cultivate their skills. Floundering in a rage of power, she still knew exactly what she was doing; she knew exactly how much power she had to hand. *I can stop this right now. I can—*

"*Atreya!* No! You can *not*—" Trevar went down under a well-placed blow from behind—always behind, the only way these men had the courage to take him on; he snarled, whipping his hand back. His knife sank hilt-deep into the side of his attacker.

I can stop this right now. I can— Thought gave way to the wail and crash of conflict splashing up against the inside of her spine, burrowing in her chest . . . sinking in through the heart of her. She could no longer breathe, only gasp—huge, ragged breaths, with the power gathering at her fingertips.

::Here! Yes yes yes!:: Sklayne dashed between Garrie and Trevarr—did a flip off the wall and dashed through again, sending out a crashing wave of energy, all incandescent ripples and a foaming wake. Trevarr flipped his head up as it hit; his eyes gleamed hard and bright. His hand barely hesitated at his boot as he stood, whirling around with an expert snap and release to pin Buffest's hand to the baseboard, small, stout knife deeply embedded.

Garrie's hands tingled; her vision bled red and gray

at the edges. "You *shot him*," she snarled, holding up such a nimbus of energy that even this half-blind fool stopped short, mouthing a curse. The room bloomed color, the nimbus of it surrounding her, bathing the room in marbled light. Garrie tipped her head, looked at him from beneath a lowered brow . . . her voice didn't quite sound like her own. "Looks like I do assholes after all."

::TreyTreyTrey!::

The man stumbled back, horror on his face. Buffest stopped his agonized cries long enough to shout warning. Sweet, sweet completion flared at her fingertips; a cry of exultation swelled in her throat.

And something slammed into her from the side. Hard and muscled and profound, taking her down—arms flying, legs akimbo, and yet somehow landing with control, rolling aside with control, intersecting with a reddish-buff blur that had far too many claws. A sizzling rainbow splash of color instantly engulfed them, and Garrie screamed—in rage, in disbelief at perfection and completion thwarted, a raw and primal sound that slapped into utter dead silence as color shifted to unrelieved velvet darkness.

Darkness dropped away; they rolled across hard rock and then thick padding over rock, furs and leather and wool and sharp evergreen spice. Garrie fought back and she screamed incoherent fury and she forgot that she should probably be afraid while she was at it—afraid of the circumstances, afraid of Trevarr, afraid most of all of herself. She jerked and struggled, and as they slammed up against intractable rock wall, she pounded fists against him—wherever she could reach, indiscriminate and packed with ethereal energies turned physical.

"*Atreya,*" he said, breathless and struggling to hold her, pure strength no match for the frenzy of her. "Find yourself!"

Find herself? It only inflamed her. *Nothing. There is*— "Nothing!" she cried—incoherent still, nothing but a morass of runaway energies and uncontrolled emotion.

Maybe it didn't have to make sense; maybe he understood her anyway. "Give it to me," he told her, rising above her while cool thick rug pressed against her back, finally capturing her punishing hands at either side of her head. "What you cannot take—"

::No, no, have care!::

The wiser voice, but Garrie had nothing left to heed it. She flung excess at him, still fighting him—wrists pinned, hips clamped between his thighs, legs hooked by his feet. She forgot he was there to help and she punished him for it, throwing the dragon at him—a dark scrape of angry pain and longing that bled at her sanity.

He stiffened; his grip on her wrists tightened against her bones. His presence expanded into the darkness, damp cave air alive with the stark, sharp wood smoke of his own inner battles. But he absorbed what she threw at him, jerking with it, making that kicked-in-the-gut sound.

Garrie fought him none the less for it, wanting nothing but freedom—the freedom to explode into something no longer Garrie at all, a demanding culmination just out of reach and beyond bearing. His eyes gleamed faintly; he snapped a harsh command of a word and across the open space of his lair, a blue-white lamp glowed to life. She saw the strain on Trevarr's face—jaw clenched, nostrils flared—and she just didn't care. She threw him more—saw the jerk of it this time, his eyes widening, his mouth finding a snarl of determination, head tipping back. Saw the truth of it this time—that he, too, wanted more . . . wanted that for which she strained.

She did the only thing she had left to her, pinned so butterfly-flat, hips rising to meet his and igniting a brand-new sweet fire in the white-hot whirlwind of the rest of her. He closed his eyes, and his groan rumbled in the backdrop of ragged breathing and Garrie's efforts to free herself.

But to her utter surprise, Garrie was the one who crumbled. "Please," she said, and the word caught in her throat, a hiccough of desperation. "I can't—"

He struggled with himself—an intimate battle, shuddering through his body until he gulped air, breaking the contact between them—if only to lean in closer, to find the side of her face and press his own against it. "Is this," he said, his voice in her ear and no less strained, "what you truly want?"

Big brave reckoner, facing her demons—cruelly using the man who'd so quickly become so important, lashing him with her retribution because she knew, she *knew* she couldn't give into this thing and she didn't know how not to. So damned if she didn't burst into tears, twisting her head aside and still pinned, his body stretching out over hers.

He instantly released her; she covered her face. "Go away!" she sobbed, not all that coherently.

"Is that," he said, "what you truly want?"

"Yes! No!"

The faintest hint of laughter trembled through his shoulders. "Ebb and flow, *atreya*."

Except this was beyond ebb and flow, beyond tolerable, beyond thinking—

Oh. No.

It . . . *wasn't*.

He'd absorbed it; he'd done what she hadn't been able to. She'd thrown everything at him and added her own wild twist, and if she knew she'd find those faint patterns on arm and torso now turned to hard texture, his eyes unearthly and his expression fierce and wild, she also knew it was exactly that part of him that had known what to do with her turmoil.

Phaser on overload. Not so pretty when it happened from the inside out.

"Atreya?"

She pulled her hands aside. She regarded him; she especially regarded his neck, so close. So convenient. She licked it, salt and tang and oh, the scent of him. And she startled a little as he stiffened, pulling back.

Too late. Oh, far too late. He shifted from his knees to his feet in a heartbeat, standing—bringing her with him. Backing her, her feet barely touching the ground, long strides until her shoulders hit hard stone—the side of the cave. "Is that," he said, his hands slapping up against rock on either side of her head, *"what you want? Is this?"*

A man with limits, after all. And if she'd been in ebb, now she found herself in flow again, intensely aware of every sensation—from the warmth of his breath in her ear to the press of his heavy belt buckle against her stomach to the push of his body against hers—the deep struggle of his breath, hips still only because he held himself so very, very tensely—and that, she knew because her hands, the greedy things, had ended up on his ass, and there she felt the quiver. Biggest muscle in the body and *so* worth all the attention it got.

"Atreya," he said, and his mouth hovered just over hers.

"You," she said suddenly, startling herself. "I want *you.* If this is *you*— If this is *us*—" Her hands, like her tongue, had a mind of their own; they flexed, pulling him closer. She blew a puff of a breeze at him—not the harsh, angry heat from moments earlier, but a light and meaningful breeze and she knew just exactly what it would do to him. *For* him.

He quivered beneath her hands; he grew harder against her, and the flush of responding warmth it brought out had nothing to do with her dragon—that which still hovered and teased and licked around the edges.

"Sometimes," he said, the raw whisper of his lips brushing hers, *"this"*—he hunted control—"is me. Sometimes other."

"Either way," Garrie breathed, and lifted her head to turn the movement into a kiss, the breeze into a nudge, her hands moving intimately on his backside.

His breath hissed in; his fingers dug into rock at either side of her head. "Be sure," he told her. "Be sure or stop—" A shiver took him, down his back to her caressing hands. "Oh gods," he said, desperate beyond any measure, *"or stop now."*

Stupid to say that fear didn't shiver through her. Fear of what she'd become—fear of his need so raw and fierce and wild, right here in her hands. But she'd stopped being surprised at herself long before this, and now—

Now—

She pulled him even closer, hands demanding. Something in him let go—a shudder, a groan . . . a surge of energy. Dark, like that he'd given her; a wave of sensation and strength, given its freedom. *Beyond stopping.*

She'd thought he would be fierce and hard and sudden, taking and demanding. She thought he'd ride the edge of control . . . that he'd lose it.

But she'd also once thought him cold and unfeeling, and she'd been wrong about that, too.

Oh, how she'd been wrong.

So he did all those things. But not until after he'd drawn her up for a deep and astonishingly tender kiss, mouth and lips and tongue. And not until his hands had roamed her body, finding every possible tender, responsive spot. Not until she'd had the chance to push aside his shirt, returning the favor and gauging success by his rumbling purrs, the tight and trembling tension in his lean body, muscles clenching into definition beneath her touch. And his breathing, oh yes, his breathing. His cries, gusting out between clenched teeth.

And by the time he did turn fierce and hard and sudden, it was all that Garrie wanted from him. By the time he lost that fine edge of control, she'd lost hers. By the time he'd given everything of himself, panting and raw and primal, she matched him cry for cry, and the dragon within her rose to grasp, at last, at incandescent completion.

And there in the height of it, lost to herself, lost to him, she breathed the clear, cutting scent of wood ash and dry hard spice; a deep and satisfied rumble echoed in her bones. Over it all, the soft, astonishing susurrus of massive wings, unfurling for flight.

13

True understanding of your companions is a gift.
—Rhonda Rose

I need some—dammit!
—Lisa McGarrity

Leftovers, mine?
—Sklayne

Garrie found herself panting in a cave on another world, bathed in an unearthly cool blue light.

Naked.

Of course.

She found herself up against the hard, smooth rock wall of that cave, her legs wrapped around damp flanks, her arms wrapped around strong shoulders, her fingers digging into a faint raised pattern of feathery scales over warm skin. She found their bodies whispering in touch as they gulped for breath, still pressed warmly together.

She found that he was naked, too. And that his legs had given way, leaving him on his knees, while one hand held the back of her head, protecting it from impact with that rock behind her.

She eased back, instantly regretting the fraction of space between them. She threaded her hands through his hair—fallen from the clip in back. Thick and loose and just crisply wiry enough to be not quite human.

Not that much different from hers, now.

The braids teased her fingers; she found one and ran her thumb along it, surprised to find in it the faint trickle of power.

His hand closed over hers. "Sah," he said. "Have a care."

The things you never knew.

He breathed against her cheek, turning it into a deliberate caress. *"Atreya."*

"Yeah," she breathed back. *Yes, I am.* Heart-bonded, he'd said once.

He'd been right.

"Hey," she said. "What happened to our clothes?"

He shrugged. "In the way."

"Hey," she said, a little more sharply. "What about protection?"

"We are safe here." He ran a hand down her side, tracing every spare line in a reverent way that, for the first time farking *ever* made her feel as if she had curves. Real curves. Besides her butt, which had at least ended up pert and round. Small favors.

"Not that kind of protection," she said, on the receiving end of a minor buzz of panic as she suspected, *highly* suspected, that there'd been no such thing between them.

He frowned only faintly, his hand spanning over her flat belly, lingering at her navel before his fingers moved on to encompass her ribs, the thumb heading for greener pastures as it traced the gently plump curve of her breast. And oh, right—still completely and totally intertwined, and they pulsed, most intimately, in a simultaneous response. He said, "What other kind of protection is there?"

She narrowed her eyes, knowing this wash of artificial moonlight was as bright as day to him. "Don't people on this world protect themselves against STDs? You know? *Diseases?*" Not that Rhonda Rose would have mentioned it; it wasn't a thing that proper ladies spoke about. Not those proper ladies from Rhonda Rose's day, anyway. "And *babies*?"

He looked truly startled. "We have no need to protect ourselves against *babies*—" But no. Understanding. "Ah. Freshening." His hands stilled; he looked aside. "That is not a concern with one such as me."

"Oh," Garrie said. *Way to go. Stomp the hell out of him when you're still sitting in—er . . . around . . . his lap.* "I'm sorry."

He gave her a startled look. "Sah," he said. "I have always known it. And the other . . . some here have such problems. But the travel . . . there is a cleansing to it."

"Whoa." She blinked, squirming a little as the coolness of the stone against her back penetrated the fading heat of exertion. "That's handy."

"It does not attend everything. But yes. There is a convenience to it."

"Well, I'm good," Garrie said. "I mean, it's been since—" No, she wouldn't say that out loud. Or she wouldn't finish saying it, anyway.

From the sudden gleam in Trevarr's eye, she thought

she'd made the right choice. From his hands, suddenly possessive again, she thought she'd *totally* made the right choice. Not that she didn't return the favor, pulling herself closer to nibble kisses across the plane of his chest and the softly raised pectoral patterns there. He growled at her, and if there was a deep laugh behind it—telling her he knew exactly what she was doing and hell yes, he approved—there was also enough swell and throb inside her to tell her just how well she'd chosen.

In an instant, all her own swell and throb had surged back to meet his, two bodies leaping for each other with a pumped fist of triumph and *oh, YEAH!* and even a little unabashed *hey, bay-BEE*. He came alive again, every bit as fiercely as she'd expected the first time. He flipped her around and loomed above her, and he took her hard and fast—hands claiming her body, mouth claiming her skin, until the dragon roared back up with a rush of power to take them both. Garrie cried out a startled white-hot explosion with his uninhibited shouts in her ear, every bit as fierce and wild as she'd ever imagined from that first moment she'd seen him and known he was oh so *not safe*.

That once she'd given him this much of herself to him, she would be lost forever.

Oh, she hadn't had a farking clue.

Sklayne extruded four extra feet on his back and fumbled his haul of the day—pungent leaves and sticky branches dragging behind him in this, his familiar self-form. Not his pure form, but the solid form he'd taken all his life . . . not so different from *cat*. Bigger . . . bigger ears, with glorious tufts. Shorter tail, brisk in its expressions. Small opposable thumbs, set beside sharp spurs. Poison there, oh yes.

Much with the teeth. Lovely long canines in paired sets. Wonderful leapy hind legs, maybe a little longer than those in front. Striking color, stark silvered patterns to hide in dappled shadows at the edges of black woods and bright clearings.

Well. What Sklayne had thought of as bright until he had been taken to other worlds. Until he had been taken to Garrie's world. Taken, taken, always taken . . . never choice. The choice had been made long before, and if he longed for his dappled shadows it made no difference at all.

Tedious, traveling distance by paw. Better to travel in ethereal form, pulsing energies soaking up sustenance and skipping over all the hard bits. But no, once he had *things,* he must walk like any being.

Trevarr's safe place sat in high rock, hidden among other rock and surrounded by the black woods and the deep black fog, thick close conifers reaching into each other, twisting upward . . . jabbing sharp dead limbs downward. Here, the land jutted into unpredictable features; here the shadows held secrets.

Here, the nature of the rock made tribunal scrying impossible.

And here, Trevarr had found and enhanced his safe place, which had a *farking narrow entrance no good for bundles sppt! Hss-spptt!*

Sklayne dropped the mass of greenery he'd gathered. He wiped unhappily at his stickied coat with both paws and tongue, until *spptt!* temper got the best of him and he expanded himself as big as everything and anything, sharing himself with a rock or two on the way through, shedding sticky before he coalesced back into solidity.

Better.

A flick of his paw at a scurry bug in the wrong place at the right time, a gulp, and he strolled into the lair.

But oh, not far.

The energies hit him like a slap of water, both refreshing and drenching. And if he drank of them, he also stopped, crouched low . . . grew wary. His short tail flicked in annoyance and concern.

These energies, he was not used to. Not here, not anywhere. Rich and profound, a mixture of fizz and depth . . . an inexplicable tangle of Trevarr and the Garrie. His nose twitched. Fizz . . .

Fizz.

His whiskers sprang forward to attention. He thought of a night on a hillside northeast of Albuquerque, waiting for Trevarr's call—because while Trevarr had taken the thing called a *plane,* Sklayne would travel through the power grid from Albuquerque to San Jose. But first, the waiting. First, the bored.

The nosy.

And there he'd come across a couple with their writhings and their mouths eating but not devouring, their groans and their seeking hands. At first he had not understood, no. For all he so casually lurked at the edges of Trevarr's frequent and casual couplings—all swift and efficient and even vicious pleasuring, done in passing— he'd never *seen* it just like that, so kept at a distance. And the feel of Trevarr in body play was nothing like the feel of those humans infatuated with one another.

It was nothing like the feel of Trevarr with the Garrie—the sweet tensions, the high fizz and crackle and pull . . . the constant undertone.

And *this* . . .

This was nothing like any of it.

Except maybe for that tiny thread of fizzy energy, weaving among the rest of it like an irrepressible glee.

And so, suddenly he knew. And he scrambled into the lair with undignified haste, threading the narrow, winding neck of a passage and only coming back to proper thought just in time to stop before barging right into the lair proper.

It was never wise to surprise Trevarr.
Never.
And never had he had someone else here.
Never.
The Rhonda Rose person didn't count. She had no longer been a body person. She had made her own decisions. And she had come uninvited . . . and stayed until no one remembered that detail, giving Trevarr company and distraction through long healing.

After all, the tribunal had been trying to kill Trevarr for a long time now. Before, they had simply disguised their efforts as *missions.* Afraid of him . . . of what he was—but too greedy to simply kill him outright. Needing to make use of him and the things he could do that so few others could accomplish.

The travel. The work.

Not that Sklayne cared.

And he didn't care about *this,* either. The way his tail puffed out, that was this silly body reacting to the energy. His back arching up to make himself oh-so-much bigger . . . that was this silly body, too. The silent hiss on drawn-back lips . . .

No. No. That was Sklayne. ::Me.:: The important one.

Taking in what he saw. Naked Trevarr, on the rudimentary cot of this place, sunk into the furs. The Garrie, naked atop him. And while Sklayne was familiar with Trevarr in every form, he was not familiar with *this*—with the other lurking so close to the surface, yet still calm.

The Garrie's form he knew not at all. Trevarr preferred not to have concern about the strength of his partners, their ability to handle what he was. He chose those like himself, what few he could find. And he chose strong beings, with stout nature.

The Garrie looked smaller than ever now. More spare, if more curve to her than clothes showed. And she straddled atop Trevarr, flattened across his chest, her hair spiked every which way and the silver-blue streaks gleaming in lamp-glow. Laughing at something. Petting Trevarr's chest—the pectorals, where the markings showed. Damp and sated and between the two of them, scenting this lair with body play and fizz and still breathing hard, so replete that Sklayne could not stop his cry of dismay.

::*You left me out!*::

Garrie started. She jerked half upright, Trevarr's hands lingering on her hips; she jerked around to find him, and she squeaked when she did. She would have moved then, sliding off Trevarr—but those hands stopped her.

"But—!" she said.

"Rude, little one," Trevarr rumbled, enough lazy satisfaction in his voice so Sklayne only belatedly realized the danger behind his half-lidded gaze. "She does not know your ways."

::You left me out!::

Fark. A creature of importance did not sound petulant.

And yet he did it again, more of a whisper. ::Left me out.:: A twitch of tail, sullen at that. ::*Important.*::

The Garrie had stopped touching Trevarr. Her hands didn't seem to know where to go, covering first her small, plump little breast parts and then down at the hairy place where she met Trevarr and then her face. "Fark," she said.

Trevarr's hand stroked her thigh. Never had Sklayne seen that. *Never.* Not the care. Not the tender. Trevarr reached down to where the extra furs were dumped against the wall, and flipped up one of the light, supple pieces. It covered the Garrie, pooling around her bottom and thighs. Trevarr tugged it into place, smoothed back the Garrie's hair where it was spikiest behind her ear—such tugging she gave it—and ran his thumb over her lower lip. Still half lidded, the silver gaze that suddenly seemed unfamiliar to Sklayne, suddenly made him uncertain, and beneath the furs his body shifted slightly.

The Garrie's eyes widened. "Oh!" she said. "You didn't! You *wouldn't*."

But when Sklayne went to check—to get a sense of Trevarr from the inside—he found himself blocked. ::Secrets!::

"Private," Trevarr said, not looking away from the Garrie.

And that's when Sklayne knew.

Knew for certain.

Things had changed.

Things that had been the same for so long, now weren't.

Things that formed Sklayne's world—his *worlds*—were no longer Sklayne's to own.

In panic, he checked the bond. He meant it to be a sly thing, a subtle thing . . . just to feel it. To confirm that which had defined his life for so long that he knew not how to live without it.

Panic made for an accidental jerk.

Trevarr winced. He sat up on his elbows, his hair an unruly mess, the shorter strands framing his face and not a few of those sticking out from the rest. "No fear, little one. It exists."

It exists. But Sklayne sent back scorn. ::Mighty,:: he said. Not little. ::As big as the world.::

"When you want to be," Trevarr agreed. And he sat, easing out from beneath the Garrie, his gaze caught on hers and something in their expressions sent Sklayne into inexplicable longing. And if the Garrie sat tucked up with the fur around her, Trevarr made no move to cover himself, perfectly comfortable—not just with

Sklayne, as so many years had made them. But with the Garrie.

Things changed.

Best to pretend not.

::Brought stalup,:: he said, and licked around the thumb of his paw, giving the spur beside it special attention. Prim and distant. Yes. Independent. Yes.

Trevarr frowned, but the Garrie sat straighter. "Is that it?" she asked. "The stuff you think will help with—" She stopped her words, but her gaze cut to Trevarr. Obvious enough to Sklayne, whose perceptions had known Trevarr for so long . . . Trevarr sick, Trevarr well, Trevarr strong. Easy enough to see skin too close to bone, to taste lingering hunger in what little of Trevarr's self he now shared.

::Eat,:: he advised Trevarr, a sniff in his tone. ::Home food. While you are here.:: This place always had such stores. This place was always ready for retreat, for hurt and tired and running.

Trevarr made a noise that might have been agreement. It more likely meant *We'll talk about the stalup later.*

Not without its risks, the stalup.

The Garrie said, "Where are my clothes?" And a look came over her face, and she tugged the hair behind her ear and said, "God, the room. What a mess. What are we going to do? Do you think any of them . . . do you think they all . . . Oh God, how could we have—"

"Because it was right," Trevarr said, with such implacable certainty that the Garrie's eyes widened slightly. So did Sklayne's. *It was right.*

But Trevarr was not one to linger over things said. "If there were deaths, then Huntington will take the bodies. He did not shrink from using his partner." For yes, that death had been used. That body had been used. "He will not shrink from using these men."

"That's sick," the Garrie said, remarkably indignant for a small naked person wrapped in furs on someone else's cot.

::Sick,:: Sklayne agreed.

"I still need my clothes."

"You may well be without them." Trevarr stood, swept up his pants, stepped into them. Too loose. The Garrie bit her lip. And then her jaw dropped slightly, for although Trevarr held up her shorts in one hand, in the other he held what was left of her two thin shirts.

Not much.

"Oh," she said. And swallowed visibly. "I guess we were in a hurry." And then winced. "Your back. Did I—" But that thought derailed for another. "You were *shot*—"

"Touched by it," Trevarr said, and turned to put his side to the light so she could see the long dark furrow and bloodstained skin. Doubtful she could see the rest of it, the bruises blooming so vivid along his back and ribs, the marks from the Garrie's fingers the least of it all.

"Mow," Sklayne said. A reminder. Of who he was, of what he could do. Of what he'd always done for Trevarr.

Trevarr glanced at him. "Yes. And the room where we fought."

Sklayne essayed a purr. That was no chore, the cleaning. That was snack. That was challenge. Cleaning Trevarr's clothes of what he did to them, that, too, was challenge. The slight mendings, the subtle reworkings of the substance of them . . . a matter of pride.

The Garrie's clothes . . . beyond his abilities. Far beyond.

"The clan things," Trevarr said suddenly. "Those were hidden in the fall of the bed. But if they were found . . ."

::We take them back.:: Sklayne purred. Not everything had changed. Trevarr needed him. Counted on him.

And they would not lose the clan things. Clan history, knotted into a belt of complexities and reverence—*kirk-irrah*. The memory stone, with its heart of blood. More important than the Eye, than the Gatherer, than the Tracker. Those things, replaceable. The clan things . . .

Never.

The Garrie accepted her shorts and sadly set the shirts aside. "This trip," she muttered, "has been really, *really* hard on my clothes." She sighed, struggling into her shorts while still on the cot and under the fur, and then stood—a tentative quality to her movement, as if she was testing out her limbs anew. "Whoa," she said. "Kinda . . . tender."

Trevarr gave her a sudden, half-sided smile, one that stopped Sklayne's so-casual grooming in its tracks. He dug around in the trunk on the other side of the room until he came up with his softest shirt, his oldest shirt, a thing of fine weaving and hand-stretched leather from the wings of the skytes who soared high in the trees. He glanced at Sklayne. "Can you size it?"

Sklayne narrowed his eyes. ::Leftovers mine?::

"Yes," said Trevarr, and Sklayne *leaped* so suddenly that the Garrie made a noise of surprise, recoiling slightly.

But then she said, "So that's what he looks like here."

Trevarr told her, "Sometimes," which was true.

But the Garrie had a thought and wasn't done with it yet. "It exists?" she said. "That's what he said to you, and you said it did. What was he worried about?" She crossed her arms beneath the fur. "You've got some kind of hold over him, don't you? He's hardly biddable, and yet he never truly argues with you. And back in San Jose, when you were . . . when you needed help . . . he acted . . ." she sought words. "Restricted. Bound, some-how."

Sklayne, busy kneading leather and weave, absorbing and changing and refining, stopped in midmotion. ::Mine,:: he said, full of alarm. ::Ours.::

The Garrie looked straight at him. "Sklayne," she said, with an understanding that both humiliated him and astonished him, "you're safe with me."

Sklayne stared, nothing but his nose twitching. Pink nose, black at the edges, refined. Handsome nose.

Trevarr gestured at the shirt . . . but not without un-derstanding. "Finish that, please."

Sklayne twitched tail instead of nose, eyeing Trevarr with more care than he had the Garrie. All that effort . . . all that energy. Much went into coupling, and this . . . this had been no ordinary play of bodies. Not with the energies still swamping around in here, with the linger-ing glow of Trevarr's eyes and the manifestations of his other. If their play had for the moment invigorated Tre-varr, Sklayne thought there would yet be a price for it.

Not that he cared. Not.

Except that his well-being and Trevarr's . . . inextri-cably entwined, all these years.

He went back to the shirt. He may have accidentally left a hole in the shoulder.

Trevarr opened the cupboard that held the dried stores, pulling out sealed and warded jerky. "I cannot offer you any," he told the Garrie. "Likely it would be safe. But now is not the time to experiment."

"No, no, that's fine," she said. "But can't you bring some back with you?"

"Better to leave it here, in case of strong need."

Yes. Because this was their lair. Their world. Even if Kehar's tribunal had served justice on them.

Justice that was not *justice* at all. The justice of frightened beings who had not expected their pawn to survive, and now suddenly truly understood what they had tried to leash. Not just strength, for others had that. Not just the advantages born of the mixed blood for those who withstood it, for others had that, too. But single-minded determination backed with a knack for surviving the unsurviveable . . .

And of course, Sklayne. ::Me.:: He purred to himself. He didn't care if Trevarr heard it. Trevarr would not bother to wonder.

Trevarr was busy. Chewing. Finding his shirt, pulling it on without bothering to tuck it in. Taking stock of his few weapons, with so much left behind in the room. And ever watching the Garrie, who stood waiting. "There is," he said finally, while Sklayne pretended not to care, "a deep-woods clan of beings. They live in places where it is not safe for anything else to go. They thrive there, for they can consume almost anything. And they have an amazing facility with energies. All energies."

"I noticed," the Garrie said dryly.

"They can take different forms; you have seen this. They have few predators . . . few things threaten them." There, it came—the first wave of a price for their play—a sudden misstep, quickly corrected. But the jerky . . . it would help. And the stalup . . . it would dry quickly in the desert air of the Garrie's home, and it would help, too.

Not that it mattered to Sklayne.

"What I don't get is how come his kind haven't taken over the world."

::Too busy,:: Sklayne muttered, surreptitiously enlarging the hole in the shirt. ::More important things to do.::

The Garrie put a hand over her mouth, covering a smile with no success at all. But Trevarr sat in his roughly crafted chair, a thing smoothed by years of use, and there was a smile at the corner of his mouth. "Just so," he said. "They are their own downfall. They are curious, and impulsive." As the Garrie drifted closer, he pulled her right into his lap—*owning* her.

Sklayne was surprised that the Garrie didn't seem to mind this, settling in against the clan designs on Trevarr's belt buckle—if only to offer him a skeptical look. There was that smile again, at the corner of Trevarr's mouth. A seldom-used smile. He said, "I told you it would ever be thus, if you were close."

"Get used to it," the Garrie muttered, although Sklayne wasn't clear if she spoke to Trevarr or to herself. "So basically, Sklayne's people are too distracted to pull a Pinky and the Brain."

It could have made no more literal sense to Trevarr than it did to Sklayne, but he seemed to see past it. "They tend to live short, through their own folly. They also live remotely—difficult to reach. But if one can survive that journey . . ."

If one is desperate enough. But Sklayne didn't say it. He simply thought of Trevarr, those years ago—still lanky in form, not yet in any harmony with his other. Having left his clan for their own sake—for the unwanted attention he had brought them—but not yet ready to survive the fierce world of Kehar. Not in the wilds, not in the populated zones where he was scorned. Knowing the tribunal was sniffing hard on his trail . . . wanting him. Wanting to use him.

Knowing how long such tribunal agents survived.

"Which you did," the Garrie surmised. "Made the journey, I mean. And you found Sklayne?"

"Mm," Trevarr said, a thoughtful noise that seemed to be related to the way the Garrie's hands slipped inside his shirt. "I let him find me."

Trevarr, lying still at the edge of the clearing where Sklayne's kind liked to play. For hours, lying still. *What is it what is it what is it?*

Yes. Sklayne had found him, all right.

"You . . . *caught* him?"

"There is a bonding," Trevarr told her. "A mutual thing. It creates structure. Prevents . . . impulsiveness." He glanced at Sklayne. "For the most part."

::Older now. Older than most. Older than any. Prevent impulses by myself.::

But Trevarr pretended not to hear. He tipped his head back to the chair, eyes closed; face weary but the rest of him . . . tucking the Garrie closer.

"We have to go back," the Garrie said, a voice of regret. A voice of worry. "There's no telling what's happening there."

Trevarr wrapped a hand around her waist, fingers spread . . . for all the world as if he were simply trying to *absorb* her.

Not smart. Sklayne was the one who could do such things. Not Trevarr.

But Trevarr was saying, "*Atreya,* this was needed. We have been changed—"

"In San Jose," the Garrie murmured, not entirely happily. But she put her hand over his and invited it up to cradle her breast on that side. Not with the twisting intense energy that had been spiraling around this lair earlier, but as a gift . . . that this was his place to touch, too. Sklayne blinked in surprise. So very *corporeal,* the Garrie was. And this that she gave Trevarr . . . something Sklayne never could. He pinned his short tail for a quick, rough washing as she nodded, acceding Trevarr's statement. "Yes. We did have to figure out how to handle those breezes. I hope . . . I hope next time . . . the breathing . . ." Her voice trailed away.

"You will do it," Trevarr said. "*We* will." And, for that moment, he rested his face against her neck.

Content.

Had Sklayne seen this in him before?

Ever?

He returned to his work on the shirt. He may have coincidentally mended the hole.

Lucia ran to the hotel room with a haste she never allowed herself in public.

No flat-out running. No unseemly stumbling, or tripping, or wild panic. She was her father's daughter; she was well turned out, she was aware of her grace and her beauty, and she knew better than to ever, ever let that public facade crack to show anyone—strangers, acquaintances, social butterflies—the simmering run of emotions always bubbling beneath her surface.

Whether they were hers or not.

But now, Lucia ran.

And Quinn ran beside her, a noise of surprise that he had to leap to keep up with her deer-fleet legs.

Because Garrie wasn't answering her cell phone. She wasn't answering her room phone. And Trevarr didn't answer at the other room, either.

And at Robin's apartment—not the shop wrecked first by those who had taken her and then by the police investigation, but the quiet apartment overhead to which Quinn had quietly produced a key, and to which the police would surely turn their attention eventually—they'd found more than they'd expected.

Not Robin, no. Not any sign of Robin.

But Robin's friend.

Still warm, still limp, eyes barely glazed over.

The room tingled with psychic aftershock. Garrie no doubt would have been able to dissect it, to read it in detail. But Lucia, reeling, could sense only that the woman had been felled by a clumsy ethereal attack in which she was likely not supposed to die at all.

And she knew the woman was still there—still spewing her fear, her shock, her grief. And her concern. And now she lingered, broadcasting warning. *Robin, beware! Robin, they know your friends are at Journey Inn!*

Not in so many words. Impressions; concepts. Emotions overwhelming all the rest, for that's what Lucia was. An emotional lodestone.

And so it had taken time—too much time—while Quinn hastily wiped their prints from the doorknob and the doorframe and then quickly, quietly, escorted Lucia away—down the very back staircase they'd used for their unobtrusive entrance.

"They don't know yet," he told her as she'd started to come out of it—gasping and trembling, upright only because he held her that way. Careful of Lucia, as were they all. They sat at the back bumper of the rental car, a block away from the store, gathering only the occasional stare from passersby. A young man consoling his sweetheart—it was the role he'd taken, and she didn't fight it.

Camouflage. For the police didn't yet understand . . . the store damage was more than just store damage. They didn't know that Robin was missing. They didn't know that her friend and partner was dead. But once they did, they'd certainly turn their attention to any unusual scenes in the area.

Like a hysterical young woman and the man who had dragged her down the street to sob by the back of their car.

So Lucia was glad, in retrospect, that Quinn had thought to escort her with an arm over her shoulders and a hand propping her up at the elbow, his head bent over her with solicitous attention. She was glad he'd supported her at the car as though she were a teary lover and not a friend come unglued.

She was glad she'd let him, instead of slapping him off to find her own space, her own equilibrium.

But the moment she had it—the moment she finally understood all that, and was able to absorb what she'd experienced, and the moment they pulled it together into comprehension—they'd dropped that facade, scrambling for the car doors and heading back up the car-and-pedestrian-jammed section of 89A to the turn-off for the Journey Inn.

And still, they'd been gone far too long. The Sin Nombres—those who had killed, those who had taken Robin—had been already heading for the inn. And so here, after a sloppy parking job that had taken not two but three spots, Lucia ran for the little split cabin.

A blur of motion to the side caught her eye; Quinn grabbed her arm, as wary as she. Not taking a single thing for granted. *Caryn.* "Hey!" Caryn called to them, jogging in to intercept them, all fresh and folksie in denim shorts and a neat polo shirt with the inn logo. "Is everything okay?"

It might have been the evasive look in her eyes. It might have been the emotions sifting through the atmosphere like falling leaves, brushing against Lucia. *Warning and regret and fear.* It might have been the way this woman had overreached herself in the past. Lucia couldn't quite stop the words that popped out of her mouth. "You! Aie, Quinn—*chueca!*" *Snake in the grass.*

"I—what?" Caryn pulled up short, but her indignance was a beat too late.

"Come on," Quinn said, grimly enough. If he didn't quite take Caryn's arm, it was nonetheless a close thing—but they were close enough to the cabin so it wasn't necessary anyway. That the door hung violently askew couldn't be plainer; that the window was veined with cracks and ready to shatter, likewise. That violence had left things that way . . . also all too clear.

"Hey," Caryn said, suddenly as wary as they. "What's going on here?"

But now Lucia was looking, and now Lucia saw the uncertainty in her eyes. She shot a look at Quinn—*watch her*—and ran the rest of the way to the cabin, already aware of the silence within, and all too aware of the ethereal emotions: the sense of violence, the shock of death. The regret from that same source that had first greeted her—the young Bobbie Ghost who had been haunting this place, Lucia thought, and who had not been able to do anything but watch this mayhem.

She'd thought it was enough to prepare her, but—

She made a choking sound and whirled away from the room.

Caryn hesitated; Quinn shoved her right up to the door behind her, where he made a sound of deep dismay.

Lucia didn't have to look again. She'd always have that memory, that image of the second bed upturned and canted partly over hers, the rest of the furniture tumbled around the room, the luggage and belongings scattered.

The blood.

Aiee, Dios, *the blood.*

Caryn made a retching noise and jerked away from Quinn.

He went after her. "What do you know about this?"

"I—*no!*" But her gaze held guilt in a pasty white face.

Unrelenting, that was Quinn. Going after information . . . whatever the source. "You got tangled with us from the moment we landed here. You have no boundaries, no ethereal etiquette. You *want*. What the hell *did you do to get it*?" He pushed her at the room. "Was it worth it, Caryn? Whatever Huntington promised you?"

"What's going on here?" The demand came from Feather, stalking toward them in full Sedona mode—strings of beads and feathers in her thin, graying hair, flowing batik outfit in earth tones and turquoise. Her voice held no alarm, but much annoyance and no little offense. "I know Caryn offended you when you arrived, but I'm afraid we've reached the point where I have to ask you to—oh—oh, my . . . *oh*." Her step faltered; her voice fluttered to a stop, then reemerged faintly. "What—?"

"Didn't anyone see anything?" Quinn asked, still driving at Caryn. "Mention anything to you? If they took Garrie and Trevarr—"

"*Took* them?" Lucia echoed in horror. Bad enough that one of them might be hurt, might be at the hospital. But overpower Trevarr?

Then again, he hadn't looked himself lately. At moments when Garrie wasn't watching. "Quinn—" she said, "someone did die here. A stranger. It was violent and he was angry, and then . . . terrified." She closed her eyes, let the feelings settle. "He wasn't expecting this. He was overconfident." A moment more, and she shook her head, brushing her arms as if she could brush the emotions away. "He regrets that now."

"I'm calling 911," Feather said.

"No." Quinn stepped in her way—but not touching her—so much more respectful than he'd been of Caryn. "This isn't something they can handle."

"But . . . Quinn . . ." Lucia found herself whispering, heartbroken in the moment. "Is it something *we* can handle?"

Not without Garrie.

Her voice strengthened a little, backed only by determination. "We can call in a tip on Huntington—the cops can bring him in. They'll find Robin. That doesn't mean we stop looking for her. Or . . . or Garrie." She kept her gaze averted from the blood.

"The lerket?" Quinn demanded—but he looked desperate. Cornered. Knew she was right.

"If nothing feeds it . . ." Lucia suggested.

But Caryn, who had been pale enough already, now reached to her aunt for support. "What do you mean, *find Robin*?"

Quinn turned on her. "What did you think would happen when you aligned with that hedonist, egotistical freak? That some of his mojo would rub off on you? That you would get the acknowledgment you craved? Reality check—Robin has been *kidnapped*. Her shop partner is *dead*." He stabbed a thumb at the room. "Someone else died here, too. And who knows about my friend!"

"Friends," Lucia corrected softly. But Quinn hadn't been in San Jose. Quinn didn't yet truly understand what Garrie and Trevarr had done together, or how it had changed her.

Caryn mustered some spirit. "That bastard. He *said*—"

"Skip it," Quinn said roughly. "He promised you ethereal treasures, right? And you already resented Garrie for what she has, and Trevarr for what he is."

Ooh—*zing!* Lucia, through watery vision, gave Quinn a moment of unadulterated admiration.

Quinn took a step closer, and if his hands were fisted, he kept them by his side. "Thing is, we don't *care* why you did it. We just want to stop whatever's happening, and we want to stop it *now*!"

Feather, very faintly, said, "Caryn. Honey. What is he talking about?"

Caryn turned away from them all. "It's complicated," she mumbled. She swiped her hands over her eyes and didn't look back at them. "I never meant for this to—"

"If your motives had been true ones, my dear, it *wouldn't* have," Feather said sadly. "Are we sure the others haven't simply left? Fled the scene?"

Lucia dared another look in the room, confirming

what her mind's eye told her. The leather duster, sprawled across her bed. The worn satchel of rugged leather, still tangled around the headboard post of the overturned bed. "However they left, it wasn't by choice."

Feather slipped a hand in her pocket and pulled out her cell phone—and if her hand shook, her voice was admirably firm. "I'm sorry, but if I don't call the police, I'll be charged with obstruction. Or worse. Especially if you're right, and a man died here."

"Ten minutes," Quinn said, but he didn't move to take the phone. "Just ten minutes, to grab my stuff and what information we can."

"Containment," Lucia said slowly, beginning to think again. "The lerket. It's mixed with our energies now. Maybe our containment procedures will affect it."

Quinn glanced at the room. "Can you pull them together?"

She straightened. She brushed herself off again— arms, shoulders, slender torso. Everywhere the emotions lingered and clung to her. "Quinnie, I am your *chica*."

"Oh," Caryn said, taking a step back from the room. "*Oh*. What—"

"What?" Quinn said, looking around—above, behind . . . everywhere.

"Oh," Feather said. "I . . . feel it, too—"

Lucia did a quick ghost check—as best she could, hunting escalating emotions and intrusions—and by then she saw it herself, and gasped.

From darkness within the room, a rainbow coalesced. Black sparks scattered everywhere, clearing out before the color, and Lucia put a hand up before her face and turned away as the brightness grew, and grew, and—

Quinn grabbed her arm, snapping something about getting to safety, but Lucia stayed rooted. "The Eye," she murmured. Garrie had spoken of it to her, whispered

into the darkness of the shared San Jose hotel room . . .
grieving for what she thought she'd lost in those days
after Trevarr had gone and before he'd returned. Lucia
grabbed Quinn's arm in return, giving him a little shake.
"The Eye!"

Before he could voice the alarmed curse so visibly on
the tip of his tongue, the light faded. In the background,
Feather hyperventilated oh so gently; Caryn muttered
a single curse, endlessly repeated.

"Garrie!" Lucia shrieked, an unabashedly girly noise.
"Chicalet!"

Garrie, indeed. And behind her, Trevarr—who
looked, as ever, ready for anything. Readier. No matter
that his shirt hung untucked and his boots weren't completely buckled and his hair—a little ragged, there—
hung loose along one side of his face.

The knife in his hand, that was ready enough. Gleaming an odd shade, as did all his metals, held with utter
conviction. Enough so Lucia took a step back, putting
herself cleanly between Quinn and Trevarr—not liking
the wild look, the clear intent—the leftover violence
showing in his bruised face and the random smears of
blood on jaw and neck.

But the moment he saw them all—Lucia and Quinn
and the two proprietors clutching each other for moral
support—he eased back. More a change in focus than
any identifiable shift of body, although—suddenly, for
a startling instant, Lucia thought—

No. Absurd. No faltering there. Tall and strong and
straight. Sunglasses gone, eyes piercing—and not . . .
quite . . . right. Not quite . . .

But she looked again, blinking as something seemed
to change . . . she couldn't tell what. Only that they no
longer baffled her.

Garrie looked at them all in vague surprise, orienting
to the wrecked room and their presence, her shorts even

250 · DORANNA DURGIN

more wrinkled than they'd been this morning and her shirt nothing Lucia had even seen before. More like something Trevarr would wear, with its sturdy and faintly iridescent weave, a deep chocolate brown inset by panels of fine leather at shoulder and waist and the cuffs rolled back to her forearms in a way that made it obvious the sleeves were much too long even if the rest of the shirt seemed tailor-made.

Lucia's eyes narrowed. She knew Garrie's wardrobe and this shirt wasn't from it. She knew *all* their wardrobes, of course. Someone had to keep track of these things.

From between them, Sklayne shook himself in an ear-popping gesture, his feet tangled up in a large pile of sticky-looking leaves with a quickly spreading pungency. "Mrrup!" he said, and dashed under the overturned bed.

"Hey," Garrie said. "You guys okay?"

"Us!" Quinn laughed, no humor there whatsoever. *"You?"*

Garrie looked at the room. "Better than *them*. Dammit. I wish we'd—" She shook her head, stopping herself. "Well, we didn't. And we didn't get the lerket, either—no sign of it and *no you would not*." That last seemed to be directed at Sklayne, still under the mattress . . . which jostled slightly, as if a cat could move a double-bed set.

Quinn took a step forward. "Robin's gone," he said. "Her friend Nancy—from the store—is dead in Robin's apartment." He shook his head, anger settling on his brow. "We could go back and try to talk to her, but the cops have probably found her by now."

"I *swear*," Caryn moaned. "I had no idea—"

"And that's just what you'll have to tell the police," Feather said, quite firmly. As firmly as any woman who finds herself clinging to reality with all her might. "You people have had your ten minutes. I'm sorry, but I have to make this call. Just *look* at this place—"

POOFPOW

Lucia staggered slightly, not sure if the flash of light, the vertiginous movement of everything and yet nothing at all, the blurring of her reality . . . not sure if those things had happened just inside her head or even at all, and then not sure if they were under attack, lifting her head to look wildly around—

"Aunt Feather!" Caryn lunged, catching the older woman just as she folded in a graceful faint. Quinn leaped to help her, but Lucia . . .

Lucia just stared.

No more blood.

Not a drop. Not a splatter. Not a single spray.

The room might be jumbled, but it was jumbled *pristine*.

"*¡Caray!*" she said. "Aie farking *caray!*"

Garrie looked as though she wanted to slap a hand over her face. Did it, in fact, hiding gamine features. "My life," she said. "Completely out of control."

Quinn left Feather to her niece's attentions. Trevarr, that knife—all business, that knife—still loosely in his grip, took a step forward, and Lucia saw it clearly—the way they caught each other's gaze; the instant the connection was made. Trevarr said, "We must find your Robin."

"Yeah," Quinn said. "As soon as fucking possible." But there was a light in his eye that hadn't been there before. Hope, maybe.

Caryn looked up from where she helped Feather to sit, flipping her aunt's phone closed. No call to the police, apparently. After all . . . no longer any trace of *trace evidence*. No witnesses. And once the jumble was flipped rightside up and the scatter of belongings dumped back into place—though to be fair, that one dresser with Lucia's jewelry and makeup was probably just how she'd left it—there would be only the broken door.

Caryn slipped the phone into Feather's tunic pocket. "I'll do what I can to help," she said. "I've made a terrible mistake, and I want to make it right."

"There isn't any making it *right*," Garrie said, and for an instant—in that strange new outfit of hers, her face only now emerging from behind her hands—she looked as resolute as Trevarr. As sure of herself. "You went over the line when we first met, and you said you were sorry, that it would never happen again, that you didn't know. And then you went right out looking for *more*. You and Huntington—"

"I'm nothing like him!" Caryn cried. "I've done nothing like this!"

"You're *exactly* like him," Garrie snapped at her. "You justified what you did to Trevarr; you found a way to justify going to Huntington. You justified pointing him at an innocent woman—someone with no defense! And now her friend is dead and she's missing." She shook her head, the frustration ramping up—a strange dark energy crackling the air around her. Caryn recoiled from her in growing horror and even Lucia took a step back, startled and wary, but Garrie took a deep breath and shook her head, and only then did Lucia see that her fingers had become tightly entwined with Trevarr's free hand.

They all somehow ignored the way the mattress again shifted of its own apparent accord, the stray puff of feathers from beneath. "Look," Garrie said, turning away from Caryn. "Assuming the police aren't going to descend on us . . . we need a plan. *She*"—a nod at Caryn—"needs to tell us what she knows. It might be enough to track Huntington down. I'll look, too, of course, but Quinn, you might find more about the ler-

ket's location if you look for power outages, a series of
freak accidents, a batch of old folks dying—"

Caryn gasped; it earned her a glare, as Garrie turned
on her. *"Yeah,"* she said, and the darkness crackled briefly
against Lucia's sensitized perception. "It's like that. That's
what you're helping."

Lucia winced. *This* Garrie . . . had hardened.

And then Garrie said, just like herself, "But I need a
shower first. I really do. And I need some under—"

She cut herself off, but too late. Lucia's eyes widened. She quite suddenly understood.

The shirt.

The dishevelment.

The way Trevarr seemed to be touching Garrie even
when he wasn't.

The changed energies, as little as Lucia could perceive what was actually there.

I need some underwear.

Lucia stepped up into the silence. "We *all* need some
under*standing*," she said, so very smooth. "So Caryn
talks to Quinnie, yes? And we grab your things and you
can shower in the boys' room." She suited brusque action to her words, stepping into the bathroom to snag up
Garrie's tidy toiletries kit, sweeping her soap and sham-
poo into it on the way out. She found little changed when
she reemerged, and she stepped smartly to Garrie's side,
threading her arm through Garrie's to take her elbow
and, again so very smooth, guide her to the side.

Before Quinn figured it out, and lost his new common ground with Trevarr. Before it became any more
obvious. "I'm sure by the time I come back, the bed will
be fixed, yes? And then I can grab clean clothes for
you."

Relief suffused Garrie's features. And yes, her hair,
the silver-blue streaks gleaming strong and unnatural,

had a particular bed-head look to it. Yes, her cheeks were flushed with more than the heat that had infused this room through the open door. And yes, her silly reluctance to leave Trevarr was going to give it all away, so Lucia shoved the toiletries bag into Garrie's hands with more than the necessary amount of force.

Garrie blinked at her, big brown gamine eyes in the gamine face beneath the gamine hair. Lucia leaned close. "Come," she said, under the cover of Feather's rising protests in the background. "Get cleaned up. It will help." Right. Lucia, Daddy's princess—what did she know? But *everything* was better after a good shower and clean clothes, so. "Also," she added, leaning even closer and stepping over what had once been a chair, "you let me know if he ever hurts you. I will break his balls."

Garrie gave her a startled look—not the words of a princess, oh no—and then cast a glance back at Trevarr. Lucia's gaze followed, an instinctive thing, and she gasped silently when she found Trevarr looking at her—straight at her, meeting her glace as though he had, yes, somehow heard her quiet words across the room and over Feather's fussing. And if for the first instant she thought *oh, caray!* with a little thrill of fear, in the second she realized that Trevarr's darkening gaze said something different altogether.

If I ever hurt her, I will let you.

14

Garrie emerged from the shower, towel-wrapped, with a cleaner body and a clearer head. Not to mention a much clearer idea of what the morning had wrung from her—her own set of bruises, rising to the surface. Tender places, within and without.

Action-Figure Reckoner, indeed.

She also emerged from the shower to find a plan taking shape without her—Lucia waiting on Trevarr's apparently unused bed, filing her nails, one leg crossed over the other and looking as cool and unruffled as ever.

Except when she looked up to meet Garrie's gaze. There, in her eyes, it showed—how baffled she was to find herself in this situation, where they somehow weren't reckoning ghosts at all. How unsettled her world had become, between here and San Jose.

She nodded at the other bed. Quinn's bed, all rumpled, the covers tangled with half a dozen cords and chargers and gizmos that Garrie had never understood and never would. "I grabbed some clothes."

Relief. "Great. 'Cause even *I* know these towels aren't my color."

Lucia raised an eyebrow. Put the nail file aside. "The boys are making plans," she said. "To get Robin. But it means trusting that *chueca*." She shook her head. "We can't do that."

"No," Garrie said, scrubbing a hand towel over her wet hair and quickly finger-combing it into place before it dried in complete disarray, a process that took approximately two minutes in this arid climate. "We can't."

Lucia looked no more settled. Not the least bit relieved. Garrie's hand stilled. Lucia said, "What about you, chic?"

What?

Lucia might as well have heard it; no doubt it was written all over Garrie's face. "You have things you're not telling me, yes?"

"No!" But as she gathered up her clothes, she thought again. Lucia already knew what had happened in Trevarr's lair . . . the gist of it, at least. Enough of it. And maybe there were things about Trevarr himself that Garrie wasn't sharing, but those weren't *her* things to share. And besides, she was still figuring half of them out. So, what—?

Impatience flickered through her, snapping into a little burst of the dark, cold heat—there, blooming right in the center of her.

And Garrie knew.

"Oh," she said. "Well. Maybe. Yes."

Lucia waited. Deeper than casual attention to her nails and that piece of lint she'd just flicked off her knee.

"It's not that I'm *not telling*," Garrie said. "It's that I'm *not knowing*. And by the time I figure something out, it's moved on. And so have we. Pretty much speed of light around here lately. Well, around us. Because we haven't even *been* around here. Am I babbling?"

Lucia gave that one a moment's thought. "Do you think?"

Garrie made a face. "I'm pretty sure." She sighed, retreating to the bathroom to drop the towels, not bothering to close the door as she dressed. "Since that first visit to the Winchester House, when the ghosts got all pissy—"

"That would be when they tried to kill you."

"That would be it." She yanked a camisole over her head, found that Lucia had brought her the shirt Trevarr had provided, and yanked that on, too . . . pausing to run a hand over it. His, now fitted to her—except for the sleeves, which Sklayne had forgotten. And now it still *felt* of him. "All those breezes flying around . . . ? Some of his got mixed with some of mine. And I don't always know how to handle it." Ahh, underwear. And her crop cargos. Still stiff from when she'd washed them out the night before, but they knew the shape of her and fell into place.

She found a comb on the sink and appropriated it, taming down what she could of her hair, then not liking it. With the silver-blue streaks, the smooth look . . . just too emo fey. So she scruffed it up again, compromising between emo fey and punk and ending up somewhere around bed-head.

When she poked herself out of the bathroom again, Lucia nodded, tossing over the collection of braided leather bracelets Garrie had pulled off before the shower. "And if you don't?" she said. "Handle it?"

Garrie stopped fussing with the bracelet. "Bad things, Lu. Places I wasn't meant to go. Things I wasn't meant to do." She found Lucia's gaze, dark and serious, perfectly made up to complement their exotic allure—and no less perceptive than ever. She took a deep breath, let it out with a whoosh, and was horrified at the sudden prick of tears in her own eyes, the betraying wobble in her voice and at her chin. "I've come so close to losing myself these past couple of days. If Trevarr—" If he hadn't taken her in, given her the buffer of his lair . . . if he hadn't held onto her in every possible way . . .

She shook her head, groping for words. "He's showing me the way through it. And he's paying for it, too."

"This morning," Lucia said evenly.

"This morning," Garrie agreed. "Huntington is a sensitive. I could have . . . if I had . . . if *Trevarr* hadn't . . ." But she stopped, shook her head . . . fiddled with the bracelet. "I'm doing this wrong. Because this—what happened—it's so much more than that. I can't even—" She stopped again, frustrated. Bereft of the words that might explain to her very good friend and very good teammate and the person who knew her best in the world with her parents gone and Rhonda Rose gone and—

"I get it," Lucia said. She did, perhaps, look a little resigned. "Maybe I don't like it, because I'm worried about you. But I get it."

"Do you?" She couldn't keep the hope from her voice.

Lucia nodded. Once, firmly. "Not because of your mastery with words, chicalet. But . . ." She nodded her head in the direction of the room beside them. "Because I saw the look on his face just now."

Oh.

Oh.

Okay then.

Garrie wiped damp eyes on the rolled-up ends of her overlong sleeves. "Let's go," she said. "We've got a *pajarito* to find."

"Little *petirrojo*," Lucia said, sadly enough so Garrie thought she had little more hope than Garrie herself.

And they gathered themselves and their emotions, bundled up the shower gear, and headed out. But when they showed up in the wrecked doorway of the room next door, they found Feather staring at her niece with horror and Quinn grim and Trevarr cold and hard, hidden again behind his sunglasses and duster.

And Caryn said, *"What?"* with her hands thrown open wide, holding her active cell phone.

::Tried to eat that tasty phone,:: Sklayne announced to anyone who could hear him, crouched down at the foot of the bed with his tail twitching. ::Too late.:: *Twitch*. ::Take off geas shackles now, yess?::

"No," Trevarr said flatly, and either everyone else had grown used to the way he spoke bluntly to thin air or they were too focused on Caryn and her phone to care.

"What?" Caryn asked again, inching toward wronged petulance.

"What?" Garrie demanded, inching toward alarm.

"They called her," Quinn said, staccato words hammering home. "She told them you were here."

Caryn nodded. "Don't you see? They'll come back for you! You won't need to find them at all!"

Garrie saw, all right. She took a quick, deep long breath—quick, to gain control before she even started to lose it. "I think," she said, slowly and deliberately, "that you're going to die."

Caryn looked at her in utter astonishment. "What! You wouldn't!"

Okay, that deserved some scorn. "Of course I wouldn't. But you've done it *again*. That wasn't *saving the day*. That was twisted justification to take control so *you* could be the one who saves the day." She breathed it in—the hard dark temper, eating at her control—and she breathed it out. "Too bad you have no clue. So mainly, I just think you're going to get yourself killed. And I think I'm going to be too busy dealing with what you've just done to stop it."

Caryn's response got stuck at her mouth, words forming and failing, her hands slowly falling to her sides. Nothing left to say there—nothing left to hear. Garrie turned to Quinn and Lucia. "This morning, he came to push us around, see what he could learn. If he comes back, I don't think he's going to waste time talking. He's got to know we're . . ."

She glanced at Trevarr. *Lethal* wasn't quite the word she wanted to use in front of Feather.

"Unpredictable," Quinn suggested darkly. And he was looking at her.

Right. Just that.

"So we need to go after him—after Robin. The problem is," Garrie said, "that lerket left traces of itself all over this area. I can tell you where it's been, but I can't tell you which of those places it still *is*."

"You're saying you can't find Robin?" Quinn asked, desperate disbelief on his features.

"I'm saying," Garrie said, ever so aware they now had mere minutes of safety, "that I think *you'll* have a better chance. You and Lucia, grab your gear and go!"

"It could be too late," Quinn said, and he closed the space between them to grab her by the shoulders, his gaze full of bright blue surfer-boy distress. "If I have to do the footwork from scratch—"

"Not from scratch," Garrie said, too aware of how Trevarr had checked himself at Quinn's movement. "Get me a map. I'll mark the likely spots. You check the scanner, check your chat rooms . . . check those reports I'm not supposed to know you hacked into."

Quinn tightened his hands on her shoulders, and when she winced, when Trevarr rumbled, seemed to realize what he'd done. He eased up, running an apologetic hand down her arm—briefly fingered the fine-spun and faintly iridescent material of this new shirt. "Who would have even thought—" Shook his head again. "If only she'd understood. If she'd just let us *do the work*."

"She made her own choices, for her own reasons," Garrie said gently. "And I don't honestly think she thought it would lead to any of this. I think she just saw an excuse to get you to Sedona."

"If she'd *trusted* me—" Quinn said, and broke off with an inarticulate noise—grief and frustration and anger, and it twisted his face up as he turned away. "Then again, that was always the problem. She always knew better."

"Quinnie," Lucia said, but nothing else. Her face troubled, wanting to make it all right . . . no more able than any of them to do it.

::Me.:: Sklayne sat nibbling something out from between the pads of his front paw, and didn't bother to look at any of them.

Garrie glanced at Trevarr, who crossed the room in even fewer strides than Quinn had taken, crouching before Sklayne with such abruptness that those perfectly cat eyes opened wide in green startlement. "You have a thing to say, little friend?"

Ears flattened. ::Not. *Little*.::

"Garrie, what—?" Quinn glanced between Garrie and Sklayne; Lucia murmured to Caryn's surprised response in the background, something matter-of-fact about Sklayne not being what Caryn and Feather thought he was and really, they did need to keep the little dog named Trickle from running around loose near this cabin.

Trevarr tipped a single finger under that stubborn cat chin. "We have only moments."

::Say it. Not little. *Mighty*.::

"Prove it," Garrie snapped at him. "You can help? Do it!"

Sklayne shot her a narrow-eyed sideways glare. ::Already saved your ass. Holy farking shit!::

"Never going to let me live down those words, are you? You *knew* I'd be surprised when you shoved words in my mind that first time!"

"He talks in *your head*?" Caryn blurted.

"Just keep the little dog on a leash, yes?" Lucia told her.

Quinn lost patience. "If we're going to go, we'd better *go*. But what're you—"

The tip of Trevarr's head stopped him. Sklayne stared back at him with ears still flat and his eyes mere slits of cat mad as Trevarr lowered to one knee before him. To Garrie's astonishment, Trevarr only tickled beneath Sklayne's chin. Gently. Along his jaw. Gently. "Little friend," he said, "we have only moments."

A faint spark shot from Sklayne's tail. His claws flexed into thin carpet. He tipped his jaw ever so perceptibly into Trevarr's fingers.

And then his eyes widened and he jerked his head away, his fur rippling down his back. Cat embarrassment. Not-cat embarrassment, apparently. His mental voice came as a mutter. ::Yes. Can find the Robin person.::

"You can do that?" Garrie asked, startled. "That would be . . . that would be . . ."

"Mighty," Trevarr suggested, completely straight-faced.

"Someone better start talking out loud." Quinn took a step toward the door. "We have no idea where Huntington was when he called. Could have been halfway to Cottonwood, could have been down the block."

Garrie gave him only a glance. "Sklayne says he can find Robin."

"You know," Lucia said slowly, lingering at the open door, "he found me in San Jose. When I was out shopping, and tangled with the goo."

::Eatsll,:: Sklayne said primly. ::Yes. Like that.::

Trevarr sat back on one heel to regard the Abyssinian form of his familiar, then glanced at Quinn. "Connections. Through me to Garrie to one whom she knows."

"Six degrees of separation," Quinn said, abrupt understanding on his face. "We wouldn't have to take the laptop. We could just head straight there—"

"Can he do it?" Garrie asked. "I mean, I don't have

enough of a connection with Robin . . . okay, face it, I have no connection at all. So that means through Trevarr and me and Quinn to Robin . . ."

::Through you, now:: Sklayne corrected her. ::Mostly.:: And at her surprise, he added, smug again, ::Things change.::

"Go, then," Garrie told him. "Do what you can."

Sklayne stood, a trail of sparks in the air behind his tail. ::Treyyy,:: he said, and hesitated.

"Go," Trevarr told him. "We will handle what has become of the lerket. We will . . . *deal* with Huntington."

"Garrie," Quinn said, uncertainty taking the place of his determination . . . warring with the desperation.

Sklayne cocked his head. ::It comes.::

"Go!" Garrie pushed Quinn at the door. "Go now!"

"This isn't right," Quinn said, drilling her with that final look. "None of this is right."

And he went.

And in his wake, Garrie muttered, "Can't argue with you there."

Feather jumped suddenly to her feet, dragging Caryn toward the door. "You have to go with them, Caryn. Hurry!"

"I—what?"

"You want to take responsibility? Here it is!" She gave her niece a little shove. "This Robin woman is in trouble because of *you*. Because of what you did." Caryn gaped at her, but she stood firm. "And you do what you're told," she said. "This is the first test of the rest of your life, do you understand? No making decisions for other people!"

"But—"

"Caryn," Feather said, her voice quavery and her face pale and legs not looking altogether too steady. "I love working with you. I love *you*. But did you think there would be no consequences?"

Garrie heard it then, loud and clear. She saw from Caryn's face that she heard the same. No free family ride here. Caryn could start working toward her redemption right now . . . or she could go back to her room and pack. Right now.

Wow. *Go, Feather.*

"Oh," Caryn said. *"Oh."* And she took a step out the door, into the bright Sedona sunlight. She looked back. In the not-too-far distance, the newly familiar sound of the Cruiser engine turned over; a car door slammed.

::It comes,:: Sklayne said, and *poof!* expanded outward, a rush of sparkling clear energy and light that made Garrie hold her breath as he shot into motion, warp speed special effects.

Caryn startled . . . and then she followed. One step, then another, then pounding feet, rushing for the parking area.

In the silence that followed, Garrie turned to Feather. "You'd better go. They could have more than the one gun, among other things. It won't be safe."

Feather stood straighter. "Consequences."

Trevarr opened his coat slightly. He'd outfitted himself from within those endless pockets and now fairly bristled with weapons—a brace of balanced throwing blades, metal knuckle guards over the half-finger gloves. The sword Lukkas hung at his side; the hand-to-hand knife jammed into its sheath on his belt, within easy reach. "You cannot fight such as this. You are sensitive, and you will drain Garrie's skills if she must protect you through what is to come."

Feather swallowed visibly, paling even more; her skin took on the cast of age. "Oh," she said.

Yeah. *Oh.*

"Besides," Garrie said, with a level of casual she certainly didn't feel, "We'll need someone on the sidelines. Someone who can wield a cell phone. Someone who knows what happened."

Feather clutched her phone to her chest in both hands. "Oh," she said again. "Yes. I can do that." She took a step toward the door. "All right, then. I'll do that."

"Good," Garrie said, straightening ever so faintly, tipping her head . . . listening. Feeling the beat of un-naturally muddy breezes, the edges of corruption . . . rippling lava ribbons, a hint of smoldering stench. The flaws of something so very hungry it could never sate itself. "Because . . . *it comes*."

15

Initiate ethereal activity from a defensible position.
—Rhonda Rose

First, we put our backs to a wall.
—Lisa McGarrity

¡Aiee! ¡Caray!
—Lucia Reyes

Sklayne sat on the Lucia person's lap, the car air-conditioning blasting feebly into the desert-heated car, water jugs at the Lucia person's feet. The problematic one had thrown herself into the back just as the car started to move, and no one looked very happy about it. Not the Lucia person; not the Quinn person. Not the problematic one.

Not Sklayne, either.

Lucia fussed with her seat belt, fussed to get herself settled. Patted her tote for reassurance, while Quinn said, "I brought my kit. Duct tape, screwdriver ... Leatherman. Don't know what good any of that will do us."

"We can always use duct tape," Lucia said, so firmly that Sklayne recognized it right away. Knew she was only convincing herself.

She certainly hadn't convinced Sklayne.

And up came their turn. ::Here,:: Sklayne said, with plenty of time to make the turn. And, ::Here.:: And, ::*Here.*:: And a slash of his tail, farking deaf humans, and he slapped his paw down on the Lucia person's right leg and squeezed down his claws. ::*Here,*:: he purred.

"¡Aiee! ¡Caray!" The Lucia person jumped beneath him. "Don't *do* that!"

Sklayne lifted his paw, so deliberately. Replaced it, so firmly. Squeezed down his claws.

"Right!" the Lucia person cried out. "Turn right!" And Sklayne eased back his claws and sat on her lap, perfectly balanced and reaching, reaching, reaching for that small thread of awareness that was Robin.

He wondered what duct tape tasted like.

"Here?" Garrie said, looking around the tidied room, the blood gone and the furniture rumpled and not quite squarely placed. A glance at Trevarr and she narrowed her eyes, for if he stood just how he'd been the last time she looked his way, he also stood *other,* as if something in him had drained right out through the soles of his feet.

And then she saw it not. Then she saw only what she'd ever seen, the strength of him. The drive behind him. He replaced his sunglasses and said, "Too confined."

They hardly had time to pick and choose. "The rock," she said, knowing it was too exposed ... hoping hard that the other Journey Inn guests were off being tourists, soaking up what was left of the vortexes and admiring the views and wearing out their jeans at Slide Rock falls.

She didn't expect him to agree. But she found herself running to keep up with his long strides, and running hard. "Wait!" she cried after him, thinking of the lerket and its mutated creepiness, thinking of Huntington and his willingness to aim whatever weapon he had where he thought it would get what he wanted as fast as he wanted it. Thinking of how she'd never faced human opposition, and how she barely knew how to handle what she had within herself.

"Little time, *atreya*." But he hesitated.

"I know, I know. But . . . what about . . ." She hesitated. If she'd grown used to his warmth, his understanding, and even his touch, she also remembered well this determination. How well it matched hers. How much grimmer it was. So it took all her nerve. "The eggs," she said. "Maybe we should—"

"The eggs." He said it so flatly that she knew without a doubt he had no idea what she was talking about.

Well, how could he? They hadn't talked about it, had they? "Those *things*," she said, oh-so-glibly. "That the Krevata left behind."

That name got his attention, all right, even as he lifted his head, all but scenting the air. The lerket's influence closed in on them, impossible to gauge.

Though she really, *really* hoped it wasn't far. Not if it was this strong already.

"The portal power," she continued, somewhat desperately. "The thingies they were using—"

One sudden, long stride and he'd caught her up, taken both upper arms and squeezed her shoulders together slightly—even given her a little shake. "You have their stones?"

Not as frightened or even annoyed as she probably should be, she nodded. "Hidden in—"

"Do they know?" he demanded. Again with the shaking. Were her feet even touching the ground? "The other two?"

Okay, now it was getting annoying. "They have no idea. Should I kick you in the shins now?"

Only then did he seem to realize how aggressively he'd responded to her. She had the impression of rustling feathers, mantled and settling but not feathers at all . . . the dry dusty scent of ash. Not an impression that came from without, but one that came from within—and one that faded quickly, leaving him unsettled and Garrie bemused.

"They wouldn't understand, anyway," she told him. "How could they?"

"No," he murmured, head lifting to stare into the distance.

She thought she heard a car.

His hands tightened on her arms again, if briefly this time. "We will talk about the stones after," he said. "But know this—that power, trapped by the Krevata as it was, will not maintain stability. It is not safe to harbor. It is not safe to use."

Garrie looked back at him, brow climbing. "Do we have a door number three, then?"

"After," he repeated, grimly enough.

Definitely the slam of a car door in the near distance.

"Okay," Garrie said. "First, we put our backs to a wall." *Get thee to the rock!*

Huntington found them there in the shaded shelter of Feather's cleansing circle. Garrie sat on the rock with her legs crossed—the flat stone hard beneath her bottom, the ground far beneath her feet, the rock itself stable and grounded.

Garrie, maybe . . . not so much. Flutters of *wild* beat against the inside of her chest; cold heat riffled goose bumps across her skin even in the full oven of the Sedona summer day.

Inside her shoes, her toes twitched.

Trevarr stood beside her, everything about him still and balanced; Lukkas slanted loosely from one hand, the knife from the other. The duster swirled around his legs, and he didn't look the least bit hot for it. He looked cold and hard and ready.

A trickle of sputtery breeze from above told Garrie they weren't alone; a trickle of rock down the bluff confirmed it. The resident ghost. Quiescent; thoughtful. She'd certainly had an eyeful these past days.

Huntington came alone, at first. He looked like exactly what he was—a banged-up, bandaged-up, bruised-up red rocks guide, tanned and fit and totally belonging at the organics section of the local health food store. If he'd gotten his hands on another gun, it didn't show.

He just looked at them.

"Kind of awkward, huh?" Garrie asked him, chin planted in her palm. "But simple, actually. It's time for you to stop messing with this land. And with these people."

His mouth twisted a little. "And you think you can stop me."

"Well," Garrie said, all modesty, "I kinda do."

"And my little pet? Do you think you can stop that?" He might have been genuinely curious.

"That lerket belongs to Trevarr. We'd like it back, now."

"To *him*?" Carefully, there, as if he wanted to be dismissive but knew better. "But he has no skills."

Garrie laughed, a little more freely. "Oh, I wouldn't say *that*." She sat up straighter. "The cops are going to get you for Jim-Bob Dandy's death—whatever you think, you left evidence—so leave that for now. But what you've done to this land . . . what you've done to the spirits resting here . . ." She shook her head. "I don't get it. You *live* here. You *know* this place."

A flush rode the sides of his neck. "With power comes sacrifice."

"That," Trevarr said, his baritone gone rugged, "is not your choice to make."

Huntington flinched, ever so slightly. "I *shot* you," he said, his gaze drifting to Trevarr's side.

Garrie kept a perfectly straight face. "He got better."

Huntington's flush crept up the side of his face, his latent redheaded complexion coming out—his self-restraint obvious. He was going to let that one pass. "Sometimes," he said again, all righteous dignity, "with power comes sacrifice."

Now Garrie sat straight, all right. Now she sat *ramrod* straight, the dragon beating wildly within her and fury coalescing into one tight, bright spot in her chest. "With power," she said distinctly, clearly, hearing Rhonda Rose's precision tones overlaying her own, "comes *responsibility*."

"Hmm," he said, unaffected . . . or maybe amused. "I guess we'll have to disagree about that."

"Do you even know how many people died last night because you played Disneyland with breezes? Do you even know how many ghosts are tearing themselves up, losing their own journeys, because *you* came along and screwed with their anchor?"

"No." He looked at her with genuine curiosity now. "Do you?"

A familiar voice drifted down from the hill. "I do. It has to *stop*."

"I do," Garrie said. "And I'm not the only one."

"The ghosts?" Huntington laughed, and this time he didn't try to hide his scorn. "They're not going to bother me. And neither are you. Not when I have *this*."

Likely, that was supposed to be a grand entrance.

But if Garrie heard a faint rattly rolling noise, it wasn't exactly the effect Huntington had been looking for.

"So hard to get good help these days." Huntington shot the sidewalk a look of pure annoyance.

Garrie scowled. "You're taking this 'Evil Overlord' thing way too seriously. I really hope you read the manual. You know, the part where it doesn't end well for you?"

"Very cute. But we know where this is going—I want to know more about you and I want you out of my way. And I don't care who gets hurt in the process. But you don't want anyone hurt, so in the end you'll give me what I want in order to avoid it. My vote is, we skip to the end."

"Well, that's a problem," Garrie told him, just that serious, just that fast. "Because I don't want to know anything about *you* and I'm not getting out of your way." She sent a puff of breeze his way, just for the startle factor. Her hands, resting over her knees, fisted. *I'm sorry, Rhonda Rose.*

I'm sorry, me. This isn't who I am.

It wasn't who she'd *been*. But maybe it was who she'd turned into. Even with her stomach churning beneath the anger and regret heavy beneath the knowing. Because if she didn't stop this man, then who? If she didn't stop the lerket, then who? And how many would die before it happened?

"Please," she said, dropping all the smart-assery. "Please don't make me do this."

Inside her, the dragon stirred and grumbled and fluttered, building icy-cold heat. That part of her had not known Rhonda Rose. That part of her wanted retribution and control and release, and didn't care about the tenets on which she'd built her life.

Please. Don't make me do this.

If she even could.

* * *

By the time they reached the outskirts of Sedona, Lucia found herself well trained to the tap of Sklayne's tidy reddish paw on her knee. "Right!" she said, then helped steady the cat as Quinn took the sudden turn.

Amazing how very much like a cat he looked. *Felt.* Soft, short fur, luxurious against her fingers, beautifully pristine in nature. Dark ticks of color on each hair turned the red-buff color into something else altogether when she smoothed it down his back; large ears flicked expressively at things Lucia couldn't discern. Long-legged, lean in body . . . a little predator, sitting in her lap, occasional growls vibrating against her fingers.

In the back, Caryn kept her thoughts to herself. Until they made that last turn, and then she said, "I can't believe it. He took her *here*?"

"Where is *here*?" Quinn asked instantly, as they passed a dirt cross street to nowhere and forged on.

Caryn pulled herself up between the front passenger and driver seats and pointed down the street—barely paved, definitely no longer on the beaten path. What passed for a back alley in Sedona, desert style—spaced out, last season's tumbleweeds collecting in an old fence corner, and quite suddenly looking as though this area barely even received electricity and might well not have running water. "Here," she said. "Not his storefront, but this building he uses to store things—camping gear for the overnighters, a couple of canoes, portable sweat lodge gear—"

"Gross," Lucia said. "Who even wants one of those?"

"He shares the space," Caryn said, even as Lucia jumped under Sklayne's sudden application of paw and motioned Quinn *left, left, left!* "With a couple of other tour places. You know . . . he specializes in the spiritual tours, and one of the others does birding, and there's one who does climbing . . ."

"Not that it's a tourist-based industry around here or

anything," Lucia added, alert for the next tap of Sklayne's paw. It came in a quick stutter of motion, so she ended up saying, "Here, here, here!" without directionals, but it hardly mattered. Not with Caryn's hand stabbing at the small row of abandoned old shops. A defunct old gas pump stood off to the side beneath a ratty lean-to; tumbleweeds loafed at the edges of the lot, and unclaimed desert spread out beyond, red soil and stark green junipers. Prickly pear jutted up between, a few blooms of outrageous magenta peeking through.

"Charming," Lucia muttered.

Quinn just looked grim. "If she's being held in there, I hope they've at least got a swamp cooler going."

Lucia doubted it. "Poor *petirrojo*!" As soon as Quinn pulled the vehicle to a stop, there in the hard stone and scattered gravel, she reached for the door handle.

"Hold on," he said, and jerked the car into reverse, swinging it around in a quick backward arc. Then he took a moment before turning off the engine—looking around. Taking stock.

"I don't think anyone else is here," Caryn said.

"Can you tell?" Lucia asked her, immediately interested.

"Tell? I—no, I . . ." Caryn trailed away. "Tell?"

"Garrie could tell," Lucia told her. "Well, never mind."

"If it was easy," Quinn said, and Lucia chimed in, "it wouldn't be the reckoner way!"

"You know," Caryn told them, sitting back and tugging her twisted shirt straight. "You people are seriously weird." She reached for the door handle, suddenly all brisk and take-charge and quite clearly prepared to march forth.

"Uh-uh," Quinn told her, sharply enough to get her attention. "You're following. Period. *Following*. That's the whole point, isn't it?"

Caryn looked a bit stunned—possibly at the correction, possibly because she realized she'd been about to charge forth all over again. She looked at Lucia—whether in search of consolation or ally, Lucia couldn't say.

Lucia didn't especially care. "That's it, *chueca*. That's the way it is."

"What—?"

"You don't want to know," Lucia told her, and made the decision, pushing her own door open. "You really don't."

Quinn dropped the keys into a cup holder. "Leave it unlocked. This way, any of us can get this thing moving."

"But no one's here," Caryn said. "What could possibly go wrong?"

"You don't want to know," Lucia told her.

You really don't.

Garrie uncrossed her legs and drew her knees up under her chin, gripping her ankles as she stared down Huntington.

"I want the lerket," she said. "And then I want you to stop what you're doing. This sucking thing. I don't care about how clever you are or that you think you're *the only one ever* to figure out how to harness these energies. You're wrong. You're just the one who's done so badly with it. And you're not harnessing them, you're stealing them."

He offered her a polite golf clap. "Very nice speech." His expression hardened. "Now get your ass off the rock and come with me. Because things are about to get very ugly for both of you."

"It comes," Trevarr murmured, the merest nod at the office. Huntington's backup. His big weapon.

It certainly did. Trundled along on a low gardening cart, ensconced in a plastic dog crate large enough for a Great Dane. Whining and grumbling and shooting off ethereal sparks that blew right through the crate, while the man and the woman handling the crate—one pushing, one pulling—swatted obliviously at bugs that weren't there.

It had gotten heavy, it seemed. Both its caretakers were sweating, their faces red in the heat. The woman carried some age and didn't look fit enough for the task at hand; the man carried some weight and didn't look steady in the heat. The lerket made a pitiful noise . . . the sound of a giant dog whining through a cardboard paper towel tube.

"That's it?" Garrie said. "That's your big *or else*?"

"Well, no," Huntington said, so modest. "I've also figured out how to make it mad."

16

Did I mention discretion, dear?
—Rhonda Rose

Fainting in three . . . two . . . one . . .
—Lisa McGarrity

"Make it *mad*? On *purpose*?" Garrie fought back that thrill of anger, the impulse to slap him down and have it over with. *Don't get cocky.* Words of wisdom to live by. *Too big for your breeches,* Rhonda Rose would have said, crediting Davy Crockett himself for that one. Because Garrie knew only what the lerket had been . . . but not what it had become.

Huntington—battered, splinted, and full of an overlord's premature triumph—he obviously lacked the advice of a Rhonda Rose—nodded at the giant crate, where gleaming puce lava lines glowing starkly in the dim space. The woman stepped back, and back again; the man reached for the latch to the wire door. "Are you certain—?"

Listen to the Sin Nombre lackeys, you idiot.

Huntington held up a hand, but his expression remained unrelenting. "Oh," he said. "I'm forgetting." And he gestured, glancing at the far end of the office cabin. Two extraordinarily fit young men emerged from around the side of the office—bursting with impatience and muscle and carrying street weapons—a baseball bat, a heavy length of chain, a crowbar. "I thought I'd already hurt your friend," Huntington said. "But I'm not stupid. And I'm not unprepared. Behave, and they'll restrain themselves to menacing looks."

"Trevarr," Garrie said, not caring if her desperation showed; she felt the growl of him in her bones. "We can't—" *We can't just* kill *people.*

No outward response from him—just that growl from the inside, caressing her bones . . . purring over her heart. A glance showed her just what she expected to see—Lukkas still held low, every bit of him bristling with warning.

That's when she realized the crate door was open. When she felt Huntington give the creature a cruel punch of his dark, toxic energy. The lerket flared within its dim confines.

"It's a vacuum!" the lurking Bobbie ghost cried out—and fled.

Not words that made sense . . . not at first. Not until Garrie felt the first touch, a startling tug at the very depth of her. A tree limb cracked as if bent by the breeze; rocks crumbled off the bluff behind her.

A bird tumbled to the ground and lay limp.

"What are you *doing*?" Her voice caught in her throat. "Are you *insane*?"

"I wanted to talk to you," Huntington said, crossing his battered arms, his head raised with a self-righteous tilt. "I needed to know who you are, what you can do. But I don't need *you*. And I don't want you in my way."

"Trevarr—" She risked another glance at him, wild-eyed this time, as the lerket hopped awkwardly from the crate—as the two men flanked the cleansing circle, as Huntington settled into his smugness.

The alarm on Trevarr's face scared her more deeply than anything else. The glimpse of *weary,* before he shut it away. Because it wasn't just her. Not just the earth, the bird, the rock.

The lerket wanted them all. It wanted *him.*

And he didn't have anything to spare.

He set his jaw; he looked away from her, the sunglasses not hiding that from her, not one bit. "I do not know, *atreya.*"

"Harmless," she said, and couldn't help but move back on the rock. "Simple creature!"

"And so it should be." He turned a steady look on Huntington. "If we deal with the one who controls it—"

Huntington shook his head without any evident regret. "I don't exactly control it." He shrugged. "I offer it opportunities."

Trevarr set his feet a little more firmly against the ground, his stance a little wider. The men moved a little closer and Garrie suddenly realized they had no idea—no idea at all. *Ethereal deaf-mutes.* The lerket might get around to them eventually, but for now . . .

It was eating dessert first.

Prickles of gray ate the edges of her vision. It was eating dessert *fast.*

Shield, idiot. Whatever it stirred up between her and Trevarr, they'd handle it.

They'd have to.

"Miss McGarrity! Lisa!"

Fark. Was that—

"Lisa!" Yes, here came Feather, dammit.

"Get out of here!" Garrie snapped at her—instantly distracted from the shielding, instantly wondering if she could protect this woman as well . . . and knowing she couldn't. "Keep everyone away from here!"

"But I—oh, my little Trickle dog! I had to see—I had to help—he's collapsed!"

Fark. A sensitive dog. *Go figure.* Six pounds of sensitive dog, no more resistant to the lerket than the bird that had been in its cone of influence.

"You can't help!" Garrie told her, desperate to keep her back.

It was too late anyway.

"What—?" Feather asked, her eyes wide and her gaze glued to the lerket and its blobby head, its dangling blobby nose, the nexus of tentacles sprouting at both ends . . . chartreuse eyes in goggly, independent rotation . . . putrescent lava veins. Everything it had been when Trevarr had called it forth, now supersized. *"What—?"*

"Something you shouldn't have seen," Huntington said, full of annoyance; he snapped out a command to the two crate lackeys. "Go watch that parking lot. If anyone else comes in, tell them there's been a gas leak. We don't need fucking spectators."

"I—" Feather said, and wavered. She looked down at her hand, as if she expected to find herself insubstantial.

Fainting in three . . . two . . . one . . .

Down she went, folding gracefully to the ground. Garrie surged back to strength while the lerket focused on Feather—intensely aware that Trevarr had shaken off the effects, his balance subtly changing and his intent clear, sizing up the lackeys and hunting for the right moment. She glared at Huntington. "She can't hurt you, you asshat! Call that thing off!"

"More of an *or else* than you expected?"

"No," she said, and started to gather her feet beneath her—but only started to, because the big guy with the bat was closest to her and he was looking at her ankles and he seemed like he'd already taken his warm-up swings. "Not more *or else*—more *stupid*! No wonder Rhonda Rose told me to stay away from the living! Who knew ghosts would be more sensible, when it comes right down to it?"

He narrowed his eyes at her. *Here it comes.* He gathered himself—gathered what he'd stolen from the land—and threw it at her, shielded as she was. The garish dart of energy left a strange fog of ugly; Huntington's head lifted, his chest lifted . . . as though he'd inhaled the best scent in the world. As though pleasure shot through his body.

Far too much information.

And it hadn't really been aimed *at* her at all. Not to harm her. To *paint* her.

The lerket's blobby trunk stuck straight out; it blatted a startled, flat trumpet and stumbled a few steps on stiff legs—redirected, it fastened hungry eyes on Garrie, the trunk reaching in her direction. *Homing in for serious action.*

Me. She knew it even as she saw the sparking glow of chartreuse eyes, aimed directly at her. She knew it even before she felt the abrupt tug, a frigid cold stab of hunger rushing like liquid weakness through muscle and soul.

She knew it even before Huntington laughed.

The lerket. Stealing from the land. Stealing from Feather. Stealing straight from Garrie herself, right through the shields.

Scrabbling back onto the rock did no good. A thin thread of panic fluttered as her heart skipped a beat, lost in the thrall of the parasitic connection. Trevarr jerked, shouting something harsh and warning—the dark of it rose between them, his struggle with what surged around and through him.

Better shields—she reached for the breezes—for what was left of them—and in desperation, reached within herself, too.

"Take care, *atreya*," Trevarr said, words ground out as he staggered a short step. "Take—"

Oh, too *late*. Oh, too *farking late*.

The lerket trumpeted a short blast, tentacles standing on end—sparks and spit flying, gaping lava cracks widening as the creature stiffened in joy, inhaling everything she'd meant to put between them—clamping onto those shields and sucking them down. Garrie made a noise she'd never thought to hear from herself—a mewling, wounded noise, faint to her own ears. In the distant background, she heard a wail, dismay and warning and *waiwaiwai* in Sklayne's distinct voice.

Garrie crumpled to the hard rock. Her shoulder buckled; her forehead hit red stone. A rumble filled the air from no apparent source at all and she thought maybe Trevarr and she thought maybe the land itself, groaning as the buff cracked in a rifle shot of unnaturally brittle, unnaturally disturbed rock. A small scrubby bush landed beside her, its precarious hold on the bluff lost.

A startling new shock wave of dark cold heat slammed against her—skin and hair and fingernails aching with it, chest echoing with it. The lerket cried out—a French horn mated with an oboe and blatting out short and sharp, a sound of distress. Garrie twisted, floundering to figure out where her body was, glad enough to discover her elbows grinding into stone and to lift her head.

For an instant, she had a glimpse of Huntington's confusion—unable to parse the energy flows, slow to understand what hung imminent. Trevarr faced the supersized lerket and she knew that tilt of shoulder, that cant of arm—he'd pulled the Gatherer on it. *Cold dark heat.*

The faint overlay of the lerket's answering energy brushed against her . . . and then nothing.

The Gatherer's effect faded in failure.

The lerket instantly lost interest in Trevarr. Its tendrils wiggled at Garrie, straightening . . . pulsing. Sucking her down again. Pulling a raw cry of useless protest from her life and soul.

Trevarr jerked as if stabbed, reaching for her, face twisted in desperation. And then he whirled back around, Lukkas no longer quiescent, movement no longer showing the weary weight of moments earlier, otherworldly metal flashing. Huntington scrabbled backward in panic—but he wasn't the target at all, and the lerket wailed as Lukkas struck its rocklike flesh, sparks flying, metal biting deep with an unnatural clang.

Garrie snapped free with a rubber-band sting, reeling with misery and implications. *I can't shield against it. The Gatherer did a crash and burn.* Only Lukkas had even touched it—

Oh, so *don't get cocky!*

If Huntington's muscle lackeys hadn't been prepared for a battle they couldn't perceive and couldn't understand—if they'd been understandably startled by the lerket's appearance—they'd also been coached well enough to recover and respond. Huntington barked out a command made illegible by his own fury and they pounced.

Trevarr evaded that first charge, a tumble and roll and straight to his feet, every bit of effort focused in on his goal beyond even his own safety. Garrie saw it in him, the blade clanging, biting deep to create a hissing vent of putrid steam. The lerket blatted in pain, an innocent creature doing only what it had been bred to do and twisted by Huntington's vile energies, fighting back as best it could, those tentacles waving. Trevarr dodged back; he ducked a whistling swing from the crowbar—and *crack!* the bat slammed against his arm. Lukkas fell to the ground.

It didn't matter that Trevarr instantly scooped the sword up with the other hand, an expert whip of blade that sliced a thin and meaningful line across one lackey's entire torso. It didn't matter that his grunt and stagger turned into a snarl of a Keharian curse; that his sunglasses, lost, showed eyes bright and silver and wild, as otherworldly as the sword. Garrie heard his pain; she *felt* it, an earthquake reverberating between them, a sudden shadow of awareness and the rising breeze, the clap of a thunderous wing.

Her fingers clawed at rock, gaining traction; blood trickled down her face from her fall. And as the bat-lackey danced back, out of reach of the sword that had marked him and wary astonishment on his features, Garrie launched herself right off the rock at him—the arm full of bat, so easy to grab, to wrench, to twist beneath her as they went down.

Huntington's face flashed through her field of view, flabbergasted. He'd thought her small; he'd thought her weak. Maybe he'd thought her fearful. Maybe she should have *been* fearful. But this time, she wasn't the one thinking *oh fark*. She wasn't the one suddenly facing less-than-certain victory as she slammed the bat across the damned stupid interfering lackey's ass. And when he cried out and rolled over—the one shoulder not quite working and the other hand clapping tight to his newly wounded, highly humiliated posterior—she wasn't the one screeching in sudden ultrasonic agony at the impact of bat against equally nether regions now newly exposed.

No. She was the one fighting a human fight with human ways and human weapons, the bat an equalizer in a wiry, highly toned body. She was the one refusing to

STORM OF RECKONING 283

play by Huntington's rules while Trevarr braced the
creature that had become such a threat to every living
thing in these canyon lands.

At least, until the other lackey reached her. Until he
grabbed the bat, used it to yank her close, and sneered
manfully in her face.

*Sudden shadow of awareness . . . the clap of a thun-
derous wing . . .*

Until he flung her hard against the rumbling stone.

"What is *wrong* with him?" Quinn hissed, while Sklayne
froze in the hot sun, stuck on the stark baking ground
between the car and the old storefront turned storage
area. Indecipherable lettering skimmed the inside of the
window, an arc of ex-words on dusty glass backed by
plywood. Stiff, immobile cat, half crouched and panting,
small jaw barely dropped, pink tongue barely showing.

"I don't—" Lucia didn't have the faintest. She glanced
at Caryn, as if they'd find any wisdom in that direction.
But Caryn had eased up to the door—another frustration
for Quinn, who clearly wanted her nowhere near it—and
gently tried the knob, oblivious to anything else.

That left Lucia. "I can try."

"But not out here! Can't you just pick him up or
something?"

Sklayne growled. All deep in his throat, with a multi-
level reverberation that just shouldn't have been there
at all. His glossy green eyes stared blankly at nothing.
Lucia took a tentative step forward.

Sklayne went, *"Mowmowmowwai!,"* sprang straight
into the air—*poof!*—and exploded into a startling cloud
of sparkling vagueness. Lucia gave up a girly shriek;
Quinn let out a startled oath.

Instantly, Sklayne re-formed right where he had
been. Just as he had been. Frozen in the hot sun, stock
still on the stark baking ground.

Lucia said, "*You* pick him up."

Quinn took a deep breath. A very deep breath. "The cat got us here," he said. "That's what we needed, right? Leave him, then."

"But what if—" No, she wouldn't finish that. She wouldn't think about the way this baffling not-cat had a direct connection to Trevarr . . . maybe, even, she thought, to Garrie. That maybe this wasn't about what was happening *here* at all. "Okay," she said, pretending her voice wasn't wobbly. "Let's get through that door."

"It's locked," Caryn said, staring warily at Sklayne.

Quinn glanced over to the dirty window—but with plywood behind it, they weren't going to smash their way in, either.

The entry door had a small window . . . Garrie could have made it. Or she could have picked the lock. Or scanned the place for resident energies, or—

"Splitting up," Quinn said. "Always such a damned bad idea." He spared Lucia the briefest of glances. "I know, I know. We didn't have any choice." His voice might even have broken a little on those last few words, but had steadied when he spoke again. "Who ever said we were prepared for this sort of thing? We work *for* people, not against them. I spout facts, that's all!"

Lucia heard her own voice from far away. "I bet it's a hundred degrees in the shade. How hot does this place get, anyway?"

Quinn didn't even pause. "Sedona has a generally mild climate. Record high is a couple of hundred and ten days—most recently in 2003. Goes over a hundred about twenty days a year and—God, Lu, you got me going, didn't you?"

Lucia just smiled thinly. "Better now?"

"Let's just do this."

Caryn said, "But the door—"

Quinn gave her a look. "If there was someone lurking here, he'd have been out to check on your door noise by now. So stealth mode is off."

"You're going to bash your way in?"

"I'm damned sure getting in one way or another." Quinn stalked to the car, flipping up the back hatch. "I *know* Robin got herself into this. I know if she'd let us work this our way, if she hadn't kept things from us, it never would have gone this far. But those were *mistakes*. She doesn't deserve to die for them."

"Mowmowmow," Sklayne said softly, a piteous thing—and as Quinn reemerged with a tire iron, he sprang abruptly to his feet, all bristling whiskers and stiff tail and mysterious thumb-claws. He glared narrow-eyed at the door.

Caryn's eyes widened, and Lucia told her, "Maybe you should—"

Too late.

Sklayne burst into a blur of speed, and before Quinn could do more than jerk out a startled exclamation and Lucia could do more than throw her hands out in protest and cry, *"¡Aiee!,"* he slammed into the door, leaping straight for the knob and lock assembly.

And quite impossibly, passing through it.

"Oh!" Caryn said, at the exact instant a faint flash came from the lock, an electric zing of energy. A sharp brittle *crack* of metal and dust poofed out around the edges of the door, out the keyhole.

After a long moment in which no one seemed to breathe, the door canted slightly open.

Quinn recovered first, hefting the tire iron. "I'll just bring this along."

Lucia eyed it with trepidation. "I'm beginning to get wistful for a good old emoting ghost. Maybe two."

"No, you're not," Quinn said, and headed inside.

Sullen heat met them at the door. No swamp cooler here. No such thing as air-conditioning. It had to be well over a hundred, and there was an awful lot of lady-like *glow* trickling down Lucia's back and between her breasts. Caryn's face quickly took on a bright shade of pink, and fair-haired Quinn flushed ruddy.

How long had Robin been in this?

Sklayne met them with impatience; the dusty floor showed evidence of his wandering, cat prints everywhere. Gear lay strewn around in more or less functional piles—camping gear and river gear, sleeping pads and life vests and one box of mass-produced quartz crystals. Old pallets, coiled rope, a tumble of water bottles strung together . . . all well used. Dead flies littered the floor. A few black widow husks lingered by the baseboards.

"Active widow web," Quinn said, pointing at the crevice where a kayak leaned up against the plywood.

Sklayne went, "Mrrp!" and burped politely.

"Maybe not," Lucia murmured.

"In here?" Caryn asked, and *ah, chueca* if she wasn't, finally, actually hanging back a little as she stood by a closed door—barely noticeable in the clutter at that. "Look at the floor," Caryn said, and they did. And they found no tracks, because there was no dust.

"If she's in there, she might not be alone." Quinn frowned at the door, hefting that tire iron again. "If it opens, I'm going in fast."

The door opened.

Quinn charged, face grim and flushed, impromptu weapon raised—but not for long. "Lu!" he said. "The water!"

And leave? "Get it," she snapped at Caryn, and rushed into the room—only to stop short. "Oh, poor *petirrojo*!"

Robin sat in this stifling little room with no ventilation and no water and no escape, tied limply to a chair . . . her hair sticking to her face and her skin gone pale and— Lucia put the back of her hand to that round cheek— clammy. Quinn tore at her bindings in frustration until

Lucia dug deeply into her tote and came up with her road kit and extracted the clippers. "Try this," she said, and while she was in there, found a teeny bottle of water from the airplane and quickly unscrewed the lid, dribbling just a bit of it into Robin's mouth—a fat lip there, a smear of blood there—and quickly lifted Robin's hair to splash the rest of it along her neck, not wasting a drop.

"Robin," Quinn said, a voice Lucia had never heard before as Robin stirred. "C'mon, honey. We're getting you out of here."

"The car A/C," Lucia said, carelessly tossing the empty bottle into a cardboard carton—and realizing only then that it was a heavily depleted wholesale display box for textured condoms of all colors. "*Ay Dios*," she muttered. "This room—"

And then she moved, quite suddenly, to divert Quinn's attention from that box. Because she didn't even want to think about the implications.

But Quinn saw. He saw it all. Lucia knew it by his suddenly stiff body, and by the way he tackled the cable tie bindings with renewed vigor.

And Caryn saw—standing in the doorway, her jaw dropped—taking in Robin's disheveled state, the shirt with its tiny floral print torn at the neckline and stretched out along the belly, bruises on her arms. Caryn fumbled the water and she said, "I—"

"Shut up," Quinn said savagely, tearing away the cable ties. When he looked at Lucia, his gaze was pleading. "We don't *know*."

"But we'll find out," Lucia said, numb for the moment, "and we'll take care of it. Come, *petirrojo*—wake now." She took the water from Caryn, dribbled out a few more precious drops and smeared them over Robin's forehead. "We should get her to the car, Quinnie."

Quinn didn't seem to hear her. His hands hovered over Robin's limp shoulders as though afraid to touch her, then settled gently. "We have to reach her," he said. "Whatever she's been through—" He stopped on that, and his jaw tightened hard enough so Lucia expected to hear it crack. "She needs to know it's safe now."

"*Reach* her?" As she sometimes reached out to raging ghosts, soothing them as best she could? "I don't do *people,* Quinnie."

"*None of us do people!*" he snapped. "None of us! But here we are!"

"I—" Caryn said.

Lucia and Quinn whirled on her in tandem, voices a chorus. "No!"

And Lucia said tightly, "You don't do people, *chueca.* You do *to* them."

Caryn gasped. "That—that's a horrible thing to say—"

But no one paid her much mind. Not even Sklayne, who had done a circuit of the exterior storage area and now appeared in the doorway, emitting a noise of extreme disapproval, ears twitching—distraction so evident it was a wonder he still stood upright.

"Lu?" Quinn said, gone pleading.

She shook her head. But she crouched to put her hand on Robin's knee. "*Petirrojo,*" she said softly, and bent her head, listening. Sifting through the emotional driftwood of other people's lives—former lives, always clinging to her, if ever so faintly—and hunting the unfamiliar. The sharper, poignant touch of live imprints, more deeply buried than those lingering breezes of surprise and sadness and anger so commonly marking ethereal presence.

Guilt and terror—

She gasped, and it was gone. She turned to Quinn, trying to sound more confident than she felt—here, with *glow* now trickling freely along parts of her body that had never thought to sweat before at all. "I really think . . . the car . . ."

He nodded, bending down to lift Robin's arm—but Robin thrashed; she jerked. She whimpered, and her eyes fluttered open briefly—and even if Lucia hadn't been able to feel her terror, she would have seen it. Quinn froze; the look he sent Lucia was stricken.

"I'll try again," she said. She blotted her cheek against her sleeve and returned to Robin. "Here," she said. "It's Lucia, yes? Are you listening?" And rather than reaching out, she *sent*. It rarely worked with spirits; she had nothing of Garrie's true control. But every now and then . . . "Are you listening?" she repeated out loud. "You're safe now. Let us take you to the nice cool car."

GUILT and TERROR—

Lucia wrenched herself away. "Ah, *caray!*" She struggled to separate her feelings from those that had assaulted her. "She's strong, your Robin."

"Mow," said Sklayne. He brushed up against Lucia's leg, sitting there; his tail wrapped around her ankle.

It had rather more grip than any cat tail should ever have. And it tingled.

"Hey," Caryn said, wary, as if the tingle wasn't clue enough. "What's that about?"

"Mer-*ow*." Impatience in narrowed eyes, canted back ears. He snagged Robin's jeans with his claws—yes, definitely a thumb on that paw, definitely his face grown a little longer, a little narrower, his ears a little bigger and tufted to boot. But then he shook off, a delicately precise movement of head and shoulder, and he looked just himself again.

"Let's just *go*," Caryn said, nerve failing.

"Just watch the door," Lucia told her. So she didn't want to be here; she'd earned every moment of penance and more. "Quinn," she said. "Sklayne helped Garrie in San Jose. I wasn't there . . . I never understood exactly how . . . but . . . ?"

"You're not Garrie," Quinn said, not unkindly, and stepped forward to take up Robin.

Sklayne swatted him. Shouldn't have been able to reach him without moving, and yet somehow did. He latched on to Lucia again, and he *tickled*.

"All right, yes," she said, not quite believing herself. "I'm not Garrie. But we'll try."

She returned to Robin, hunting those human undertones of feeling—finding the fear rippling along her scalp, the guilt leaden in her stomach. Feeling it deeply, clearly. Robin stirred, an uneasy sound in her throat. Lucia pretended Robin was a ghost, and she siphoned away what she could of the terror and shed it, flicking it away; she sent soothing comfort. Sklayne panted beside her, sparks roiling off his dark-ticked red coat. Working hard.

"Now talk to her," she murmured to Quinn, knowing Quinn would never interrupt the work by speaking directly back to her. "I think she'll hear you."

What Quinn said, she didn't hear—didn't try to hear. What Sklayne did through her, she couldn't feel—didn't try to feel. But within moments the fear soothed over into ripples.

"Robin," Quinn said, an urgency coming into his voice. "Wake up, sweetheart. We have to get you out of here. You're okay now."

Far from it. But if they could get her out and get her cool and get her to help . . .

"The cat!" Caryn said, even as Robin croaked something about *water* and Quinn fumbled to get it for her. "What happened to the cat?"

No more impatience, no more haughty stance. Just a limp little Abyssinian puddled beside her feet. "Aiee!" she said. "No, no, no!" She picked him up, daring that which she wouldn't have considered had those bright green eyes been aimed her way.

Instead the green showed through barely slitted lids,

third eyelids drawn up halfway. His head lolled; his tail hung limp. "Oh, this can't be good."

"Put him down by an outlet," Quinn said shortly, words that didn't match his gentle manner with Robin. "Or haven't you noticed the way things lose power when he's around?"

Lucia pet the slick, tiny-short hairs between Sklayne's eyes, there where they came together in the faintest cowlick up the center. "Please be okay," she whispered to him. "I didn't mean to hurt you. I didn't know."

Working blind, that's what she'd been. Big clumsy human, no true idea what she'd even been doing . . . just what she wanted to accomplish.

"Lu," Quinn said, his voice sharp. "Look!" He held the water bottle for Robin, restricting her attempt to down it in a gulp. "Give us another minute and we're outta here—"

"Huh," said a voice that could have belonged to Beavis or Butthead or both, still standing outside the door where only Caryn could see him. "Huh. I don't think so. Did you *really* think we left this place completely unwatched?"

"Caryn!" Lucia snapped, instinctively holding Sklayne close. Caryn, standing by the door. Caryn, watching for them. Caryn, all caught up in what was happening and not the least caught up in what she'd agreed to do.

And she knew it. Her mouth turned hard; her shoulders straightened. "It's okay," she said. "I can fix this."

"No!" Quinn shouted.

"Aiee! No!" Lucia cried.

"Stop her," Robin said, alarmed voice a rasp.

But no. Of course it was too late.

17

Know your strengths; accept your weaknesses.
—Rhonda Rose

I *so* don't do people . . .
—Lisa McGarrity

Garrie crumpled beside the rock with her head roaring and shocked lungs rattling for air. And if deep in the back of her thoughts she felt a fizzling spark of Sklayne's aghast dismay, it made no impact next to the hard stone and the foot that followed, slamming into her side to lift her from the ground.

She retched, grabbing at dirt, and yet another roar filled her mind, filling her body with dull glowing cold and fire.

Trevarr. Aware of her peril; flinging himself with fury at the lerket so he could reach her—

The lackey jerked her up by the shirt, ripping at it—or trying to. That otherworldly material held fast and he moved to her belt, yanking it with such a look in his eye—

Garrie flailed at him—so aware of Trevarr fighting to break away, his sword biting deeply into the monstrous lerket but his position gone defensive—and never had she felt so small, so ineffective, so ninety pounds sopping wet . . . so vulnerable.

Why? Why *this*? Why *now*?

Because it's what Huntingdon does best. Leeching from a thing pure and joyful, turning it foul in the process. Twisting power from what should be pleasure, and control from what should be love.

She'd be damned if she'd have anything to do with it.

She kicked, she squirmed, she flipped herself to her belly and scrabbled away, one hand seeking, seeking, *seeking* at her thigh pocket. The lackey jerked her back with a grunt, flipped her over, and yanked on her pants as if he could get the low-rise cargos off without unsnapping them at all.

Panic rose. The gust of ash filled her senses; a dark shadow washed through her mind. Huntington nodded at the lackey, radiating utter confidence—in himself, in the lerket, in Trevarr's battered state and his failure.

Trevarr broke away from the lerket and its glowing ichorous blood of sparks and lava, one useless hand jammed into his belt, the sword whipping around to find its new target. His eyes burned hard bright metal, his neck dappled with rising tattoos, and his face turned grimly, darkly determined—Garrie's mind flushed full of beating wings and thunderous noise, her body filled with rushing, foreign power. Trevarr stalked for them, the sword in a low guard and ready with heft and swing.

The lackey glanced behind at that flash of sword, an instant of distraction. And Garrie's hand finally found that thigh pocket, ripping away the buttoned flap; fingers closed around the cool black horn handle and came free with a slice of sound that cut through the roar and the panic both.

The preternaturally sharp blade sank deeply into the lackey's calf, in and out so smoothly she didn't quite believe it had gone in at all. So cleanly that he didn't even seem to know why his leg buckled until he found the gushing blood. Rage distorted his face into thicknecked ugly as Garrie scrabbled back, clutching a knife handle gone slippery.

Huntington's face darkened, distorted in fury. He gave the lerket a quick glower, and Garrie braced for her own surging snap of response—out-of-control energies that had seemed so very manageable only hours earlier, when Trevarr had shown her how to coax them into submission.

She almost missed the lerket's startled, prodded reaction—a creature bleeding ethereal ichor and ready for retreat but too mindlessly frantic to withstand Huntington's sharply sent stimulus. Its stubby trunk stood straight out; its tentacles stood on end, stiff and bristly and full of sparks.

Trevarr had no warning when it charged.

Garrie screamed—pure wordless horror as the look on Huntington's face told her, the sparks among the tentacles told her, the lerket's very posture told her *no, no, no* and yet *too late.*

It slammed into Trevarr from behind, wrapping tentacles around his leg with the sickening slap of flesh.

Trevarr stiffened. He lost Lukkas as his fingers splayed open in shock; a strangled noise made its way from between clenched teeth. His eyes rolled back in his head and he thumped to the ground, landing hard.

Garrie sobbed on fear; she found her fingers already drying to sticky on the knife. She bolted past her own still whimpering bat victim, found Trevarr's jaw clenched and his nostrils flared with agony, breath coming panting-fast through involuntarily gritted teeth, the lerket latched on tight.

Huntington's words came mocking. "No one's lasted more than three minutes so far."

What? "No!" she said, an animal snarl of incoherence. Not just like that. Not *just like that!*

But even so the scent of wood smoke eased; the clapping rush of wings faded from her mind.

Rage suffused her. She snatched up the knife and launched herself at the lerket, stabbing it to the hilt. It grunted faintly and ichor surged out, burning her hand. She snatched it away and saw she'd had no effect at all—that the tentacles still pulsed slightly where they wrapped around Trevarr's knee and thigh, sparking gently each time.

She stared at the gory knife for only a moment, then she planted one foot and lifted the other and kicked the lerket in the face as hard as she could. Once, twice— over and over, aiming for the bulbous eyes—*connecting*—aiming for the snout. "Let—him—*go!*" Making it startle, making it flinch. "Let—him—*go!*"

"Got you, little bitch!" A hand grabbed her wrist, numbing it; the knife stayed in her grip only because of the sticky gore. The other hand wrapped cruelly around her ribs, dragging her away—and then holding her back, when she suddenly realized that the lackey with the battered balls had found his feet, and now she faced them both; that Busted Balls held her in a tight grip and the man she'd stabbed was still coming for her; that he still intended to have her.

"Yes," Huntington said, excitement raising his tone. "There's no telling what I can get from this! Take her, you fool—right there, where he can see—"

Dimming eyes and fading scent and receding energies—

"Do it quickly, before he dies!"

"He won't die!" Garrie spat at him. "Oh, you're going to be so very sorry when *he doesn't die!*"

But this time she couldn't escape—not when the limping, bleeding lackey grabbed her belt and jerked it free, or when he grabbed her pants and ripped them open. And it didn't matter how much she twisted, she couldn't evade the brutal crush of his mouth. Not that he lingered—not when she tried so hard to bite his lips off; he drew back to give her a little shake by his cruel hold on her jaw, only smiling when Trevarr spat out foreign threats between horrifyingly harsh breaths.

Huntington cried out in triumph; the earth groaned around them, the red rock bluff cracking a gunshot report of stressed rock. And when the lackey reached down to fumble with his own zipper, he kept his face right there in hers, sneering at her, showing her his power—such deliberate cruelty that no ghost, no matter how dangerous or difficult, had ever shown her.

I so don't do people . . .

But she stared right back. She saw his anticipation and she met his power and she narrowed her eyes. Because she was still what she was, and she still *knew* what she was. She gathered every breeze that she could, and she sent it spearing at the lerket.

He didn't get it at first.

Not when the lerket spasmed, not when it gave its eager little honk. Not even quite when the tentacles snapped audibly away from Trevarr's leg, blindly seeking.

Garrie sent another spear of energy at it, and it made up its mind.

It charged.

Then the lackey realized it had released Trevarr. *Then* the lackey realized it was coming for Garrie.

And only then did he realize he was in the way.

"Robin!" Quinn cradled Robin's blotchy pale face between his hands. "You're okay," he said, quite seriously. "We'll get you out of here."

She reached up to pull him closer. Her ruined sleeves fell back from her wrists, revealing bloody welts and abrasions from the cable ties and he held her, so carefully.

"Yeah, yeah, yeah," said the man who pushed into the doorway, shoving Caryn back so hard she stumbled. A big man, hirsute and hefty. "You," he said, looking at Robin. "You ready for the real thing now?"

She frowned. "I don't . . . what?"

Lucia's eyes widened; she took a cautious ethereal glance and her eyebrows shot up. Fatigue and concern and yes, the guilt—the awareness that she'd created a situation in which they'd all become vulnerable and compromised. But the terror, gone. Lingering whispers of horrified anticipation, gone.

She glanced at Quinn, gave the merest shake of her head in response to his puzzled, silent query. *No. She doesn't remember.* Whatever had happened that morning—preliminaries?—Robin didn't have a clue.

She looked down at the limp cat in her arms. "What have you done, *gatito*?" she asked him, a mere murmur. "At what price?"

The man said, "I hear you're all the real deal. You may think that's an advantage, but then, you haven't been on Huntington's turf long enough to know, have you?" His nasty grin accompanied a surge of . . .

Ewww.

Nausea swept through Lucia. "Quinnie," she said, as Robin gasped, already vulnerable and used; Caryn, whatever she'd had in mind, now only reeled against the wall.

"Yeah," Quinn said, utterly unaffected if plenty grim. He took out his cell phone, took a photo of the man, and returned the phone to his pocket. "Let's go."

"Always gotta be one," the man grumbled. He opened his arms, made a beckoning motion—a challenge, and an extra leer at Robin in case it just wasn't clear enough. "Come on, then."

Slowly, Quinn stood; he retrieved the tire iron on the way up and the set of his jaw made all things clear—just how badly he wanted this man. Lucia held limp Sklayne a little more closely, her own expression just as eloquent. *We have to* go. *Just because you can take this guy doesn't mean you should.*

Quinn took a deep breath, his hands tightening on the tire iron—knuckles going white, and then easing again. He put himself between Lucia and Robin. "Get her to the car, Lu. He won't bother you."

Right. As simple as all that.

"*Petirrojo,*" she murmured to Robin, taking her arm—taking a whole lot more of her weight than she'd intended as Robin stood on shaky legs. Her tote slipped; she shifted Sklayne into the cradle of one arm and planted her feet. "*Walk* now, yes?" She glared at Caryn. "Some help?"

But Caryn watched the hefty man, to all appearances frozen in the wash of his nasty energies. There, along the wall beside the door, she had a clear shot at escape—but she made no move to take it, or to help Lucia. Nor did she respond to the trickle of brand-new emotion in the room—pure anger, pure resentment. Purely spiritual. *Ghosts.*

Lucia ducked down beside Robin on her own. "Arm over my shoulder, there you are—" She snagged onto the sturdy jean belt loops, jostled Sklayne back into place, and went for it. Pretending they might even make it.

But the moment they passed directly behind Quinn, the hefty man charged them with a bellow and clear intent—to mow them all down with brute force. Quinn hit a football blocking stance, the tire iron before him as Lucia tried to spurt away with Robin . . .

It might even have worked, had not Quinn given an inexplicable shout, stiffened, and jerked back, slamming Lucia down and Robin with her. Lucia curled around to protect Sklayne, trying to crawl away—but not with all those people on her legs.

The man heaved himself up, flung the tire iron away, and hit Quinn again with the boxy device suddenly evident in his hand, and only as Quinn convulsed again did Lucia understand. *Aiee, caray! Stun gun!* What *was* it with this town?

She popped free, shoving Sklayne into the corner and grabbing Robin's shoulders—"Come, come!"—and hardly pausing to glare at Caryn. "Help *now, chueca!*"

"I can fix this," Caryn said, a delayed echo of her earlier words.

Lucia's hackles rose; she hesitated in her fumbling attempts to tug Robin free even as the man hit Quinn *again*. Lucia's temper, a mild thing, flared hot—

And then stuttered and abruptly died, as an unfamiliar tug of feeling twitched into her. *Caryn.* "What are you doing?" she asked, but Caryn didn't answer and the tug only intensified. "*¡Chueca!* What are you *doing*?"

The man laughed. "You stupid crystal-loving woo-woo hounds," he said, and added mockingly, "Can't we all just get along?" Meaty jowls quivered as he shook his head. "As a matter of fact, *no*. But it is *so* kind of you to feed me."

Feed him . . . "*¡Chueca!* Caryn! *No!* Stop!" Lucia left Robin, left Quinn—poor Quinn, a jerking, spastic and uncoordinated heap of human—and scrambled for Caryn, grabbing her shoulders, shaking her. Shaking her *hard*. "Don't you ever *think*? You can't *fix* him! You can only make him—"

"Stronger," the man said, so smugly. "Strong enough to take you all. Goody little crystal gazers with no sense of the real power this world holds."

"I know exactly what power this world holds," Lucia said, pulling herself up to full princess posture—never mind the dirt or the sweat or the disarray. "You will *never* see the things I have seen, you arrogant, despicable, donkey-balled *troll*."

Troll. Maybe not the smartest thing to say.

"Fine," he snarled. "Die, then. But suffer a whole lot first."

Robin cried out first, twisting away from him, still trapped beneath Quinn. He managed to do little more than shove a limp hand along the floor in her direction, fingers twitching. The nausea hit Lucia; her strength drained away and she stumbled back against the wall.

Caryn gasped and Lucia said through her teeth, "You see? You *see*?"

And then the man said, "Oh-ho. Oh-*ho*. What have we here?" and he looked at Sklayne.

"Leave him alo—" Lucia snapped at him, or tried to. It turned into a gag, and suddenly her senses dipped and rolled and she felt herself sliding into a faint—and just as suddenly she understood. He was throwing ugly energies at them, prodding out a reaction . . . scooping that up for himself. Just what Garrie had described from the arch, where Huntington's group had corrupted a feedback loop of emotion and pleasure to harness energy and grown it to the point where they could slowly suck away the very life of the land.

Just as this man would do to them.

She fumbled in her tote. Surely her little pepper spray was in here. Surely her nail file was within reach, or her PDA stylus, or *something* with which she could gouge his eyes out. Surely—

"What the fuck?" the man said, and if the assault faded with his words, it didn't give Lucia any clues. She looked up, hand in her tote . . . guilt on her face. *I'm not looking for something to gouge your eyes out, really I'm not—*

He stood braced in the middle of the room, stout and hearty and despicable, head cocked—completely baffled. "What *the* . . ."

She suddenly understood, sensing the swoop of feeling, the roar of anger . . . the things that had been simmering and building and homing in and now turned to resentment released, one last gathering of *nothing to lose* spirits. Those who had swirled down around her in the shop in town, plucking and snatching. Those who had covered the arch with ghost poop effluvia. Those who had been disturbed and distressed and who knew more than anyone how very much *wrong* Huntington's people had done. And she answered the man with some satis-faction: "Ghosts."

Short-lived satisfaction.

Oh, *angry* ghosts.

And Lucia also knew better than anyone just how much damage a pack of berserker ghosts could do. A living body ran on energy . . . a dead body ran on en-ergy. The two, forced together . . .

Didn't mix well.

"Dumb-ass things don't know when to stay dead," the man grunted. But he frowned as Lucia's hair stirred and Caryn slapped a hand to her cheek and Quinn, with a great groan, rolled over, tried to get up, and fell on his face.

"Oh, protect yourself," Lucia said to Caryn. "Quiet yourself. They are so very, very—"

Angry. It stormed against her; it raised the hair on her arms. It snaked thin threads of panic through her mind and sent her heart rocketing, shallow and insubstantial in her chest. And the man in the middle of the room lost his cocky sneer, slapping at his body as if mice ran around under his clothes. Caryn gasped, shrinking down the wall to her heels, covering first her head and then her shoulders and then any part of her she could reach, try-ing to protect every inch from a stinging sandstorm of ethereal energy.

No hysteria. *No.* For Lucia was the one who knew what was going on. She. Lucia. *Reckoner.* And her hand was still in her tote, and in her tote she also kept the secret herbs and spices they used in ghost containment bags. And if the secret recipe kept the ghosts *in,* then surely . . .

Suddenly she was fumbling, again digging franti-cally through the tote, strewing the contents around on the floor until she found the storage bag and then fum-bling with that until she abruptly got it open, spilling precious contents. Not enough here, not really. She'd have to be careful, so hard to do with her hands shaking this hard and her mind and body reeling—

She dipped long fingers into the bag, removed a pinch . . . scattered it over herself and then didn't wait to see if it would work before moving on to Quinn and Robin—lather, rinse, repeat—and then, finally, Caryn.

And by then she knew.

Not perfect, no. But she could think. She could breathe.

She could see a man self-destructing before her eyes—slapping at himself, caught in an immense feedback loop of his own making. Stealing from the ghosts and throwing cruel energy at them, not realizing he only *fed* them, then stole from them, then fed them— each round of energy growing even more putrid. She blinked—hard. She reached for Sklayne without thinking about it, hunting comfort just in the touch. Was the man getting *bigger*? Expanding? Wavering around the edges? Hastily, she scattered more secret recipe, pungent herbs and spices settling in her hair and over Robin's skin, Quinn's lips . . . Sklayne's fur.

He writhed from it; she muttered a curse and brushed it away. "Sorry, sorry—" but never truly took her eyes from the man in the middle of his own maelstrom, the energies pulsing around him so quickly, so strongly, she could all but see it with her plain old Lucia vision. She swallowed hard on the sick response from her tender stomach and she said, "*Chueca* . . . when they finish with him . . ."

They're going to come for us.

The man gargled. He'd stopped trying to fight—he was trying to scream. It came out a spew of black goo— caught in his beard, splatting down his chest—bubbling up endlessly from inside. No longer enlarged at all, but shrinking down on himself, everything that had been contained within him . . .

Pounded into puree.

"*Caryn*," Lucia said suddenly, low and urgent and

holding fast under Caryn's huge-eyed response, her astonished hurt. "*You* did this. And the secret recipe isn't going to hold against them, do you understand? So you *do* something about it!"

"But—"

"Yes!" Lucia said. "For once! You broke it, you fix it!"

"I don't—" Caryn started, flinching at a particularly loud gargle as the man slowly went to his knees, goo splashing against the floor— "I don't *do ghosts!*"

"No? Well, I *don't do people* but I had to, didn't I? Because of you!" She steeled herself—against pity, against the empathetic understanding that came so naturally, whether she wanted it to or not. "We're *here,* aren't we, because of you? Do you think I care if it frightens you to try? *Do it anyway!* You *cleanse them* like you tried to do to Trevarr and you *do it now!*"

Or we will all die, and then the ghosts will be loose in this world.

18

Many things *should* be. Few things *are.*
—Rhonda Rose

If this was a bad movie, that would have worked!
—Lisa McGarrity

Light-speed lerket. Charging.

Charging straight for Garrie and ready to *eat her brains.*

Garrie screamed. *Lisa McGarrity, Girlie Reckoner.* But the lerket came on with the inexorable force of a charging bull, and it leaped with unexpected agility—

snout raised, tentacles stiffened, mouth open and hidden pincers extruding. Blinded and yet perfectly oriented, coming *ahhhhh straight for my face—!*

She didn't need to duck. The man clutching her from behind ducked and took her with him, and the lerket latched onto the back of her attacker's neck and bit down with an audible, gristly crunch.

The man didn't even scream. He just went down.

And the other man, startled beyond thinking, gave her just enough freedom to take the sticky hand holding her freakishly sharp knife and jam it into his torso up to the hilt. Shock loosened his grip further; she tore away, bolting from carnage still in process to haul her pants back together and stumble for Trevarr.

A glance showed Huntington lost in rapture, the red rock bluff spitting dust and pebbles as the big boulder in the cleansing circle cracked nearly in two, and Feather still crumpled to the ground and looking suddenly older.

Trevarr lay flat—twisted face down, one hand tucked into his belt, the other clawing hard dirt—taking agony out on whatever he could reach, his body working to suck in and spit out those harsh breaths.

"The Gatherer," she said as she reached him, pretending her voice didn't quiver and her mouth didn't quiver and emotion didn't strangle her. She reached for him, patting down his pockets. "We have to try again!"

Words seemed beyond him; he caught her gaze with eyes gone to dull gray stone, dust and blood smeared on his face—and then they flickered hard and desperate, and Garrie knew better than to stay in his way. She spun aside on one knee as he levered up—and by the time she realized he'd slipped a knife from the brace harness, flipped it into a good grip, and flung it into a smooth release, he'd fallen, wrenching around to his back, gulping for air.

She whirled, throwing herself in front of him—and

found Huntington staggering away, bat in hand and not the least cowed. Not even with a knife jutting out of his thigh and the ground cracking open behind him. "It doesn't matter," he said, but his voice didn't sound sane and his face didn't look it. "I have what I wanted—what I've earned!"

"Not yet you don't," Garrie muttered. Seriously. *Evil Overlord.* She set the knife aside and returned to Trevarr, hoping beyond hope that she could find the Gatherer without actually delving into his infinite duster pockets. She found something bulky, pulled at the coat to reach it—froze when he cried a short, raw sound.

Pincers. Those horrible, horrible pincers, and now his leg lay in a wash of black-red blood against gritty ground. "You aren't even going to tell me that thing is venomous," she said, warning in her voice. From up the bluff, something howled—loud and anguished, a woman's voice; stone rained down.

Brief, dark humor showed on his face, the bloody corners of a mouth she'd been kissing just that morning, words impossible beyond straining breath.

She took it for the answer it was. *"Shit,"* she said, with feeling. One hand resting lightly on his stomach and the other tugging—more carefully—at the coat, she guided his hand into the pocket, stiffening as her hand hit a cool wash of air and unconfined freedom. He opened his hand wide; her fingers twitched, showered by spark and tingle.

And the Gatherer *came to him.* Hit his hand solidly, nestling there. And if it was Garrie who drew their hands out again, it was Trevarr who held this one last chance. "Now?" she asked him. *"Now* can we kill this thing?"

She felt rather than heard his short laugh—affirmation. But when she reclaimed the freakishly sharp knife and moved to keep an eye on Huntington, he caught her eye. "Both of us," he said, face tight with effort, breathing still shallow and harsh. "It is too—*Klysar's farking blood!*" His hand clamped down on the Gatherer until Garrie thought metal would buckle in his grip; his body arched beside hers. But he somehow found his voice again. "It is too . . . changed. We both do this."

Garrie gave the lerket a startled look—found it done with its first victim and moving more slowly to the second. Either getting full, or . . . wanting something tastier. *Like us.*

That second man wouldn't last long . . . his shirt already utterly soaked with blood, his body slumped up against the constantly flaking rock and not reacting to the rain of shards building up around him like sand.

Trevarr flipped the device onto his stomach—bright hard metal set with pulsing sections of pure color, too intense to be of this world or even to be stone at all, delineated by thin lines of metal into exotic mosaics. A snick, a rasp of smooth metal . . . the device opened. Half weapon, half tool, and yet another part art, all fitting into the curve of his hand.

The lerket lifted its head, tentacles whirling briskly. Healing. No longer leaking ethereal matter, unconcerned by its battered face or blindness. It didn't even glance at Huntington, so lost in his power rapture. Not, she thought suddenly, recognizing the man as something separate or different from itself.

But Garrie and Trevarr, it recognized.

"Trevarr," she said uneasily. He fumbled the Gatherer and she slipped in behind him, propping him up. With that contact the whole of her world suddenly turned to the brush of leather between them, the emphatic effort of his breathing against her, the shudder of his frame . . . her whole body clenched in empathy.

Huntington's interference pressed in on her . . . made things suddenly sway and dip. *Not much time left.*

Not for Trevarr; not for this wondrous place of red rocks and green conifers and wind-carved sandstone. The fallen rock cracked sharply, spitting off shrapnel— Garrie jerked as it peppered her arm. *No time at all.*

She stretched around him, put her hand over his, and over the Gatherer. *"Trevarr."*

Snuffling lerket, tentacles questing the air . . . searching quiescent breezes.

"Trevarr!"

But his struggle had gone purely just to . . .

Living. Breathing. Twisting in the grip of poison.

She closed her eyes against the sick touch of Huntington's breezes crawling over her skin, the slam and batter of these last moments against her focus while the red-hot poker of her forehead, split and still trickling blood, finished the job. Rock split in a shuddering land; dirt rained down upon them.

She couldn't handle the lerket on her own.

We both do this. That's what he'd said. Because maybe there was now enough of this world infused into the gluttonous creature that Garrie could affect it, if there was even enough of Sedona left for her to draw on . . .

But she couldn't trigger the Gatherer by herself. Couldn't force its shift from hard copy to ethereal.

And Trevarr jerked slightly against her, staring out with glassy, unfocused eyes—jaw working, lips forming words she couldn't hear and weren't English anyway. And then he sighed, and in that moment she thought how very cold he'd gone . . . and how very wrong that was. Not Trevarr, living furnace. Not *cold.*

No, no, no. "No!" She grabbed his shoulders and shook him, that broken arm notwithstanding. The bluffs howled, the sound of wind in the eaves and a banshee in the distance. *"No!* I am *not* done kissing you yet, you fool!" Surely she had something left of herself, enough to make that spark of a difference—carefully not so much that the lerket would leap for it in its already sated state. *Surely.*

And oh, surely she wasn't about to lose the very thing that had taught her anew how to be who and what she was . . . who had *become* who and what she was.

Surely.

"Damned farking right," she said, and kissed him. Bloodied lips, tasting of bitter venom and dull pain. She deliberately roused that from which she'd been running, and sent it into him. Whatever it was, whatever part of him it had come from . . . it had become enough a part of her, these past days, so she could offer it in return. Her dragon.

Just . . . enough.

Should have been.

That kiss alone . . . *should have been.*

Wasn't.

Venom in that bite. Dark, bitter venom, and his eyes rolled back.

"That's not fair!" she cried, despair raw in her voice. "If this was a bad movie, that would have worked!"

A little help here, Rhonda Rose.

Oh, I lie. A lot of help.

"Excuse me," Feather said, her tone arch and offended and as matter-of-fact as if she'd been there all along. "You there," she said. "*Ugly thing.* You are *in my cleansing circle.*"

Garrie lifted her head, blinking through watery vision. Feather as ghost. Perfectly realized, perfectly cohesive—but not Feather as she'd been moments earlier, crumpled to the ground. Feather as she'd been ten years ago, maybe fifteen—hair glossy and complexion fresh, slender rather than spare, just a hint of transparency around her edges. She held the small Yorkie—and though it fit neatly into the crook of her arm as before, it now sported

large fangs and projected a fierce gold and orange aura
in the direction of the lerket.

Oh, be careful.

The lerket stopped its hunt, the tentacles whirling
fiercely, blindly shifting between Garrie and Feather . . .
settling on Feather. Huntington cursed—a faint thing,
as if he was too caught up in his own manipulated feedback to interfere. Feather said calmly, "Don't waste it,
girl."

Garrie didn't.

No more tragic kisses; no more Ms. Nice Reckoner.
Freed to use the energies so profoundly hovering between them, she stabbed Trevarr with a spear of piercing hard cold heat—and she rammed a very solid thumb
into his ribs.

He jerked; he snarled. It came from so deep in his
chest that she felt it through her own, and if she flinched,
she didn't quail.

"Get *back here,*" she told him, and jabbed another
snarl out of him, the faded marks of feathery scales
flushing up along his neck and going dark before her
eyes, the faint scent of him rising strong once more, his
eyes opening to a bright flare. When he lifted his lips to
grin a feral challenge, he exposed teeth gone wild as
well, primary and secondary canines distinctly sharp.
The exotic angles of his face showed fierce in a way that
struck her to the core, her own atavistic recognition of
power and grace and raw strength.

"Holy farking shit." Words whispered, as she realized what she'd done—what she'd wakened in a man
too bound by venom to fight it. That which she had never
truly understood. *The other.*

And it was all she had to work with. It didn't matter
that he looked at her with the same predatory glint
he'd so recently aimed at mortal enemies. Didn't matter

that he'd probably kill her if he could get his hands on her.

Or that he was about to try.

She jabbed him again. "Get over it!" she snapped. "And use the damned Gatherer! On *that*—over there!"

But Trevarr—*the other*—wrenched himself away, and damned if he wasn't—mindlessly, stupidly—lunging for Lukkas, no thought for the Gatherer at all.

"Fark," she snarled, a perfectly human snarl at that. And then again when he sprawled awkwardly, because like it or not, that body of his wasn't in working order.

Garrie snatched up the Gatherer and threw herself at him. Right on top of him, small and insignificant and clinging, her arm stretched out for a Hail Mary pass, shoving the Gatherer back into his hand at the same time she gave the lerket a desperate, daring glance and *pushed*—what few breezes she had left in her, pinging directly off the lerket as Huntington cried raw objection, futilely slapping ill-aimed energies to redirect it.

"Here it comes!" she told Trevarr, stabbing a finger at the invigorated, fully oriented lerket. The vibrating, pulsating, voracious lerket. The *charging* lerket. "Get it, dammit, *get it*."

Or else.

"No!" Huntington cried—more of a howl, distorted by undertones of fear and sick ecstacy, his every attempt to interfere only sucking back into his own cycling energy maelstrom. "No, you can't!"

A blazing hot metal gaze seared hers, leaving her gasping. And then it found the lerket, and it lit anew.

"Get it," she whispered, not a whole lot else left in her.

And he got it. Swift clasp and shift of metal, a sudden vibration she felt up his arm and through her body . . . the lerket stumbled. It strobed, phasing from solidity to eerie phosphorescence to solidity—until it staggered to a stop a mere foot away and shook itself like a dog. Lava slime hissed off skin and clothing, droplets mixed with another spattering rain of rock shard shrapnel. The lerket made a mournful trumpet of a noise and wrenched into its ethereal form—and hung there, caught by the Gatherer but going nowhere.

Too changed. Too damaged. Too tainted.

Garrie wanted to sob with utter exhaustion. But this was her part. This was the moment she pulled out every breeze, every hint of wafting ethereal movement, every faint memory of a gust that Sedona still had to offer. The moment she proved she was what Rhonda Rose had once made her believe of herself—a reckoner, body and soul. A reckoner unparalleled.

She didn't believe it any longer. Not after this. But she'd fake it.

So she found those breezes and those gusts and those hints of movement, and she gathered them up tight, centering them in the struggling lerket ball of captive effluvia and light. A brief moment of exacting concentration . . . ethereal inhalation, focus . . .

Release.

Breezes exploded in all directions. *Dissolution.* Lerket scattered to the ethereal winds.

And silence.

It would have been nice, then, to collapse. To lie there in limp relief. To think, *hey, maybe I saved the world after all.*

But no. Not with Huntington still connected to whatever pipeline he'd tapped. Not with the canyon lands still self-destructing around her, the land crying out in pain, Feather's dog yapping furious ghostie warning, and Huntington groaning in a rapturous undertone. And especially not because even before she opened weary eyes, Trevarr dropped the Gatherer, shrugged her off,

rolled back over the top of her—*oh my God squish*—
and flipped over to trap her facedown between his
knees, his single good hand clamping down on the back
of her neck.

It would break bone, that grip.

Her face pushed against hard ground and fine gritty
soil; it mashed against her lips.

It would break bone, that grip.

The growl of him reverberated through her body,
rumbling with breath in, breath out. Predator with prey,
hovering at that final moment.

"*Atreyo*," she breathed. No real sound behind it; no
air in her lungs to make it. Not knowing if he'd hear
it . . . knowing only that she had to say it before she lost
the chance to say it at all. *Heart partner.* She closed
her eyes; she waited.

It would break bone, that grip.

Except it didn't.

That grip instead eased ever so slightly. Trevarr said,
"What?"

There was such utter confusion in his voice that
Garrie laughed, a short and very smothered sound that
might have had a sob on the end of it. "*Atreyo*," she said
again, through those tears. "Now let me up."

"You *stabbed* me," he said with a wondering air.

"With my *thumb*. And let me up *now* or I'll do it
again." Already she breathed more easily. The split on
her forehead bore ground-in dirt; her cheekbone pounded
in steady accompaniment. Her lips felt numb. So awkwardly—so carefully—he moved his weight from her.
She squirmed forward, recapturing her pants where
she'd never actually gotten them fastened again, and
flipped herself over and up to her knees to give him a
critical eye.

Battered and reeling, and not quite able to meet her
gaze. She took his face between her hands, brushed back

the silly bits of hair that had escaped the tie-back. *"Atreyo,"* she said once more, and kissed him.

And after a moment, he released his breath on a mighty shudder and wrapped that one good arm around her, and pulled her in.

19

Know your strengths; accept your weaknesses.
—Rhonda Rose

Oh so very yes!
—Lisa McGarrity

Can I not leave you even for a moment?
—Lucia Reyes

"That's quite lovely," Feather said, with an impatience that suggested maybe in fact it wasn't. "But this is my *cleansing circle,* thank you very much, and I won't have that man messing with it! Not with my circle, my hotel, or my town!"

This version of Feather definitely had new asperity.

Well, death did that to some people.

Garrie rested her cheek against Trevarr's. "Feather," she said, "I got nothin'."

"Oh!" Feather said, a complete non sequitur. "Oh, oh, *no!*"

But the outrage in her voice didn't quite match her reaction to Huntington, and it didn't seem tied into the popping dry crackle of the juniper that disintegrated on the slope above her and rained down in bits of tinder and acrid turpentine scent. And then, in the parking lot, a car approached; its engine revved. Shouting ensued, first demanding, then frantic—and then outright fear, the warning blare of a horn covering all and growing louder, louder—

The front end of the rental car bounced over landscaped grounds and sidewalk, plowed through several bushes, grounded out on high flagstone, and bore on until it filled Garrie's entire field of view as she hunched over Trevarr in a futile gesture.

The horn stopped; she risked a glance to find the front grill far too close and still bouncing with the abrupt braking action. Lucia jumped out from behind the wheel and stopped short, fists going to her hips. "Oh . . . my . . . Dios," she said. "Can I not leave you for even a *moment*?"

Not that she waited for an answer, leaving Garrie open-mouthed. She returned to the car, emerging with Sklayne in her arms. His tail hung limply; his head hung limply. Ducking a rain of rock shards, she put him next to Trevarr. "I don't know," she told him simply, and left to haul Quinn from the back—pale and uncoordinated and staggery.

"A stun gun uses high voltage and low amperage," Quinn said, with no apparent awareness of the chaos around him. "This energy causes muscles to do a lot of work really fast. The rapid cycle instantly depletes blood sugar, and there is no energy left for the muscles. A stun gun also interrupts the tiny neurological impulses that direct voluntary muscle movement. The longer the contact, the stronger the effects." He scrubbed his hands over his face.

Lucia pushed him onto the circle seating. "It was a very long contact."

Quinn said to no one in particular, "It also hurts like a bitch." And then he blinked, and looked around, and said, "What the hell happened?"

"What the hell is *happening*," Garrie said, even as the bluff gave a great earthy groan and a larger tree, high up on the hill, blew itself into splinters; they performed a group duck and cover. "The lerket is scattered, but Huntington—"

"So I see," Lucia said, brushing wood from her hair as she aimed a narrow-eyed glare at Huntington. "You?"

"Tapped out." Garrie glanced at Trevarr. That uncertainty, that vulnerability . . . now shuttered away as if it had never been, leaving only silence and a thin presence, pain stretching a tight veil over all. "Kind of broken."

"That is so very much not the right color for blood," Lucia told Trevarr.

"Stop this!" Feather demanded. "You young people! You brought this to my home, my inn . . . my circle! Now you fix it!"

Lucia's eyes widened. She seemed to see Feather's crumpled body for the first time. "Oh, no! Ooh, chicalet, she's mad!"

"*My* home," said Bobbie from up the hill. "My unborn *baby's* home! You won't harm her!"

Say what?

Lucia glanced up the hill. "The other one is back? She feels different . . . also angry, but . . . mother bear, chicalet. Tread lightly."

"It's too late for that," Feather snapped. "Now do something!"

Garrie snapped right back at her, one hand curving around Trevarr's shoulder. She knew protective, all right. "Don't you get it? I'm done! There isn't anything left here to work with!"

"It's okay," Caryn said, finally emerging from the car, a gulp in her voice as she overcame the grief that had pinned her there until now. She lent a hand to a seriously ragged-looking Robin, and . . . she looked different.

Drawn and somber and . . . more solid. "Really. It's okay. I brought help."

Oh, that couldn't be good.

Sklayne's nose tickled. The air was full of rock grit and sawdust; sick energy glittered dimly in his mind's eye.

For the moment, his mind's eye was all he had. This body . . . so fragile. So ill-suited to distasteful human energies. Disrupted and disconnected from itself, none of its pieces talking to its other pieces.

Home. He wanted home. He wanted hot sullen air and heavy black fog and spicy taste on his tongue. He wanted familiar energies and familiar enemies. He wanted how it had always been—Trevarr on the hunt and Sklayne prowling and gamboling and not quite doing as he was told but truly, just where he needed to be, when he needed to be there.

Not free, no matter what he told Trevarr. Just . . . *home.*

Unbound, he could make the journey himself. All these years of learning, all these years of journey . . . older than so many of his kind already. So many things, he knew. Things Trevarr never guessed and never needed to.

Because bound, he couldn't go even though he could. Even given the permission . . . bound, that distance was too great for either of them to bear over significant time.

And yet . . .

"Mow," he said—except he didn't, because this body wouldn't do it yet. His mind's eye showed him putrid darkness, a seething murk shot through with bruised violet and streaks of brimstone scent. The Huntington person. It revealed the dull dead land, all its vivid color leeching toward the Huntington person, the fizzy resistance of the bluff, the hard heavy vibration of the stone. Bright Feather person, light dancing blues and golds and pretty frills, gentle edges and hard core. Not far up the hill, two more energies danced, ethereal witnesses—one growing in protective anger and one small, bright and pure . . . never born.

Ah. And two following them from the parking lot. Dull little beings of the Huntington person's taint, trying to look bigger.

Hot sunlight washed across his lids; Sklayne forced his eyes open to it. He found Trevarr, both inside and out; the hair on his tail stood on end and every claw he had popped free. Leg of fiery agony, arm so very wrong . . . venom burning down his throat and through his chest and raging through his blood. The darkness within, now a small lingering ember—and nonetheless the only thing keeping him alive at all. *Atreyvo,* he wanted to say. *Let me fix,* he wanted to say.

"Mow," he said; his tail flailed. Oh stupid small body, so fragile. No energies here to feed upon. No way to do just what he needed to do, just when he needed to do it.

Trevarr found him, and if he had no means to reach out physically, he nonetheless reached out with his thoughts. *Peace, little friend. Be easy.*

Sklayne lifted his lip to show a sharp little fang. ::*Mighty.*::

But the dull little persons from the parking lot were here—in person, a stout woman and an unfit man. And there was the Quinn person, staggering to his feet—weary but resolute, and snagging a long wooden bludgeon from the ground to stand, legs braced wide, before the Garrie and Trevarr.

"A bat applies between six to eight thousand pounds of pressure on the ball," he said, his voice full of scraping sound as he faced the dull new persons. "My friend already knows how that feels. How about you? Curious?"

The dull new persons hesitated. The man said something that Sklayne would recognize as a curse in any language. The woman responded high and thin and anxious . . . and disgusted.

And they left. Not at all mighty.

For the first time, he found the bright clean spark of the Lucia person, awash in the eddies of others. And the Robin person, muted, a wavering glow. The Caryn person, startling in a new clarity of defined edges and confined self and . . .

Not alone.

Not at all alone.

"Holy farking crap," the Garrie said. "The *ghosts*—"

"Amazing what one can do when properly inspired," the Lucia person said dryly. "Garrie, they want to help. They tanked up on Robin's watchdog and now they want to help."

The Garrie looked past them all to the ghosts, a wavering mass of pulsing energies—some vibrating, some steady, the growing strength of a young spirit coming to his self-awareness, the steadying influence of the older spirits, reclaiming their own. The Jim-Bob Dandy entity hovered right there in the front, his tangled knots of conflicting energies wrapped tightly enough to form the shape of him, features and all. Maybe not just what the Garrie saw with her Garrie eyes, but close enough.

"Yes," said the Feather ghost.

"Yesss," said the Bobbie Ghost from up on the bluff.

And the Garrie grinned, so big. "Damned farking *yes*!"

One of these days Sklayne would tell her exactly what *farking* meant.

Oh, so very yes!

Garrie couldn't use much energy from them, not as individuals—not without harming them. But some of it . . . from *all* of them . . . might be enough . . .

"Give it to *me*!" Feather urged, and looked up the

cliff. "Give it to her!" And when Garrie looked at her in surprise, she said, "This is our home! Ours! We know it better than you. *We can do this!*"

Be a channel. Just as she'd been in San Jose. A channel, this time to *ghosts.*

Here, in this body full of conflict and uncertainties and dark new corners she still knew nothing about.

"Oh, they hope," Lucia said, following only the emotions of it. "They *want.*" She looked at Garrie. "From you? What?"

"Everything," Garrie said, her throat suddenly dry. Realizing it, with startling clarity. *"Everything."* She looked at Trevarr, found more understanding than she'd expected in his eyes even as he had to struggle to look at her at all. "Everything," she said to him, and this time her voice broke.

"Ebb and . . . flow," he said to her, rasping and hunting air, and her breath caught in her chest to hear it. "As we did."

"We can do this!" Feather repeated, crowding her. "We *have* to—do you not see this land dying? All the magic of it fading? Do you think he's going to stop *here*?"

Huntington glowed black now, the center of his personal maelstrom. Barbed and swirling lines spiraled around him and hooked into the earth, drawing out the life of it; cracks spread through the ground around him as a small bird imploded into a puff of down and delicate crunch of bone. The very substance of the red rocks groaned into submission.

"Do you?" Feather demanded.

"Do you?" Bobbie cried from above.

"Do you?" The ghosts, all the ghosts, a massive swell of anguish and fear, chafing to take action . . . needing direction. Needing aim.

"Ebb . . . flow," Trevarr said to her, even as his eyelids

fluttered. She grabbed his duster, clutching it to keep him upright—scooting back into place behind him. He slipped the Gatherer back into his pocket and his hand found Lukkas, settling perfectly around the grip. "As we did," he said, and didn't flinch as a scatter of rock shards landed on them both.

"Sklayne—"

::I got nothin',:: he told her, limp sand-red cat stretched out beside Trevarr's leg, parroting her own earlier words to Feather.

"You weren't even here when I said that!" Outrage fueled her. "Eavesdropping—!"

Great green eyes slitted at her. ::This *place*,:: he said. ::He gives everything to you in this place. I give everything. Now *you*.:: A mental glare. ::*Do!*::

She choked on that.

And then she *did*.

Come on in, she said, and opened herself to the ghosts. Beckoned. *Give it up*.

Give it up, and she'd pass it on.

Easy to say.

She'd had ghosts around her; she'd pushed ghosts away from her. She'd touched them, consoled them, controlled them . . . destroyed them. She'd never let them *in*. She gasped at that first clammy whispering touch, startling and bitter cold. Cobwebs in the back of her throat, damp sucking sounds in her mind's ear, bitter rust on her tongue, her skin crawling in sloughing waves. A sudden rush of intense brain freeze, sinuses clamping down in radiating pain . . . she bent over her knees, pressing her palms to her eyes.

A hand landed on her leg, leaving the sword beside it, all but encompassing her thigh. Hot even through the sun-warmed khaki, far from steady . . . and still, somehow strong.

::Breathe, *atreya*,:: Sklayne advised her, his narrator's

voice making it clear he spoke Trevarr's words, reaching her in the only way they could, now. ::As it was with us.::

She buried her face in the crook of her arm, finding his hand and clutching it. Breaking it, for all she knew— all her fear, all the building pressure and energies, piling in and piling on and nowhere to go and nowhere to *be*—

::You see,:: Sklayne said, his own voice now, bitter edged. ::You *see*—:: and "Mow!" and grumble, prodded into silence. He added in a very small voice, ::Sorry.::

Fear, and building pressure and energies, piling in and piling on . . .

Living through this. You're doing it wrong.

"He's coming for you!" Feather said, her newly assertive voice rising to sudden alarm—Huntington, all putrescent streaks and heavy globs of clinging, transformed energies in her ethereal sight.

"Quinn!" Lucia shouted, even as Trevarr's warmth disappeared from her side. "Quinn, no—be careful—!"

"More!" Caryn told the ghosts, and before Garrie could cry denial, a pure typhoon of energies rolled on through.

She might have fallen on her face. Hard to tell. An impact of some sort, and another; her physical world wrenched around, and her ethereal world pounded itself out on her being, incompatible and billowing forces with nowhere to go and she—

She—

She started to get mad.

Not this.

Not *again*.

And the mad brought up a hint of cold fiery darkness, and Garrie snatched at it. Uncomfortable, difficult, *familiar* cold fiery darkness—and now she knew just what to do with it. *Ebb and flow.* Let it in, breathe it—

Out.

::Yesss,:: Sklayne said, entirely his own voice. ::*Yess,* atreyvo, *do this thing*—::

And *yes*! the dark cold fierce punched a hole through those incompatible and billowing internalized forces and *yes!* she sent the suddenly pouring channels of it straight to Feather, straight up the hill to Bobbie Ghost—pure, clean arrows of organized power against a backdrop of unfamiliar panic.

Sklayne's panic? Sklayne's distant voice, wailing words she couldn't understand? And Trevarr's name, alarming her beyond rational thought.

But the energy had her now. Ebb and flow, channeling chaos into order, sending it outward to those who knew this land so well. Feather churned the energy right back into the earth, drilling it in beside the rock. From above them, cycled breezes washed down the hill like a gentle mud slide, renewing ground and leaf and life. And every bit of it flowed back into Garrie, mingling with what the ghosts fed her, churning and driving and finding release in the punch of cold hard fierce—a take-no-prisoners fierce that sucked out the darkness and left only the purity.

"Quinnie," Lucia said, dimly in the background. "Quinnie, can you *see*?"

And Quinn said, "Holy. Goddam. Fucking. *Shit.*"

And Caryn said, "It's—it's what happened at the storage area, only—"

"Oh, so much *better*!" Lucia finished for her. "They're cleaning it! They're cleaning *him*!"

Garrie, caught up in being a pillar of light, saw none of it. Nothing but chaos churning into order, darkness stripped by light, and Huntington—so much closer than she'd thought—flailing for ethereal balance, fighting back. Distantly, she heard him screaming, all anguish and terror and thwarted fury. And so distantly, Quinn said, "The rock . . . the *rock*—"

Feather's voice chimed in with ringing tones. "This is *my home*."

And from above, Bobbie's ringing voice. "You will *not touch my daughter!*"

A boy's voice, new and unfamiliar. "You leave my mom and dad *alone*!

"Run! Robin, *run!* Quinnie! Caryn—"

"Almost done," Caryn shouted.

And for some reason they were all shouting, except Sklayne, who wailed, wailed, wailed into Garrie's mind. ::*Almost done!*:: he cried, and he meant something entirely different. ::*Trey!* Atreyvo!::

Almost done. The energies would be gone. The purifying action, gone. Garrie quite abruptly became aware of it all, from both inside and out. Spiraling pillar of light, taking and giving, ever in, ever out . . . the siphon of it all finally starting to ease. And there she was, buried inside it all—a tight little bundle of one wiry small person, slight of body and uncontainable with power.

By herself.

Because Trevarr sprawled on the ground as if he'd made some great effort, and not far away she found Huntington, a shriveled and twisted version of what had been a man, pinned to the ground by a familiar sword.

Not a fatal wound—too low and awkward, as though he'd been wrenching aside to avoid it. Beside him, the tire iron . . . and the chain wrapped around Quinn's bat.

All evidence of another kind of battle, barely won— and now Trevarr lay contorted beside her, all his fierce gone to fading all over again, a small pale blot of cat stretched out beside him.

Living through this. Time to do it totally right.

Time to do it *now*.

She threw herself over them both. Dragon dark met light mixed with chaos and a tightening spiral of barbed intensity. Dragon dark met light mixed with memory and hot cries and wild strength now arching beneath her and crying out in a startled scrape of pain, a slash of startled, snarling ferocity.

Dark met light, and spun entirely out of control.

20

Ponder all potential outcomes.
— Rhonda Rose

It seemed like a good idea at the time.
— Lisa McGarrity

Boom!
— Sklayne

The voices came as a babble of discordant sound. "Garrie, will you open your eyes, dammit—I have to take care of my aunt's body—Robin needs a hospital *now*—Garrie, *wake up*—just get her in the car—my *aunt*—Trevarr—did you see that oh my God did you *see*—?"

::Small person of much power,:: Sklayne said, somewhere deep in Garrie's head. ::Be here, now.::

Water trickled down her neck; gentle knuckles passed over it, spreading coolness. Okay, that felt good, here in the heat and sweat and bright hot sun, tucked up against the blessedly familiar solidity of Trevarr. The scent of pine clued her in—they were against a tree, unshaded in the midday sun. He brushed the side of his face against her ear, whispered into it. "*Atreya*. You worry them."

Quinn's voice came more decisively. "I'll carry her, then."

Trevarr's arm, folded around her shoulder, tightened slightly. Garrie's eyes popped open, not without annoyance. *"What?"*

Lucia, crouched beside her, her eyes flicking from Garrie's face to Trevarr behind her. "Chicalet? Are you back?"

Garrie checked. Arms, legs, hands and feet, all where they should be, covered with bright nicks and rock dust. And ah, pants, still not snapped up. "Oh, for pete's sake," she muttered, and finally zipped that last inch over the girlie pink flowered underwear she *really* hadn't meant for anyone to see when she'd put them on. She buckled the belt, looked her hands over front and back . . . ran them over her face and hair to make sure everything felt familiar. She found the goose egg on her forehead and the grimy trail of dried blood along that side of her face, and winced. "Maybe I'm back," she said. "Maybe not. Depends on what anyone wants of me." She squinted into the sunshine, decided it was altogether too bright. "Ugh," she said, full of visceral memory. "I suck! I kicked its *eyes* off. I suck *so bad.*"

Lucia had the experience to ignore that non sequitur. And the focus. "Chicalet . . . you're all right?" Lucia had an expression that Garrie couldn't quite decipher. Sure, maybe the mountain had just almost come down around their ears, and sure, the lerket had almost sucked them dry, and sure, Huntington had almost finished the job. But this . . . this was something else. And then Lucia's eyes drifted to her recently snapped pants, and Garrie knew.

"I'm fine," she said firmly. Not going there.

"I would find him in his hell," Trevarr said, low in her ear, "and bring him back to kill again."

Lucia eased closer. "Robin's looking better. Not remembering . . . that helps. But she has to go to the hospital."

Garrie's gaze flickered over to Robin sitting against the Cruiser's grill, pale and folded in on herself, the flush high on her cheeks and looking more feverish than healthy. "What do you mean, she doesn't remember—?"

::Me,:: Sklayne said. ::I did it. Ate her memories.::

"You did *what*?" Garrie stared at him, and could only shake her head. "I didn't need to know you can do that." She looked up at Lucia. "He says he ate her memories."

Dark eyes went wide. "Is *that* . . ." Her mouth stayed tight. "I thought I had done something. I had to . . . she needed help . . . oh, I don't *do* people!" She took a deep breath, shaking her hands out. "Okay. We did what we had to, yes? And now Robin needs the hospital, and so does Quinn—"

Quinn left the Cruiser with swift steps, and he would have been convincing in his fierceness had he not stumbled over nothing on the way. "Quinn is fine," he said. "A stun gun stuns. That's the way it is. I'll get over it."

Lucia protested, "That burn—"

"I'm *fine*," Quinn said. "But I need to be with Robin."

Trevarr's voice rumbled briefly against Garrie's back. "He should go with Robin," he said, and earned Quinn's surprise—blue eyes, bright in the sunshine, locking onto Trevarr's for a moment before Quinn nodded, ever so faintly.

Right. A guy thing.

"But," Garrie said, taking the discussion somewhere else altogether as she sat up straighter to take better stock of the area, "You and Quinn and Robin . . . what *happened*?"

"Another time, chicalet." Lucia gave Trevarr a pointed look. A changing-the-subject look. "He's a lot better than he was, thanks to you."

::And me. To me.:: Sklayne's deep green gaze followed the haphazard trail of a blue swallowtail butterfly several yards away.

No, Garrie told him. *Let it thrive. That's why we saved this place.*

His tail twitched along her arm.

Lucia said, so patiently, "I can tell when you do that, you know. Silent talking. So, the hospital, yes? Quinn goes, Robin goes . . . and Treva—"

"No!" Garrie said, panicked at the very thought.

"No," Trevarr said, his fingers stilling on Garrie's neck.

"Mow!" Sklayne said, and hissed for good measure. He seemed to like the effect; he did it again, more thoughtfully.

Lucia threw her hands up. "Whatever, then. Caryn's going to call 911—she has to take care of her aunt. And there are all these bodies—"

Sklayne purred.

Loudly.

Lucia looked a little ill; she stood, her entire body an exclamation of disbelief. "*No.* They're *gone.* They're all—" She pivoted a circle, and Garrie could only cover her face, knowing that Lucia would find nothing. Nothing but disturbed ground and exploded rock and—

"Please," Garrie said tightly, not daring to look, "tell me he left Feather."

::Respect for the Feather person,:: Sklayne said. And then he ruined the effect by purring again, so smug.

"Yes," Lucia said, relieved. "Caryn's with her. Holding her open cell phone. And we're leaving. On your own, Garrie."

And leave they did, in the slightly battered rental car with the inexplicably cracked windshield, leaving deep gouges in the landscape and bushes crunched to the ground.

Garrie pressed her hands against her face again, so aware of the grime, the sweat, the blood . . . the mists of lingering emotion. The ghosts, aside from Feather—

aside from the quiet presence up the hill—were gone. "What . . ." A deep breath. "What even happened?" she asked Trevarr, not looking. And then, when he didn't answer, she twisted to take him in—finally brave enough for that.

Amusement touched his features—eyes hardly bright, but reassuring in pewter, smoky at the rims and the pupils with their pinpoint glamour. All the bruising still evident from that unfair battle of beast and brute force and power. His hair tipped in blood, strands sticking to his neck and jaw.

His leg, resting *just so* against the ground—painful, but no longer gushing hot blood. Glimpses of raw flesh visible beneath torn leather. And his opposite arm, resting against his stomach—gently cradled, but undistorted. "Sklayne's help," he said. "But only because of your courage, *atreya*. What the lerket did . . ."

::Fatal,:: Sklayne said, cheerfully enough. He'd found and flipped an armored stink beetle, and now watched intently, nostrils twitching, to see if it could right itself. Ants by his toes, birds in the trees, the rustle of a natural breeze overhead . . . all as it should be. ::Changed, it was. A true lerket . . . :: He graced her with a mental sniff. ::Stupid little squealie, bristly face, cutesy sparks. No *tentacles*. No *big*. No *venom*.::

"Oh," Garrie said, a small voice. "You know . . . using it seemed like a good idea at the time."

::Good,:: Sklayne agreed. ::Until the mixing. Until *this* mixing. Us and them and you.:: His voice held the merest hint of admiration. *::Boom!::*

Garrie felt resentment settle into place around her mouth and chin, the draw of her brow. "We were healing this place," she said. "We were even cleansing Huntington." Right, until suddenly there'd been nothing left, because without the depraved corruption of energies in which he'd been marinating, he'd been nothing but a shell. "What the lerket did to Trevarr *came* from Huntington. It made sense to bring him into the loop!" Even if it had brought Trevarr's wild *other* into the mix, too. The darkness that they both now strove to balance.

::Stupid sense,:: Sklayne agreed, but there was a purr behind it—pleased to be scolding. *::Boom!::*

"Little friend," Trevarr said, the mildest of warning in his voice. And to Garrie, "Not without risks. But you knew that, I think."

She looked away from him. Not so different from Caryn, perhaps. Making decisions for all of them, when it came down to it. Her voice came out smaller now. "Do we even know if it's safe now?"

The smile rested at the corners of his eyes. "We may not know just how, *atreya*. But see what you have done."

She didn't, not right away. She watched his face. Hard in anger, closed when wary, and—now she knew— fiercely expressive in passion. But at the moment, hard to read at all. Weary. Hurting. And something gentler than she'd expected . . . an understanding.

Finally, resolute, she climbed to her feet—away from his trailing touch and warmth, but not away from the presence. Not quite. She took a breath and she turned around, and she—

"Holy farking . . ." But for once, she couldn't finish it. Not with the giant rock gone, shattered and blown apart, the shards of it scouring the ground clear. Behind the rock, the bluff itself had been whirled away— wind-carved, spirit-carved . . . the work of ages done in a matter of moments, revealing a fantastical swirl of shape and stone and shifting sandstone layers.

And between here and there—the spot where they'd been, where she'd flung herself over Trevarr and Sklayne and thrown them into siphoning conflagration—

Garrie's mouth dropped open. It stayed that way for a while.

For there churned a brand-new vortex, a thing of power and beauty and grace. A thing fulfilling the wistful hopes of every vortex hunter in the canyons. Mesmerizing, crystal clean curves of motion and grace, glassy layers of ethereal breezes sliding over and around each other as they made their way from the ground to the infinite sky and back down again.

Feather spoke without regard for the awe, pointing at the spot where the massive rock had been. "There, a memorial," she said. "For our young woman. For her daughter. Bif Tillotson. I did learn that much."

"Is that—?" Garrie pulled her thoughts together. "That's what it was all about?" She recalled the woman's ghost, the vague area in her pelvic girdle that Garrie had taken as the point of the fatal injury . . . bones broken, blood vessels sheared.

"I couldn't bring myself to face it," Bif said, suddenly standing right there—right where the rock had been. Now she was completely formed, down to the flat belly above her hip-huggers. "I'd only just found out. I didn't want to change my life—I didn't want to *not do* everything I'd always done. So I went hiking that day. And I killed her." She put a hand—all rings and string bracelets and henna swirls—on her belly. "I have to face that. I killed her." But sudden fury crossed her face. "Don't let anyone ever say I did this *to* myself! To her! That's what I want from this. What I need."

"I think you have what you need," Garrie told her. "When you protected this place, you protected her. You could have fled, or hidden in the safety of all the others. You didn't. And you know it."

Bif smiled. "Hmm," she said. "Groovy. I *do*."

Feather declared, "And we'll have the memorial anyway. Caryn, are you listening?"

Caryn crouched by Feather's body like a deer in the

headlights. "I can't believe I'm saying this, but . . . yes. I—oh God. Yes."

"You can tell them I was racing to the cleansing circle after Trickle collapsed, and the upset was apparently too much for me. I'd like to be remembered that way, as trying to save him." Feather thought about this, and nodded. "Yes, that's good. Then, the memorial goes over there, and move the cleansing circle to the new vortex. The Journey Vortex."

"But—" Caryn touched her aunt's body, a tentative motion. "How can I . . . how can I possibly stay here? Knowing it's all my fault that you . . . that you're—"

Feather's smile was a little tight. Garrie found herself glad that Caryn couldn't see it. "That's your penance, isn't it? Staying. And gathering up this community— start with Theo and his wife, first—I think you'll find they're willing to help, now. And then you help the spirits in this area—you do it *right*. I gather you've learned the difference?"

"What if I haven't?" Caryn hid her face in her hands. "What if I forget or lose track or . . ."

"Come out here. I think you'll find your reminders." Feather lifted her head, looking around—pride on her face for what her little inn had been through—what had been created here on this day. Another layer of age seemed to fall away—she seemed a little taller, lithe instead of thin, healthy instead of dulled. "Caryn . . . I was dying anyway, child. It wouldn't have been too much longer. This was, in its way, a mercy." As Caryn lifted her tear-tracked face in surprise, Feather gave a final nod. "That's it, then. I didn't name this place the Journey Inn for nothing. I'm headed out!"

"But—!" Caryn said, reaching out to thin air as if there might possibly be something to grasp.

"Groovy," Bif said. "Want some company?"

"We've been living in each other's hair for a while now," Feather said. "It only seems right."

No fanfare, no glamour. Just gone. Caryn looked to Garrie for confirmation, stricken.

Garrie shrugged. "It happens that way sometimes," she said. "Not everyone hangs around."

Or maybe not quite gone.

"Thank you," Feather's voice said, light as a breeze in Garrie's ear. "You and your friends . . . and your little cat, too . . ."

Sklayne hissed and stalked away.

21

Learn not just from the living.
—Rhonda Rose

Gahhh.
—Lisa McGarrity

Garrie closed the door behind her—*Yes, Caryn, thank you Caryn, we're fine, Caryn, we appreciate the rooms, Caryn*—and regarded Trevarr with more clarity than she thought she ought to have in this dim light.

Here. In their room.

Because Feather's death had closed the inn, at least officially. And Garrie and Lucia's room still lacked a door. So Lucia had taken a new room, and Garrie no doubt could have had a room all to herself if she wanted, too. But with Quinn still ninety minutes away at the Prescott hospital with Robin, Garrie had instead tucked away his accumulation of cords, power bricks, and devices and made herself at home right there.

The next day, they would probably be at work again—following through, smoothing things out. Especially when it came to the local community, the members of which had been sensitive enough to perceive the uproar—and who were now variously offended, abashed, and embarrassed at the way they'd treated Lucia, at their failure to handle the situation without outside help. One couple in particular . . . Theo and his wife, tendering apologies, wanting to help . . . coming to terms, perhaps, with their own needs and recent losses— the young son who had come through so strongly this day.

And *especially* when it came to the new cleansing circle and the memorial—but that was fine with Garrie. She needed to settle herself, and there was no better way than to work through it.

After a wicked long-distance workout on the elliptical to get things started.

For tonight, she simply eyed Trevarr, and the words burst out of her. "You look like Mad Max."

He sat upright against the bed headboard and frowned ever so faintly. *"Mad?"*

At Garrie's call, Lucia had brought back a hinged elbow splint, not to mention a sleek sporty knee stabilizer. Black metal and plastic, Velcro and neoprene . . . she wondered if it would mutate to hard leather just from his proximity.

The tall leather boots sat discarded by the bed, leaving him charmingly barefoot but otherwise clad— rugged dark pants with their narrow fall front, leather belt riding slouchy low on his hips, shirt of darkest indigo and faintly iridescent, paneled with butter-soft leather similar to that in her own new garment.

She tipped her head at him, then shook it. "Nah. Wrong accent. But I hope those braces help."

No instant healing, as had happened in San Jose, or

almost instant healing, as had happened when he returned to Kehar, a bullet still lodged in dangerous places. Too much, too fast, Sklayne had said. Too costly, for a body already faltering, even after Sklayne had tanked up on bodies, gone off to suck on a power line, and then done what he could. The rest would come as it did.

So he'd told her, before stalking out to see what small creatures he could torture in the night . . . muttering something inexplicable about *protect the Garrie*.

From what, she didn't know. Huntington was dead, the lerket was dead, the vortex was in full whirl.

"Oh! The tea!" The plant Sklayne had worked so hard to gather, and that—although the desert sun had made a good fast start on it—he'd personally finished desiccating so Garrie could steep it in strong black Irish tea. It still sat in the microwave. She locked the door behind her and went for it. "And that was kind of obviously evasive, by the way."

She came out of the tiny kitchenette area, careful with the tea. Good and dark—no doubt he'd be more satisfied with the stuff in some sort of espresso tea form, the way he practically sucked tea bags down whole—and garnished with a stalk from Sklayne's sticky, stinky plant.

Mad, maybe not. But it looked precariously close to a glower. "Ah," she said, handing him the mug—figuring it out. "Not used to healing up the hard way, are you?"

He looked away as she sat on the edge of the bed. His jaw hardened; his eyes narrowed. She'd learned to look for such subtle things in him. No Latina drama for Trevarr; no guileless in-your-face Quinn.

Just *what you see is what you get*—if you could see it at all.

And there, looking closer, she suddenly did. Enough to understand. That he, too, connected the braces to thoughts of Robin and Quinn in Prescott. To what Robin had been through, whether she remembered it or not.

To what he'd almost seen Garrie go through.

"Hey," she said. "It's okay."

He sipped the tea, wincing a fleeting grimace. Yummy, then. But it didn't change the shadow in his expression. He said, after a long moment of silent emotion, "It is *not*." And finally, he looked at her. "What if you hadn't—" *Hadn't made it? What if I had failed you? What if being willing to die for you hadn't been enough?*

"Whoa," she said, going suddenly cold. "Who ever said you were the baby-sitter of me? And who got *whom* into that situation?"

He closed his eyes. His hand tightened around the mug. "The lerket—"

"Because *I* asked you to bring it out! And I'm the one who lost control of the situation. All those different energies . . ." She flushed. She'd been so unprepared, so overwhelmed.

Her words were supposed to help. But the brief glance he managed showed her a man stricken beyond what she'd imagined this particular man could ever be. Just a glimpse, before he brought the tea up—knuckles white and hand threatening to crack the mug; draining it.

"Whoa," she said again. She floundered a moment, not understanding . . . not seeing how to understand. She climbed onto the bed again, enough room there to kneel and sit back on her ankles beside his good leg, and she took his hand. Carefully, because of his arm, but persistently.

For that moment, it was the bravest thing she had ever done—holding her ground against his resistance and the hard shell of rejection behind it, and for that instant wondering if she'd ever really known him at all.

Absorbing the very fact that she sat on this incredibly mundane bed beside him, the air-conditioning not turned down quite as low as she might have it and the warmth of him flushing her further. This stranger, the same man who'd pushed her up against a wall and taken her, eyes literally blazing with need, hands invading her body for his own. Tender, wicked, astonishing demand, and wringing the same right back out of her.

Did that happen, with two strangers? And if it did, didn't they then know each other on some level in a way that no one else ever could or would?

And so she stayed brave, sitting beside him there until his hand softened, ever so slightly, beneath hers.

Garrie said, very carefully, "I don't do *what ifs,* Trevarr. I do the best I can. That's all. And you . . . you do better than anyone."

Almost as if she'd hit him, and she didn't know why. The tightening of his mouth; the flare of nostril. He pulled his hand back . . . she didn't let go. *And didn't let go.* Until he looked at her, something of defeat behind his gaze. Something of acceptance.

She relaxed. Then, she released his hand. She found his thigh instead, and ran her hand down the length of it. Hard muscle, twitching in surprise at her touch and then relaxing. She raised her eyebrows at him. "Your problem," she told him, giving him a moment to absorb that she thought he had a problem at all, "is that healing like the rest of us is annoying. It's tedious. It's *inconvenient.*"

"Farking right it is." That scowl would have intimidated the boldest conversationalist.

"I mean, seriously." She checked within herself, to the quiescent recesses that had been satisfied and peaceful since she'd woken to find the land cleansing at the touch of a vortex she'd somehow created. Dark power, lurking along her bones, simmering deep . . . and yet flicking instantly awake to spread a burning chill from her low belly and down, her diaphragm and up. Having sought it out, she didn't run from it. She welcomed it. She breathed it up . . . breathed it out. And then she added her own breezes, light and clean and precise. She pushed those out, too, skimming them along his leg.

The scowl turned startled. Maybe a little wary.

She followed his leg to the hard line of his hip, trickling breezes out along the way. He shifted beneath her touch. *"Atreya . . ."*

"Breathe," she said, so innocently. "You know. Ebb and flow."

He understood, then. He could have stopped her; maybe he *should* have stopped her. She understood the line she was treading . . . the push and shove, the things she stirred within him . . . within herself. Not in the distant safety of some warded, shielded Keharian cave, but here in this cabin with both of them vulnerable and both of them needing.

He could have stopped her.

He didn't.

His hand, moving to halt hers, instead stilled and subsided. His breathing quickened; his body quickened. He caught her eye and held it, submitting to her touch. There, along his sides, lean flanks that would fill out as he healed, the thickened skin where a bullet had so recently carved a path. Along the curve of rib to the flat planes of his chest, feeling every tensing muscle. She slipped her hands beneath his shirt and imagined she discerned the faint tracery of tattoos that weren't, watching diamond pupils widen—watching the very moment when he floundered for composure and control—a flutter of eye, head tipping back, the sudden intake of breath. He gave in return that which had almost been taken from her this day—a sense of self, a sense of control . . . a sense of intimate belonging.

Because this was the way it should be done. Giving, not demanding. Accepting, not taking. And doing it until what whirled between them ceased to belong to one or the other but only to both, and whatever control she'd had was fraying fast.

Along the way she'd somehow pulled her shirt off and shucked her pants, mastered the secondary knot and unfamiliar fastening of his sharply incised belt buckle, and rediscovered just exactly how convenient those front fall pants could be. And if he'd understood her unspoken rules—clamping his good hand down hard on the side of the creaking headboard to keep himself from interfering with her touch, the other, braced or not, finally reached for her.

She let energies gather and swell into something far, far, bigger than them both—the dark wood smoke rising, the bright spark of reckoner clarity, the gathering sweep of wings and shadows. Gather and build and pulse and flame, until finally he twisted beneath her with a sound both beseeching and demanding, and until she finally locked her mouth onto his, all strong tea and bitter herb and canine teeth sharp against her tongue. She plunged them together, letting him take them the rest of the way.

No, not a taciturn man in love, her Trevarr.

She lay gasping on his chest, trying to feel her toes again and clinging to the lingering sense of what she brought out in him—what she brought out in herself. *Oh yeah. Groovy.* He made her feel small—he'd always made her feel small. But also . . . just right. And if she just lay here draped over and around him, catching her breath and pretending the rest of the world didn't exist, maybe she could feel it forever.

"Mow." The voice was weak and dazed and wondering. Familiar and small and questioning.

And in this room.

Garrie stiffened. Trevarr—his one good hand already conveniently palming her posterior—clamped down just enough to keep her from levitating off him. Not enough, by far, to keep her from twisting around.

Sklayne. There against the front door sill like a draft-stopping cat, stretched out and limp. "Mow," he said.

"You!" Garrie's indignation rose as quickly as had the passion. "*You!* You were on the *other side* of that locked door!"

Sklayne froze, as if just now realizing where he was, or that he was visible at all. "Mow!" he said, and *poof!* big-as-the-world to small again, under the sill and out before she could say anything else at all.

"Gahhh." Garrie rested her face on Trevarr's chest, fully aware that the new catch in his breathing was repressed amusement, if not outright laughter. Again, laughter from this man. What was the world coming to? "Easy for you to say. Next time, *you're* going to be the naked one." And she gave his chest a thoughtful lick along the patterned edge of etched feathered scales, and as his fingers flexed into her bottom, she thought . . . maybe . . . sweet beckoning temptation . . . But instead he pulled the quilt over them both just as they were and, just as they were, they relaxed toward sleep.

She thought she heard something, or someone, purring around her, and the world dropped away to the steady rise and fall of Trevarr's chest. *Atreyo.*

Purring, but aghast. *No, no, no.* Floundering. *No and no again.*

That was not as it should have been.

Mindless. Physical. Sometimes mutually brutal.

That was Trevarr with body pleasures.

Not this new ferocity. Not this *blending.* Not this tapping into that which together Trevarr and Sklayne had always controlled, always hidden.

Not *reveling* in it.

And not this other thing. That which had drawn Sklayne in all unknowing, leaving him stunned, awash in energies he could only feel and somehow not absorb. Clarity and darkness and pleasure unto exquisite, tightly drawn longing. *Completion.*

All the signs had been there, those differences. Since the Garrie had first shoved her defiance at Trevarr, they'd been there. And then Trevarr's reluctance to use the Garrie for the hunt and then walk away, as he knew so well to do. His growing protectiveness, his attachment . . . the liberties he allowed her. Sklayne had warned him. *Warned you.* The body games themselves . . . those had been inevitable. After too many years of the hunt, of the road, of the run . . . Sklayne knew how it went.

Except when he suddenly didn't.

Because Trevarr hadn't pushed. Had made it the Garrie's decision. Had given so very much of himself along the way. Almost everything, so many times.

Blind, blind Sklayne. Telling himself they'd come back to this place because it was the best place to run. The best place to hide, even as it held just what the tribunal wanted. Never letting himself truly see that which had poured over him this night.

Truth that changed everything.

22

Hold fast, child.
— Rhonda Rose

Just barely predawn and Garrie slipped back into the cabin, easing past the brokenly ajar door of her old room and into the one she and Trevarr now shared.

The violence of the previous day seemed far away, her body still purring from the night—love and sleep, and time during which Trevarr dutifully drank the horrid tea and, played out or not, continued to heal faster than anyone had a right to.

Or so it would have seemed, the way he was using his arm that last—

Garrie turned her back to the door she'd gently closed behind her and took a breath. A deep breath. *Get over it. This isn't a honeymoon.*

Or maybe it kinda was. For once, it had taken only an hour of running before she settled enough to face the day. Love and sleep, it seemed, did a body good. *Groovy.*

Trevarr still slept deeply—something else she'd never seen. Except now he was shirtless, the brace carefully reapplied. The pants had somehow been too much bother, especially given the convenient way they were put together.

Not to mention the way they came apart.

Garrie took another breath, long and silent. But smiling.

She toed her sneakers off and eased past the kitchen; she dropped two bags into the tea mug. Not without a grimace, but . . . ugh. Who knows what they drank on Kehar anyway. She eased into the bathroom, where she hesitated at the potential snick of the light switch and then realized she didn't need it anyway. There, she found her brush, gave her hair a few pointless licks. Meg Ryan hair at its shortest and bed-headiest . . . except hers was nut brown with silvered blue streaks that she no longer had to create herself.

Her skin still did the shimmer thing it had acquired in San Jose, but if the vortex had left a mark, she had yet to find it. Spaghetti-strap tank top over a sport bra with no attempt to hide the one with the other, running shorts she'd gotten in the juniors sale department complete with *Sweet!* inscribed across one cheek. Always just a little too spare, curves too subtle. But they were *there,* she realized, in a way she hadn't seen until Trevarr had traced them so reverently during the night, and then possessed them so fiercely.

Yeah. She looked . . . *relaxed.* Huh. Until this moment, she hadn't realized just what that was like.

She set the brush back into her toiletries bag, quietly . . . all too aware that the bag still shared counter space with the gift bag from Robin's store. Geodes, crystals, and several otherworldly plasmic energy storage devices joining in to pass off as basic tourist trap crap.

Well. She *did* like the geodes.

She left the rest of her as she was—still flushed from the exercise and ready for a shower, but waiting until Trevarr woke.

She didn't think he slept like this very often.

Like, in a *bed.*

He still hadn't stirred. Sprawled across the whole bed, covers everywhere. Just enough room, she thought, to curl up beneath that out-flung arm and soak up another moment or so of quiet before the day started. To ponder the fading bruises and ugly abrasions . . . feel the unusual warmth and smile to herself, thinking of

that which had reached out to her through the wild ferocity of what he carried within—the flinging sensation
of freedom, a soaring through darkness and strength.
Absorbing it, as if she could simply soak it into her
being and have it forever, whenever.

He opened his eyes, looking straight at her. No muzz-
iness there, just the clear, alert gaze in a face of hard
male beauty, oddly softened by the faint hint of beard.
The whole of him came awake, just like that—an
awareness thrumming through him that hadn't been
there moments earlier.

"Shh," she said. "It's quiet. That's all. We're being
quiet."

And he said nothing, but shifted his arm slightly to
encompass her.

Quiet.

Just *being*.

::Trey!::

We're being quiet, she thought at Sklayne.

::No no nono—:: No more warning that that and here
he came, *poof!* into the room, condensing into red buff
cat again, black-ticked hair and green eyes and regal
face, much with the ears. *::They come—::*

Garrie spent a precious moment frowning—not understanding.

But Trevarr understood.

All his repose, gone in an instant; all his ferocity filling the room. He threw off the tangled covers, rolled off
the bed to his feet—except even with the brace, the leg
gave way beneath him.

It hardly slowed him. Even as he wrenched himself
back into balance, he snatched his leather satchel from
the headboard, his duster from the chair. He dumped
the contents of the satchel—scattered tangles of metal
and bright color, the belt of intricate beading, personal
sundries. By then Sklayne was on the bed, too, using

all his dexterous claws and the sporadically forming thumb to pull out the items with which Garrie was most familiar. The Gatherer. The Eye. The knotted *kirkhir-rah* belt and the metallic tracking disk she'd seen once or twice—unwary, that pickpocket had been, and unsuccessful—but never understood.

By then Garrie had bounced out of bed, too—not exactly speechless, but knowing better. *Something.* Something big. So she waited until they had what they wanted—until Trevarr had shoved those chosen things into his duster's infinite pockets, his hands unerringly retrieving Lukkas while he was at it—before she asked, "What can I do?"

"Be quiet," Trevarr said, finally tending his pants flap. And to Sklayne, "How much time?"

::*No* time.::

"What do you mean, *be quiet*?" Garrie had a temper, too; she let it show.

He glanced at her, testing his leg . . . backing off it. Nothing on his face but a pure, hard desperation. "As we spoke. *Quiet.* Keep of yourself inside."

Oh, fark. It was never good when he starting putting sentences inside out. "Keep of myself—"

Blinding understanding. How casual that conversation had been. *"Can you keep yourself from them?"* Did she ever shield herself so tightly, so completely, that she became imperceptible?

He hadn't meant the ghosts at all.

Because this was not a surprise to him. This was what he had been concealing from her all along. *This moment.* "This is what you were talking about," she blurted. "What you've been ready for all along. *Your people.* And now you want me to hide myself from them."

"Yes," he said, blunt grimness. "Physically, you cannot hide. Physically, they will find you. Ethereally, they *cannot*."

::Told you! Told you!:: Sklayne chanted, as panicked as Garrie ever seen him—his outline shifting slightly, his coat sparking . . . claws peeking into existence and subsiding, talons, flexing and fleeing. ::Cannot save us if saving her!::

And then, as the first wave of spicy dark energy washed through the breezes, Garrie quite suddenly understood it all. Stood stunned and stupid and disbelieving and *knowing* all at the same time. "They *did* accept the Krevata as bounty," she said. "They *did* call that debt filled. And then they wanted something more."

::You! The Garrie! They wanted the Garrie!::

Trevarr moved around the bed to snag her arm—not a smooth stride, but a lurch. He jerked her in close, held her tight—and she saw in him the fear that she would not hear him, could not listen. "They felt you, when you very first left the cave. They felt something of what occurred between our worlds. They had the shattered memories of the broken Krevata. They wanted—"

"Me," she breathed, suddenly so frightened she couldn't move. "Oh my God. They want *me*. But then . . . you came back . . ."

::Would not tell them. Would not bring you. Bullies, they are.:: Sklayne paced frantically along the wall, sipping from the wall socket. ::*Ran* to you. Free the geas shackles, Trey. *Free!* Let me take them!::

No! Trevarr's vehement refusal hit Sklayne strongly enough to echo through. "And if they find out about all of you, little friend? On Kehar? Your entire people would be forfeit." He glanced at Garrie. "Double for her. Shield her. Keep her as quiet."

"Mrrrr." It came out as a sad little sound, almost washed away by a second gust of rising breeze and thickening air. ::Yes.::

"You weren't exiled because you failed to clear the debt," Garrie said, still trying to understand. "Your people weren't shunned because of it. You were exiled because you wouldn't give me up. And you came here—"

"*Atreya,*" he said, and quite suddenly that was enough. To protect her. He'd come here to protect her. Not from Huntington and his psychic bullies, but from a dictatorial tribunal on another world. One that treated Trevarr as less than a person, when Garrie . . .

Garrie knew he was *more.*

"If I'm quiet," she said, her tone making it clear she wasn't sure she'd be any such thing, "I can't help you."

His hand tightened on her arm—awkward, as he balanced on one leg, held her with one arm . . . only emphasizing that he still struggled to stay upright at all. That if he'd been anyone else . . .

We wouldn't even still be here.

"Do *not,*" he said, his eyes gone pewter dark, the pupils wide with intensity. "Do not think it. If you are *not* quiet, not safe, then it was wasted."

Nothing to clear the head like a good kick of guilt. He'd given up everything to be here. To protect her. He'd given up his people's chance at security—if not given up fighting for it—and his own chance to be with them. To be there, on his own world, a free man. Not a hunted man.

"They sent probes, but they weren't sure. Not until yesterday," she realized. "And now they've sent *you* after you. Hunters."

::Hunters,:: Sklayne said, and it was a scoff. ::*Not* like Trey.::

They didn't *feel* like him. Not the clarity of his presence, as they grew closer. Not the clean nature of it. They spewed their arrogance and their intentions and their crude energies.

"Trevarr," she said, suddenly so scared it was all she could manage—searching his face for the determination she knew, the reassurance.

Not finding it.

"Remember," he said, growing fierce again, pulling her close again. "What comes now. It is what *must* be done. *Remember.*" And he kissed her, hard and thoroughly and with poignant desperation that made her cry even as she clung to him, fear-cold fingers on warm flesh.

And the door blew open.

Open and off the hinges, slamming against the wall and crashing to the floor. Three of them stood there blocking all the diffuse morning light with size and strength and confident intention.

Trevarr acknowledged them with maddening slowness—not bothering, at first, to break away from her. But he was someone else, then. Cooler, colder, more calculating. Selfish lips, giving nothing of himself and asking nothing of her but to be there.

The men looked everything like him and nothing like him. Harsher in feature, taller . . . two of them beefier and the third bigger all around. One wore his hair shorn, tattoos heavy on his scalp.

Or not tattoos at all, she realized. Hard, tight scales, etched so sharply she thought they might peel right away. Another's hair pulled back in a rough ponytail, while the oldest had so many little tiny braids—just like Trevarr's, silvered and tight—that there was little free hair left at all.

They bore knives and swords; they bothered with neither, garnished in black leather gloves with weighted metal knuckles; studded wrist guards, and protective collars. The oldest scraped his eyes over Garrie and made a derisive comment, harsh words with a thick tongue.

Sklayne hissed bravely from under the bed.

Translate! she demanded of him.

::Quiet! Be you his *atreya* and be quiet!::

It was a stinging scold she hadn't expected to hear from that quirky being. She buttoned herself up tight, tight, tighter—there in Trevarr's arms, trembling and not even pretending she wasn't. He kept her tucked up close and tight—every bit the man interrupted in plea-sure, and not at all impressed by the interruption at that. He returned derision with words of disdain.

Garrie caught Sklayne peeking; she glared. Message clear enough. *Translate for me, or there will be no quiet.*

His energy, a touch of cool crystal breeze, circled her; clamped down tight. Annoyance and frantic aware-ness of the threat about to be made good, revealing them all, and his words spurted out to her. ::Raxl says we should have known we would find you with a—like this. Trey says you might as well leave, because I've already ruined her for other men and there will be nothing left of her for them when I am done anyway.::

Okay. She'd asked, hadn't she?

Raxl, he'd said. He knew the man. Probably knew all three of them, but the oldest . . . he spoke for them. With impatience, now.

::You know what we want, you—:: Sklayne hesitated, didn't translate that last. ::Rudeness. Heritage slander. Killing words.::

And indeed, the tension hummed through Trevarr—the impulse. He snapped a reply, dutifully translated: ::I told them he's dead.::

He pushed Garrie away—roughly, at that, and onto the bed. Hard enough so she bounced. But she'd heard. She'd understood. *I told them he was dead.* He'd just informed them that the being for which they searched was male.

She scrabbled across the width of the bed and over to the other side, looking as stunned and stupid as she could. Not far enough from the truth anyway. But here, on the other side of the bed, were some of her things.

STORM OF RECKONING   349

The knife. Truly hers, now. Blooded. Her hand closed over it.

Sklayne's head popped up in front of her. *::No!::*

No doubt he'd meant to startle her into dropping the thing.

Trevarr was without cover, now—his uneven stance revealed, his braced leg revealed . . . his sword revealed. The bald hunter lifted his lips into a derisive sneer, rumbled a few words in a voice almost too low to hear. ::Now, that's the tribunal's favorite we expected to find. Not so distracted by your scrawny little piece of—:: Hesitation. ::Sorry. Forgot to make nicer.::

It didn't matter. Nothing mattered but what happened next.

Trevarr's voice, quiet enough. ::Never *that* distracted. But the one they want is dead. You tell them that when you leave this place.::

Raxl snorted. ::They didn't believe it the first time. They didn't believe it when you ran. They won't believe it now.:: Like the other man, he showed his teeth. Really, really ugly teeth. ::We don't believe you, either. Take us to him, or we take you back now and the tribunal will get what they want, their way.::

Trevarr shrugged. He said, slowly and so deliberately, ::He. Is. Dead.::

And then he raised his hands from his sides, ever so slightly. *Come and take me, then.*

What are you doing*!* She wanted to scream it, to throw herself between them. Sklayne's paw snaked up the side of the bed to prick her skin where she still stretched for the knife.

And even if she didn't want to, she understood. Trevarr had taken things this far, this fast, because she couldn't stay *quiet* forever. She couldn't hide forever. And they couldn't talk their way out of this at all.

Come and take me, then.

They did.

Three of them, hale and hearty and large, working as a precision team. The first took a swift deep hit in the arm, but Garrie knew better than to hope. He'd be used to pain, as was Trevarr. He was strong. He'd heal. They'd *all* heal.

And it meant they had little respect for a blade, as sharp and quick as it was, in the hands of a man with one good leg and one good arm.

Trevarr went down hard. He went down fast.

Garrie groped for the knife . . . she groped for courage and for wits, and she couldn't take her eyes off jumbled arms and legs and bodies, a glimpse of Trevarr twisting beneath them, pinned tight and anger rising. She felt it, the cold rush of heat, the dark slash of unfurling wing—she felt what it evoked in her, and she panicked, knowing she couldn't quiet it. She couldn't hide it, not her response to him. And Sklayne couldn't hide it.

Trevarr wrenched his head around—he found her gaze . . . and he knew it.

I'm sorry, she said—not loud enough for it to go anywhere, but enough to come through in her eyes—her response, her imminent loss of control to it—

She saw when he realized it. She saw the decision shutter his expression, the desperation that came before. He shouted something—not at the hunters, not at Garrie, but at the shadows under the bed. Ritualized words, rhythmic and fast and suddenly overridden by a terrible, terrible feline howl of sorrow. Then his eyes flared bright and hard and fierce and the defiance exploded from his throat, all roar and bellow. Disarmed, buried under their collective weight, weakened and broken—

He went for them.

And she saw the fear on their faces. She saw fear as Raxl rolled away, stunned and streaming blood; she saw it as another cursed with pain, a small wicked knife sprouting from his chest. They shouted discordant fury, and as the third man spun away with an arcing spray of black blood, Raxl threw himself back into the fight, eyes pulsing red and gold. He brought his weighted fists down with the force of his body behind them.

Trevarr grunted, a raw deep sound, and went limp.

No.

Atreyo, no!

A rake of unkind claws across her mind, stinging reminder and rebuke thick with sorrow.

They wasted no time. They climbed to their feet; they exchanged a few curt, harsh words as Raxl snapped scorn at those wounded by their own weapons, barely giving them time to whip a quick leather tourniquet on the bald man's arm.

No!

Garrie's hand closed around the knife.

Raxl gestured at Trevarr; the two men limped over and hefted him up between them, careless with his arm, careless with his leg, careless with his head as it hung slack, his hair trailing the ground.

And then they took him away.

"No!" She screamed it, finally, bouncing up on the bed and rushing to the end of it, oblivious to Sklayne's claws digging into her ankle. She would have launched herself off and after Trevarr, had Raxl not plucked her lightly out of the air and flung her effortlessly back to the bed.

::Quiet,:: Sklayne hissed from beneath the bed, his mind's voice sounding ragged and wounded. ::Quiet, quiet, quiet, *atreyva.*::

As if she could do anything but scrabble away, the knife slicing through bedding and mattress alike in her wake.

Raxl looked at her. He looked hard; he looked with

threat and intent, decision hovering. He shifted his belt,
a meaningful gesture—his buckle so like Trevarr's and
yet patterned completely otherwise. But he lifted his lip
in a sneer. ::Scrawny,:: he said, words coming through
Sklayne in a voice numbly rote. ::Dragon-bait.::

And he left her.

Sklayne crying soft cat-wails under the bed, Trevarr's belongings littering the room, disaster scattered
around them . . .

They took Trevarr, and they left her.

23

Waiting is for when you've already let go.
—Lisa McGarrity

Lucia strolled down the curving path between the Journey Inn's widely spaced units, stretching out muscles
still sleepy as she headed behind the office cabin to the
room that had originally been Quinn's but now, she
was sure, had been thoroughly occupied by Garrie and
Trevarr.

Thoroughly.

She smiled. Here in the light heat of the early day, the
sun was just coming up and the birds were still active;
a hummingbird strafed past her head and away. And
Lucia—fresh, clean, lightly splashed with a crisp citrus
scent and her hair sleek on her shoulders—thought it all
good.

She also thought she had best not hurry. She suspected she would interrupt something no matter when
she reached Garrie's cabin, and if Trevarr wasn't natu-

rally an early riser . . . well, he would be today. All puns intended.

And she'd never seen that look on Garrie's face before.

Or Quinn's, if it came to that. She hadn't told Garrie yet; Robin hadn't quite decided. But with repairs to do on Crystal Winds, insurance claims in the works, healing to do . . . Robin might just close the store for this hottest of summer months and recover in Albuquerque. Recover, assess. Plan. Albuquerque and Sedona . . . not so very far away, really.

Butterflies fluttered off to the side, in Feather's carefully tended xeriscaping, along with honeybees and morning birds, and the rustle of a squirrel off to the side. "I am in Bambiville," she announced to it, and it flicked its tail at her and ambled a few steps away. "If you all burst into song, I—I'll . . . Well, don't. Just don't do it."

And yes, still smiling. Right up until the moment she glanced at her former cabin and realized that not just one door hung askew, but both.

Broken. Shattered inward. Violently breached.

Lucia faltered . . . and then she ran. Girlie sprinting in her dainty sandals, listening for sounds of trouble or conflict, hearing nothing.

She flung herself at the door—used the frame to stop her motion, and peered, panting, into the studio space of the room. *"Madre de* Dios." Blood, more blood.

At least, she thought it was blood. Black, even hardly dried. Black and thick and full of musky odor.

And Garrie. Crumpled in the middle of one heavily used bed, sheets tangled everywhere, her shirt twisted up her torso. She sprang up when she realized she wasn't alone, that the world's sharpest knife was gripped in her hand as if she had quite suddenly grown used to using it, her eyes fierce and wild and her teeth bared. But just as suddenly she saw Lucia, and all that fight fled right out of her.

From beneath the bed, something made the noise of a child moaning.

Garrie fell back to the bed, sitting heavily; she dropped the knife and buried her face in her hands. But just that fast, she jerked her head up to look at Lucia with a new kind of light in her eyes. "I have his things. I can—"

What, she didn't quite say.

Lucia picked her way into the room, past the newly stained carpet, so carefully not touching anything. Trevarr's duster, there. His ugly old satchel, stout and ill-used leather. His *boots*. His shirt, and . . . even his belt. Lucia bent to pick up the belt; she ran her fingers, feather-light, over the design of the buckle. Swooping lines and angles. "Wings and fang," she murmured.

Garrie jerked to life; she snatched the belt away, abrupt and not apologetic for it. *"What?"* And she, too, traced her fingers over the design, and she whispered, "You're right. I never saw it. But you're right."

Lucia gathered herself . . . as brave as she'd ever been brave. "Chicalet, what—?"

Garrie turned on her, clutching the belt tightly. "They took him," she said, a voice so raw and strained, her eyes bright and chin trembling. "Hunters, from his world. They were looking for *me*. He wouldn't give me up and *they took him*." She dropped the belt, as suddenly as she was doing everything, and then dropped to her hands and knees—groping under the bed until she pulled out a creature who had been cat but who at the moment looked more other. Larger, stumpy-tailed, big tufted ears and a short, sleek coat of darkly dappled sheen . . . stunned and mourning, his eerie green eyes half open and dazed. She held him, crooning something—lightly smoothing back his whiskers and the ruffled hair between his ears.

Lucia thought—oddly—that Garrie deeply inhaled the furry scent of him, her eyes closing.

When she looked at Lucia, tears caught the light. "I can do this," she said. "I have the three—" She stopped herself. Whatever she had, she wasn't saying. Lucia's flicker of resentment faded with the realization that she might just not want to know. Garrie stuck her chin out, just a little. Not-crying, even if her lower lip still gave her away. "I'm not just going to wait," she said. "I'm not just going to wonder."

Lucia could understand that, except . . . hunters from another world. Violent men, *Trevarr*-like men. From *another world.*

"We're *reckoners,*" she said. "*You're* a reckoner. Better than anyone—maybe better than anyone *ever.* But . . . *this* . . ." She gestured helplessly, encompassing Sklayne, the gaping doorway, Trevarr's scattered belongings . . . the blood. The evidence of what had happened . . . the reality of it crawling cold down her spine. She closed her eyes.

He hadn't gone without a fight. She knew that. The blood wasn't his, either—dark as his was, it wasn't *this.* So he'd fought and he'd lost, a thing she'd somehow come to believe simply didn't happen—not even weakened, not even battered.

What could Garrie do against that? Was she even five feet tall? Pushing a hundred pounds? Could she use or even withstand the energies of Trevarr's dark world?

"But nothing," Garrie said, that new look in her eye. She had a small rash on her neck . . . a lover's mark. Faint fingerprint bruises peeking up from her shorts and wrapping around her hip. Lisa McGarrity, Reckoner . . .

Lisa McGarrity, changed.

Maybe not the only one. Maybe not, after what they'd seen in San Jose, what they'd done there. After what they'd seen here . . . and somehow lived through. *Together.*

For suddenly, Lucia understood. "Okay, chicalet,"

she said. "I . . . I don't know if I'm *with* you. I don't know if I can be. But I'm behind you."

What Garrie saw when she looked at that doorway, glaring bright against the shelter of the room, Lucia couldn't guess. But she wasn't surprised by the words. Not anymore. *"I'm not just going to wait,"* Garrie said again, her glance hitting Lucia hard, with a sudden hard shine to it. "I'm going to find him."

Lucia thought, quite suddenly, that she felt a sudden brush of air . . . heard a faint flap of giant wings.

And then it was silent.

Or perhaps in order to live, you do have to die just a little after all.
—Rhonda Rose

He'll be back.
—Lisa McGarrity

Come and get me, then.
—Trevarr